ARIS AND PHILLIPS CLASSICAL TEXTS

HOMER

Iliad

Books VIII and IX

Christopher H. Wilson

LIVERPOOL UNIVERSITY PRESS

This edition published in the United Kingdom in 1996 by Aris & Phillips.
Currently published by Liverpool University Press, 4 Cambridge Street,
Liverpool L69 7ZU.

Hardback ISBN 978-0-85668-627-6

Paperback ISBN 978-0-85668-628-3

A CIP record for this book is available from the British Library

Cover image: The embassy to Achilles (*Iliad*, Book 9): Phoenix and Odysseus in front of
Achilles. Attic red-figure hydria, Kleophrades Painter, c. 480 BC. Staatliche
Antikensammlungen, Room 4, Inv. 8770. Photograph by Bibi Saint-Pol, public domain via
Wikimedia Commons.

Contents

Preface   v

Abbreviations   vi

Bibliography   vii

INTRODUCTION
    A.   Homer and the *Iliad*
        1. The Mycenaean and Dark Ages   1
        2. The Epic Cycle   2
        3. Homer   4
        4. Oral Poetry: Formulas and Themes   7
    B.   Books VIII and IX
        5. Books VIII and IX and the *Iliad*   10
        6. Book VIII   12
        7. Book IX   17

Basic Homeric Grammar   30

Scansion: The Homeric Hexameter   43

TEXT AND TRANSLATION
      Iliad VIII   50
      Iliad IX   110

COMMENTARY
      Iliad VIII   177
      Iliad IX   208

Index   251

Preface

This edition is intended primarily for students. The text is that of Allen's 1931 edition (Oxford), with one or two small changes, all of which follow at least one of Allen's Oxford Classical Text and Willcock's 1978 edition. There is no *apparatus criticus*, but it is hoped that the grammatical and linguistic notes at the bottom of each page of the text and translation will help to make *Iliad* VIII and IX accessible to students who are not yet very familiar with Homer's Greek.

In anglicizing Greek proper nouns and their derivatives, I have usually transliterated; but I have retained familiar forms such as Argive, Helen, Hellespont, Peloponnese, and Priam.

Professor J. Griffin's *Homer Iliad IX* (Cambridge, 1995) was unfortunately not available to me before I had finished my own work.

I should like to thank the General Editor of this series, Professor Malcolm Willcock, for encouraging me to undertake this work, for the great help that he has given me over matters both large and small and for saving me from a great number of mistakes. There is the usual caution to be made about the errors that still remain in my work.

Christopher H. Wilson

Tonbridge, Autumn, 1996

Abbreviations

acc. accusative
act. active
adj. adjective
adv. adverb

AJP *American Journal of Philology*
aor. aorist
BICS *Bulletin of the Institute of Classical Studies*
CQ *Classical Quarterly*
dat. dative
fem. feminine
fut. future
G&R *Greece and Rome*
GB *Grazer Beiträge*
gen. genitive
GRBS *Greek, Roman & Byzantine Studies*
HSCP *Harvard Studies in Classical Philology*
Il. *Iliad*
imperat. imperative
imperf. imperfect

infin. infinitive
intrans. intransitive
JHS *Journal of Hellenic Studies*
LSJ The Greek-English Lexicon of Liddell & Scott
m. masculine
mid. middle
ms(s). manuscript(s)
n. neuter
nom. nominative
Od. *Odyssey*
optat. optative
part. participle
pass. passive
perf. perfect
pers. person
pl. plural
plupf. pluperfect
pres. present
s. singular
subjunc. subjunctive
trans. transitive
voc. vocative

Bibliography

Adkins, AWH   (1960) *Merit and responsibility*, Oxford.

----------- ------   (1972) 'Homeric gods and the values of Homeric society', *JHS* 92, 1–19.

Ameis, KF, Hentze, C & Cauer, P (1965) *Homers Ilias*, reprinted, Amsterdam.

Andersen, Ø and Dickie, M, eds. (1995) *Homer's World*, Bergen.

Andrewes, A (1961) 'Phratries in Homer', *Hermes* 89, 124–35.

Arend, W (1933) *Die typischen Scenen bei Homer*, Berlin.

Blegen, CW (1963) *Troy and the Trojans*, London.

Boardman, J (1985) *Greek Art²*, London.

Bremer, JM, de Jong, IJF & Kalff, J eds. (1987) *Homer: beyond oral poetry. Recent trends in Homeric interpretation*, Amsterdam.

Burkert, W (1976) 'Das hunderttorige Theben und die Datierung der Ilias', *Wiener Studien* N.F. 10.

-------------- (1985) *Greek religion*, trans. J. Raffan, Oxford.

Camps, WA (1980) *An introduction to Homer*, Oxford.

Carpenter, TH (1991) *Art and myth in ancient Greece*, London.

Chantraine, P (1968–80) *Dictionnaire étymologique de la langue grecque*, Paris.

Coffey, M (1957) 'The function of the Homeric simile', *AJP* 78, 113–32.

Davies, M (1989) *The epic cycle*, Bristol.

Davison, JA (1962) 'The Homeric question', in Wace & Stubbings (1962), 234–65.

de Jong, IJF   (1987) *Narrators and focalizers: the presentation of the story in the Iliad*, Amsterdam.

Denniston, JD (1934) *The Greek particles*, Oxford.

Dickinson, O (1994) *The Aegean bronze age*, Cambridge.

Dindorf, G & Maass, E (1875–88) *Scholia Graeca in Homeri Iliadem*, Oxford.

Dodds, ER (1951) *The Greeks and the irrational*, Berkeley & Los Angeles.

Dowden, K (1992) *The uses of Greek mythology*, London.

Easton, D (1985) 'Has the Trojan war been found?', *Antiquity* 59, 188–96.

Edwards, MW   (1970) 'Homeric speech introductions', *HSCP* 74, 1–36.

---------------- (1987) *Homer poet of the Iliad*, Baltimore & London.

---------------- (1991) *The Iliad: A Commentary. Volume V: books 17–20*, Cambridge.

Emlyn-Jones, C, Hardwick, L & Purkis J eds. (1992) *Homer: readings and images*, London.

Erbse, H (1969–77) *Scholia Graeca in Homeri Iliadem*, Berlin.

Evelyn-White, HG   (1936) *Hesiod, the Homeric Hymns and Homerica*, Loeb, Cambridge, Mass.

Fagles, R trans. (1991) *Homer; The Iliad*, London.

viii

Fenik, B (1968) *Typical battle-scenes in the Iliad,* Hermes Einzelschriften 21, Wiesbaden.

Finkelberg, M (1991) 'Royal succession in heroic Greece', *CQ* 41, 303–16.

Fitzgerald, R trans. (1984) *Homer; The Iliad,* Oxford.

Foxhall, L & Davies, JK eds. (1984) *The Trojan war: its historicity and context,* Bristol.

Greenhalgh, PAL (1973) *Early Greek warfare: horsemen and chariots in the Homeric and archaic ages,* Cambridge.

Griffin, J (1976) 'Homeric pathos & objectivity', *CQ* 26, 161–87.

---------- (1977) 'The epic cycle and the uniqueness of Homer', *JHS* 97, 39–53.

---------- (1980) *Homer on life and death,* Oxford.

---------- (1986) 'Words and speakers in Homer', *JHS* 106, 36–57.

Hainsworth, JB (1966) 'Joining battle in Homer', *G&R* 13, 158–66.

------------ (1968) *The flexibility of the Homeric formula,* Oxford.

------------ (1984) 'The fallibility of an oral heroic tradition', in Foxhall & Davies (1984), 111–28.

------------ (1990) *The Iliad: A Commentary. Volume III: books 9–12,* Cambridge.

Hammond, M trans. (1987) *Homer: The Iliad,* London.

Heubeck, A, West, S and Hainsworth, JB (1988) *A commentary on Homer's Odyssey. Volume I,* Oxford.

Hooker, JT (1987) 'Homeric society – a shame-culture?', *G&R* 34, 121–5.

Hope Simpson, R and Lazenby, JF (1970) *The catalogue of the ships in Homer's Iliad,* Oxford.

Janko, R (1992) *The Iliad: A Commentary. Volume IV: books 13–16,* Cambridge.

Jones, PV (1988) *Homer's Odyssey: a companion,* Bristol.

Kakridis, JT (1949) *Homeric Researches,* Lund.

------------- (1971) *Homer Revisited,* Lund.

Kirk, GS (1962) *The songs of Homer,* Cambridge.

------------- (1985) *The Iliad: A Commentary. Volume I: books 1–4,* Cambridge.

------------- (1990) *The Iliad: A Commentary. Volume II: books 5–8,* Cambridge.

Lattimore, R trans. (1951) *The Iliad of Homer,* Chicago.

Leaf, W (1900) *The Iliad. Vol. I: Books I–XII²,* London.

Liddell, HG and Scott, R (1940) *A Greek-English Lexicon⁹,* revised by Jones, HS, Oxford (referred to as LSJ.).

Lloyd-Jones, H (1983) *The justice of Zeus²,* Berkeley & Los Angeles.

Lohmann, D (1970) *Die Komposition der Reden in der Ilias,* Berlin.

Lord, AB (1960) *The singer of tales,* Cambridge, Mass.

---------- (1991) *Epic singers and oral tradition,* Cornell.

Lorimer, HL (1950) *Homer and the monuments,* London.

Luke, J (1994) 'The *krater, kratos,* and the *polis*', *G&R* 51, 23–32.

Macleod, CW (1982) *Homer: Iliad Book XXIV,* Cambridge.

Manning, S (1992) 'Archaeology and the world of Homer: introduction to a past and present discipline', in Emlyn-Jones, etc. (1992), 117–44.

Monro, DB (1891) *A grammar of the Homeric dialect²*, Oxford.

––––––––––– (1894) *Homer: Iliad Books I–XII*, Oxford.

Monro, DB and Allen, TW (1920) *Homeri opera I: Iliad I–XII³*, Oxford Classical Text, Oxford.

Moorehead, C (1994) *The lost treasures of Troy*, London.

Moulton, C (1977) *Similes in the Homeric poems*, Hypomnemata 49, Göttingen.

Murray, O (1993) *Early Greece²*, London.

Nilsson, MP (1932) *The Mycenaean origins of Greek mythology*, Berkeley & Los Angeles.

–––––––––––– (1933) *Homer and Mycenae*, London.

Owen, ET (1947) *The story of the Iliad*, London.

Page, DL (1959) *History and the Homeric Iliad*, Berkeley & Los Angeles.

Parry, A (1971) *The making of Homeric verse: the collected papers of Milman Parry*, Oxford.

–––––––––– (1989) *The language of Achilles and other papers*, Oxford.

Pfeiffer, R (1968) *History of classical scholarship*, Oxford.

Pinsent, J (1984) 'The Trojans and the Iliad', in Foxhall & Davies, (1984).

Pötscher, W (1993) 'Die homerische Presbeia in religioser und in poetischer Sicht - ihre Duale und deren Sinn', *GB* 19, 1–33.

Redfield, JM (1975) *Nature and culture in the Iliad: the tragedy of Hector*, Chicago & London.

Reinhardt, K (1961) *Die Ilias und ihr Dichter*, Göttingen.

Richardson, N (1993) *The Iliad: A Commentary. Volume VI: books 21–24*, Cambridge.

Rosner, JA (1976) 'The speech of Phoenix: *Iliad* 9.434–605', *Phoenix* 30, 314–27.

Rutherford, RB (1986) 'The philosophy of the *Odyssey*', *JHS* 106, 145–62.

Schadewaldt, W (1965) *Von Homers Welt und Werk⁴*, Stuttgart.

Segal, C (1968) 'The Embassy and the Duals of *Iliad* 9. 182–98', *GRBS* 9, 101–14.

Sherratt, ES (1992) 'Reading the texts: archaeology and the Homeric question', in Emlyn-Jones, etc. (1992), 145–66.

Silk, MS (1987) *Homer: the Iliad*, Cambridge.

Snodgrass, AM (1964) *Early Greek armour and weapons*, Edinburgh.

–––––––––––––––– (1971) *The dark age of Greece*, Edinburgh.

–––––––––––––––– (1974) 'An historical Homeric society?', *JHS* 94, 114–25.

Taplin, O (1992) *Homeric soundings: the shaping of the Iliad*, Oxford.

Taylour, Lord W (1983) *The Mycenaeans²*, London.

Wace, AJB and Stubbings, FH eds. (1962) *A companion to Homer*, London.

West, ML (1981) 'The singing of Homer and the modes of early Greek music', *JHS* 101, 113–29.

–––––––––– (1988) 'The rise of the Greek epic', *JHS* 108, 151–72.

x

Willcock, MM (1964) 'Mythological Paradeigma in the *Iliad*', *CQ* 14, 141–54.
--------------   (1970) 'Some aspects of the gods in the *Iliad*,' *BICS* 17, 1–10.
--------------   (1976) *A companion to the Iliad*, Chicago & London.
--------------   (1978) *The Iliad of Homer Books I–XII*, and (1984) *The Iliad of Homer Books XIII–XXIV*, London.
--------------   (1990) 'The search for the poet Homer', *G&R* 37, 1–13.
--------------   (1995) 'The importance of *Iliad* 8', in Andersen & Dickie (1995), 113–121.
Wood, M (1985) *In search of the Trojan war*, London.
Yamagata, N (1991) 'Phoinix's speech – Is Achilles punished?', *CQ* 41, 1–15.
Zanker, G   (1992) 'Sophocles' *Ajax* and the heroic values of the *Iliad*', *CQ* 42, 20–25.
------------   (1994) *The heart of Achilles: characterization and personal ethics in the Iliad*, Michigan.

Introduction

Note: Dates throughout are B.C. unless otherwise stated

A. Homer and the *Iliad*

1. The Mycenaean and the Dark Ages

Homer announces the subject of the *Iliad* with the invocation to the Muse with which he begins the poem – 'Sing, goddess, the anger of the son of Peleus, Akhilleus, the accursed anger, .. – from the time when they first separated in quarrel, the son of Atreus, the lord of men, and the godlike Akhilleus' (I 1–7).

The son of Atreus was Agamemnon, who was the commander-in-chief of a punitive expedition which the Greeks, or, as Homer commonly calls them, the 'Akhaians', launched against the city of Troy, in the north-west corner of Asia Minor. Akhilleus was the leading warrior on the Akhaian side. When the poem begins the Akhaians are encamped, as they have been throughout the previous nine years since the war began, on the shore outside the walls of Troy. As it is related by Homer, the story of the quarrel occupies a space of about twenty-four days, during which time the war drags remorselessly on, the warriors kill and are killed, and the gods intervene on behalf of their favourites, now on one side and now on the other. When the poem ends, the Akhaians have not yet taken Troy, as they will eventually do. The *Iliad*, therefore, gives us no more than an insight into the Trojan war as a whole. Homer gives hints, both of how the war began and of how it will end; and some of his scenes may be thought of as generic ones, which convey a typical picture of incidents that must have been continually repeated throughout the ten years of the war. The poem seeks to give a flavour of what the whole war was like; but the *Iliad* is very far from being a historian's account of the war.

The questions of whether there ever was a Trojan war, and of whether any germ of truth underlies the events of the *Iliad*, were raised in ancient times, and are still a matter of much debate today. We do not yet know of a historical Agamemnon or Akhilleus. But we do know that during the later Bronze Age, from, very approximately, 1600 to 1100, a number of palace centres were established in Greece, including one at Mukenai, the site in the north-east of the Peloponnese which Homer represents as the capital of Agamemnon. During this period, which is commonly called 'the Mycenaean age', the Greek language was first spoken on the mainland, and the mainland Greeks, Homer's Akhaians, established considerable trading contacts overseas. Judging from the Greek pottery discovered there, one overseas centre where such contacts were particularly flourishing was that at Hissarlik, in north-west Turkey, just inland from the entrance to the Dardanelles from the south. It was at Hissarlik that the celebrated Heinrich Schliemann in the 1870's uncovered a massive ancient site that he himself had no doubt was Troy. Schliemann's archaeological methods were, by modern standards, primitive, and his attitude to the truth sometimes cavalier; but few scholars would now be disposed to doubt that the identification of the Hissarlik site with Troy is correct. The site has been the subject of extensive excavation since Schliemann's day, up to and including the present; and it seems highly likely that it underwent violent destruction somewhere around 1220, a date which on other grounds seems a likely one for a possible Trojan war. But indisputable evidence for such a war remains absent; that the *Iliad* represents a war that really did take place remains no more than an assumption, albeit an attractive and interesting one.

The end of the second millennium was a period of widespread destruction throughout the eastern Mediterranean world. If the Mycenaean Greeks did sack Troy, then this must have been one of their final achievements. Somewhere around 1100 the palaces on the mainland were destroyed – it is not known for certain by whom; and with them their culture perished too. The art of writing was lost, overseas trade declined, and there ensued a period that is known as the Dark Age – partly because our knowledge of it is so scanty, and partly because such knowlege as we do have shows an age that was much inferior culturally and economically to the ages before and after. This Dark Age continued into the eighth century.

For Greece in the Bronze Age, and for the Mycenaeans, see Dickinson, and Taylour. For the archaeology of the site of Troy, see Manning; for archaeology and the Trojan war, Easton; and for Schliemann, Moorehead. Wood gives a colourful account of the story of the archaeologists' search for the Trojan war. On the Dark Age, see Snodgrass 1971. See also Section 3 of this Introduction.

2. The Epic Cycle

The *Iliad* narrates directly no more than 24 days or so of the final year of the Trojan war; but there are frequent references in it to episodes of the war that occurred outside this brief period. At IX 129 and 366–7 we hear of the raiding operations that Akhilleus had carried out in the towns and islands around Troy; from the moment that Akhilleus finally decides to rejoin the fighting his eventual death in it is referred to, or at least hinted at, repeatedly; and at II 701–2 and XV 704ff. Homer recalls the very first incident in the fighting, when Protesilaos was killed as he leapt ashore when the Akhaian fleet first arrived at Troy. And often Homer relies on his audience's knowledge of episodes that he does not himself narrate. When, for example, Helen appears in Book III, Homer takes for granted that we already know how she was abducted by the Trojan prince Paris from her husband Menelaos, king of Sparta and brother of Agamemnon, and how this led to the present war.

Homer also alludes to many incidents from outside the Trojan war. At VIII 364–70 Athene recalls how Herakles went down to the underworld to recover the hound

Kerberos and bring it back to his master Eurustheus; and in his speech at the embassy in IX Phoinix recalls his tutelage of the youthful Akhilleus (478–94), and then tells the story of the war between the Aitolians and the Kouretes, and of Meleagros' withdrawal and return, including within this references to the Kaludonian boar, the discord within Meleagros' family, and some excerpts from the family history of Meleagros' wife Kleopatre, or Alkuone (529–99). Elsewhere, Glaukos, a warrior on the Trojan side, details the adventures of his grandfather Bellerophontes at VI 155–202; and in the course of a long speech to Patroklos at the end of XI (668–761) Nestor recalls exploits from his now far-distant youth, when he led his fellow-men of Pulos against the neighbouring Eleians. Homer has at his disposal a great body of mythological stories, which he draws on as occasion offers, and often in an allusive and elliptical way which assumes that his audience is already familiar with the story.

The chronological span of Homer's repertoire is really quite limited. He does not tell us of the creation of the gods, or of the universe; and rich and diverse as his stories are, they fall within no more than the three or four generations that led up to the Trojan war. Such post-war stories as he gives (these are more common in the *Odyssey* than the *Iliad*) do not go more than one generation beyond the war. The setting of the stories is the Mycenaean age; and there is considerable evidence to suggest that many, at least, of the stories originated then – rather, that is, than originating later and being set in what is by then a past age. There was a body of epic poems (all of them considerably shorter than the *Iliad* and the *Odyssey*), which later came to be known as the Epic Cycle, which between them told the whole story of the Trojan war – from the gods' original decision to cause the war through to the quarrel between Agamemnon and Akhilleus with which the *Iliad* begins, and then from the death of the Trojan leader Hektor (the final event in the fighting of the *Iliad*) through to the end of the war, the return home of the various Akhaian heroes, and ultimately to the death of Odusseus, whose return is the subject of the *Odyssey*. Only small fragments of these poems have survived; but their subjects are known from summaries that were later made of them. We also hear of epics on such subjects as the story of Thebes, the family of Oidipous, and the adventures of Herakles, and of the Argonauts, some of which may, though this is not certain, have been included in the Epic Cycle; and when Homer tells us of, for example, the Kaludonian boar, and the exploits of Nestor in his youth, it is often assumed that these stories must go back to, respectively, an Aitolian and a Pulian cycle of epic, even though explicit evidence of such cycles has now disappeared. Homer's poems are part of a network of tales which surround the Trojan war as a whole.

It seems that the poems of the Epic Cycle, though precise dates are usually very difficult to arrive at, were composed later than the *Iliad*, but that the material which they contained did already exist at the time of the *Iliad*, and would have been available to Homer. When, therefore, we find in Homer stories whose details are at odds with the tradition as it has come to us from elsewhere, it is difficult to be certain whether Homer is giving what in his day was the received version of the tradition, and the variations from it arose later, or whether Homer is himself introducing variations, and our other version, although itself composed later than Homer, represents a tradition from which Homer has departed. All we can be entirely certain of is that the tales clearly did not exist in canonical form; the fact of variations in the different accounts that have survived of what is basically the same story is undeniable. A great deal of work has been done on Homer and the tradition as it may have existed in his day; and when the details of the stories as he gives them are closely examined, there are sometimes some grounds for believing that Homer is responsible for the departures that his version represents from the tradition as we find it elsewhere, even though our other sources are all later than Homer. In his examination of the Meleagros story in Book IX, Willcock 1964 makes a strong case for believing that Homer's paradigmatic use of this story – Phoinix is presenting it to Akhilleus as an example of conduct which he should, or more accurately should not, follow – has led him to reshape it in such a way that it fits his paradigm better than the probable received version would have done; and he draws the same conclusion from the other stories of Homer's that he discusses. The story of Nestor in his chariot being rescued by Diomedes at VIII 80ff. has aroused particular discussion in this connection. One of the poems of the Epic Cycle, called the *Aithiopis*, continued the story of the Trojan war from immediately after the burial of Hektor; and we know that it contained a story of Nestor's chariot being immobilised when one of its horses was shot by an arrow from Paris, whereupon Nestor was rescued by his son Antilokhos, a success which, however, cost Antilokhos his life. At VIII 81 it is again Paris who has shot one of Nestor's horses; and though it is this time Diomedes who saves Nestor, and without losing his life, yet a number of scholars argue that the *Iliad* episode is a refashioning of a tale whose original form is the one that was followed in the *Aithiopis* – though this is to be regarded as controversial.

On the Epic Cycle, see Davies; for the surviving fragments, see the Loeb edition, *Hesiod, the Homeric Hymns, and Homerica*, of Evelyn-White. On Greek mythology and the Mycenaean age, see Nilsson 1932; on Greek epic before Homer, West 1988. Kakridis 1949 and 1971 examines Homer's tales in relation to the tradition as he may have found it. On Meleagros, see Willcock 1964. Griffin 1977 considers differences in approach between Homer and the poets of the Epic Cycle. On the *Iliad* and the *Aithiopis*, see Willcock 1976, Appendix D, 285–7.

3. Homer

We know virtually nothing of the author of the *Iliad* other than what we can gather from the poem itself. Already to the Greeks of the classical period of the fifth century Homer was a shadowy figure, little more than a name; and such stories as we hear about him are unreliable, and often implausible. When the *Iliad* was composed, and what other works, if any, are to be attributed to the same composer, are questions which are still debated. But the following points are more or less generally agreed –

a. The date of composition is most probably towards the end of the eighth century. There are occasional references to objects and customs that on archaeological grounds seem to rule out an earlier date – hoplite fighting tactics are a commonly given example; and the very few passages which might seem to suggest a date later than 700 are commonly explained away as later interpolations.

In the eighth century, Greece was reawakening after the hardships and impoverishment of the Dark Age. The century was one of much colonization – i.e. founding of new cities – overseas; and this must have led to a considerable rise in trading and cultural contacts with the world outside Greece. The Greeks were becoming more conscious of themselves. The Olympic games, held every four years and open to entrants from all over the Greek world, are supposed to have begun in 776; and there was a great upsurge in the importance of the oracle at Delphi (see IX 405), which, like the Olympic games, was a panhellenic institution, i.e. attended from all over the Greek world. At the same time, a new Greek alphabet evolved, probably from Phoenician sources; and in painted pottery the rigid geometric patterns of the Dark Age began to give way to more lively designs, many of them featuring real or imaginary animals, that came to Greece from the east, and by about the end of the century the first representations of scenes from mythology were beginning to appear. The century also saw greatly renewed interest in graves from the Bronze Age, and in the hero-cults that were associated with them. It is appropriate that such a period should have produced the *Iliad*, an epic that commemorates the earliest known action of a panhellenic force against a foreign power. Homer more than once explicitly distances his heroes and their exploits from his own times, saying that they performed feats which would be beyond his contemporaries; and in historical terms, he is looking back across the Dark Age, from the reawakening of Greece in his own day back to the late Mycenaean age.

b. The *Iliad* was composed, not in mainland Greece, but somewhere in the eastern Aegean or on the western seaboard of Asia Minor. The simile at IX 4–7, where the north and west winds are described as blowing from Thrace, which is the eastern half of the Balkan peninsula, is one of several passages which suggest a composer with a viewpoint from the eastern Aegean rather than from mainland Greece. The island of Khios has since ancient times been suggested as Homer's birthplace – we hear of a guild of reciters known as the *Homeridae*, 'descendants of Homer', there in the sixth century; and Smyrna, the modern Izmir, opposite Khios on the Asiatic mainland, also has some claims.

c. The poem is an oral composition. Both the poet and his audience may well have been illiterate. (Literacy had been one of the casualties of the Dark Age.) The text of the *Iliad* is basically the record of a *performance* of the poem, and in this respect is quite unlike the texts of later epic poems such as Virgil's *Aeneid* or Milton's *Paradise Lost*. The poet does not read from a text, nor does he recite from memory (except in a passage such as Odusseus' delivery of Agamemnon's offer to Akhilleus at IX 264–99, which is an almost verbatim recall of the original offer which Agamemnon presented to the Akhaian leaders, in the absence of Akhilleus, at 122–57). Rather, he improvises as he performs; a parallel has been suggested between the oral poet and the jazz musician. The exact nature and circumstances of the performance are completely obscure; but it is tempting to suppose – though it can be no more than supposition – that, apart from the great difference in scale of the *Iliad*, the performance may have resembled the performances of Phemios at the court of Odusseus in Ithaka, and of Demodokos at the court of Alkinoos in Skherie, which are described in Books I and VIII of the *Odyssey* respectively. These men are professional bards, who are at the beck and call of their masters, and are summoned to ceremonial occasions to sing what their audiences require of them, accompanying themselves on the lyre as they do so. They rely for their knowledge on the Muse of poetry, who 'knows all things' (*Il.* II 485); and their songs are what we should now call 'heroic poetry'. Phemios sings of the homecomings of the Akhaian heroes from Troy, and Demodokos gives three separate tales, two from the Trojan war, and one from the life of the gods in their home on Mount Olumpos.

d. We do not know when the text of the *Iliad* was first put into writing. This could have been immediately, or very soon, after its composition; or the poem may at first have been committed to memory, and passed on from one singer to the next, with the text only taking written form some considerable time after the performance of which it is a record. We hear of public performances of the poem being given at the Panathenaic festivals at Athens in the sixth century, which would seem to presuppose some sort of official text. But our manuscripts of the poem derive from the work of the scholars at the great library of the Ptolemies in Alexandria in the third and second centuries, who established a text that is known as the vulgate. The history of the transmission of the text before that is a vexed subject; but it seems probable that there was no standard text prior to the vulgate. Many extracts from the poem survive from before the time of the vulgate, both in quotations by other authors and in papyrus fragments; and the many discrepancies that these reveal make the existence of a standard text seem unlikely.

e. How far our text is a faithful record of the original composition, and how far it has been overlaid by amendments and interpolations, are questions that have produced enormous debate. Most scholars nowadays would feel that this debate has been pursued to excessive lengths, and that, while one or two passages in our texts of the *Iliad* and *Odyssey* have stolen in from elsewhere (in the *Iliad,* Book X is usually regarded as an intruder), the fundamental integrity of the text is not in dispute.

On the date of the *Iliad*, see Silk, 2–5; on the historical background, Kirk 1962, Part 1, 3–51. On the development of art in the eighth century, see Boardman, chaps. 1 and 2, and Carpenter, chap. 1. On oral poetry, see the next section of this introduction. On bards, see West 1981, 101 and 113–29. On the 'Homeric question', and the transmission of the text, see J.A. Davison, in Wace-Stubbings, 234–66; also Parry 1971, Introduction, ix–lxii, and *Have we Homer's Iliad?*, in Parry 1989, 104–40.

4. Oral Poetry: Formulas and Themes

Our understanding of the way in which Homer's language and diction reflect the oral method of his composition was significantly advanced by the work of Milman Parry. Parry directed his attention to Homer's use of the *formula* – which he defined as 'a group of words which is regularly employed under the same metrical conditions to express a given essential idea' (Parry 1971, 272). Parry began with the name-plus-epithet formulas, such as 'swift-footed Akhilleus' and 'long-suffering god-like Odusseus'; and he showed that such formulas were the building-blocks of Homer's versifying repertoire, metrically convenient expressions which he calls on as required and which help him to keep his song going.

For an understanding of what follows, knowledge of the scansion of the Homeric hexameter is essential. This is set out at pp. 43–47 of this Introduction.

Suppose that Homer has some action of Akhilleus to describe, something that he did, thought, or felt, and that the description of this action fills the first four feet of his hexameter line.

Then the formula 'godlike Akhilleus', δῖος Ἀχιλλεύς, is available to make up the final two feet of the line. But if the description of the action ends at the second syllable of a three-syllable third foot, then this formula is expanded to

'swift-footed godlike Akhilleus', ποδαρκὴς δῖος Ἀχιλλεύς. Or, from the second syllable in the fourth foot, Akhilleus is again 'swift-footed', but the vocabulary

is different – πόδας ὠκὺς Ἀχιλλεύς. These three positions, the third syllable of the third foot, the second syllable of the fourth foot, and the beginning of the fifth foot, are very common ones at which the description of an action with which the line has begun comes to an end, and a formula begins and runs on from there to the end of the line. So, depending on the length of the description of an action which he has

done in the first part of the line, Odusseus may be 'godlike', δῖος Ὀδυσσεύς, or

'long-suffering godlike', πολύτλας δῖος Ὀδυσσεύς, or 'resourceful', πολύμητις

'Οδυσσεύς . Diomedes may be either 'strong', κρατερὸς Διομήδης, or 'good at the war-cry', βοὴν ἀγαθὸς Διομήδης. And so on. Each of the important characters, divine as well as human, has his epithet, and this epithet with his name makes up a formula which completes the line after the character's action has been described in the first part of the line; and there are different epithets to match the different positions in the line from which the formula may begin. When the character is in some other case than the nominative, then metrical considerations may require a formula with a different epithet. In the nominative, Diomedes is 'strong', or 'good at the war-cry'; but in the genitive he is 'horse-taming', Διομήδεος ἱπποδάμοιο. The epithets in these formulas are *generic* ones – they refer to general characteristics of the character to whom they are attached, without any necessary application to the particular situation at which the formula occurs. But the epithets are not normally interchangeable between different characters. From a metrical point of view, Akhilleus and Odusseus are equivalent; but, while both may be 'godlike', δῖος, Odusseus is not 'swift-footed', nor Akhilleus 'resourceful'.

Once this system of metrically convenient epithet-plus-name formulas has been grasped, one may see how the system is extended, and is at work throughout the whole poem. Consider the more frequent common nouns. To fill the fifth and sixth feet of the line, a ship in the dative singular is 'black', νηῒ μελάινη, but ships in the accusative plural are 'well-balanced', νῆας ἐίσας; and when something is happening in ships, then they are 'hollow', and the line begins, ἐν νηυσὶ γλαφυρῆσι. And when someone is going to the ships, then the line begins, νῆας (acc. pl.) ἔπι γλαφυράς.   We also see a comparable use of formulaic expressions to fill the first half of the line with a description of some common action. τὸν (or τὴν) δ' ἀπαμειβόμενος, 'and answering him/her', is used over and over again, taking the verse up to the break in the third foot, and leaving the rest of the line to be completed with a verb for 'spoke', and then an epithet-plus-name formula; and expressions like ὣς ἄρα φωνήσας and τὸν δὲ μέγ' ὀχθήσας, 'having spoken thus' and 'greatly angry with him', operate in the same way.

These formulas and patterns of phrases are the oral poet's stock-in-trade; he calls on them, and either uses one of them individually, or puts several of them together, as his subject-matter requires. As an example, consider the five lines giving the Akhaians' reception of Odusseus' report of the failure of the embassy to Akhilleus and the beginning of Diomedes' response at IX 693–7:

"Ὣς ἔφαθ', οἱ δ' ἄρα πάντες ἀκὴν ἐγένοντο σιωπῇ   IX   693
μῦθον ἀγασσάμενοι· μάλα γὰρ κρατερῶς ἀγόρευσε.   694
δὴν δ' ἄνεῳ ἦσαν τετιηότες υἷες 'Αχαιῶν·   695
ὀψὲ δὲ δὴ μετέειπε βοὴν ἀγαθὸς Διομήδης·   696
"'Ατρεΐδη κύδιστε, ἄναξ ἀνδρῶν 'Αγάμεμνον,   697

There is almost nothing here that has not already occurred in this book. Lines 693 and 695–6 repeat 29–31, the reception of Agamemnon's speech at the beginning of the book. The first half of 694 has appeared at 51, the reception of Diomedes' rejoinder to Agamemnon's initial proposal that the Akhaians should, in view of the desperate straits that they are now in, take to flight forthwith. Lines 693–4, with ἀγόρευσε for ἀπέειπεν, repeat the sequel to Akhilleus' response to Odusseus at 431–2. The first half of 696 is repeated from 432, and 697 repeats 163, the beginning of Nestor's response to Agamemnon's offer. The whole sequence is a pattern of phrases which Homer has to hand, and which he applies when the situation that he has reached in his narrative warrants it.

Is Homer's use here of building-blocks that appear elsewhere just a matter of his own convenience; or is he also aiming to remind us of the earlier scenes by his repetition of lines from them? Certainly, he *could* here be reminding us that the Akhaians' situation now, when Akhilleus has refused the offer of recompense, is just as bleak as it was at the beginning of the book, before the offer had been made. And he could also be underlining that it is once again Diomedes who has practical advice to offer; and the respectful tone of 697 could be a contrast with the less than respectful tone towards Agamemnon that Diomedes had struck in his previous speech. In a literary epic, one would expect repetitions like this to have some especial significance. In the oral poetry of Homer, this cannot be more than a possibility, a matter of interpretation and debate.

A comparable use of elements that he already has to hand is also found in Homer's accounts of recurring incidents. The Homeric heroes frequently do such things as perform sacrifices, arm themselves, welcome and entertain visitors, and deliver and receive messages; and one account of such actions is very much like every other one. The same actions are performed, in the same order, and with similar vocabulary. Such repeated incidents are called 'themes', or 'typical scenes'. It is most important to be alive to such differences from the standard pattern as the different examples of these scenes presents. In, for instance, the reception of the disguised Athene at Odusseus' palace by Odusseus' son Telemakhos at *Od.* I 102ff., and in

Agamemnon's arming himself at *Il.* XI 15ff., the scene follows the regular course, but is in each case pursued to unusual length; and this is no doubt due to the especial importance of this example. But it is fair to suppose that here too, as with the formulas and repeated phrase-patterns, Homer is in each case drawing on his stock-in-trade, which gives him the basic ingredients of what he now wishes to say, even though that by no means prevents him from introducing variations and innovations that are appropriate to each particular example.

Milman Parry's papers were collected after his untimely death and edited by his son, Parry 1971. On formulas and phrase-patterns, see Willcock 1978, XIX–XXII, Edwards 1987, 45–53, Hainsworth 1968, and 1993, 1–31. Schadewaldt and Reinhardt find more significance in some of Homer's repetitions than many English-speaking scholars have done. On typical scenes, see Fenik, Lord 1960, 68–98, and 1991, 26–37, Hainsworth 1966, Willcock 1990.

B. Books VIII and IX

5. Books VIII and IX and the *Iliad*

a. The introduction to the *Iliad* announces the quarrel between Agamemnon and Akhilleus as the theme of the poem; and the narrative goes into the quarrel straightaway. Agamemnon has offended a priest of Apollo, Khruses, by refusing to allow him to ransom back his daughter Khruseis, whom Agamemnon is keeping as a slave. Apollo sends a plague to punish the whole Akhaian force, and Agamemnon then publicly agrees to give up Khruseis, but insists on taking Briseis, the prize of Akhilleus, in compensation. Angry and dishonoured, Akhilleus withdraws from the war, taking his close friend Patroklos and all his forces with him; and he appeals to his mother, the sea-nymph Thetis, to persuade Zeus to support the Trojans in revenge for the insult that he has sustained. Zeus promises Thetis that he will do so (Book I).

In II the Akhaian army advances from its camp to the plain outside Troy. But before battle is resumed the two sides agree to a truce, and it is arranged that the war shall be settled by a duel between Agamemnon's brother Menelaos and the Trojan prince Paris (or Alexandros), whose abduction of Menelaos' wife Helen was the cause of the war. However, the duel ends inconclusively when Aphrodite, the goddess of love, rescues Paris and spirits him back to Helen in the city (III). In IV Zeus raises the possibility of saving Troy from eventual destruction, but he is over-ruled by his wife Here. Athene, Zeus' daughter, causes the Trojan Pandaros to break the truce by treacherously shooting an arrow at Menelaos, and general fighting begins. Despite the splendid exploits (ἀριστεῖα) of the Akhaian warrior Diomedes, and several interventions by the gods, this fighting is inconclusive. In VII there is another duel, this time between Aias and the Trojan leader Hektor, but this again has

no clear result. At the end of VII a truce is arranged for the burial of the dead, and
the Akhaians fortify their camp.

b. Book VIII covers one full day of operations. The book begins with Zeus at last
fulfilling the promise that he made to Thetis in I, by firmly forbidding the gods from
further interference in the war, a ban which Athene immediately – and correctly, as
the ensuing action makes clear – interprets as spelling disaster for the Akhaians.
Battle is resumed; and though the Akhaians at first do badly, and signs from Zeus
confirm that the tide of war is now running against them, their fortunes are
temporarily restored, first by Diomedes and then by the archer Teukros. But Teukros
is wounded, and the Trojans recover the initiative. Here and Athene attempt to defy
Zeus' ban and bring help to the Akhaians, but Zeus sends the messenger-goddess Iris
to call them off. The goddesses are cowed into reluctant submission, and the day
ends with the Trojans so firmly in control that they now prepare to camp outside the
city-walls, and Hektor delivers a rousing speech to them.

c. The action of Book IX takes place in the Akhaian positions on the following
night. The day's fighting has reduced Agamemnon to despair, and he calls an
assembly of the full Akhaian force, at which he proposes that they abandon their
campaign at Troy and return home forthwith. Diomedes protests that he at least will
not give up; and the aged Nestor, the king of Pulos, successfully proposes that this
general assembly should now end, and that the Akhaian leaders should meet among
themselves for further discussion. At this meeting Nestor sensitively but firmly
reminds Agamemnon of the insult that he has done to Akhilleus, and suggests that
they immediately seek ways of placating him. Agamemnon agrees, and specifies the
enormous reparations that he is now prepared to pay if Akhilleus will resume
fighting; and Nestor's proposal that Odusseus, Aias, and Akhilleus' friend Phoinix,
along with the heralds Eurubates and Odios, should straightaway convey this offer to
Akhilleus is promptly accepted.

The ambassadors set forth for Akhilleus' tent, where they are welcomed eagerly;
and after they have taken a meal together Odusseus conveys Agamemnon's offer.
But Akhilleus is quite unappeased, and uncompromisingly refuses to rejoin the
Akhaians; and the following speeches by Phoinix and Aias have little success in
persuading him to abandon this position. Phoinix stays with Akhilleus, but the other
ambassadors return to report the failure of their mission. The Akhaians are
dismayed; but Diomedes suggests that there is nothing more that they can do about
Akhilleus, and that in the morning they should resume the fighting without him.

d. There are important hints in VIII and IX of the course that the later fighting is to
take. At VIII 471–7 Zeus begins his speech to the now subdued Here and Athene by
declaring that the present success of the Trojans and Hektor is to continue, and will
only be halted when the fighting has reached the Akhaian ships and Patroklos has
been killed; and in his reply to Aias, the last of the three ambassadors to address him,

Akhilleus says that he will consider re-entering the fighting, but only when Hektor has stormed his way through to the Akhaian encampment and set fire to their ships (IX 650–3). The next day's fighting sees these foreshadowings of future events fulfilled. In Akhilleus' continuing absence from battle the Trojans smash through the Akhaians' defensive wall and begin to set fire to their ships; and in this desperate situation Patroklos at the beginning of XVI persuades Akhilleus to lend him his armour and lead out his men. Patroklos succeeds in driving the Trojans back to their wall, but he is killed, and Hektor, who has been instrumental in killing him, strips the corpse of the armour that Patroklos had borrowed from Akhilleus.

Akhilleus learns of Patroklos' death in XVIII. He is overwhelmed with grief, and now at last undertakes to fight again, determined to take his revenge on Hektor. Thetis warns him that he will himself be killed soon afterwards, but nothing can now stop Akhilleus. Fresh armour is made for him at Thetis' request by the blacksmith god Hephaistos; Akhilleus and Agamemnon go through a formal reconciliation in XIX; Zeus rescinds the interdict on the gods intervening that he had issued at the beginning of VIII; and Akhilleus rages mercilessly and unstoppably through the Trojan ranks, until in XXII he finally tracks Hektor down and kills him in single combat. He drags Hektor's body round the walls of Troy from his chariot, and in XXIII holds a funeral and funeral-games for Patroklos. But still his anger is unappeased, and he abuses Hektor's corpse mercilessly. So in XXIV the gods arrange that Hektor's father, Priam, the aged king of Troy , should go by night to Akhilleus' tent with a ransom for Hektor's body. Akhilleus accepts the ransom, and during the same night Priam brings Hektor's body back to Troy. The poem ends with the funeral of Hektor.

For the story of the *Iliad*, see Owen.

6. Book VIII

a. When Zeus begins this book by forbidding the deities to intervene in the human action, Athene interprets this as spelling certain catastrophe for the Akhaians; and we may interpret it as Zeus at long last fulfilling the promise that he made to Akhilleus' mother Thetis in I that he would grant her request and bring success to the Trojans as a means of honouring Akhilleus. Zeus' interdict, which he does not withdraw until the beginning of XX, gives new direction to the action of the poem after the inconclusive fighting of Books IV–VII; and the situation at the end of the book, where the Trojans are firmly in the ascendant, leads naturally into IX, where Agamemnon's despair at the present position causes the Akhaians to make a new approach to Akhilleus. By that stage, moreover, Zeus has delivered his important prophecy at 471–7, in which he foreshadows the course that the action will take in the next day's fighting, and the death of Patroklos at the end of XVI.

b. The book is therefore firmly connected to what has gone before and what is to follow; and it also has an overall logic of its own, beginning with Zeus making an edict that will bring disaster to the Akhaians, and ending with a situation where disaster does indeed stare the Akhaians in the face. But the action within the book has often seemed less satisfactory, in that, while the position at the end of the Trojans in complete ascendancy is clear enough in itself, it does not appear to arise very well from what has gone before. In ancient times the book was entitled Κόλος Μάχη, 'The Unfinished Battle'; and on both the divine and the human fronts the book is a series of false starts and frustrated initiatives which hardly seem to warrant the clear ascendancy of the Trojans to which they in fact lead. Zeus expresses his edict in unmistakeably forthright tones which seem to rule out all possibility of contradiction; but he has no sooner done so than Athene remonstrates with him, and he appears to give way to his daughter's distress (28–40). When the fighting begins, he weighs the scales, which assure him of Trojan success, and he then sends terrifying lightning and thunder among the Akhaians (69–77); but when Agamemnon appeals to him, he sends the portent of the eagle and the fawn to revive the spirits of the Akhaians (245–52). The performance of Here is equally puzzling. She holds her peace at her husband's opening edict, but then appeals to Zeus' brother Poseidon for help in rescuing the Akhaians (198–211). This is quite unsuccessful. But when later she appeals successfully to Athene, their preparations for intervention are described at some length, only for their undertaking to be called off the moment the goddesses receive from Iris the stern command from Zeus, and they return to Olumpos to receive the scorn and mockery of Zeus. The sequence has been a long one (350–483), but it has apparently accomplished nothing.

The human action appears similarly inconsequential. It may be summarised thus:–

53–65	The battle begins; heavy casualties on both sides, and no advantage to either.
66–98	After Zeus weighs the scales and sends thunder and lightning from Ide, the Greeks take to their heels, and Nestor is narrowly saved from death by Diomedes.
99–129	Diomedes retrieves the situation and kills Hektor's charioteer.
130–197	Further thunder and lightning from Zeus. The Trojans regain their superiority, and Hektor speaks exultantly to his men and to his horses.
212–244	Further Akhaian setbacks. Agamemnon prays despairingly to Zeus.
253–334	Their spirits revived by the portent of the eagle and the fawn, the Akhaians recover, and Teukros distinguishes himself with his archery.
335–349	Zeus breathes spirit into the Trojans, and Hektor restores their supremacy.

At this point there follows the long episode of the futile attempt at intervention by Here and Athene, and no more is heard of the situation on earth until 485ff., when night begins to fall, and so ends the action of the day, to the great dismay of the

Trojans and the relief of the Akhaians. This obliges us to suppose that Teukros' archery was a last-ditch attempt to retrieve the Akhaian fortunes, and that the wounding of Teukros that brought his archery to an end, and the consequent revival of the Trojans, marked a decisive turning-point. But little or nothing of this was suggested by the narrative at the time when these events occurred (324–49).

c. Homer has here been put in a difficult position by the requirements of his narrative. He needs a sequence of Akhaian setbacks, both so that Thetis' request to Zeus may be fulfilled, and so as to occasion the attempt to placate Akhilleus that follows in Book IX. But hitherto he has regularly maintained that, even in the absence of Akhilleus, and whatever the momentary fluctuations in the fortunes of the two sides, the Akhaians are more than a match for the Trojans. At the beginning of Book III, as the forces are preparing to re-engage, the Trojans are likened to clamouring wild fowl and cranes, whereas the Akhaians 'advanced in silence, breathing strength, eager in their hearts to help one another' (III 1–9, where one of the ancient commentators observes, 'Homer characterises the two armies, and maintains this characterisation to the end'). These preparations for war are curtailed by Paris' proposal that the war should be settled by the issue of a duel between himself and Menelaos; but then, when this duel has got under way and defeat stares Paris in the face, he is spirited away by the goddess of love, Aphrodite. In IV the Trojan treachery which had given rise to the war, when Paris abducted Helen from Sparta, is re-enacted when the Trojan Pandaros treacherously shoots Menelaos with an arrow during a time of truce; and as the forces finally proceed to war, the advance of the Greeks is likened to the relentless surge of the waves of the sea, while the Trojans are likened to bleating sheep, with no common language (IV 422–45). The ancient commentators, or scholia, over and over again observe that Homer is φιλέλλην, 'the friend of the Greeks'; and while this does not prevent him from viewing the individual Trojans who are the victims of the war with the utmost compassion (e.g. Gorguthion at VIII 302–8), it does give him difficulty when his theme requires that the Trojans should momentarily get the upper hand in the fighting. So in this book he produces a battle-narrative which in itself appears to show the fortunes of war just about even between the two sides, but ends it somewhat peremptorily with the picture of total Trojan success.

d. One also needs to bear in mind the relation between the divine and the human action. It is sometimes difficult to take Homer's gods seriously. They bicker among themselves constantly, and are one discordant family, as both the first and the last god-scenes of this book make clear (1–40, 438–84). But their influence on the human events is nevertheless decisive. Zeus makes a decree that will cause things to go badly for the Akhaians; and things do go badly for the Akhaians. Athene wins a concession from Zeus; and Zeus momentarily relaxes his pro-Trojan stance when he sends the portent of the eagle and the fawn to revive the spirits of the Akhaians. Where a change in the human fortunes occurs, this is regularly caused, at least partly, by some action of the gods. The opening exchanges in the fighting are even; but then Zeus sends thunder and lightning among the Akhaians and they take to their heels (75ff.). Diomedes restores the Akhaian cause, but Zeus sends more thunder and lightning, whereupon Diomedes and Nestor take to flight (130ff.). The Trojans pen the Akhaians behind their ditch, whereupon Here causes Agamemnon to rouse his men with a speech, in the course of which he prays to Zeus, and in response Zeus revives the spirits of the Akhaians with the portent of the eagle and the fawn (218ff.). And so on. There is thus more significance in the final god-scene of the book than may at first be apparent. When Zeus browbeats Here and Athene into submission, he is finally establishing his authority as he had insisted on doing at the beginning of the book. The resistance of the pro-Akhaian divinities is exhausted, and broken; and in consequence the outlook for the Akhaians on the ground is indeed grim.

e. The human action of the book is largely comprised of scenes of battle, which share a number of characteristics with the battle-scenes elsewhere in the poem. The fighting takes the form either of a σταδίη, 'mêlée', as at 60–5, or of a φόβος, 'rout', as at 78–9. Frequently the course that the fighting is taking is expressed indirectly, or left to us to infer for ourselves; and when the focus is on individual warriors we must often suppose that their success or failure is common to their army as a whole. Thus at 78–9 we are told that neither Idomeneus, Agamemnon, nor the two Aiantes stood their ground, and we are to conclude that the Akhaians generally are in retreat, and further, that this is the consequence of the terror that Zeus' thunder and lightning at 75–7 has struck into them. At 131 we are told that 'the Trojans would have been penned within Ilion like sheep', and from this we may conclude that Diomedes' success in killing Hektor's charioteer, even though he missed his first target of Hektor himself (this missing of one's first target is a common motif of the battle-scenes), has momentarily given the advantage to the Akhaians. Then Zeus sends thunder and lightning again, and the ensuing section (136–97) contains very little narrative at all; but by the despairing speeches of Nestor and Diomedes, and Hektor's exultant addresses to his men and to his horses, it is made clear that the Trojans have now recovered the initiative. In the next sequence of fighting (212ff.), we find for the first time that the Akhaians have now given way so far that they are hemmed in between their ditch and the ships (213–7); but Teukros' successes with his archery must have enabled them to advance from there, because when Teukros is stunned by Hektor the Trojans push forward over the ditch and oblige the Akhaians to make a stand by their ships (335–49). Other than in his general scenes of fighting such as the first battle-scene of this book at 60–5, Homer focusses on individual scenes of battle, and individual warriors; and he leaves it to us to make the necessary inferences and the connections with what is happening elsewhere that enable us to build up a general picture of the fighting.

f. The text of *Iliad* VIII has received a fair measure of critical attention. The book contains a considerable number of verses that occur elsewhere in Homer, and the view has been expressed that where these appear in Book VIII at least some of them are post-Homeric additions – lines that are appropriate when they appear elsewhere have, so it is alleged, been inappropriately introduced into VIII. Thus, for example, Aristarkhos, the critic who was in charge of the Ptolemaic library at Alexandria in the early second century, *athetised* lines 28–40 – i.e. he included the lines in his text, but marked them in such a way as to make his suspicions of them clear. The lines are all to be found elsewhere; and Aristarkhos thought that their subject-matter, Athene's protest to Zeus and Zeus' conciliatory reply, had no place here after the stern and uncompromising tone that Zeus has struck in his opening speech. Likewise the scene of Here and Athene arming themselves at 381–96 (where Aristarkhos athetised 385–7). This has already appeared at V 719–52, and it has been felt that the lines are appropriate there, where the goddesses' preparations do lead to their intervention in the human action, but less so here, where they do not.

Doubts have also been voiced over a number of apparent inconsistencies in the text. E.g. at 71–2 Zeus appears to have one fate for each of the armies, but then at 73 the plural is used for the fate of the Akhaian army; at 113 Nestor's horses are feminine (Νεστορέας), whereas they were masculine (βραδέες) at 104; and at 185 Hektor addresses four horses, but in the following line he uses the dual (ἀποτίνετον), as though he were addressing no more than two.

It would be unwise to make too much of this. It does not always make things easier if we simply delete lines that may appear suspicious. When, for example, Here appeals to Poseidon at 201ff. and to Athene at 352ff., she repeats the theme of Athene's address to Zeus at 30–40 that the Akhaian situation has been rendered desperate by Zeus' decree; and we may feel that Here's expression of the theme is made more effective by this repetition, an effect that would be lost if we were to delete Athene's appeal to Zeus. The argument about 'more appropriate' and 'less appropriate' occurrences of the same lines in different parts of the poem is a hazardous one. Repetition is a fundamental feature of the oral procedure; and the oral poet is not giving a performance of a text that he has already edited in his study. He will therefore commonly repeat motifs; and we may perhaps find the appearance of the motif more appropriate in one place than in another. But we need stronger grounds than that if we are to say that the allegedly less appropriate appearance was not part of the original performance at all. Likewise with the inconsistencies over the number of fates, and of Hektor's horses. A fully edited version might perhaps have eliminated such inconsistencies; but we are not here considering a fully edited version, and so while the inconsistency may be noted it can hardly be used on its own as an argument for rejecting the passage in which it occurs.

The remains of ancient texts written on papyrus that have been discovered, and still are being discovered, in Egypt contain a great number of quotations from the *Iliad*;

and those that quote from *Iliad* VIII contain an unusually large number of lines that either do not appear in our manuscripts of the book at all, or only in the inferior ones. Thus for example a papyrus known as P7 after VIII 54 adds the three lines II 477–9, 'to go into the fray, and among them mighty Agamemnon, with eyes and head like Zeus who rejoices in thunder, with girth like Ares, and with chest like Poseidon', and after the following line, 55, it adds the four lines XI 57–60. And numerous other 'plus-verses' are found elsewhere. After VIII 131, for example, the scholia tell us that some editions included the extra lines

Τρῶες ὑπ' 'Αργείων, ἔλιπον δέ κεν 'Εκτορα δῖον

χαλκῷ δηιόωντα, δάμασσε δέ μιν Διομήδης

'the Trojans by the Argives, and they would have left Hektor slaying (men) with his bronze, and Diomedes would have overcome him'. The appearance of such plus-verses makes clear how fluid the transmission of Homer's text for a long time was, and that of Book VIII unusually so. But we again need further criteria beyond this if we are to call the manuscript tradition of the text into question.

On *Iliad* VIII, see Willcock 1995; on the contrast between the Akhaians and the Trojans, Griffin 1980, 4–5 and 23. The scholia, which are the the remains of the ancient commentaries which are found between the lines and in the margins of the manuscripts, are to be found in Dindorf & Maass and in Erbse. On the battle-scenes, see Hainsworth 1966, 158–66, Fenik, and Willcock 1976, Appendix B, 279–80. On suspicions over repetitions from elsewhere in the *Iliad* and over inconsistencies, see the introductions to VIII in the editions of Ameis-Hentze and Leaf; on the plus-verses, see Kirk 1990, 293–4.

7. Book IX

a. The division of the *Iliad* into books was virtually certainly not by Homer, but was much later. According to a *Life of Homer* which is included in the mss. of Plutarch, although it is probably not by him, the division was the work of the Alexandrian critic Aristarkhos, and this may well be right – see Pfeiffer, 115–6. With some books there is room for doubt over whether the division has been made in the best place; but both VIII and IX are clearly self-contained, VIII giving one whole day's fighting, and the reaction to it on the Trojan side, IX the embassy to Akhilleus.

Book VIII is almost entirely scenes of battle, or of the gods, with which Book IX, with no such scenes at all, is in the sharpest contrast. The book has been judged 'in many ways the finest in the *Iliad*' (Willcock 1976, 94); and Reinhardt 228–9 calls it 'the most consummate ring-composition'. The book begins with the three speeches at the Akhaian assembly by Agamemnon, Diomedes, and Nestor, and ends with the three speeches in Agamemnon's tent by Agamemnon, Odusseus, and Diomedes, when it is again Diomedes who has practical proposals to make in the face of the immediate crisis. Much of the book is composed of speech, and Homer's characterisation of the speakers is consistently closely observed, and the characterisation of one speaker sharply contrasted with that of the others. Thus in the opening scenes we have Agamemnon as the leader who is possessed by the sense of failure, the comparatively youthful Diomedes for whom defeat is unthinkable, and the mature Nestor whose commitment to the Akhaian cause enables him to see the way ahead and how to present this to the commander-in-chief; and at the embassy to Akhilleus each of the ambassadors adopts a different approach to Akhilleus and draws a different response from him. Among the many other fine passages in the book there are, for instance, Phoinix's story-within-a-story of Meleagros (529–99), and on a smaller scale such touches as the picture of Nestor, whose idea the embassy had been, unable to leave it alone but burdening it with last-minute instructions as it sets forth (179–81), and the scene that greets the ambassadors on their arrival, when they find Akhilleus reduced to singing to his lyre of 'the famous deeds of men' – rather than, which would come more naturally to him, performing such deeds, for later bards to sing about – with only Patroklos for company (186–9). Nor should the intense exchanges once the embassy gets down to business allow us to forget the silent presence throughout in the background of Patroklos, the man who, in consequence of Akhilleus' present refusal of Agamemnon's offer, will himself in due course enter the fighting and there lose his life. No wonder that in ancient times Homer was called ἀρχηγὸς τραγῳδίας, 'the originator of tragedy'.

b. But towering above all the other fine features of the book is the tremendous speech that Akhilleus makes after Odusseus has conveyed Agamemnon's offer to him (308–429). This is the longest speech in the *Iliad*, apart from those which include, which Akhilleus' does not, extended sections of the speaker's personal reminiscences; and it is often adjudged the finest. Agamemnon's attempt at reconciliation, the enormous material rewards that he now promises, and the polished diplomacy with which Odusseus has presented Agamemnon's offer, – these only make Akhilleus even more angry than he was before. He unleashes an overpowering outburst of fury, in which he re-enacts every item of his rage against Agamemnon for having deprived him of Briseis. Agamemnon's offer of recompense he quite rejects; rather, Agamemnon's seizure of his own γέρας, the prize that he had won by his exploits in warfare, leads him to call into question the whole basis of his presence at Troy. Why should he fight in Agamemnon's army, and for the purpose of recovering Menelaos' wife? What is the point of the prospect of further κῦδος that Odusseus has held out to him if he will rejoin the fighting, when what his mother has told him about his two κῆρες offers the prospect of a life at home which, though it will bring him no glory, will at least be a long one? Akhilleus' speech has a power and a logic and an intensity of emotion all of its own; there is nothing like this anywhere else in the *Iliad*.

Akhilleus responds to Odusseus with emotion very much more than with logic; how is his explosion of rage to be accounted for? Consider the final four lines (158–61) of the speech that Agamemnon had made to the Akhaian leaders when he set forth the recompense that he was now prepared to offer to Akhilleus. Agamemnon concludes, 'Let him (Akhilleus) give in – it is Hades who is indeed unyielding and implacable, and for that reason he is the most hateful of all the gods to men as well. And let him place himself under me, as I am the more kingly, and claim to be the more distinguished in ancestry'. The offer that Agamemnon has just made could not in material terms be more handsome; but Agamemnon has completely overlooked Nestor's final instruction to him at 113, that Akhilleus is to be approached 'with soothing words'. For Agamemnon the issue between Akhilleus and himself is a matter of his own superior status, just as it had been at the start, when he pulled rank on Akhilleus and insisted on seizing Briseis from him. And for Akhilleus too that is the matter at issue. Akhilleus has not, of course, heard what Agamemnon said at the βουλή, and Odusseus understandably makes no mention of this section of Agamemnon's speech when he presents Agamemnon's offer. But the very size of Agamemnon's offer, extending far beyond what it would be within the powers of anyone else to offer, is for Akhilleus nothing more than a renewed attempt on Agamemnon's part to reassert his authority over him; it is for that reason utterly insulting and utterly unacceptable.

On the language and form of Akhilleus' reply to Odusseus, see Lohmann 236–45, Griffin 1986, 52–7, and Parry 1989, 1–7, *The Language of Achilles*. The thought of the speech has been the subject of a great many studies, coming to many different conclusions; see, for instance, Lloyd-Jones, chapter 1, Redfield 11–19.

c. Odusseus delivers the official message to Akhilleus, and he does so with the greatest diplomacy and skill. His 'highly rhetorical and calculated speech employs the arguments that would convince *him*: gifts, glory and gain, with added touches of flattery' (Rutherford 149, n.26). But with Akhilleus' total rejection of Odusseus, an impasse is arrived at. Akhilleus has made it abundantly clear that if one approaches the subject of the quarrel as Odusseus, the official spokesman for Agamemnon, has approached it, then there is nothing more to be said. Within the story of the quarrel which is the declared subject of the *Iliad*, the importance of the ensuing speeches lies in the way that the other two ambassadors, Phoinix and Aias, extend the issue beyond the quarrel purely between Agamemnon and Akhilleus that it has so far been.

In a much discussed speech at XII 310–28 Sarpedon, a warrior on the Trojan side, considers the question of why the heroes risk their lives by fighting. For Sarpedon it is a matter of *noblesse oblige*; the men over whom the heroes are appointed honour them with such things as feasts and gifts of land, and in return the heroes fight in the forefront of battle, even though this will almost inevitably lead to an early death. This philosophy Akhilleus, uniquely in the whole poem, rejects in his reply to Odusseus; there is, so he maintains, no reason at all why he should now fight and risk his life. This he is able to do because, unlike Sarpedon, he considers the matter entirely from his   own   point   of   view;   and   Phoinix   and   Aias   take   the   matter further by proposing that this is not the only way in which the matter is to be considered. Akhilleus has very little to say to the fresh approaches of Phoinix and Aias; he cannot answer them as he has answered Odusseus. But that must not be allowed to obscure the significance of the new dimension that is now given to the quarrel.

d. Phoinix begins by reminding Akhilleus at length of the strong personal bond that exists between Akhilleus and himself. All the service that he rendered to Akhilleus in his youth was rendered 'so that you may one day save me from shameful ruin' (495). He then makes his first, brief, appeal, 'Tame your mighty passion', which he follows immediately with the parable of the *Litai*, where he strives to show that the giving and receiving of an apology is not just a matter between the parties concerned, but one that involves regard for none other than the daughters of Zeus as well. Akhilleus, that is, has an obligation to Phoinix, and, now that Agamemnon has made his offer, he has an obligation to provide τιμή, 'honour', to the daughters of Zeus, an obligation which he will discharge if he now renounces his anger and helps the Argives (513–8, especially 513–4) – the Argives, not Agamemnon, who was the only member of the Argive army other than himself whom Akhilleus considered in his reply to Odusseus.

Phoinix then proceeds to the third and final part of his speech, the paradigmatic story of Meleagros, a man who, like Akhilleus, once withdrew in anger from fighting with his fellow-countrymen, but then when disaster stared his side in the face gave way to the pleas of his wife, and re-entered the fray just in time. Had Phoinix wished to do no more than repeat what he has already said, he would have concluded the paradigm with, 'As Meleagros gave way to entreaties, so too should you'. But Phoinix does not conclude thus. What he says (597–605) is that Meleagros' change of heart came too late, when the gifts he had been promised were no longer on offer; this is the fate which Akhilleus must now avoid, because the loss of the gifts will diminish the enhanced τιμή which Agamemnon's offer has now made available to him. Phoinix's position is thus ultimately very close to Sarpedon's. He ended the parable of the *Litai* by declaring that Akhilleus should serve his fellows by saving them from the disaster which now faces them; and he ends the Meleagros paradigm by declaring that the gifts which are on offer are the τιμή which he will receive in return. His position is also totally different from that which Akhilleus has just taken in his reply to Odusseus; Agamemnon's offer is not a matter between Akhilleus and Agamemnon alone.

On Phoinix's speech, see Rosner, Yamagata, and Hainsworth 1993, 55–7, and his notes on 430–605 and 502–12.

e. After Akhilleus hardly responds to Phoinix's arguments at all, beyond reasserting his continuing anger towards Agamemnon, there is little for the straightforward military man Aias to say – so little, in fact, that he begins (624) by addressing Odusseus, and only turns to Akhilleus in the middle of 636. But Aias' plain speaking very much builds on the fresh lines that Phoinix has introduced. By his refusal of the offer Akhilleus is betraying the φιλότης, 'friendship', of his companions (630). Akhilleus must show αἰδώς – αἴδεσσαι at 640 is the word that Phoinix has used of the man who gives heed to the *Litai* at 508; he should remember that by entertaining the ambassadors under his roof he has established a bond of friendship with them. Like Phoinix, Aias is concerned with the social aspects of the situation, and with the obligations that Akhilleus is betraying by isolating himself from the rest of the army and refusing the gifts. He speaks more bluntly than Phoinix, and whereas Phoinix expressed himself largely in general terms all that Aias says is related to the immediate situation; but the connection in thought between the two speeches is clear.

On Aias' speech, see Zanker 1992, 20–5, and 1994; on αἰδώς in Homer, Hooker 1987.

f. Akhilleus' replies to Phoinix and Aias (607–20 and 644–55) do nothing at all to take further the points they have advanced. For Akhilleus there is just one, constant, factor in the situation, and that is his anger with Agamemnon, which he therefore repeats in both of his replies. He acknowledges that Phoinix has spoken of τιμή – but he has enough τιμή already, and is prepared to share this with Phoinix; and he acknowledges that Aias has spoken κατὰ θυμόν, 'in accordance with my feelings', but having done so returns immediately to his anger, and then dismisses the embassy. When, therefore, Odusseus reports back to the Akhaian leaders, it is to say that Akhilleus rejects Agamemnon and his gifts (679). That is, of course, true, and is all that matters for the present situation. But it does leave unsaid how Phoinix and Aias have nevertheless made some headway in causing Akhilleus to modify the position of flat rejection that he adopted in his first reply to Odusseus. His tone to both of them is a great deal more open than it had been to Odusseus; and, whereas to Odusseus he declared uncompromisingly that he would take his men back with him to Greece on the following morning (356–63), to Phoinix he says that this is a matter for later decision (618–9), while to Aias, his threat to return home now apparently forgotten, he says that he will return to battle, but only when Hektor has fought his way through to the Akhaian ships and is setting fire to them (650–5) – a promise that is in fact fulfilled, though not exactly in the way that Akhilleus anticipates. This, though less than what the Akhaians had been hoping for, is nevertheless a significant concession. After Akhilleus' tour de force in reply to Odusseus, Homer is not content to leave things as they are, or to allow the embassy to end in the total impasse that has there been reached.

g. While *Iliad* IX has in itself never lacked admirers, its position within the poem as a whole has caused much uneasiness and debate. Agamenon's offer to Akhilleus, and Akhilleus' rejection of it, are nowhere mentioned again; and there are even a number of passages later in the poem which have been taken to imply that no such offer had ever been made – i.e. that Book IX cannot have been part of the original version of the *Iliad*, but must have been imposed onto it at some later date. Thus, at XI 608–10 Akhilleus begins a speech to Patroklos, 'Godlike son of Menoitios, you who delight my heart, now I think that the Akhaians will stand about my knees, imploring me', which has been taken to imply that the Akhaians have not implored Akhilleus already and Agamenon has not made his offer to him. And in the course of another speech to Patroklos at XVI 49–100, Akhilleus three times says things which have been taken to imply that the events and the words of Book IX have not taken place. Patroklos had wondered (XVI 37) whether Akhilleus' continuing refusal to fight is because 'your royal mother has told you something from Zeus'; and Akhilleus replies (51), 'my royal mother has told me nothing from Zeus' – a reply that seems discordant with what Akhilleus had said at IX 410–6, that his mother had told him about the two different fates that were awaiting him. Then at 72 Akhilleus says that the Trojans would now be in full retreat 'if Agamemnon had treated me kindly', as though Agamemnon had never made his offer of reparations. And at 84–6 Akhilleus, granting Patroklos the permission he had requested to fight in Akhilleus' place, says that he may do this 'so that I may gain great honour and glory from all the Danaans, and they may bring back to me the very beautiful girl (Briseis)', words which again seem to disregard Agamemnon's offer, which explicitly included the promise that Briseis would be restored (IX 131–2, 273–4).

This sort of argument, in which quite short passages are used as the foundation for mighty conclusions about a supposed 'original version' of the *Iliad* which was substantially different from the one we have now, were once a common feature of Homeric scholarship, though they are very much less so nowadays. Particular passages have been interpreted and then counter-interpreted, but for all their ingenuity the interpretations have not led to the certainty or the consensus that had been hoped of them. It is possible to take each of the passages mentioned above, and to suggest interpretations of them that do not lead to denying the authenticity of Book IX in the way that has been claimed. Akhilleus may not be thinking very carefully of what he is saying; and/or he is perhaps adapting what he says to the requirements of the present situation, and so exercising some economy with the truth; and/or there may be some inconsistencies between Book IX and the rest of the *Iliad*, and the book may be less well edited within the poem as a whole than it might have been. That may be granted; but to conclude any more than that seems misguided and unwise. It is tempting to think of the difficulties that have been found in XI and XVI vis-à-vis IX as arising, not out of different compositions by different poets at different times, but from different stages in the composition by one poet. One might want to argue that at least some sections of IX are later than the problematical passages of XI and XVI, and that Homer's editing has been less thorough than would be expected of a literary, not an oral, composer. I return to this possibility in the following section.

On the supposed inconsistencies between IX and the later books, see Page, 297–315, with his notes at 324–335. For later discussion of the particular passages see Willcock 1976 on XI 608 ('This line has caused extreme and unnecessary difficulty') and XVI 49–86; Janko on XVI 49–50; and Hainsworth 1993 on IX 410–6 and XI 609. On the composition of the *Iliad* as a long drawn-out process, and the application of this idea to IX, see Reinhardt, 212–42.

h. No single passage in the entire *Iliad* has caused more discussion than IX 182–198. The difficulty lies in Homer's use of the duals – the pronouns at 182, 192 and 196, adjectives and participles at 183 and 192, and verbs at 182, 185, 192, 197 (twice) and 198. The dual is used of two, so that the passage appears to record the journey of two men along the shore, and their welcome and reception in Akhilleus' tent. The plural verbs at 186 and 193, and the plural adjective at 198, are not in contradiction of this view, as the plural is quite commonly used for two instead of the dual. But when Nestor proposed the embassy at 168 he named not two, but five, members of it – Phoinix, Aias, Odusseus, and the two heralds, Odios and Eurubates; and this proposal was gladly accepted (173), with no indication at all that two of these men should travel separately from the rest, let alone of what point there might be in such a procedure. Also, after 199 the duals are discarded completely – they do not even reappear at 656ff., when Phoinix has remained with Akhilleus, and the other ambassadors make their way back to Agamemnon's tent; and there is no suggestion anywhere that Akhilleus has not received the full embassy, and every suggestion that he has. We thus apparently have an embassy of two persons at 182–200, and of five persons everywhere else. Many scholars have found it easy to explain away the heralds, who are entirely silent throughout the ensuing proceedings; but even so we still have one embassy of two persons, and another one of three.

This difficulty was recognised in ancient times, and two different explanations of it were put forward. The Alexandrian critic Zenodotos apparently thought that in Homer the dual may at times be used instead of the plural, i.e. to designate more than two, so that here it is being used of the embassy as a whole; and Aristarkhos, basing himself on Nestor's Φοῖνιξ ... ἡγησάσθω at 168, supposed that Phoinix went on ahead, and that 182ff. describe the subsequent journey and arrival with Akhilleus of Aias and Odusseus. Neither of these views has found unqualified favour from modern scholars. Zenodotos' view of the dual in Homer has been challenged most recently by Pötscher, 2–7, who examines those passages where the dual is supposedly doing duty for the plural, the so-called *dualis pro plurali*, and concludes that they do not justify the view that Zenodotos took of the dual; and against Aristarkhos it is urged that Akhilleus' surprise at the arrival of the two ambassadors at 193 is inexplicable if Phoinix has already preceded them and arrived with Akhilleus.

Nevertheless, the approaches of the Alexandrian critics are the ones that in one form or another have usually been followed by modern scholars. Either, the duals here do not refer to only two, but describe the journey and arrival of the full embassy; or, the duals are to be accepted in their normal meaning, as referring to two ambassadors only, and it is the task of scholarship to explain who these two are, and what has happened to the other three. Thus Edwards 1987 and Pötscher, both supposing that the full embassy is meant throughout 182–200, suggest, Edwards that the duals may give 'an air of honourable antiquity' to the embassy, Pötscher that with the use of the dual there is a gain in 'hieratic dignity'. Scholars who have followed Aristarkhean lines have produced innumerable solutions, even extending to the view that the duals do not always refer to the same two men. But Phoinix has been the ambassador whom the duals have most often been taken to be excluding – either on the grounds advanced by Aristarkhos, or as part of something more sweeping. For some scholars, Phoinix is a figure who arouses the gravest suspicions. Nestor's nomination of him to lead the embassy at 168 is most unexpected, seeing that he has not hitherto appeared in the poem at all; and from what we learn of him later it is surprising to find him at the *boulē* of the Akhaian leaders in Agamemnon's tent, rather than with Akhilleus, which is where he remains at the dispersal of the embassy, and where, from his close association with Akhilleus, we might expect him to have been all the time. These scholars therefore, many of whom are the same ones who also raise the points about the authenticity of Book IX that were referred to in the previous section, take the view that Phoinix had no place in the 'original version' of the book at all. There were originally two ambassadors, Odusseus and Aias, and the dual is rightfully used to describe their progress to Akhilleus. At a later stage some other poet added Phoinix to the embassy, but in doing so failed to make the adjustments to lines 182–99 that this adddition of a third ambassador required.

None of the very many solutions that have been proposed to the problem of the duals has found universal acceptance; and the one just outlined concerning Phoinix seems hopelessly far-fetched, not least in assuming that a poet who was good enough, presumably, to compose Phoinix's speech at the embassy could nevertheless have left lines 182–99 so grievously un-aligned with his new version. We may, however, perhaps tentatively accept the allegation of insufficient editing, but suppose that this reflects, not some later poet working on Homer's original, but rather different stages in Homer's own process of composition. We may, that is, here be getting a glimpse into Homer's 'workshop', and looking at some draft which could be entitled 'The journey of two ambassadors', and which has here been set into a narrative where it does not properly belong. While there can be no certainty about this, it can nevertheless perhaps be taken a little further. It has often been observed that at the beginning of our passage the language is closely similar to I 327–30, where the dual is quite unexceptionably used for the journey that Agamemnon's emissaries Talthubios and Eurubates make to the tent of Akhilleus for the purpose of taking away Briseis. Might 'The journey of two ambassadors' be one of the themes that Homer already has at his disposal (a scholiast's note on IX 168 reads, 'Two was the usual number for an embassy', and as well as I 327–30, there are also embassies of two men at III 205–6 and XI 139–40)? And might this be a theme which Homer calls up entirely appropriately at I 327, and calls up again at IX 182, but there only at a preliminary stage of his work, where the theme still awaits adaptation to the embassy of three (or five) men that Nestor had proposed at 169–70?

The discussions of Edwards 1987, 218–21, Hainsworth 1993 on IX 182, and Pötscher include extensive references to earlier work on the question of the duals at 182–99. On the workshop of Homer, see Reinhardt, as cited at the end of the previous section. On IX 182ff. and I 320ff., see especially Segal.

i. *The speech of Phoinix.*
There are a number of difficulties of interpretation in all three parts of Phoinix's speech, his own story, the parable of the *Litai*, and the story of Meleagros. He is somewhat rambling and inconsequential, and in his stories he seems to assume that the outlines are already known to his audience, so that he sometimes abbreviates in a way that would otherwise appear wilful. Where Phoinix departs from the tradition as it elsewhere comes down to us, it may be that Homer is adapting the tradition to his own requirements; this suggestion has been made in connection with all three sections of the speech.

I. Phoinix's own story (434–95)
(i) For Phoinix as the tutor of the young Akhilleus, and for the name of Phoinix's father, Amuntor, and the location of his domain in Hellas, see the notes to IX 442 and 447–8.
(ii) The course of events that led to Phoinix's flight from home seems to be –
    Phoinix's father Amuntor took a concubine, to the indignation of his wife, who urged Phoinix to lie with the concubine himself, so that she and Amuntor might become estranged from each other. This he did, whereupon Amuntor cursed him, successfully asking the Erinues, the avenging spirits that concern themselves especially with crimes against parents, that Phoinix should ever after be childless. Phoinix planned to kill Amuntor (assuming 458–61 are genuine), but was forestalled by one of the deities. His family then kept him at home for nine days, but thereafter he made his escape.
    The family's insistence that Phoinix remain with them is left unexplained; it is perhaps aimed at closing ranks, and so disguising the family strife beneath an outward appearance of solidarity. But even so it must be accepted that both the gathering of the family in such numbers, and the length at which Phoinix gives this part of the narrative (464–73), seem curious. The prayers that his kinsmen address to him (λισσόμενοι 465) are presumably to the effect that he should stay, and/or should abandon his anger against his father. Lines 458–61 are not in any of our manuscripts, but they are recorded by Plutarch, who says that Aristarkhos removed them because of the grossness of Phoinix's plan to kill his father. The story can stand without

them; but Phoinix's plan does give a stronger motivation for his subsequent flight. At XXIII 83–90 we find that what brought Patroklos to the same destination as Phoinix, the home of Akhilleus' father Peleus, was a murder he had committed previously.

II. The Litai (496–523)

The second part of Phoinix's speech is again a paradigm, in which he personifies *Atē* and the *Litai*, and draws from what he says about them the conclusion (513–23) that Akhilleus should abandon his anger and accept Agamemnon's offer. *Atē* is a kind of momentary madness, which is sent on a man by a god, and causes him to act quite out of character, and with disastrous results; when Akhilleus says (IX 377) that Zeus has taken away Agamemnon's wits, he is saying that Agamemnon has been possessed by *Atē*. The word is also sometimes used of the disastrous consequences that ensue from this external possession. By the *Litai*, whom he represents as being the daughters of Zeus, Phoinix means 'Apologies'. Personifications are quite common in Homer – Panic and Fear appear at IX 2, Sleep plays a full part in Here's design to beguile Zeus at XIV 231ff., Sleep and his brother Death carry away the corpse of Sarpedon at XVI 681–3, and *Atē* is personified again when Agamemnon finally makes things up with Akhilleus at XIX 87ff. But there is nowhere else anything quite like what we have here, the sustained use of personified abstractions to make up a paradigm; and the underlying thought of the passage, that apologies should be met with forgiveness, has also been felt to be hardly characteristic of the *Iliad* elsewhere. So Homer may once again be innovating for the sake of his immediate purposes.

What Phoinix says is clear in itself – the *Litai* follow in the wake of *Atē*, and put things right again. The man who pays due court to the *Litai* benefits greatly therefrom; but when the *Litai* are disregarded, they approach their father Zeus, and implore him that *Atē* should again go into action, and join the man who has disregarded them (502–512). What is less clear is how this applies to the present situation. Phoinix presumably has in mind that Agamemnon, as he himself has bluntly admitted at 116, has been misled by *Atē* into his seizure of Briseis, but that now he is apologising with his offer of reparations, and Akhilleus ought to accept the offer, as an act of honour to the *Litai*. That indeed is what Phoinix says – 'But do you too, Akhilleus, provide that honour attend the daughters of Zeus' (513–4). But what is the significance of what Phoinix says about the reappearance of *Atē* if the *Litai* are rejected? Akhilleus has already rejected Agamemnon's offer; and neither Phoinix nor Aias will succeed in getting him to change his mind. Are we then to suppose that Homer is here foreshadowing some *Atē* that will in due course visit Akhileus? If *Atē* were to be taken as simply 'disaster', then this might be so; Akhilleus' refusal will lead to the disastrous death of his dearest friend Patroklos when Patroklos has asked to be allowed to fight in Akhilleus' place. But *Atē* is in fact nowhere used of Akhilleus' despatch of Patroklos, and it was certainly no momentary loss of his wits that caused Akhilleus to send Patroklos to his death; Patroklos lost his life when he took it upon himself to assault the Trojan wall, which was something which Akhilleus had explicitly and forcefully told him not to do (XVI 87–100). So either the meaning of *Atē* has changed from what it was at 505, the sort of momentary loss of one's wits that caused Agamemnon to take away Briseis, or, more plausibly, this passage on *Atē* following on behind when the *Litai* are dishonoured is included only to complete Phoinix's parable, and with no intended reference to the action of the poem.

On *Atē* in Homer, see especially Dodds, chapter 1.

III. *The story of Meleagros*

The third of Phoinix's paradigms falls into two parts – the background story to the fighting in which Meleagros was involved at 529–49, followed by the paradigm proper at 550–99. Initially, Phoinix appears to be using the paradigm to illustrate the statement that he makes at 526, 'the heroes of old were open to gifts, and could be persuaded by words' (note the similarity of this to what he had said about the gods when introducing the *Litai* paradigm at 497); but in the telling of the story this is significantly modified (see Section **d**. above) into, 'Meleagros left it too late before accepting the offered gifts; do not you, Akhilleus, do the same'.

Phoinix says that he remembers the story 'from long ago' (πάλαι, 527), and we must therefore envisage it as taking place some time before the Trojan war, although in fact Meleagros had a half-brother Tudeus, who was the father of the Akhaian hero Diomedes (see the *stemmata* given by Hainsworth 1993 in his note on 555–8). Meleagros' father Oineus was the king of Kaludonians, whose opponents in the war, the Kouretes, came from nearby Pleuron (though this city is not named here). Both these cities are in Aitolia in its wider sense, the area of Greece north of the gulf of Corinth at its western end. The narrative background is given in clear, if somewhat compressed, form, and by Homer's common method of ring-composition –

a¹. 529–32.   The Kaludonians were at war with the Kouretes.
b¹. 533–4.   Artemis had sent an 'evil' on Oineus,
c. 534–7.   because he had omitted her from his sacrifices.
b² 538–46.   So she sent the wild boar, which did terrible damage until it
                was at last killed.
a² 547–9.   Quarrelling over the spoils of the boar led to war between the
                Kaludonians and the Kouretes.

In the paradigm, the parallels between Meleagros and Akhilleus are also clear; and they refer not only to Akhilleus' present situation, but also to what is to come –
   Meleagros withdrew from the fighting in anger.
   In his absence, the fighting went very badly for the Kaludonians.
   In their danger, his people approached him with offers of gifts.
   Meleagros at first refused these gifts.

Eventually, when the danger was at its greatest, he gave way to the person closest to him (his wife Kleopatre in Meleagros' case, his friend Patroklos in Akhilleus').

But there are a number of difficulties in the working-out of this section of Phoinix's speech. Phoinix speaks allusively, as though assuming that the story is already known to his hearers; and modern discussions have commonly suggested that Homer has here taken an already existing story of Meleagros, which he has adapted, but not always entirely successfully, to match the situation of Akhilleus. See especially Willcock 1964, 147–53; and note lines 524–8, suggesting that the story of Meleagros is an old one. The major difficulties are:–

(i) The confused account of the fighting at lines 550–2, on which see the note to 552.

(ii) Lines 557–64, on the previous history of the family of Meleagros' wife. Note once again the ring-composition; 565–6 takes us back to 555–6. Kleopatre is going to play a crucial part in the story, in that it is she who will finally succeed in persuading Meleagros to re-enter the fighting, and this digression into her family history is perhaps intended as a means of establishing her importance. But the digression is exceedingly allusive. The story seems to be – Kleopatre was the daughter of Idas, a man who had once drawn his bow against Apollo, and of Marpesse, who was herself the daughter of Euenos. Marpesse used to weep as a kingfisher weeps for its mate, because Apollo had once snatched her away. (This was the occasion of Idas drawing his bow against Apollo.). And so Idas and Marpesse used also to call Kleopatre by the name of Alkuone, 'Kingfisher'. But it does look as though Phoinix has somewhat lost grasp of his narrative in this section, which seems to do little to advance the paradigm of Meleagros.

But there may be something more to Kleopatre. It is curious to find a Greek with two different names, as Kleopatre is also known as Alkuone; and it has been noted that the name *Kleo-patre* reverses the two elements of the name of Akhilleus' friend *Patro-klos*. Patroklos will, by his death, cause Akhilleus to abandon his anger and re-join the fighting; and it is Kleopatre who will persuade Meleagros to do the same. It seems possible that originally the daughter of Idas and Marpesse may have only had the name Alkuone, and that Homer has introduced the second name of Kleopatre to hint at the similar roles of her and Patroklos and thereby to improve the fit with his own story, and that in doing this he has felt obliged to introduce the digression on how his Kleopatre also had the name of Alkuone.

(iii) *Althaie and her curse, lines 566–72.* Meleagros is cursed by a parent – just as Phoinix himself had been (453–6); and his anger at this curse is what causes him to withdraw from battle. But Homer says no more in explanation of Althaie's curse than that it was for 'the murder of her brother' (567) – there is once again the suspicion that he knows more than he here chooses to say. Elsewhere, we learn that Meleagros had more than one uncle, and that they came from Pleuron, and so were Kouretes. So it was presumably in the fighting that followed the Kaludonian Boar episode that Meleagros killed one of them, and so provoked the curses of his mother.

But why then does Althaie, her anger with Meleagros now apparently forgotten, subsequently join the suppliants who plead with him to return to the defence of Kaludon (584)?

The main surviving versions of the story of Meleagros are those of the fifth century poet Bakkhulides, at V 94–135, and of the early first century A.D. Roman poet Ovid, at *Metamorphoses* VIII 270–444. Both of these differ substantially from the version of Phoinix. They do not mention Althaie's curse, or Meleagros' withdrawal from battle, but say instead that when Althaie heard of her brothers' deaths, she cast onto the fire a firebrand that represented Meleagros' life, and that thereupon Meleagros collapsed and died. Let us suppose, while acknowledging that certainty is not possible, that this different version was already current in Homer's day. Then when Homer turned to it, he would have found this form of it unsuitable for Phoinix's paradigm for Akhilleus on at least two counts – in that Althaie's anger with Meleagros leads to his death, and that it does not provide a motive for the most important part of the paradigm, Meleagros' withdrawal from the fighting. Homer therefore discards the firebrand element of the story, but retains Althaie's anger at Meleagros killing one of her brothers, and makes her consequent curse on Meleagros the reason for his withdrawal. Homer's paradigm also requires that Meleagros must be implored to resume fighting, as Akhilleus is being implored now; and he includes Althaie among those who come to implore him, but in doing so fails to account for the change of heart that Althaie must have undergone since her curse on Meleagros. In the absence of pre-Homeric sources, this cannot be more than a supposition; but it is certainly a tempting and interesting one.

On Homer's use of paradigm in general, see the whole of Willcock's 1964 article, and also Ø. Andersen, *Myth, paradigm, and spatial form in the Iliad*, in Bremer, de Jong & Kalff, 1–14.

Basic Homeric Grammar

Note: *The grammatical, etc., help at the foot of the pages of the Greek text is linked to this Basic Homeric Grammar; and points on metre are linked to the Section on Scansion, Introduction, pp. 43–47.*

A. For many words, Homer has two (or more) different forms, which scan differently. Thus in many words, either $-\pi-$ or $-\pi\pi-$, $-\sigma-$ or $-\sigma\sigma-$, $-\tau-$ or $-\tau\tau-$ may be used, e.g. ὁπ(π)ως, ὅσ(σ)οι, ὅτ(τ)ι, where the ὁ– is scanned short before the single consonant, but long when the consonant is doubled. Likewise an initial ε– may be doubled in words like εἶπε and εἴκοσι, giving ἔειπε and ἐείκοσι.

NOUNS AND ADJECTIVES

B. <u>First declension</u>

<u>Feminine in –α and –η</u>

(1) Nom s.: ends in –η, even after ε, ι, and ρ. This –η ending is retained throughout the sing., e.g. ἀγορήν, κλισίης, γαίῃ.

(2) Gen. pl.: usually ends in –αων or –εων, e.g. ῥοάων, ἀγορέων.

(3) Dat. pl.: usually ends in –ῃς or –ῃσι(ν), e.g. αὐγῆς, θεῆσι, for αὐγαῖς, θεαῖς.

<u>Masculine in –ης</u>

(4) Nom. s.: some endings in –α, e.g. ἱππότα.

(5) Voc. s.: ends in –η, e.g. Κρονίδη.

(6) Gen. s.: ends in –αο or –εω, not –ου, e.g. Ἀτρείδαο, Ἀΐδεω.

(7) Gen. pl.: ends –αων, e.g. αἰχμητάων.

(8)   The ending –ίδης, meaning 'son of', or 'descendant of', is very common –
e.g. Ἀτρείδης, 'son of Atreus'.

C.   <u>Second declension</u>

(1)   νόος not contracted to νοῦς.

(2)   Gen s.: ends –οιο, e.g. θανάτοιο.

(3)   Dat. pl.: ends –οισι(ν), e.g. Δαναοῖσι(ν).

(4)   Dual: Nom. and acc. –ω, e.g. ἵππω;

        Gen. and dat. –οιιν, e.g. ὤμοιιν.

D.   <u>Third declension</u>

    <u>Sing.</u>

(1)   Voc.: –ις words end in –ι, e.g. γλαυκῶπι;

(2)   Acc.: <u>a</u>. –ις words end in –ιν, e.g. Ἶριν;

        <u>b</u>. –ηα for –εα, e.g. ἡνιοχῆα;

        <u>c</u>. –εα for –η, e.g. περικαλλέα.

(3)   Gen.: <u>a</u>. –ηος and –ιος for –εως, e.g. Ἰδομενῆος, πόλιος;

        <u>b</u>. –εος for –ους, e.g. τείχεος.

(4)   Dat.: –εϊ and –ηϊ for –ει, e.g. σάκεϊ.

    <u>Plur.</u>

(5)   Nom.: <u>a</u>. m. and f.: –εες and –ηες for –εις, e.g. ὠκέες, ἱππῆες;

        <u>b</u>. n.: –εα for –η, also in acc., e.g. ἔπεα.

(6)   Acc.: –εας and –ηας for –εις, e.g. ὠκέας, βασιλῆας.

(7)　Gen.: <u>a</u>. –ηων and –ιων for –εων, e.g. βασιλήων, πολίων;

　　　<u>b</u>. –εων for –ων, e.g. ὀχέων.

(8)　Dat.　–εσσι(ν)　for　–σι(ν),　–εσι(ν),　and　–ξι(ν),　e.g.　Τρώεσσι, πάντεσσι (from πᾶς), κηρύκεσσι.

Dual

(9)　Nom. and acc.: ends –ε, e.g. κῆρε;

　　　Gen. and dat.: ends –οιϊν, e.g. ποδοῖϊν.

(10)　Three frequent nouns –

	Ἀχιλ(λ)εύς			ναῦς	Ζεύς
		Sing.	Plur.		
Nom.	Ἀχιλ(λ) –εύς	ναῦς	νῆες		Ζεύς
Voc.	–εῦ	–	–		Ζεῦ
Acc.	–έα, –ῆα	νῆα	νῆας		Ζῆνα, Ζῆν, Δία
Gen.	–έος, –ῆος	νηός	νεῶν, νηῶν		Διός
Dat.	–εῖ, –ῆϊ	νηΐ	νήεσσι(ν), νηυσί(ν)		Ζηνί, Διί

E.　The suffix –φι(ν) is used for the gen. and dat., s. and pl., e.g. διὰ στήθεσφιν, 'through the chest'.

F.　<u>Possessive adjectives</u>

2 s. can be τεός;

1 pl. can be ἀμός;

3 s. and pl. ὅς ἥ ὅν and ἑός ἑή ἑόν.

Possessives are often expressed by the dative of the noun or pronoun – G.3, H.3.

G. <u>Some uses of the cases</u>

(1) Acc.:
<u>a</u>. n. adj., s. and pl., used adverbially, e.g. σμερδαλέον ἐβόησεν, 'he shouted terribly'.
<u>b</u>. 'to', especially after ἱκάνω, ἱκνέομαι, ἵκω, e.g. "Αργος ἱκέσθαι, 'to come to Argos'.
<u>c</u>. the 'seat of the emotions', e.g. τετιημέναι ἦτορ, 'downcast *in* heart'.
<u>d</u>. the 'part affected', e.g. αὐτὸν ἔβαλε στῆθος, 'he struck him *in* the chest'.
<u>e</u>. acc. 'of respect', e.g. βοὴν ἀγαθός, 'good in respect of the shout'.
<u>f</u>. 'to take away X from Y', with X and Y both acc., e.g. ἵππους Αἰνείαν ἀφελόμην, 'I took away the horses from Aineias'.
<u>g</u>. duration of time, e.g. ἤματα πάντα, 'for all the days'.

(2) <u>Gen</u>.:
<u>a</u>. time in the course of which, e.g. ἠοῦς, 'in the morning'.
<u>b</u>. space over which, e.g. πεδίοιο, 'over the plain'.
<u>c</u>. causal gen., often for the source of anger and grief, e.g. παλλακίδος ἐχώσατο, 'he was angry about his mistress'.
<u>d</u>. 'full of', 'fill with', and similar expressions, e.g. πλεῖαι οἴνου, 'full of wine'.
<u>e</u>. for separation, or ceasing from, e.g. πολέμου ἀφεξόμεθα, 'we shall hold ourselves back from war'.

(3) <u>Dat</u>.:
Possesive, e.g. "Ηρῃ στῆθος, 'Here's breast'. Often like this with pronouns, e.g. τοι γούνατα, 'your knees'.

PRONOUNS

H. <u>Personal pronouns</u>

(1)	1 s.	2 s.	1 pl.	2 pl.
nom. & voc.	ἐγώ, ἐγών	σύ	ἡμεῖς	ὑμεῖς
acc.	ἐμέ, με	σέ, σε	ἡμᾶς, ἡμέας, ἄμμε	ὑμᾶς, ὑμέας, ὔμμε
gen.	ἐμοῦ, μοῦ, ἐμεῦ, μεῦ, ἐμέθεν, ἐμεῖο	σεῖο, σέο, σεῦ, σέθεν	ἡμέων, ἡμείων	ὑμέων, ὑμείων

| dat. | ἐμοί, μοι | σοί, σοι, τοι ἡμῖν, ἄμμι(ν) | ὑμῖν, ὔμμι(ν) |

| dual: nom. & acc. | | νῶϊ | σφῶϊ, σφώ |
| gen. & dat. | | νῶϊν | σφῶϊν |

(2)   3 s.   3 pl.

acc.   ἔ, μιν   σφε, σφέας, σφας

gen.   εἷο, ἕο, εὗ, ἕθεν, εὑ   σφείων, σφέων

dat.   οἱ, οἷ when reflexive   σφι(ν), σφισί(ν)

dual: nom. & acc.   σφωέ

gen. & dat.   σφωΐν   (Note difference in accentuation
                                              from 2 dual above.)

(3) The dat. of the personal pronoun is often used possessively, e.g. τοι σθένος,
'your strength'.

I.   ὁ ἡ τό and ὅς ἥ ὅ

    (1)   <u>a.</u> Gen. s. m. and n. can be τοῖο;
        <u>b.</u> gen. pl. f. τάων;
        <u>c.</u> dat. pl., m. and n. τοῖσι(ν), f. τῇς, τῇσι(ν);
        <u>d.</u> Dual nom. and acc. τώ, gen. and dat. τοῖν;
        <u>e.</u> The relative pronoun often retains the initial τ–.

    (2) ὁ ἡ τό rarely 'the', a word Homer usually omits. Usually, it is 'he', 'she',
'it', pl. 'they'; also demonstrative, 'that'.

    (3) ὅ and ὅ τε,'because', 'that'. E.g. VIII 32, ἴδμεν ὅ τοι σθένος οὐκ
ἐπιεικτόν, 'we know that your strength is irresistible.'

    (4) τῇ 'there': τῶ 'therefore'.

J.   τίς, 'who?', 'what?' and τις, 'a', 'someone'

(1)   Gen. s.: τέο, τεῦ;

Dat. s.: τέῳ;

Gen. pl.: τέων.

(2) τί 'why?'; τί ποτε, τίπτε, 'why ever?'; τι 'at all', after negative words.

(3) ὅστις usually appears as ὅτις, with o– unchanged throughout.

K.   αὐτός

(1) 'him', 'her', 'it', pl. 'them': not so in nom., or at beginning of clause.

(2) 'himself', 'herself', etc. Often so of Zeus; and often when the narrative has been concerned with a less important character, and now returns to a more important one. E.g. VIII 319–20, 'Hektor's charioteer ..., αὐτὸς δ' (Hektor) ...

(3) 'on one's own', e.g. VIII 99, Diomedes αὐτός περ ἐών, 'although being on his own.'

(4) In dat., αὐτῇ γαίῃ, 'earth and all', αὐτοῖσιν ὄχεσφιν, 'chariot and all', etc.

(5) αὐτοῦ, αὐτόθι, 'there'.

·VERBS

L.   <u>Person endings</u>.

(1) –εαι for –ει, –ῃ, in 2 s. mid. and pass., e.g. ὄψεαι for ὄψει;

(2) –εο for –ου in 2 s. mid. and pass., e.g. βούλεο for βούλου;

(3) –ομεσθα and –ωμεσθα for –ομεθα and –ωμεθα in 1 pl., e.g. φραζώμεσθα for φραζώμεθα.

(4) –αται and –ατο in 3 pl. mid. and pass., e.g. βεβολήατο for βεβόληντο;

(5) –εν for –ησαν in 3 pl. aor. pass., e.g. ἔφανεν for ἐφάνησαν;

<u>Subjunctive</u>

(6) –ωμι for –ω in 1 s. act., e.g. ἐθέλωμι for ἐθέλω;

(7) –ῃσθα for –ῃς in 2 s. act., e.g. ἐθέλῃσθα for ἐθέλῃς;

(8) –ηαι for –ῃ in 2 s. mid. and pass., e.g. γένηαι for γένῃ;

(9) –ῃσι(ν) for –ῃ in 3 s. act., e.g. μάρπτῃσι for μάρπτῃ;

(10) The –η and –ω at the beginning of the ending may be shortened to –ε and –ο, e.g. ἴομεν, εἴδετε, for ἴωμεν, εἴδητε.

M.   <u>Dual</u>

(1) –τον, –σθον, in pres., fut., 2 aor., perf., imperat.: e.g. ἀποτίνετον, μέματον;

(2) –την, –σθην, in imperf. and 1 aor.: e.g. βήτην, μεδέσθην;

(3) –των in imperat., e.g. κομείτων.

N.   <u>Augment</u>

(1) The augment is often omitted, e.g. ποιήσατο for ἐποιήσατο; also in compound verbs, e.g. κάββαλε, κάλλιπον, for κατέβαλε, κατέλιπον.

(2) After the augment, a consonant at the beginning of the root is sometimes doubled, e.g. ἔλλαβε for ἔλαβε.

O.   <u>Contraction</u>

(1) Verbs are often in their uncontracted forms, particularly after a consonant at the end of the future root; e.g. ὑπερθορέονται, 'they will jump over, VIII 179.

(2)   Some non–Attic forms –

    <u>a</u>. αα instead of ᾳ, e.g. ἐάᾳ for ἐᾷ;

    <u>b</u>. οω instead of ω, e.g. ὁρόων for ὁρῶν;

<u>c</u>. ωο instead of ω, e.g. ἱδρώοντες for ἱδρῶντες;

<u>d</u>. αα instead of α from αε, e.g. ἠγοράασθε for ἠγορᾶσθε.

P.   <u>Infinitives</u>

–μεν and –μεναι for –ειν and –ναι, e.g. ἐχέμεν for ἔχειν, δόμεν and δόμεναι for δοῦναι.

Q.   <u>The Aorist</u>

(1)   A *gnomic* aorist is sometimes used in general statements and similes, where English uses a present. E.g. VIII 556–8.

(2)   The aorist is sometimes used for the pluperfect, eg. VIII 323–4, ἐξείλετο, ἔθηκε, 'had been taking out', 'had been placing'.

(3)   The σ in the ending of the 1 aor. act. and mid. is sometimes doubled, e.g. ἐφράσσαντο.

R.   <u>Tmesis</u>

Compound verbs sometimes have their prefix separated from their root by intervening words, e.g. ἐν δ' ἐτίθει for ἐνετίθει δέ.
But it is sometimes difficult to judge whether there is tmesis, or whether the first word is an adverb and the verb is being used in its root form.

S.   <u>Frequentative verbs</u>

σκ– is sometimes added to the root of a verb to indicate continued action, e.g. σώεσκον, 'I kept on saving', δόσκον, 'I kept on giving' (from σώζω, δίδωμι).

T.   <u>Reduplicated forms</u>

Several verbs have a reduplicated aorist, e.g. κέκλυτε (κλύω), πεπιθεῖν (πείθω).

U.   <u>εἰμί, 'I am', and εἶμι 'I shall go'</u>

These are some of the forms that appear in *Iliad* VIII and IX:–

εἰμί   εἶμι

(1) Pres.:   2 s. ἔσσι; 1 pl. εἰμέν;
              3 pl. ἔασι; 2 dual ἔστον;

(2) Part.:   ἐών;   ἰών;

(3) Infin.: εἶναι, ἔμεν, ἔμεναι, ἔμμεναι;   ἰέναι;

(4) Imperf.: 1 and 3 s. ἔην;   3 pl.   ἴσαν;
              3 s. ἦεν, ἔσκε;
              3 pl. ἔσαν;

(5) Imperat.: 3 s. ἔστω; 2 pl. ἔστε;   2 s.   ἴθι;

(6) Fut.: 2 s. ἔσεαι; 3 s. ἔσσεται;

(7) Subjunc.: 3 pl. ἔησι (ν);   3 s. ἴησι(ν), 1 pl. ἴομεν;

(8) Optat.: 2 s. εἴης, ἔοις; 3 s. εἴη, ἔοι.

The same forms may also appear in the compounds.

V.   <u>'Speak (to)' and 'say (to)'</u>

Many of these forms also appear in compounds.

(1) 'I say' – φημί;

(2) 'I shall speak' –ἐρέω, φησώ;

(3) 'he spoke (to), 'he said (to)' –ἦ, ἔφη, ἔφατο, εἶπε, ηὔδα, ἐφώνεε, ἐφώνησε;

(4) 'having spoken' – εἰπών, φάς, φωνήσας;

(5) 'having been spoken' – εἰρημένος;

(6) 'speak!' (pl.) – φάσθε.

W. <u>ἄν and κεν (also κε, κ', χ')</u>

I. <u>Conditional sentences with ἄν or κεν</u>

(1) <u>a</u>. ἄν and κεν sometimes appear in the 'if' (*protasis*), as well as the main (*apodosis*), clause of a conditional.

   <u>b</u>. 'if' – εἰ, αἴ, ἤν. Negative in 'if'–clause μή.

(2) <u>Conditionals with 'would' in the apodosis in English</u> –

   <u>a</u>. ἄν or κεν in the apodosis.

   <u>b</u>. Past time: aor. indic. E.g VIII 217–8, καί νύ κ' ἐνέπρησεν .. εἰ μὴ Ἥρη ἔθηκε; 'And now he would have burned..., if Here had not put ..'.

   <u>c</u>. Present and future time: imperf. or optat. E.g. IX 515–7, εἰ μὴ δῶρα φέροι, . . . οὐκ ἄν ἐγώ σε ... κελοίμην, 'If he was not bringing gifts, I would not be ordering you'.

(3) <u>Future conditionals with 'shall' or 'will' in the English apodosis</u> –

   <u>a</u>. εἰ with subjunc. in protasis, with or without ἄν, fut. in apodosis; e.g. IX 359, ὄψεαι, αἴ κ' ἐθέλησθα, 'you will see, if you wish'. But sometimes the sense requires a different mood in the apodosis, e.g. imperat. at IX 137.

   <u>b</u>. Optat. with κε(ν) in both clauses., e.g. IX 141–2, εἰ κεν Ἄργος ἱκοίμεθα ... κεν ἔοι, 'if we come to Argos, he will be'.

   <u>c</u>. At IX 362–3 we have subjunc. in protasis, optat. in apodosis.

(4) <u>Potential conditionals</u>

Sometimes the protasis is not expressed, but the main clause follows one of the procedures above, and so makes its conditional nature clear. E.g. VIII 451, οὐκ ἄν με τρέψειαν, 'they would not divert me (if they tried to)'.

(5) εἰ κεν with subjunc., 'in the hope that'. E.g. VIII 282, βάλλ' οὕτως, αἴ κεν ... γένηαι, 'Shoot like this; in the hope that you become'.

<u>II. Other uses</u>

(6) With subjunc. in indirect questions. E.g. IX 680–1, φράζεσθαι . . .
ὅππως ·κεν ... σαῷς, 'Take counsel as to how you may save'.

(7) With subjunc., for future. E.g. VIII 34, οἵ κεν ὅλωνται, 'who will be
destroyed.'

(8) <u>a</u>. In *indefinite* clauses with subjunc., e.g. ὅττι κεν εἴπω, 'whatever I
say'. (But κεν omitted at VIII 391.)

<u>b</u>. But indefinite clauses referring to the past take optat. without ἄν; e.g.
VIII 189, ὅτε θυμὸς ἀνώγοι, 'whenever their heart bade'.

X.   <u>Other uses of subjunc. and optat.</u>

(1)   <u>a</u>. For purpose, after ἵνα, ὅπως, ὄφρα, ὥς, negative μή. E.g. VIII 5–6,
κέκλυτέ μευ, ὄφρ' εἴπω, 'Listen to me, that I may say'..

<u>b</u>. Purpose may also be expressed by the future participle, e.g. VIII 365,
398; and at VIII 111 it is expressed by ὄφρα and *fut*.

(2) Jussive subjunctive, 1 and 3 s. and pl. E.g. VIII 509, καίωμεν, ... σέλας
δ' ... ἵκῃ, 'let us burn, and let the light come.'
The same meaning also comes from 1 and 3 s. and pl. imperat., e.g. IX 47,
φευγόντων, 'let them flee'. Also dual imperat. at VIII 109, κομείτων, 'let the
two of them attend'.

(3) μή with subjunc. and optat. for 'I fear lest'; e.g. VIII 244–5.

(4) μή and aor. subjunc.   <u>a</u>. 'Be careful that .. not.. ', e.g. VIII 95.
                                 <u>b</u>. 'Don't', e.g. IX 33, 522.

(5) Optative expressing a wish for the future. E.g. VIII 512, μὴ ... ἐπιβαῖεν
..., ἀλλ' ... τις ... πέσσοι, 'May they not board, but may one of them tend'.
This sort of expression may (but need not) be introduced by εἰ γάρ, as at VIII
538.

Y.   ADVERBS AND PREPOSITIONS

Adverbs

(1) –δε, –ζε, –σε of movement towards; e.g. ἅλαδε, 'to the sea', ἑτέρωσε, 'to the other side', χαμᾶζε, 'to the ground'.

(2) –θεν, 'from' (but often preceded by ἀπό or ἐκ); e.g. οὐρανόθεν, 'from heaven'.

(3) –θι, 'where', e.g. κηρόθι, 'in his heart'.

(4) περί frequently 'exceedingly', 'especially'.

(5) Note ὥς and ὧς, 'thus'. In its other meanings, ὡς is normally not accented, unless it comes after what it governs, e.g. θεὸν ὥς 'like a god'.

(6)   Adjectives are sometimes better translated as adverbs, e.g. ὅτε ... πρόφρων ἐθέλοιμι, 'whenever I wanted in earnest'.

(7) Neuter adjectives frequently function as adverbs. G.1.

(8)   Prepositions may be used adverbially. E.g. VIII 547, ἐπὶ δὲ ξύλα ... λέγοντο, 'they gathered wood *besides*'.

Prepositions

(9) These are some alternative forms –

ἀμφί : ἀμφίς

ἀνά : ἄμ

εἰς : ἐς

ἐν : εἰν, εἰνί, ἐνί

ἕνεκα : εἵνεκα

κατά : κάδ, κάκ

παρά : πάρ

πρός : ποτί, προτί

(10) περί + gen. is often 'superior to'.

(11) When a preposition comes after what it governs, this sometimes changes its accentuation. E.g. ποταμῷ ἔπι (ἐπί when the preposition precedes its noun).

Z.   PARTICLES

These are some of Homer's commonest particles –

ἄρα, ἄρ, ῥα: 'so', 'next', 'as is now clear'

γε : 'at least', often intensifying; e.g. VIII 7, τό γε, '<u>this</u>, at least'

γάρ: 'for'. Sometimes used *elliptically*, when a word like 'yes' or 'no' has to be supplied before 'for'

δή: 'indeed'

ἦ: 'surely', 'indeed', particularly in speech. Sometimes joined with τοι (see below) to make ἦτοι, 'indeed, I tell you'

καί: 'even', 'as well', besides 'and'

μέν: 'on the one hand', often followed, not by δέ, but some other word such as ἀλλά or αὐτάρ

μήν – also μάν and μέν (this is different from the μέν above): 'indeed'

περ: a. concessive, often with a participle. E.g. VIII 99, αὐτός περ ἐών, 'although being on his own'; and often in this sense preceded by καί;

      b. 'at least', e.g. VIII 242–3;

      c. intensive, 'indeed'

που: 'I suppose'

τε: the 'generalising' τε is often used in general statements and similes, when it is not to be translated. E.g. IX 5–6

τοι: 'let me tell you'

Scansion: The Homeric Hexameter

A. Metre

1. Each line of the *Iliad* follows the same metrical pattern. The line has six metrical feet, and each foot consists of an initial long syllable, followed and completed, either by a second long syllable, or by two short syllables – except that the last, sixth, foot, is always a two-syllable foot, and the second of these syllables may be short.

The pattern may therefore be represented thus:–

```
    1        2        3        4        5        6

-  ⌣ ⌣  | -  ⌣ ⌣  | -  ⌣ ⌣  | -  ⌣ ⌣  | -  ⌣ ⌣  |  -  ⌣  |
-   -   | -   -   | -   -   | -   -   | -   -   |  -  -  |
```

The - ⌣ ⌣ foot is called a *dactyl*, the - - one a *spondee*.

In the fifth foot, a dactyl is more common than a spondee.

2. The caesura.

a. *Caesura* is the name given to a break between words that occurs within, rather than at the end of, the foot. There may be a caesura in any of the feet; but Homer almost invariably has one within the third foot, either after the first syllable (the *strong* caesura), or after the second syllable of a dactylic foot (the *weak* caesura). Where reference is made to 'the caesura' of a particular line, it is this third foot caesura that is meant, unless there is explicit indication to the contrary.

Thus VIII 1 scans –

```
- - |  -    ⌣ ⌣ | -  ⌣    ⌣|- ⌣ ⌣ | -  ⌣    ⌣ | - ⌣ |
```
Ἠὼς μὲν κροκόπεπλος ‖ ἐκίδνατο πᾶσαν ἐπ' αῖαν

with a weak caesura; and IX 1 scans –

```
-   - | -    - |-    ⌣ ⌣ |-  ⌣ ⌣ | - ⌣    ⌣ |- - |
```
ὣς οἱ μὲν Τρῶες ‖ φυλακὰς ἔχον αὐτὰρ Ἀχαιοὺς

with a strong caesura.

The caesura may, or it may not, coincide with a break in the sense. In the two lines above it does not; it comes when the subject of the verb has been given, but the verb has not. But at IX 2 we have –

    ‒ ◡ ◡|‒ ◡ ◡ | ‒ ◡   ◡ |‒   ◡◡|‒ ◡   ◡|‒ ‒ |
    θεσπεσίη ἔχε φύζα, ‖ φόβου κρυόεντος ἑταίρη

with the caesura at a place where one would naturally insert a comma.

<u>b</u>. Postpositives and prepositives

In determining where the caesura of a line occurs, care must be taken over certain monosyllabic words that attach themselves to either the preceding word (*postpositives*) or to the succeeding one (*prepositives*). A caesura does not occur immediately before a postpositive, or immediately after a prepositive.

Postpositives include –

Enclitic words – i.e. words that throw their accent back to the previous word, such as κε, μιν, νυ, τις;
Particles that cannot stand first word in the sentence, e.g. γάρ, δέ, μέν, οὖν.

Prepositives include –

Monosyllabic prepositions, such as εἰς and ἐν;
Conjunctions which come first in the sentence, such as εἰ, ἤ, καί, ὡς;
Interrogative words, such as ποῦ and τίς.

For the effect of this, consider VIII 5 –

    ‒ ◡◡ | ‒   ‒ | ‒ ◡   ◡|‒   ‒|‒   ◡ ◡|‒ ‒ |
    κέκλυτέ μευ, πάντες τε ‖ θεοὶ πᾶσαί τε θέαιναι

with caesura after τε, not before; and VIII 57 –

    ‒ ◡ ◡|‒ ‒ |‒   ◡   ◡ | ‒ ‒ | ‒   ◡ ◡|‒ ‒ |
    χρειοῖ ἀναγκαίῃ ‖ πρό τε παίδων καὶ πρὸ γυναικῶν

with caesura before πρό, not after it, both because it is a prepositive, and because it is followed by a postpositive, τε.

B.   Prosody

Prosody is the word given to the rules which determine how each word fits into the metre of the line.

1. A syllable is normally scanned long (the commonest exceptions are given below) when it contains, or is comprised of –

one of the long vowels (η, ω);
a vowel that is pronounced long, e.g. πᾶσα (any vowel marked with a circumflex is long);
a diphthong, or a vowel with an iota subscript beneath it.

2. But a vowel may also be *long by position* – that is to say, the vowel is itself pronounced short, but the syllable in which it occurs is scanned long because of the nature of the consonants following the vowel. Consonants that cause a preceding vowel to be long by position include –

the *double* consonants – ζ, ξ, and ψ; also ῥ at the beginning of a word;
the same consonant repeated, e.g. βάλλω;
all combinations of three consonants;
many, but not all, combinations of two consonants.

These consonants exercise their effect on the vowel whether they occur within the same word, or at the beginning of the next word.

3. Subject to what is said above, the short vowels ε and o, and a vowel that is pronounced short in the word in which it occurs, are scanned short.

4. Thus in VIII 1, scanned above, both syllables of Ἡώς are naturally long, as are the first syllables of πᾶσαν and γαῖαν; but in μὲν, κροκόπεπλος and ἐκίδνατο we have vowels that are long by position.

5. The following circumstances sometimes produce unexpected effects of prosody –

a. Correption
A long vowel or diphthong at the end of one word which is followed by a vowel at the beginning of the following word may be scanned short by *correption*. E.g. VIII

8,   διακέρσαι ἐμόν.

b. Synizesis

Two vowels together, either in the same word or in successive words, may come together to form a single long syllable. E.g. IX 537, ἦ οὐκ.

c. Certain words that begin with a single consonant, particularly λ and μ, originally began with this consonant doubled; and the effect of this still sometimes makes itself felt in Homer's verse by lengthening the final vowel of the previous word. E.g. IX 9. ἄχεῑ (μ)μεγάλῳ.

d. The digamma

The Greek language originally contained a letter called the digamma, written as *F* and pronounced as *w*. This letter does not occur in the transmitted text of Homer, and it was already falling out of use in his time. But its effect is still sometimes felt, when a vowel is scanned long when it is followed by what is now only one consonant, but where this consonant was originally preceded or followed by a digamma. E.g. καλ(*F*)ός (first syllable always long in Homer); and at VIII 8, ἐμῶν (*F*) ἔπος.

C.   Effects of Sound

Within the system outlined above, Homer has infinite opportunity, both for artistic variation in such matters as, e.g., the distribution of the caesuras within the lines, and for special effects that in some way relate to the sense of what is being said. His verse needs to be read aloud for these effects to be felt to the full; here one can do no more than give examples of some sense-related sound-effects.

    i) In Zeus' speech at VIII 5–27, the first 8 lines, 5–12, all have the caesura after the second, not the first, syllable of the third foot; and none of these caesuras coincides with a break in the sense. One would not normally have such a long uninterrupted run of weak caesuras. In these lines, Zeus sets forth the main burden of his speech to the assembled gods and goddesses – that he is in no mood now for contradiction, and absolutely forbids the deities to intervene on either the Akhaian or the Trojan side. The unusual caesura arrangement helps to convey the authority and the urgency of Zeus' words. He knows exactly what he wants to say, and is in no mood for interruptions. He will say just what he wants to say, and will say it in just the way that he wants to say it.

The authoritative tone of these lines is reinforced by the last of them (12) ending with a four-syllable word, Οὐλυμπόνδε, of which the first two syllables are long, thus making a spondee, rather than the more common dactyl, for the fifth foot of the line. Exactly the same effect is achieved by the last two words of the whole speech,

εἴμ' ἀνθρώπων, four long syllables, at 27. This line also contains the following effects for the same purpose –
The line is a complete sense-unit in itself;
The third-foot caesura after εἰμὶ is over-ridden by the sense, which runs on to the fourth-foot caesura after θεῶν.
The last syllable before this caesura is identical to the last syllable of the line.
περί τ' εἰμ(ὶ) before the third-foot caesura is repeated after the fourth-foot caesura.

Individually, each of these features may be paralleled in other lines where they do not appear to have any sense-related effect. But taken together they help significantly to reinforce the sense of what Zeus is saying.

ii) In bringing his sentences to an end, Homer's most common practice is to end the sentence at the end of the line ('end-stopping'). Where a sentence runs on over the end of the line, this is called 'enjambment', and is sometimes done for special effect. IX 337–341, from Akhilleus' speech to Odusseus, is a celebrated example, where the effect of repeated enjambment is strengthened by the run-over into the second line always taking the form of a single word of three long syllables, after which the sentence, or question, comes to an end. This structure helps to convey the overpowering crescendo that Akhilleus' anger against Agamemnon has now reached.

iii) Sometimes Homer will create an effect with an unusual number of dactyls or spondees. In the final section of VIII, 553–565, of the first seven lines (553–9), which include the famous simile of the Trojan watch-fires like the stars on a clear night, all but 557 have five dactyls, the maximum possible within a line, and 557 has 4. But in the last line, Homer again indicates that an ending has been reached by having Ἠῶ as a spondaic fifth foot.

HOMER
ILIAD– BOOKS 8 & 9

ΙΛΙΑΔΟΣ Θ

Ἠὼς μὲν κροκόπεπλος ἐκίδνατο πᾶσαν ἐπ' αἶαν,
Ζεὺς δὲ θεῶν ἀγορὴν ποιήσατο τερπικέραυνος
ἀκροτάτῃ κορυφῇ πολυδειράδος Οὐλύμποιο·
αὐτὸς δέ σφ' ἀγόρευε, θεοὶ δ' ὑπὸ πάντες ἄκουον·
"κέκλυτέ μευ, πάντές τε θεοὶ πᾶσαί τε θέαιναι,   5
ὄφρ' εἴπω τά με θυμὸς ἐνὶ στήθεσσι κελεύει.
μήτε τις οὖν θήλεια θεὸς τό γε μήτε τις ἄρσην
πειράτω διακέρσαι ἐμὸν ἔπος, ἀλλ' ἅμα πάντες
αἰνεῖτ', ὄφρα τάχιστα τελευτήσω τάδε ἔργα.
ὃν δ' ἂν ἐγὼν ἀπάνευθε θεῶν ἐθέλοντα νοήσω   10
ἐλθόντ' ἢ Τρώεσσιν ἀρηγέμεν ἢ Δαναοῖσι
πληγεὶς οὐ κατὰ κόσμον ἐλεύσεται Οὔλυμπόνδε·

---

2. ἀγορὴν = ἀγορὰν (B.1) | ποιήσατο = ἐποιήσατο (N.1)

3. Οὐλύμποιο = Ὀλύμπου (C.2); Οὐλ- for Ὀλ- again at 12, 25

4. αὐτὸς: 'he himself', contrasted with the other gods (K.2) l σφ' = σφι, 'to them' (H.2) | ὑπὸ ... ἄκουον, tmesis, for ὑπήκουον (R)

5. κέκλυτε: imperat. of a reduplicated aorist of κλύω (T) | μευ: gen.s. ἐγώ (H.1), gen. after a verb of hearing | τε ... τε: a common alternative to τε ... καί

6. εἴπω: 'I may say'; subjunc., 2 aor. after ὄφρ' (X.1) | τά: relative pronoun (I.e), with antecedent omitted – 'those things which' | ἐνὶ στήθεσσι = ἐν στήθεσι (Y.9, D.8)

7–8. μήτε τις θεὸς πειράτω: 'don't let any god try' (X.2); πειράτω 3 s. imperat. πειράω

7. θεὸς: with a f. adj., θήλεια, but to be supplied also with ἄρσην | τό γε: '*this*, at least' (Z), to be defined in the next line | τό demonstrative (I.2)

8. διακέρσαι: aor. infin. act. διακείρω; final syllable short, by correption (Scansion, B.5a.)

9–10. τελευτήσω, νοήσω: both aor. subjunc. act., τελευτήσω after ὄφρα (X.1a), νοήσω after ὃν ἂν, 'whomsoever', in an indefinite clause (W.8a)

10. ὃν: relative pronoun, m., but referring to the goddesses as well as the gods

11. ἐλθόντ': acc. s. m. 2 aor. part. ἔρχομαι; 2 aor. indic. ἦλθον at 89, etc. | ἀρηγέμεν = ἀρήγειν, infin. (P); 'coming, to help', i.e 'to come and help' | Τρώεσσιν = Τρῶσιν (D.8)

12. πληγεὶς: nom. s. m. aor. part. pass. πλήσσω | οὐ: with κατὰ κόσμον, not with the verb of the sentence | ἐλεύσεται fut. ἔρχομαι | Οὔλυμπόνδε: '*to* Olumpos' (Υ.1); likewise πεδίονδε, 21, etc.

ILIAD VIII

1   Yellow-robed Dawn was spread over all the earth, and
Zeus, who delights in thunderbolts, made an assembly of
the gods on the highest summit of many-ridged Olumpos.
He himself began to address them, and all the gods took
heed –

5   "Listen to me, all you gods and all you goddesses, so
that I may say what my heart in my breast orders me. Let
no female god, nor any male one, try this – to confound my
word; but all of you together accept it, so that very quickly I
10   may end these actions. Whomsoever I spot wanting to go
off apart from the gods to help either the Trojans or the
Danaans, he, struck (by my thunderbolt), will come back
ingloriously to Olumpos. Or, having caught him, I shall

ἤ μιν ἑλὼν ῥίψω ἐς Τάρταρον ἠερόεντα
τῆλε μάλ', ἧχι βάθιστον ὑπὸ χθονός ἐστι βέρεθρον,   15
ἔνθα σιδήρειαί τε πύλαι καὶ χάλκεος οὐδός,
τόσσον ἔνερθ' Ἀΐδεω ὅσον οὐρανός ἐστ' ἀπὸ γαίης·
γνώσετ' ἔπειθ' ὅσον εἰμὶ θεῶν κάρτιστος ἁπάντων.
εἰ δ' ἄγε πειρήσασθε, θεοί, ἵνα εἴδετε πάντες·
σειρὴν χρυσείην ἐξ οὐρανόθεν κρεμάσαντες
πάντες τ' ἐξάπτεσθε θεοὶ πᾶσαί τε θέαιναι·   20
ἀλλ' οὐκ ἂν ἐρύσαιτ' ἐξ οὐρανόθεν πεδίονδε
Ζῆν' ὕπατον μήστωρ', οὐδ' εἰ μάλα πολλὰ κάμοιτε.
ἀλλ' ὅτε δὴ καὶ ἐγὼ πρόφρων ἐθέλοιμι ἐρύσσαι,
αὐτῇ κεν γαίῃ ἐρύσαιμ' αὐτῇ τε θαλάσσῃ·
σειρὴν μέν κεν ἔπειτα περὶ ῥίον Οὐλύμποιο   25
δησαίμην, τὰ δέ κ' αὖτε μετήορα πάντα γένοιτο.
τόσσον ἐγὼ περί τ' εἰμὶ θεῶν περί τ' εἴμ' ἀνθρώπων."

 Ὣς ἔφαθ', οἱ δ' ἄρα πάντες ἀκὴν ἐγένοντο σιωπῇ
μῦθον ἀγασσάμενοι· μάλα γὰρ κρατερῶς ἀγόρευσεν.

---

13. μιν: 'him' (H.2) | ἑλὼν: nom. s. m. 2 aor. act. part. αἱρέω | ἐς = εἰς (Y.9)

15. ἔνθα: supply εἰσί

16. Ἀΐδεω: gen. s. (B.6), gen. after ἔνερθ'; scan Ἀΐδεω with synizesis (Scansion, B.5b)

17. γνώσετ': fut. act. γιγνώσκω | ἔπειθ' = ἔπειτα

18. εἰ δ' ἄγε: 'but come now', with εἰ in this expression not having the sense 'if' | πειρήσασθε: aor. imperat. mid. πειράομαι | εἴδετε: subjunc. οἶδα, after ἵνα (X.1a), with –ετε for –ητε (L.10)

19. ἐξ οὐρανόθεν: 'from the sky' (Y.2), as 21 | κρεμάσαντες: aor. part. act. κρεμάννυμι

21. οὐκ ἂν ἐρύσαιτ': ἐρύσαιτ' 2 pl. aor. optat. act. ἐρύω; potential conditional (W.4) – 'you would not, (if you tried)'

22. Ζῆν': acc. Ζεύς (D.11) | κάμοιτε: 2 aor. optat. act. κάμνω, optat. in a 'would' conditional (W.2c)

23. ἐθέλοιμι: optat. ἐθέλω, optat. after ὅτε, 'whenever' (W.8b) | ἐρύσσαι: aor. infin. act. ἐρύω; aor. optat. act. in next line

24. αὐτῇ γαίῃ, αὐτῇ θαλάσσῃ: 'earth and all', 'sea and all' (K.4)

26. τὰ πάντα: 'all these things', τὰ demonstrative (I.2) | μετήορα = μετεῶρα | γένοιτο: 3 s., 2 aor. optat. γίγνομαι; 2 aor. indic. at 28

27. περί: 'superior to' (Y.9)

28. Ὣς: 'thus' (Y.5) | ἔφαθ' = ἔφατο, 'he spoke' (V.3) | ἄρα: 'so' (Z.1) | ἀκὴν .. σιωπῇ: a common tautology

29. ἀγασσάμενοι: aor. part ἄγαμαι (Q.3)

hurl him into murky Tartaros, far, far away, where the
15 deepest pit lies beneath the earth, where there are gates of
iron and a threshold of bronze, as far beneath Hades as
heaven is from the earth. Then he will come to know how
much I am the strongest of all the gods. But come, try it,
gods, that you may all know. Hanging a golden cord from
20 heaven, take hold of it, all you gods and goddesses. But
you would not drag Zeus, the supreme master of counsel,
from heaven to earth, not even if you laboured most
mightily. But whenever I wanted in earnest to drag (you), I
25 would drag (you) with the earth and the sea itself. Then I
would bind the cord around the peak of Olumpos, and
everything would be in mid-air. So much am I superior to
gods and to men."

Thus he spoke, and they all became silent, stunned by his
30 speech – for he had spoken very forcefully.

ὀψὲ δὲ δὴ μετέειπε θεὰ γλαυκῶπις ᾿Αθήνη·   30
"ὦ πάτερ ἡμέτερε Κρονίδη, ὕπατε κρειόντων,
εὖ νυ καὶ ἡμεῖς ἴδμεν ὅ τοι σθένος οὐκ ἐπιεικτόν·
ἀλλ᾿ ἔμπης Δαναῶν ὀλοφυρόμεθ᾿ αἰχμητάων,
οἵ κεν δὴ κακὸν οἶτον ἀναπλήσαντες ὄλωνται.
ἀλλ᾿ ἤτοι πολέμου μὲν ἀφεξόμεθ᾿, ὡς σὺ κελεύεις·   35
βουλὴν δ᾿ ᾿Αργείοις ὑποθησόμεθ᾿, ἥ τις ὀνήσει,
ὡς μὴ πάντες ὄλωνται ὀδυσσαμένοιο τεοῖο."

    Τὴν δ᾿ ἐπιμειδήσας προσέφη νεφεληγερέτα Ζεύς·
"θάρσει, Τριτογένεια, φίλον τέκος· οὔ νύ τι θυμῷ
πρόφρονι μυθέομαι, ἐθέλω δέ τοι ἤπιος εἶναι."   40

    ῝Ως εἰπὼν ὑπ᾿ ὄχεσφι τιτύσκετο χαλκόποδ᾿ ἵππω
ὠκυπέτα, χρυσέῃσιν ἐθείρῃσιν κομόωντε,
χρυσὸν δ᾿ αὐτὸς ἔδυνε περὶ χροΐ, γέντο δ᾿ ἱμάσθλην
χρυσείην εὔτυκτον, ἑοῦ δ᾿ ἐπεβήσετο δίφρου,

---

30. μετέειπε: 'spoke' (V.3) | θεὰ ..᾿ Αθήνη: note the omission of 'the', as normally in Homer
31. Κρονίδη: 'o son of Kronos', voc.; –ιδη 'son of' (B.5,8)
32. ἴδμεν: 1 pl. οἶδα | ὅ: 'that' (I.3) | τοι σθένος: 'your strength', τοι dat. of personal pronoun, used possessively (H.1,3); supply ἐστί after σθένος
33. αἰχμητάων = αἰχμητῶν (B.7), gen. after ὀλοφυρομεθ᾿
34. οἵ: 'who', | ὄλωνται: 2 aor. mid. subjunc. ὄλλυμι; κεν and subjunc. for fut. (W.7)
35. ἤτοι: 'indeed' (Z.1) | πολέμου: gen. for 'from' (G.2e)
36. ὑποθησόμεθ᾿: fut. mid. ὑποτίθημι | ἥ τις: 'some one which'; relative pronoun and indefinite (I & J), in the reverse order from what we translate them | ὀνήσει: fut. act. ὀνίνημι
37. ὀδυσσαμένοιο τεοῖο: gen. absolute, 'you having become angry'; τεοῖο a very unusual form of the gen. of the 2 s. personal pronoun.
38. Τὴν: 'her' (I.2) | προσέφη: 'spoke to' (V.4) | νεφεληγερέτα: nom.s. (B.4)
41. εἰπὼν: 'having spoken' (V.4) | ὄχεσφι: fromὄχος, equivalent to dat. pl. (E) | χαλκόποδ᾿ ἵππω: dual acc., as ὠκυπέτα and κομοῶντε in 42 (C.4, D.9)
42. χρυσέῃσιν ἐθείρῃσιν: dat. pl. f., –ῃσιν for –αις (B.3) | κομοῶντε = κομῶντε (O.2L), dual pres. part. κομάω
43. χροΐ: dat. s. χρώς | γέντο: 'he grasped'; 2 aor. mid. in form, but this is the only form in which the word is found
44. ἑοῦ: 'his', gen. s. m. ἑός (F) | ἐπεβήσετο: 3 s. aor. mid. ἐπιβαίνω, with gen., 'he mounted on', as 105, etc.

But finally the grey-eyed goddess Athene spoke –

"O father of ours, son of Kronos, highest of the mighty, well indeed do we know that your strength cannot be resisted. But nevertheless we pity the Danaan spearmen, who are to perish, having fulfilled a miserable fate. But we shall indeed keep ourselves away from the war, as you order. But we shall suggest a plan to the Argives, some one which will help them, so that they will not all perish because you are angry."

Smiling at her, Zeus the cloud-gatherer said –

"Take heart, Tritogeneia, dear child. I certainly do not speak with my heart in earnest, and I want to be kind to you."

So speaking, he harnessed a pair of bronze-footed horses to his chariot, swift-flying ones, with flowing manes of gold, and he put clothing of gold on his body, grasped his whip, golden and finely wrought, and mounted his

μάστιξεν δ' ἐλάαν· τὼ δ' οὐκ ἀέκοντε πετέσθην 45
μεσσηγὺς γαίης τε καὶ οὐρανοῦ ἀστερόεντος.
Ἴδην δ' ἵκανεν πολυπίδακα, μητέρα θηρῶν,
Γάργαρον, ἔνθά τέ οἱ τέμενος βωμός τε θυήεις.
ἔνθ' ἵππους ἔστησε πατὴρ ἀνδρῶν τε θεῶν τε
λύσας ἐξ ὀχέων, κατὰ δ' ἠέρα πουλὺν ἔχευεν. 50
αὐτὸς δ' ἐν κορυφῇσι καθέζετο κύδεϊ γαίων,
εἰσορόων Τρώων τε πόλιν καὶ νῆας Ἀχαιῶν.

 Οἱ δ' ἄρα δεῖπνον ἕλοντο κάρη κομόωντες Ἀχαιοὶ
ῥίμφα κατὰ κλισίας, ἀπὸ δ' αὐτοῦ θωρήσσοντο.
Τρῶες δ' αὖθ' ἑτέρωθεν ἀνὰ πτόλιν ὁπλίζοντο, 55
παυρότεροι· μέμασαν δὲ καὶ ὣς ὑσμῖνι μάχεσθαι,
χρειοῖ ἀναγκαίῃ, πρό τε παίδων καὶ πρὸ γυναικῶν.
πᾶσαι δ' ὠΐγνυντο πύλαι, ἐκ δ' ἔσσυτο λαός,
πεζοί θ' ἱππῆές τε· πολὺς δ' ὀρυμαγδὸς ὀρώρει.

 Οἱ δ' ὅτε δή ῥ' ἐς χῶρον ἕνα ξυνιόντες ἵκοντο, 60

---

45. ἐλάαν: pres. infin. act. ἐλάω, a form of ἐλαύνω; infin. after μάστιξεν, 'he whipped them, so that he drove them on' | τὼ: 'the two of them' (I.2), nom. dual ὁ (I.1d and 2) l ἀέκοντε = ἄκοντε, nom. dual (D.9) | πετέσθην: 3 dual imperf. πέτομαι (M.2)

48. Γάργαρον: either m. or n., 'Gargaros' or 'Gargaron' | τέ: generalising (Z.1) | οἱ: dat. 3 s. personal pronoun; supply εἰσί– 'there are to him', i.e. 'he has' (H.2,3)

50. ὀχέων = ὄχων, as 105, etc. (D.7b) | κατὰ .. ἔχευεν: tmesis (R), aor. act. καταχέω | πουλὺν = πολὺν, as often

51. κύδεϊ = κύδει, dat. s. κύδος (D.4)

52. εἰσορόων = εἰσορῶν, pres. part. εἰσοράω (O.2b) | νῆας: acc. pl. ναύς (D.11)

53. ἕλοντο: 2 aor. mid. αἱρέω | κάρη: acc. s. κάρα; acc. of respect, 'long-haired in respect of their heads' (G.1e)

55. ἑτέρωθεν: 'from the other side' (Y.2) | πτόλιν = πόλιν; πτ– lengthens the previous syllable (Scansion, B.2)

56. μέμασαν: 3 pl. plupf. (with imperf. meaning) of a form of μέμονα | καὶ ὣς: 'even so' (Y.5) | ὑσμῖνι: dat. s. ὑσμίνη

57. χρειοῖ: dat. s. χρείω = χρέω

58. ὠΐγνυντο: 3 pl. imperf. pass. οἴγνυμι | ἐκ .. ἔσσυτο: 3 s. plupf. ἐκσεύομαι (N.2)

59. ἱππῆες = ἱππεῖς (D.5a) | ὀρώρει: 3 s. plupf. act. ὄρνυμι

60. ἕνα: acc. s. m. εἷς, 'a single' | ξυνιόντες = συνιόντες, nom. pl. part. σύνειμι (U.2), acting as pres. part. συνέρχομαι | ἵκοντο 2 aor. ἱκνέομαι

45   chariot. He whipped (the horses) into a run, and they flew on eagerly between earth and starry heaven. He came to Ide with its many springs, the mother of wild animals, and to Gargaros, where he has a precinct, and an altar fragrant with sacrifice. There the father of men and gods stopped his

50   horses, releasing them from the chariot, and poured much mist over (them). He himself sat down on the summits, exulting in his glory, looking on the city of the Trojans and the ships of the Akhaians.

    The flowing-haired Akhaians took their meal hurriedly in

55   their tents, and after it they began arming themselves. And the Trojans for their part were arming themselves in the city, fewer in number, but even so they were eager to fight in battle, because of compelling necessity, for their children and their wives. The whole gate was opened, and the host rushed out, foot-soldiers and horsemen, and much din arose.

60   And when, coming together, they reached a single spot,

σύν ῥ' ἔβαλον ῥινούς, σὺν δ' ἔγχεα καὶ μένε' ἀνδρῶν
χαλκεοθωρήκων· ἀτὰρ ἀσπίδες ὀμφαλόεσσαι
ἔπληντ' ἀλλήλῃσι, πολὺς δ' ὀρυμαγδὸς ὀρώρει.
ἔνθα δ' ἅμ' οἰμωγή τε καὶ εὐχωλὴ πέλεν ἀνδρῶν
ὀλλύντων τε καὶ ὀλλυμένων, ῥέε δ' αἵματι γαῖα.   65
  Ὄφρα μὲν ἠὼς ἦν καὶ ἀέξετο ἱερὸν ἦμαρ,
τόφρα μάλ' ἀμφοτέρων βέλε' ἥπτετο, πῖπτε δὲ λαός.
ἦμος δ' Ἥέλιος μέσον οὐρανὸν ἀμφιβεβήκει,
καὶ τότε δὴ χρύσεια πατὴρ ἐτίταινε τάλαντα·
ἐν δ' ἐτίθει δύο κῆρε τανηλεγέος θανάτοιο,   70
Τρώων θ' ἱπποδάμων καὶ Ἀχαιῶν χαλκοχιτώνων,
ἕλκε δὲ μέσσα λαβών· ῥέπε δ' αἴσιμον ἦμαρ Ἀχαιῶν.
αἱ μὲν Ἀχαιῶν κῆρες ἐπὶ χθονὶ πουλυβοτείρῃ
ἑζέσθην, Τρώων δὲ πρὸς οὐρανὸν εὐρὺν ἄερθεν·
αὐτὸς δ' ἐξ Ἴδης μεγάλ' ἔκτυπε, δαιόμενον δὲ   75
ἧκε σέλας μετὰ λαὸν Ἀχαιῶν· οἱ δὲ ἰδόντες

---

61. σύν .. ἔβαλον: 3 pl. 2 aor. act. συμβάλλω; supply ἔβαλον with the second σὺν | ἔγχεα,
μένε' = ἔγχη, μενη (D.5) | note how συνέβαλον, having been followed by ῥινούς and ἔγχεα,
which is quite natural, is then followed by μένε', which is much less so. This is called a *zeugma*
62. ὀμφαλόεσσαι: nom. pl. f. ὀμφαλόεις
63. ἔπληντ': 3 pl. aor. pass. πελάζω; 'they were brought near to', i.e. 'they clashed'
65. ὀλλύντων, ὀλλυμένων: gen. pl. pres. part. act., mid. and pass. ὄλλυμι | ῥέε: imperf. act. ῥέω,
neither contracted nor augmented (N.1, O.1)
66. ὄφρα: here (and 87, etc.) 'while' | μὲν: balanced by the δὲ in 68, not 67; 'while, on the one
hand, it was early morning ..; but when the sun .. .' | ἀέξετο: imperf. mid. ἀέξω, a form of
αὐξάνω | ἦμαρ: a common Homeric alternative to ἡμέρα
68. Ἥέλιος = Ἥλιος | ἀμφιβεβήκει: 3 s. plupf. act. ἀμφιβαίνω
69. καὶ: 'indeed'
70. ἐν ... ἐτίθει: 3 s. imperf. act. ἐντίθημι | κῆρε: dual acc. κήρ (not κῆρ, 'heart') |
τανηλεγέος = τανηλεγοῦς, gen. s. (D.3b)
72. μέσσα = μέσα (A); supply τάλαντα, 'taking them *by* the middle' | λαβών: 2 aor. act. part.
λαμβάνω
74. ἑζέσθην: 3 dual imperf. and 2 aor. ἕζομαι (M.2); Homer is now thinking of *two* fates for each
side | Τρώων: supply αἱ κῆρες | ἄερθεν: 3 pl. aor. pass. αἴρω, ἀείρω, –εν for –ησαν (L.5)
75. μεγάλ': n. pl. μέγας, acting as adverb (G.1a)
76. ἦκε: 3 s. aor. act. ἵημι | μετά: 'among' | ἰδόντες: nom. pl. m. 2 aor. act. part. ὁράω

they clashed their ox-hide shields together, and they clashed together their spears, and the might of the warriors with bronze breastplates. The bossed shields encountered one another, and much din arose. Then there were at the same time groans and shouts of triumph, from men killing and being killed, and the ground flowed with blood.

While it was morning, and the sacred day was progressing, so long were the weapons of both sides surely finding their targets, and the men were falling. But when the Sun had crossed the middle of the sky, then indeed the Father was holding forth the golden scales, and putting in them the two fates of death which brings long sorrow, one for the horse-taming Trojans and one for the Akhaians of the bronze tunics. And taking them by the middle he lifted them up; and down sank the fateful day of the Akhaians. The fates of the Akhaians settled on the earth, the nourisher of many, and those of the Trojans rose towards the broad sky. And Zeus himself thundered mightily from Ide, and sent a blazing flash among the host of the Akhaians. And they, seeing it, were dumbfounded, and pale fear seized them all.

θάμβησαν, καὶ πάντας ὑπὸ χλωρὸν δέος εἷλεν.

   Ἔνθ' οὔτ' Ἰδομενεὺς τλῆ μίμνειν οὔτ' Ἀγαμέμνων,
οὔτε δύ' Αἴαντες μενέτην, θεράποντες Ἄρηος·
Νέστωρ οἷος ἔμιμνε Γερήνιος, οὖρος Ἀχαιῶν,   80
οὔ τι ἑκών, ἀλλ' ἵππος ἐτείρετο, τὸν βάλεν ἰῷ
δῖος Ἀλέξανδρος, Ἑλένης πόσις ἠϋκόμοιο,
ἄκρην κὰκ κορυφήν, ὅθι τε πρῶται τρίχες ἵππων
κρανίῳ ἐμπεφύασι, μάλιστα δὲ καίριόν ἐστιν.
ἀλγήσας δ' ἀνέπαλτο, βέλος δ' εἰς ἐγκέφαλον δῦ,   85
σὺν δ' ἵππους ἐτάραξε κυλινδόμενος περὶ χαλκῷ.
ὄφρ' ὁ γέρων ἵπποιο παρηορίας ἀπέταμνε
φασγάνῳ ἀΐσσων, τόφρ' Ἕκτορος ὠκέες ἵπποι
ἦλθον ἀν' ἰωχμὸν θρασὺν ἡνίοχον φορέοντες
Ἕκτορα· καί νύ κεν ἔνθ' ὁ γέρων ἀπὸ θυμὸν ὄλεσσεν   90
εἰ μὴ ἄρ' ὀξὺ νόησε βοὴν ἀγαθὸς Διομήδης·
σμερδαλέον δ' ἐβόησεν ἐποτρύνων Ὀδυσῆα·
"διογενὲς Λαερτιάδη, πολυμήχαν' Ὀδυσσεῦ,
πῇ φεύγεις μετὰ νῶτα βαλὼν κακὸς ὣς ἐν ὁμίλῳ;

---

77. ὑπὸ .. εἷλεν: 3 s. 2 aor. act. ὑφαιρέω
78. τλῆ: 3 s. aor. act. τλάω | μίμνειν: a form of μένω
79. μενέτην: 3 dual imperf. act. (M.2) | Ἄρηος: gen. s. Ἄρης (D.3a)
81. τὸν: relative pronoun (I.1e)
82. ἠϋκόμοιο: gen. s. (C.2); a *two-termination* adjective – i.e. f. the same as m. throughout
83. κὰκ = κατά (Y.9)
84. ἐμπεφύασι: 3 pl. perf. act. ἐμφύω, here intransitive, 'grow'
85. ἀνέπαλτο: 3 s. aor. pass., either ἀνα–πάλλομαι or ἀν– ἐφ– ἅλλομαι, it is not certain which |
δῦ: 3 s. aor. act. δύ(ν)ω
86. σὺν ... ἐτάραξε: 3 s. aor. act. συνταράσσω | χαλκῷ: literally, 'bronze', hence here the bronze
arrowhead
87. ἀπέταμνε = ἀπέτεμνε
88. ὠκέες = ὠκεῖς (D.5a)
90. κεν ἀπόλεσσεν: 'would have lost' (W.2b) | ἀπὸ .. ὄλεσσεν: 3 s. aor. act. ἀπόλλυμι (N.1)
91. βοὴν: acc. of respect (G.1e)
92. Ὀδυσῆα: acc. s. (D.2b)
94. μετά: either 'behind', in which case supply 'shield' as object of βαλών; or, which most editors
prefer, tmesis (R) with βαλών | κακὸς ὥς: 'like a coward'; a common meaning of κακός; ὥς
accented because it goes with the *preceding* word (Y.5)

Then neither did Idomeneus dare to stand his ground, nor Agamemnon, nor did the two Aiantes stand firm, the servants of Ares. Nestor alone stood his ground, the Gerenian, the guardian of the Akhaians – not indeed willingly, but his horse was in trouble, which the godlike Alexandros, the husband of Helen of the beautiful hair, had struck with an arrow at the top of its head, where the first hairs of horses grow on the skull, and it is a particularly vital spot. The horse reared up in agony, the arrow pierced its brain, and the horse threw the (other) horses into confusion as it writhed around the bronze (arrowhead). While the old man was cutting away the traces of the horse, thrusting with his sword, Hektor's swift horses came through the mêlée, carrying their bold master, Hektor. And the old man would have lost his life there and then, had not Diomedes, good at the shout, promptly noticed (him). He gave a tremendous shout, urging on Odusseus –

"Child of a god, son of Laertes, resourceful Odusseus, – Where are you fleeing to, turning your back like a coward in

μή τίς τοι φεύγοντι μεταφρένῳ ἐν δόρυ πήξῃ·   95
ἀλλὰ μέν' ὄφρα γέροντος ἀπώσομεν ἄγριον ἄνδρα."

Ὣς ἔφατ', οὐδ' ἐσάκουσε πολύτλας δῖος Ὀδυσσεύς,
ἀλλὰ παρήϊξεν κοίλας ἐπὶ νῆας Ἀχαιῶν.
Τυδείδης δ' αὐτός περ ἐὼν προμάχοισιν ἐμίχθη,
στῆ δὲ πρόσθ' ἵππων Νηληϊάδαο γέροντος,   100
καί μιν φωνήσας ἔπεα πτερόεντα προσηύδα·
"ὦ γέρον, ἦ μάλα δή σε νέοι τείρουσι μαχηταί,
σὴ δὲ βίη λέλυται, χαλεπὸν δέ σε γῆρας ὀπάζει,
ἠπεδανὸς δέ νύ τοι θεράπων, βραδέες δέ τοι ἵπποι.
ἀλλ' ἄγ' ἐμῶν ὀχέων ἐπιβήσεο, ὄφρα ἴδηαι   105
οἷοι Τρώϊοι ἵπποι, ἐπιστάμενοι πεδίοιο
κραιπνὰ μάλ' ἔνθα καὶ ἔνθα διωκέμεν ἠδὲ φέβεσθαι,
οὕς ποτ' ἀπ' Αἰνείαν ἑλόμην, μήστωρε φόβοιο.
τούτω μὲν θεράποντε κομείτων, τώδε δὲ νῶϊ
Τρωσὶν ἐφ' ἱπποδάμοις ἰθύνομεν, ὄφρα καὶ Ἕκτωρ   110

---

95. μή: 'be careful that .. not', with subjunc. (X.4a) | τίς: 'someone' (J); accented here because of the following enclitic word | τοι: dat. s. 2 pers. pronoun, possessive with μεταφρένῳ (H.1,3) | ἐν .. πήξῃ: 3 s. aor. subjunc. act. ἐμπήγνυμι

96. γέροντος: gen., '*from* the old man' (G.2e) | ἀπώσομεν: 1 pl. aor. subjunc. act. ἀπωθέω, -ομεν for -ωμεν (L.10)

98. παρήϊξεν: aor. act. παρ– αἴσσω

99. Τυδείδης : 'son of Tudeus', i.e. Diomedes (B.8) | αὐτός: 'on his own' (K) | περ: concessive (Z) | ἐὼν = ὤν, nom. s. pres. part. εἰμί (U.2) | ἐμίχθη: 3 s. aor. pass. μείγνυμι

100. στῆ: 3 s. 2 aor. act. ἵστημι, intransitive | Νηληϊάδαο: gen. s., –αο for –ου (B.6); 'the son of Neleus', i.e. Nestor

101. ἔπεα = ἔπη (D.5b) | προσηύδα: 'he spoke to' (V.3)

105. ἐπιβήσεο: 2 s. aor. mid. imperat. ἐπιβαίνω, –εο for –ου (L.2) | ἴδηαι = ἴδη (L.8), 2 s. 2 aor. subjunc. mid. ὁράω

106. οἷοι: supply εἰσί | ἐπιστάμενοι: 'knowing *how to*' | πεδίοιο gen., '*over* the plain' (C.2, G.2b)

107. διωκέμεν = διώκειν (P)

108. ἀπ' .. ἑλόμην: 1 s. 2 aor. mid. ἀφαιρέω, followed by double acc. (G.1f) | μήστωρε : dual acc., in apposition to οὕς

109. θεράποντε, νῶϊ: dual nom. θεράπων and 1 pl. personal pronoun (D.9, H.1) | τούτω, τώδε: dual acc. οὗτος, ὅδε (C.4, I.1d) | κομείτων: 3 dual imperat.. act. κομέω (M.3, X2)

110. ἰθύνομεν: pres. subjunc., jussive (X.2), –ομεν for –ωμεν (L.10) | καὶ Ἕκτωρ: 'even Hektor (as well as all the other Trojans)'

95   the throng of battle? (Be careful that) no one plants his
spear in your back while you flee. But stay, that we may
drive the wild fellow away from the old man."

So he spoke, but the much-enduring godlike Odusseus
did not hear, but shot past towards the hollow ships of the
Akhaians.

But the son of Tudeus, although being on his own,
100   mingled with the front-line fighters, and stood in front of the
horses of the aged son of Neleus, and addressing him he
spoke winged words –

"O old man, indeed the young warriors are certainly
oppressing you, your strength is weakened, and harsh old
age is upon you. And your driver is weak, and your horses
105   slow. But come, get into my chariot, so that you may see
what my horses from Troy are like, which know how to
make pursuit very rapidly this way and that over the plain,
and how to flee – horses which I once took from Aineias,
and which drive men to flight. Let our lieutenants attend to
110   these (horses of yours), while the two of us steer these two

εἴσεται εἰ καὶ ἐμὸν δόρυ μαίνεται ἐν παλάμῃσιν."
    Ὣς ἔφατ', οὐδ' ἀπίθησε Γερήνιος ἱππότα Νέστωρ.
Νεστορέας μὲν ἔπειθ' ἵππους θεράποντε κομείτην,
ἴφθιμοι Σθένελός τε καὶ Εὐρυμέδων ἀγαπήνωρ.
τὼ δ' εἰς ἀμφοτέρω Διομήδεος ἅρματα βήτην·   115
Νέστωρ δ' ἐν χείρεσσι λάβ' ἡνία σιγαλόεντα,
μάστιξεν δ' ἵππους· τάχα δ' Ἕκτορος ἄγχι γένοντο.
τοῦ δ' ἰθὺς μεμαῶτος ἀκόντισε Τυδέος υἱός·
καὶ τοῦ μέν ῥ' ἀφάμαρτεν, ὃ δ' ἡνίοχον θεράποντα,
υἱὸν ὑπερθύμου Θηβαίου Ἠνιοπῆα   120
ἵππων ἡνί' ἔχοντα βάλε στῆθος παρὰ μαζόν.
ἤριπε δ' ἐξ ὀχέων, ὑπερώησαν δέ οἱ ἵπποι
ὠκύποδες· τοῦ δ' αὖθι λύθη ψυχή τε μένος τε.
Ἕκτορα δ' αἰνὸν ἄχος πύκασε φρένας ἡνιόχοιο·
τὸν μὲν ἔπειτ' εἴασε, καὶ ἀχνύμενός περ ἑταίρου,   125
κεῖσθαι, ὃ δ' ἡνίοχον μέθεπε θρασύν· οὐδ' ἄρ' ἔτι δὴν
ἵππω δευέσθην σημάντορος· αἶψα γὰρ εὗρεν
Ἰφιτίδην Ἀρχεπτόλεμον θρασύν, ὅν ῥα τόθ' ἵππων

---

111. εἴσεται: fut. οἶδα; fut., rather than subjunc., unusually after ὄφρα for purpose (X.1) | καὶ
'my spear also' (i.e. as well as his)
112. ἱππότα: nom. s. (B.4)
113. κομείτην: 3 dual imperf. act. κομέω
115. τὼ, ἀμφοτέρω: both dual nom. (I.1d, C.4); 'they both' | εἰς: with ἅρματα, not ἀμφοτέρω
 | ἅρματα: pl. for. s.; so too with ὄχος | βήτην: 3 dual aor. act. βαίνω
117. Ἕκτορος: gen. because governed by ἄγχι
118. τοῦ: 'him', gen. with ἀκόντισε; and in 119 τοῦ gen. with ἀφάμαρτεν | ἰθὺς: adverb |
μεμαῶτος: gen. s. m. of the participle of μέμονα (see on 56) | Τυδέος: gen. s. (D.3b)
119. ἀφάμαρτεν: 3 s. 2 aor. act. ἀφαμαρτάνω
120. Ἠνιοπῆα: acc. s. Ἠνιοπεύς (D.2b)
121. στῆθος: acc. of part affected, 'in the chest' (G.1d)
122 ἤριπε: 2 aor. act. ἐρείπω, here intransitive | ὑπερώησαν: 3 pl. aor. act. ὑπ–ερωέω | οἱ
ἵπποι: 'his horses' (H.3)
124. φρένας: acc. pl. φρήν; acc. of the seat of the emotions (G.1c), 'grief covered H. in his heart'
 | ἡνιόχοιο: 'grief for his charioteer' (G.2c); likewise ἑταίρου, 125 –'grieving for his companion'
125. εἴασε: 3. s. aor. act. ἐάω | καὶ .. περ: 'although' (Z)
127. δευέσθην: 3 dual imperf. δεύομαι, = δέομαι, followed by gen. | εὗρεν: 3 s. 2 aor. act.
εὑρίσκω

(of mine) against the horse-taming Trojans, so that even Hektor may know whether my spear too rages in my hands."

Thus he spoke, and the Gerenian charioteer Nestor did not disobey. Then the lieutenants attended to the mares of Nestor, strong men, Sthenelos and the manly Eurumedon.
115 The two of them went into the chariot of Diomedes, and Nestor took the shining reins in his hands, and whipped on the horses, and they quickly came close to Hektor. The son of Tudeus hurled a spear at him as he rushed straight on. He missed Hektor, but hit his lieutenant and charioteer
120 Eniopeus, the son of the great-hearted Thebaios, as he was holding the reins of the horses, in his chest by the nipple. He crashed from his chariot, his swift-footed horses shied back, and his life and strength collapsed there and then. Bitter grief closed over Hektor's heart for his charioteer.
125 Then he let him lie, even though he grieved for his companion, and he went to find a bold charioteer. Nor did his horses go short of a driver for long, for he quickly found the bold Arkheptolemos, the son of Iphitos, whom he then mounted on his swift-footed horses, and gave him the

ὠκυπόδων ἐπέβησε, δίδου δέ οἱ ἡνία χερσίν.

Ἔνθα κε λοιγὸς ἔην καὶ ἀμήχανα ἔργα γένοντο,　130
καί νύ κε σήκασθεν κατὰ Ἴλιον ἠΰτε ἄρνες,
εἰ μὴ ἄρ' ὀξὺ νόησε πατὴρ ἀνδρῶν τε θεῶν τε·
βροντήσας δ' ἄρα δεινὸν ἀφῆκ' ἀργῆτα κεραυνόν,
κὰδ δὲ πρόσθ' ἵππων Διομήδεος ἧκε χαμᾶζε·
δεινὴ δὲ φλὸξ ὦρτο θεείου καιομένοιο,　135
τὼ δ' ἵππω δείσαντε καταπτήτην ὑπ' ὄχεσφι·
Νέστορα δ' ἐκ χειρῶν φύγον ἡνία σιγαλόεντα,
δεῖσε δ' ὅ γ' ἐν θυμῷ, Διομήδεα δὲ προσέειπε·
"Τυδεΐδη, ἄγε δὴ αὖτε φόβονδ' ἔχε μώνυχας ἵππους.
ἦ οὐ γιγνώσκεις ὅ τοι ἐκ Διὸς οὐχ ἕπετ' ἀλκή;　140
νῦν μὲν γὰρ τούτῳ Κρονίδης Ζεὺς κῦδος ὀπάζει
σήμερον· ὕστερον αὖτε καὶ ἡμῖν, αἴ κ' ἐθέλησι,
δώσει· ἀνὴρ δέ κεν οὔ τι Διὸς νόον εἰρύσσαιτο
οὐδὲ μάλ' ἴφθιμος, ἐπεὶ ἦ πολὺ φέρτερός ἐστι."

Τὸν δ' ἠμείβετ' ἔπειτα βοὴν ἀγαθὸς Διομήδης·　145
"ναὶ δὴ ταῦτά γε πάντα, γέρον, κατὰ μοῖραν ἔειπες·

---

129. ἐπέβησε: 3 s. aor. act. ἐπιβαίνω, transitive, and followed by gen., 'whom he set *on* his horses' | δίδου: 3 s. imperf. act. δίδωμι

130. ἔην: 3 s. imperf. εἰμί (U.4); with κε for 'there would have been', as also 131 (W.2b); this normally requires the aor. (so, γένοντο) rather than imperf.; but εἰμί does not have an aor. . Hom. means that the Trojans would have suffered a setback, and the result of Zeus' weighing of the scales would not have come to pass | γένοντα the pl. verb after n. pl. subject is irregular, although this occurs again at 137

131. σήκασθεν: 3 pl. aor. pass. σηκάζω (L.5) | ἄρνες: nom. pl. ἀρήν

133. ἀφῆκ': 3 s. aor. act. ἀφίημι; so 134, κὰδ .. ἧκε for καθῆκε

134. χαμᾶζε: 'to the ground' (Y.1)

135. ὦρτο: 2 aor. mid. ὄρνυμι | θεείου = θείου, gen. s. θεῖον

136. δείσαντε: dual nom. δείσας, aor. part. δείδω | καταπτήτην: 3 dual aor. act. καταπτήσσω | ὄχεσφι: for dat. pl. (E)

137. φύγον: 3 pl. 2 aor. act.

138. προσέειπε: 'spoke to' (V.3)

139. φόβονδ': 'to flight' (Y.1); in Hom. φόβος is 'flight', rather than 'fear'

140. ὅ: 'that' (I.3) | τοι: dat. after ἕπετ' | Διὸς: gen. (D.11)

142. αἴ = εἰ, here with κ' for fut. conditional without 'would' (W.3a) | ἐθέλησι: 3 s. pres. subjunc. act. ἐθέλω, -ῃσι for -ῃ (L.9)

143. δώσει: 3 s. fut. act. δίδωμι | κεν .. εἰρύσσαιτο: potential conditional (W.4), 'would not thwart (if he tried)' | νόον = νοῦν (C.1) | εἰρύσσαιτο = ἐρύσαιτο (Q.3), aor. optat. mid. ἐρύω

reins in his hands.

130   Then there would have been disaster, and deeds beyond control, and they would have been penned in Ilion like lambs, had not the father of men and gods quickly spotted (it). Thundering terribly, he let loose a vivid flash of lightning, and sent it down to earth in front of Diomedes'
135 horses. A terrible flame of burning sulphur rose up, and the two horses, terrified, cowered back against the chariot. The shining reins dropped from Nestor's hands, and he was frightened in his heart, and said to Diomedes –

"Son of Tudeus, come, turn your horses, uncloven of
140 hoof, to flight. Do you not realise that support from Zeus does not follow you? For now the son of Kronos, Zeus, grants glory to this man for today; but later he will, if he wishes, grant (it) to us. A man would not thwart the intention of Zeus, not even a very strong one, since he is indeed much more powerful."

145   Then Diomedes, good at the shout, answered him –
"Yes, indeed, old man, you have said all this as is right.

ἀλλὰ τόδ' αἰνὸν ἄχος κραδίην καὶ θυμὸν ἱκάνει·
Ἕκτωρ γάρ ποτε φήσει ἐνὶ Τρώεσσ' ἀγορεύων·
Τυδείδης ὑπ' ἐμεῖο φοβεύμενος ἵκετο νῆας.'
ὥς ποτ' ἀπειλήσει· τότε μοι χάνοι εὐρεῖα χθών."　　　　　　150

　　Τὸν δ' ἠμείβετ' ἔπειτα Γερήνιος ἱππότα Νέστωρ·
"ὤ μοι, Τυδέος υἱὲ δαΐφρονος, οἷον ἔειπες.
εἴ περ γάρ σ' Ἕκτωρ γε κακὸν καὶ ἀνάλκιδα φήσει,
ἀλλ' οὐ πείσονται Τρῶες καὶ Δαρδανίωνες
καὶ Τρώων ἄλοχοι μεγαθύμων ἀσπιστάων,　　　　　　155
τάων ἐν κονίῃσι βάλες θαλεροὺς παρακοίτας."

　　Ὣς ἄρα φωνήσας φύγαδε τράπε μώνυχας ἵππους
αὖτις ἀν' ἰωχμόν· ἐπὶ δὲ Τρῶές τε καὶ Ἕκτωρ
ἠχῇ θεσπεσίῃ βέλεα στονόεντα χέοντο.
τῷ δ' ἐπὶ μακρὸν ἄϋσε μέγας κορυθαίολος Ἕκτωρ·　　　　160
"Τυδείδη, περὶ μέν σε τίον Δαναοὶ ταχύπωλοι
ἕδρῃ τε κρέασίν τε ἰδὲ πλείοις δεπάεσσι·
νῦν δέ σ' ἀτιμήσουσι· γυναικὸς ἄρ' ἀντὶ τέτυξο.
ἔρρε, κακὴ γλήνη, ἐπεὶ οὐκ εἴξαντος ἐμεῖο
πύργων ἡμετέρων ἐπιβήσεαι, οὐδὲ γυναῖκας　　　　　165
ἄξεις ἐν νήεσσι· πάρος τοι δαίμονα δώσω."

　　Ὣς φάτο, Τυδείδης δὲ διάνδιχα μερμήριξεν,
ἵππους τε στρέψαι καὶ ἐναντίβιον μαχέσασθαι.

---

147. ἱκάνει: 'comes *to*' (G.1b)
148. φήσει: 3 s. fut. φημί, as 153 (V.2)
149. ἐμεῖο = ἐμοῦ (H.1) ǀ φοβεύμενος = φοβούμενος
150. χάνοι: 3 s. 2 aor. optat. act. χανδάνω; optat. for wish for the future (X.5)
154. ἀλλ': 'yet' ǀ πείσονται: fut. mid. πείθω, 'will be persuaded'
156. τάων: gen. pl. fem. relative pronoun (I.1b)
157. φύγαδε: 'to flight' (Y.1) ǀ τράπε: 2 aor. act. τρέπω
158–9. ἐπὶ … χέοντο: 3 pl. imperf. mid. ἐπιχέω
160. τῷ: 'at him', i.e. Diomedes
163. ἄρ': 'as I now see', followed by plupf. when in Eng. we would use perf. ǀ ἀντὶ: 'as good as', 'the equal of', with γυναικός ǀ τέτυξο: 2 s. plupf. pass. τεύχω
164. εἴξαντος: gen. s. m. aor. part. act. εἴκω; gen. absolute with ἐμεῖο, 'me having yielded'
165. ἐπιβήσεαι: 2 s. fut. mid. ἐπιβαίνω, –εαι for –ει or –ῃ (L.1)
166. νήεσσι: dat. pl. ναῦς (D.11)
167. μερμήριξεν: in translation, supply after this 'whether or not'
168. στρέψαι: aor. infin. act. στρέφω ǀ μαχέσασθαι: aor. infin. μάχομαι

But this deep sorrow comes upon my heart and spirit – for
Hektor will one day say as he holds assembly among the
Trojans: 'The son of Tudeus, put to flight by me, came to
150   the ships.' Thus he will one day boast; may the wide earth
then gape open for me."

Then the Gerenian charioteer Nestor answered him –

"Alas, son of warlike Tudeus, what a thing you have
said! For if Hektor calls you a coward and a man of no
spirit, yet the Trojans and the descendants of Dardanos will
155   not believe him, and neither will the wives of the great-
hearted Trojan warriors, whose strong husbands you have
hurled in the dust."

Speaking thus, he turned his horses of uncloven hoof
back through the mêlée, and the Trojans and Hektor with
tremendous cries poured showers of missiles that cause
160   grief at them. Great Hektor of the flashing helmet shouted
loudly at him –

"Son of Tudeus, the Danaans of the swift horses used to
honour you in particular, with your seat, and the meat, and
the full cups. But now they will dishonour you. You have
clearly become the equal of a woman. Off with you, you
165   feeble puppet, since you will not scale our defences with me
having given way, nor lead off our womenfolk in your
ships. Before that, I will deal out fate to you."
Thus he spoke, and the son of Tudeus was in two minds,
whether (or not) to turn his horses about and fight face-to-
face.

τρὶς μὲν μερμήριξε κατὰ φρένα καὶ κατὰ θυμόν,
τρὶς δ' ἄρ' ἀπ' Ἰδαίων ὀρέων κτύπε μητίετα Ζεὺς 170
σῆμα τιθεὶς Τρώεσσι, μάχης ἑτεραλκέα νίκην.
Ἕκτωρ δὲ Τρώεσσιν ἐκέκλετο μακρὸν ἀΰσας·
"Τρῶες καὶ Λύκιοι καὶ Δάρδανοι ἀγχιμαχηταί
ἀνέρες ἔστε, φίλοι, μνήσασθε δὲ θούριδος ἀλκῆς.
γιγνώσκω δ' ὅτι μοι πρόφρων κατένευσε Κρονίων 175
νίκην καὶ μέγα κῦδος, ἀτὰρ Δαναοῖσί γε πῆμα·
νήπιοι, οἳ ἄρα δὴ τάδε τείχεα μηχανόωντο
ἀβλήχρ' οὐδενόσωρα· τὰ δ' οὐ μένος ἁμὸν ἐρύξει·
ἵπποι δὲ ῥέα τάφρον ὑπερθορέονται ὀρυκτήν.
ἀλλ' ὅτε κεν δὴ νηυσὶν ἔπι γλαφυρῇσι γένωμαι, 180
μνημοσύνη τις ἔπειτα πυρὸς δηΐοιο γενέσθω,
ὡς πυρὶ νῆας ἐνιπρήσω, κτείνω δὲ καὶ αὐτοὺς
Ἀργείους παρὰ νηυσὶν ἀτυζομένους ὑπὸ καπνοῦ."

Ὣς εἰπὼν ἵπποισιν ἐκέκλετο φώνησέν τε·
"Ξάνθε τε καὶ σύ, Πόδαργε, καὶ Αἴθων Λάμπε τε δῖε, 185
νῦν μοι τὴν κομιδὴν ἀποτίνετον, ἣν μάλα πολλὴν
Ἀνδρομάχη, θυγάτηρ μεγαλήτορος Ἠετίωνος,
ὑμῖν πὰρ προτέροισι μελίφρονα πυρὸν ἔθηκεν

---

170. ὀρέων: gen. pl. ὄρος, –εων for –ων (D.7b) | μητίετα: nom. s. (B.4)

171. τιθείς: nom. s. m. aor. part. act. τίθημι | ἑτεραλκέα: acc. s. f., –εα for –η (D.2c) | νίκην: in apposition to σῆμα, and so in the same case – 'a sign of victory'

172. ἐκέκλετο: a reduplicated 2 aor. (T) of κέλομαι, a verb connected with κελεύω

174. ἀνέρες = ἄνδρες, nom. pl. ἀνήρ; with long α | ἔστε: 2 pl. imperat. εἰμί (U.5) | μνήσασθε: 2 pl. aor. imperat. μιμνήσκομαι, followed by gen.; aor. indic. of this word at 252, etc.

177. μηχανόωντο: 3 pl. imperf. μηχανάομαι, –οω for –ω (O.2b)

178. ἁμόν: 'our' (F) | ἐρύξει: fut. act. ἐρύκω

179. ὑπερθορέονται: fut. mid. ὑπερθρώσκω (O.1)

180. ὅτε: 'whenever', followed by subjunc. (W.8a) | γένωμαι: 1 s. 2 aor. subjunc. γίγνομαι; in next line, γενέσθω 3 s. 2 aor. imperat.

182. ἐνιπρήσω: 1 s. aor. subjunc. act. ἐμπίμπρημι; aor. indic. at 217, fut. at 235 | κτείνω: pres. subjunc. act. Both subjuncs. after ὡς, 'in order that' (X.1a)

186. ἀποτίνετον: 2 dual pres. imperat. act. ἀποτίνω; from this dual we must suppose that H. is now addressing two horses, despite the four in 185

188. πὰρ .. ἔθηκεν: 3 s. aor. act. παρατίθημι | προτέροις with ἢ ἐμοί in 190 – 'to you first, before me' | μελίφρονα πυρόν: in apposition to ἣν, 186 – 'which, consisting of delicious wheat'

Three times he pondered in his mind and his heart, and three
170 times Zeus, the deviser of counsel, thundered from the
mountains of Ide, giving a sign to the Trojans of victory that
.changes sides in the fight. And Hektor called on the Trojans
with a great shout –

"Trojans and Lukians and Dardanians who fight at close
quarters, be men, my friends, and remember your furious
175 fighting spirit. I see that Zeus has willingly promised
victory and great glory to me, but to the Danaans disaster.
Fools! – who have devised these walls that are feeble and
worthless, and will not thwart our strength. My horses will
180 easily leap over the ditch that has been dug. And when I am
at the hollow ships, then let there be some memory of the
consuming fire, that I may burn the ships with fire, and kill
the very Argives themselves at their ships while they are
bewildered by the smoke."

Speaking thus, he called to his horses, and said –

185   "Xanthos, and you, Podargos, and Aithon and noble
Lampos, now repay me for the provisions which
Andromakhe, the daughter of great-hearted Eetion, set
before you first in great abundance, the delicious wheat –

οἶνόν τ' ἐγκεράσασα πιεῖν, ὅτε θυμὸς ἀνώγοι,
ἢ ἐμοί, ὅς πέρ οἱ θαλερὸς πόσις εὔχομαι εἶναι.   190
ἀλλ' ἐφομαρτεῖτον καὶ σπεύδετον, ὄφρα λάβωμεν
ἀσπίδα Νεστορέην, τῆς νῦν κλέος οὐρανὸν ἵκει
πᾶσαν χρυσείην ἔμεναι, κανόνας τε καὶ αὐτήν,
αὐτὰρ ἀπ' ὤμοιιν Διομήδεος ἱπποδάμοιο
δαιδάλεον θώρηκα, τὸν Ἥφαιστος κάμε τεύχων.   195
εἰ τούτω κε λάβοιμεν, ἐελποίμην κεν 'Αχαιοὺς
αὐτονυχὶ νηῶν ἐπιβησέμεν ὠκειάων."

Ὣς ἔφατ' εὐχόμενος, νεμέσησε δὲ πότνια Ἥρη,
σείσατο δ' εἰνὶ θρόνῳ, ἐλέλιξε δὲ μακρὸν Ὄλυμπον,
καί ῥα Ποσειδάωνα μέγαν θεὸν ἀντίον ηὔδα·   200
"ὢ πόποι, ἐννοσίγαι' εὐρυσθενές, οὐδέ νυ σοί περ,
ὀλλυμένων Δαναῶν ὀλοφύρεται ἐν φρεσὶ θυμός;
οἱ δέ τοι εἰς Ἑλίκην τε καὶ Αἰγὰς δῶρ' ἀνάγουσι
πολλά τε καὶ χαρίεντα· σὺ δέ σφισι βούλεο νίκην.
εἴ περ γάρ κ' ἐθέλοιμεν, ὅσοι Δαναοῖσιν ἀρωγοί,   205

---

189. τ': this is ungrammatical; in translation, either omit it, or treat ἐγκεράσασα as though it was not a part., but aor. indic. | ἐγκεράσασα: nom. s. f. aor. part. act. ἐγκεράννυμι | πιεῖν: 2 aor. infin. act. πίνω – '(for you) to drink' | ἀνώγοι: optat. after ὅτε 'whenever' (W.8b)

190. εὔχομαι εἶναι: literally, 'I claim to be', but little, if anything, more than 'I am'

191. ἐφομαρτεῖτον, σπεύδετον: 2 dual pres. imperat. act. ἐφομαρτέω, σπεύδω

193. ἔμεναι: infin. εἰμί (U.3); infin. after κλέος – 'the fame .. it to be', i.e. 'the fame .. that it is'

194. ὤμοιιν: gen. dual ὦμος (C.4)

195. κάμε: 2 aor. act. κάμνω

196. εἰ .. ἐελποίμην: 'if we take, I should hope' (W.3b) | τούτω: i.e. Nestor's spear and Diomedes' breastplate | ἐελποίμην: 1 s. pres. optat. mid. ἔλπω, ἐέλπω, a verb connected with ἐλπίζω | 'Αχαιοὺς: object of ἐπιβησέμεν, 197

197. νηῶν : gen. pl. ναῦς (D.11) | ἐπιβησέμεν: fut. infin. ἐπιβαίνω | ὠκειάων: gen. pl. f. ὠκύς, –αων for –ων (B.2)

199. εἰνὶ = ἐν (Y.9)

200. Ποσειδάωνα: acc. s. Ποσειδῶν. Hom. usually uses the –αων form, which is often easier to fit into the hexameter

201. εὐρυσθενές: voc. s.; so ἀπτοεπές, 209

202. φρεσὶ: dat. pl. φρήν

204. βούλεο = ἐβούλου, –εο for –ου (L.2); 2 s. imperf. βούλομαι

205. γάρ: here used elliptically (Z), with something like, 'Why don't you pity the Danaans?' to be supplied beforehand | ὅσοι: supply ἐσμέν

and she mixed in wine for you to drink whenever your heart
190   prompted you, (and she did this) before she served me,
even though I am her strong husband.   But come on with
me, and make haste, that we may take the shield of Nestor,
the fame of which reaches to the sky, that it is all gold, its
staves and the shield itself, and then (we may take) from off
195   the shoulders of Diomedes the finely-wrought breastplate,
which Hephaistos wore himself out in making.   If we could
take these two (prizes), I would hope to set the Akhaians on
their ships this very night."

So he spoke boasting, and queen Here was angry, and
she shook on her throne, and caused mighty Olumpos to
200   quake, and she spoke directly to the great god Poseidon –

"Alas, strong shaker of the earth, does not even your
heart in your breast pity the Danaans as they are being
destroyed? Yet they bring gifts to you at Helike and Aigai,
many and pleasing, and you used to want victory for them.
205   For if we wanted – all those of us who support the Danaans

Τρῶας ἀπώσασθαι καὶ ἐρυκέμεν εὐρύοπα Ζῆν,
αὐτοῦ κ' ἔνθ' ἀκάχοιτο καθήμενος οἶος ἐν "Ιδη."

Τὴν δὲ μέγ' ὀχθήσας προσέφη κρείων ἐνοσίχθων·
"Ἥρη ἀπτοεπές, ποῖον τὸν μῦθον ἔειπες.
οὐκ ἂν ἔγωγ' ἐθέλοιμι Διὶ Κρονίωνι μάχεσθαι   210
ἡμέας τοὺς ἄλλους, ἐπεὶ ἦ πολὺ φέρτερός ἐστιν."

Ὡς οἱ μὲν τοιαῦτα πρὸς ἀλλήλους ἀγόρευον·
τῶν δ', ὅσον ἐκ νηῶν ἀπὸ πύργου τάφρος ἔεργε,
πλῆθεν ὁμῶς ἵππων τε καὶ ἀνδρῶν ἀσπιστάων
εἰλομένων· εἷλει δὲ θοῷ ἀτάλαντος Ἄρηϊ   215
Ἕκτωρ Πριαμίδης, ὅτε οἱ Ζεὺς κῦδος ἔδωκε.
καί νύ κ' ἐνέπρησεν πυρὶ κηλέῳ νῆας ἐΐσας,
εἰ μὴ ἐπὶ φρεσὶ θῆκ' Ἀγαμέμνονι πότνια Ἥρη
αὐτῷ ποιπνύσαντι θοῶς ὀτρῦναι Ἀχαιούς.
βῆ δ' ἰέναι παρά τε κλισίας καὶ νῆας Ἀχαιῶν   220
πορφύρεον μέγα φᾶρος ἔχων ἐν χειρὶ παχείῃ,
στῆ δ' ἐπ' Ὀδυσσῆος μεγακήτεϊ νηΐ μελαίνῃ,
ἥ ῥ' ἐν μεσσάτῳ ἔσκε γεγωνέμεν ἀμφοτέρωσε,
ἠμὲν ἐπ' Αἴαντος κλισίας Τελαμωνιάδαο
ἠδ' ἐπ' Ἀχιλλῆος, τοί ῥ' ἔσχατα νῆας ἐΐσας   225
εἴρυσαν, ἠνορέῃ πίσυνοι καὶ κάρτεϊ χειρῶν·
ἤϋσεν δὲ διαπρύσιον Δαναοῖσι γεγωνώς·

---

206. ἀπώσασθαι: aor. infin. mid. ἀπωθέω; aor. indic. at 295, etc. | εὐρύοπα Ζῆν: both acc. s. (D.11)

207. αὐτοῦ: 'there' (K.5) | ἀκάχοιτο: 3 s. 2 aor. optat. mid. of a reduplicated aorist (T) of ἀχέω

211. ἡμέας = ἡμᾶς (H.1)

213. τῶν: 'of them', 'their'. i.e. the Greeks', going with ἵππων and ἀνδρῶν in 214 | ἔεργε: 3 s. imperf. act. εἴργω

214. πλῆθεν: 3 s. imperf. act. πλήθω, intrans. | ὁμῶς: 'alike', 'equally'

215. εἰλομένων, εἷλει: pres. part. mid. εἴλω, imperf. εἰλέω

219. ποιπνύσαντι: with Ἀγαμέμνονι; lit., 'having rushed, to urge on', i.e. 'to rush, and to urge on'

220. βῆ: 3 s. aor. βαίνω | ἰέναι: infin. εἶμι (U.3); 'he went to go', i.e. 'he went forth'

222. ἐπί: with νηΐ, not Ὀδυσσῆος; and in 224 with κλισίας, not Αἴαντος | νηΐ: dat. s. ναῦς (D.11)

223. ἔσκε: 3 s. imperf. εἰμί (U.4) | γεγωνέμεν: an explanatory infin. – 'it was in the middle, so that one could shout' | ἀμφοτέρωσε: 'in both directions' (Y.1)

225. Ἀχιλλῆος: gen. s. (D.11), and κλισίας to be supplied with it | ἔσχατα: adverbial, 'at the ends'

– to drive back the Trojans and thwart the far-seeing Zeus, then he would feel sorry, sitting there alone on Ide."

Greatly angered, the royal earth-shaker addressed her –

210 "Rash-speaking Here, what a word you have spoken! I would not want the rest of us to fight with Zeus the son of Kronos, since he is certainly much stronger."

Thus they were saying such things to each other. And as much (space) as the ditch, beyond the ships, separated from the wall was filled equally by the horses and by the men, 215 armed with shields, and hemmed in. Hektor, the son of Priam and the equal of rapid Ares, was hemming them in, since Zeus had granted him glory. And he would indeed have burned the well-balanced ships with blazing fire, had not queen Here put it into the mind of Agamemnon to rush 220 around speedily on his own and urge on the Akhaians. He went on his way to the tents and ships of the Akhaians, holding a great purple cloak in his massive hand, and stopped at the huge black ship of Odusseus, which was in the middle, so that one could shout in both directions, both 225 to the tents of Aias the son of Telamon and to those of Akhilleus, the men who had drawn up their well-balanced ships at the extreme ends, confident in their prowess and in the strength of their hands. Agamemnon called with a piercing shout to the Danaans –

"αἰδώς, Ἀργεῖοι, κάκ' ἐλέγχεα, εἶδος ἀγητοί·
πῇ ἔβαν εὐχωλαί, ὅτε δὴ φάμεν εἶναι ἄριστοι,
ἃς ὁπότ' ἐν Λήμνῳ κενεαυχέες ἠγοράασθε,   230
ἔσθοντες κρέα πολλὰ βοῶν ὀρθοκραιράων,
πίνοντες κρητῆρας ἐπιστεφέας οἴνοιο,
Τρώων ἄνθ' ἑκατόν τε διηκοσίων τε ἕκαστος
στήσεσθ' ἐν πολέμῳ; νῦν δ' οὐδ' ἑνὸς ἄξιοί εἰμεν
Ἕκτορος, ὃς τάχα νῆας ἐνιπρήσει πυρὶ κηλέῳ.   235
Ζεῦ πάτερ, ἦ ῥά τιν' ἤδη ὑπερμενέων βασιλήων
τῇδ' ἄτῃ ἄασας καί μιν μέγα κῦδος ἀπηύρας;
οὐ μὲν δή ποτέ φημι τεὸν περικαλλέα βωμὸν
νηΐ πολυκλήϊδι παρελθέμεν ἐνθάδε ἔρρων,
ἀλλ' ἐπὶ πᾶσι βοῶν δημὸν καὶ μηρί' ἔκηα,   240
ἱέμενος Τροίην εὐτείχεον ἐξαλαπάξαι.
ἀλλά, Ζεῦ, τόδε πέρ μοι ἐπικρήηνον ἐέλδωρ·
αὐτοὺς δή περ ἔασον ὑπεκφυγέειν καὶ ἀλύξαι,
μηδ' οὕτω Τρώεσσιν ἔα δάμνασθαι Ἀχαιούς."

---

228. εἶδος: acc. of respect (G.1e) – 'as far as your appearance is concerned'

229. ἔβαν: 3 pl. aor. act. βαίνω | φάμεν: 1 pl. imperf. φημί | εἶναι ἄριστοι: 'that we were best'; ἄριστοι superlative ἀγαθός, nom. because it refers to the subject of φάμεν

230. Either supply something like 'you were making' with ἃς; or take ἠγοράασθε with ἃς, and supply 'you were' with ὁπότ' | κενεαυχέες: nom. pl. (D.5) | ἠγοράασθε: 2 pl. imperf. ἀγοράομαι, –αα – for – α – (O.2d)

232. ἐπιστεφέας: acc. pl., –εας for –εις (D.6)

233–4 Τρώων .. πολέμῳ: this defines the εὐχωλαί of 229 – 'boasts .. that each (of us) would stand ..'

233. ἄνθ' = ἄντα, governing Τρώων

234. στήσεσθ': fut. infin. mid. ἵστημι | οὐδ' : 'not even' | ἑνὸς: gen. s. εἷς, as 355, etc., gen. after ἄξιοι | εἰμεν: 1 pl. pres. εἰμί (U.1)

236. Ζεῦ: voc. (D.11) | βασιλήων: gen. pl., –ηων for –εων (D.7a)

237. ἄασας: 2 s. aor. act. ἀάω | ἀπηύρας: 2 s. of a 2 aor. act. tense ἀπηύρων; with double acc. (G.1f), 'took away κῦδος from μιν'

238. οὐ μὲν: take these with παρελθέμεν, not φημι | τεόν: 2 s. possessive adj. (F)

239. παρελθέμεν: 2 aor. infin. παρέρχομαι (P); infin. after φημι, 'say that I passed by' | ἐνθάδε: '(to) here' (Y.1)

240. δημὸν: N.B. accent; 'people' would be δῆμον | ἔκηα: 1 s. aor. act. καίω

241. ἱέμενος: pres. part. mid. ἵημι

242–3. περ: 'at least' (Z) | ἐπικρήηνον, ἔασον: 2 s. aor. imperat. act. ἐπικραίνω, ἐάω

243. ὑπεκφυγέειν: 2 aor. infin. act. ὑπεκφεύγω | ἀλύξαι: aor. infin. act. ἀλύσκω

244. Τρώεσσιν: 'by the Trojans' | ἔα: 2 s. pres. imperat. act. ἐάω

"Shame, Argives, feeble targets of reproach, wonderful in your appearance (alone). Where have the boastings gone,
230 when we said that we were the best — (the boastings) which you vainly uttered when (you were) in Lemnos, eating much meat of straight-horned oxen, drinking bowls brim-full of wine, (claiming) that each one (of you) would stand in war against one hundred and two hundred of the Trojans? But
235 now we are not even worth Hektor alone, who will quickly burn the ships with blazing fire. Father Zeus, have you before now deluded any of the mighty kings with delusion such as this, and taken away great glory from him? I declare that never once have I passed by any of your very beautiful altars in my many-benched ship as I came on my
240 journey here, but at every one of them I burned the fat and the thigh-bones of oxen, as I hastened to sack Troy of the fine walls. But, Zeus, this wish at least accomplish for me — Allow us at least to flee away and escape, and do not allow the Akhaians to be subdued by the Trojans like this."

Ὣς φάτο, τὸν δὲ πατὴρ ὀλοφύρατο δάκρυ χέοντα,   245
νεῦσε δέ οἱ λαὸν σόον ἔμμεναι οὐδ' ἀπολέσθαι.
αὐτίκα δ' αἰετὸν ἧκε, τελειότατο͞ πετεηνῶν,
νεβρὸν ἔχοντ' ὀνύχεσσι, τέκος ἐλάφοιο ταχείης·
πὰρ δὲ Διὸς βωμῷ περικαλλέι κάββαλε νεβρόν,
ἔνθα πανομφαίῳ Ζηνὶ ῥέζεσκον Ἀχαιοί.   250
οἱ δ' ὡς οὖν εἴδονθ' ὅ τ' ἄρ' ἐκ Διὸς ἤλυθεν ὄρνις,
μᾶλλον ἐπὶ Τρώεσσι θόρον, μνήσαντο δὲ χάρμης.

 Ἔνθ' οὔ τις πρότερος Δαναῶν πολλῶν περ ἐόντων
εὔξατο Τυδεΐδαο πάρος σχέμεν ὠκέας ἵππους
τάφρου τ' ἐξελάσαι καὶ ἐναντίβιον μαχέσασθαι,   255
ἀλλὰ πολὺ πρῶτος Τρώων ἕλεν ἄνδρα κορυστήν,
Φραδμονίδην Ἀγέλαον· ὁ μὲν φύγαδ' ἔτραπεν ἵππους·
τῷ δὲ μεταστρεφθέντι μεταφρένῳ ἐν δόρυ πῆξεν
ὤμων μεσσηγύς, διὰ δὲ στήθεσφιν ἔλασσεν·
ἤριπε δ' ἐξ ὀχέων, ἀράβησε δὲ τεύχε' ἐπ' αὐτῷ.   260

 Τὸν δὲ μετ' Ἀτρεΐδαι Ἀγαμέμνων καὶ Μενέλαος,
τοῖσι δ' ἐπ' Αἴαντες θοῦριν ἐπιειμένοι ἀλκήν,
τοῖσι δ' ἐπ' Ἰδομενεὺς καὶ ὀπάων Ἰδομενῆος

---

246. ἀπολέσθαι: 2 aor. mid. infin. ἀπόλλυμι. Both this and ἔμμεναι are after νεῦσε – 'assented his army to be safe and not to be destroyed', i.e. 'assented that his army should be saved and not destroyed'

248. ὀνύχεσσι: dat. pl. ὄνυξ, -χεσσι for -ξι (D.8)

249. πὰρ = παρά (Y.9), with βωμῷ, not Διός | κάββαλε = κατέβαλε (N.1), 2 aor. act. καταβάλλω

250. Ζηνὶ: dat. s. Ζεύς (D.11), with -ι long before ῥ- at the beginning of the next word (Scansion, B.2) | ῥέζεσκον: 'kept on sacrificing' (S)

251. εἴδονθ': 3 pl. 2 aor. mid. ὁράω | ἤλυθεν: 3 s. aor. act. ἔρχομαι; so ἐπ – ήλυθε, 488

252. θόρον: 3 pl. 2 aor. act. θρώσκω

253. οὔ τις: 'not anyone' (J), i.e. 'no one' | ὄντων: gen. pl. pres. part. εἰμί (U.2)

254. Τυδεΐδαο: gen. s. (B.6), gen. after both πρότερος and πάρος | σχέμεν: 2 aor. infin. act. ἔχω (P), after εὔξατο

255. ἐξελάσαι: aor. infin. act. ἐξελαύνω – so ἔλασσεν, aor. indic. ἐλαύνω, 259; consecutive infin. after σχέμεν – 'direct the horses, so as to drive them out ..'

258. See on 95

259. στήθεσφιν: for gen. pl. (E)

260. τεύχε': nom. pl. n. (D.5b)

261-5. Supply ἦλθε or ἦλθον as verbs | μετ', ἐπ': go with Τὸν, τοῖσι before them

262. θοῦριν: acc. s. f. (D.2a) | ἐπιειμένοι: nom. pl. m. perf. part. mid. ἐπιέννυμι

245   Thus he spoke, and the father pitied him as he was pouring forth a tear, and he assented that his army should be saved and should not be destroyed. Straightaway he sent forth an eagle, the most sure of winged creatures, with a fawn in its talons, the young of a swift doe. The eagle set
250   the fawn down at the most beautiful altar of Zeus, where the Akhaians used to sacrifice to Zeus, the god of all omens. And they, when they saw that the bird had come from Zeus, rushed more (fiercely) at the Trojans, and recovered their fighting spirit.

       Then not one of the Danaans, many though they were, claimed that he had steered his swift horses ahead of the son
255   of Tudeus, so as to drive them across the trench and to fight at close quarters; but far in front (of the rest), he took a helmeted warrior of the Trojans, Agelaos the son of Phradmon. Agelaos had turned his horses to flight, but when he had wheeled about Diomedes fixed his spear in his back between his shoulders, and drove it through his chest.
260   Agelaos crashed from his chariot, and his armour clattered over him.

       After him (came) the sons of Atreus, Agamemnon and Menelaos, and after them the Aiantes, clothed in the spirit of the fight, and after them Idomeneus and Idomeneus'

Μηριόνης, ἀτάλαντος Ἐνυαλίῳ ἀνδρειφόντῃ,
τοῖσι δ᾽ ἐπ᾽ Εὐρύπυλος, Εὐαίμονος ἀγλαὸς υἱός·   265
Τεῦκρος δ᾽ εἴνατος ἦλθε παλίντονα τόξα τιταίνων,
στῆ δ᾽ ἄρ᾽ ὑπ᾽ Αἴαντος σάκεϊ Τελαμωνιάδαο.
ἔνθ᾽ Αἴας μὲν ὑπεξέφερεν σάκος· αὐτὰρ ὅ γ᾽ ἥρως
παπτήνας, ἐπεὶ ἄρ τιν᾽ ὀϊστεύσας ἐν ὁμίλῳ
βεβλήκειν, ὁ μὲν αὖθι πεσὼν ἀπὸ θυμὸν ὄλεσσεν,   270
αὐτὰρ ὁ αὖτις ἰών, πάϊς ὡς ὑπὸ μητέρα, δύσκεν
εἰς Αἴανθ᾽· ὁ δέ μιν σάκεϊ κρύπτασκε φαεινῷ.

    Ἔνθα τίνα πρῶτον Τρώων ἕλε Τεῦκρος ἀμύμων;
Ὀρσίλοχον μὲν πρῶτα καὶ Ὄρμενον ἠδ᾽ Ὀφελέστην
Δαίτορά τε Χρομίον τε καὶ ἀντίθεον Λυκοφόντην   275
καὶ Πολυαιμονίδην Ἀμοπάονα καὶ Μελάνιππον.
πάντας ἐπασσυτέρους πέλασε χθονὶ πουλυβοτείρῃ.
τὸν δὲ ἰδὼν γήθησεν ἄναξ ἀνδρῶν Ἀγαμέμνων
τόξου ἄπο κρατεροῦ Τρώων ὀλέκοντα φάλαγγας·
στῆ δὲ παρ᾽ αὐτὸν ἰὼν καί μιν πρὸς μῦθον ἔειπε·   280
Τεῦκρε, φίλη κεφαλή, Τελαμώνιε, κοίρανε λαῶν,
βάλλ᾽ οὕτως, αἴ κέν τι φόως Δαναοῖσι γένηαι
πατρί τε σῷ Τελαμῶνι, ὅ σ᾽ ἔτρεφε τυτθὸν ἐόντα,
καί σε νόθον περ ἐόντα κομίσσατο ᾧ ἐνὶ οἴκῳ·

---

264. Ἐνυαλίῳ: a name of Ares, the god of war. In scansion, the final -ῳ and the ἀ- at the beginning of the next word are the subject of synizisis (Scansion, B.5b), so that they are treated as a single long syllable.

266. εἴνατος = ἔνατος

268. ὑπεξέφερεν: imperf. act. ὑπεκφέρω

269. παπτήνας: aor. part. act. παπταίνω | τιν᾽: acc., 'someone' (J)

270. βεβλήκειν: 3 s. plupf. act. βάλλω | ὁ μὲν .. ὄλεσσεν: this clause referring to the victim interrupts the main sentence about Teukros, which is resumed by αὐτὰρ ὁ in 271 | πεσὼν: nom. s. m. 2 aor. act. part. πίπτω

271-2. δύσκεν, κρύπτασκε: frequentatives (S), from δύ(ν)ω, κρύπτω

273. τίνα: 'whom?'; with accent (J)

279. τόξου ἄπο: i.e. with the arrows from his bow; ἄπο, not the usual ἀπό, because it follows the word it governs (Y.11) | ὀλέκοντα: acc. s. m. pres. part. act. ὀλέκω, a form of ὄλλυμι

282. αἴ κεν: 'in the hope that', with subjunc. (W.5) | φόως = φῶς | γένηαι: 2 s. 2 aor. subjunc. γίγνομαι, -ηαι for -ῃ (L.8)

283-5. ἐόντα = ὄντα, acc. s. m. part. εἰμί (U.2)

284. κομίσσατο = ἐκομίσατο (Q.3), aor. mid. κομίζω | ᾧ : dat. s. m. 3 possessive adj. (F)

comrade Meriones, the equal of the man-slaying Enualios,
265 and after them Eurupulos, the splendid son of Euaimon.
And ninth came Teukros, brandishing his taut bow, and he
took his position under the shield of Aias, the son of
Telamon. Then Aias would move his shield slightly to one
side, and the hero, glancing rapidly around, when, having
270 shot, he had struck someone in the throng of battle, – and
he, falling on the spot, had given up his spirit – then
Teukros, returning as a child returns to the protection of his
mother, would go back to Aias, and Aias would cover him
with his bright shield.

Which then of the Trojans did the excellent Teukros take
275 first? Orsilokhos first, and Ormenos and Ophelestes, and
Daitor and Khromios and godlike Lukophontes, and
Amopaon the son of Poluaimon and Melanippos – all of
these, one after the other, he brought to the earth which
nourishes many. Seeing him as he destroyed the ranks of
the Trojans from his mighty bow, Agamemnon the lord of
280 men rejoiced, and coming to his side he stopped, and
addressed a word to him –

"Teukros, dear man, son of Telamon, leader of people,
keep on shooting like this, in case you may become a light
to the Danaans and to your father Telamon, who brought
you up when you were little, and, although you were a

τὸν καὶ τηλόθ' ἐόντα ἐϋκλείης ἐπίβησον.   285
σοὶ δ' ἐγὼ ἐξερέω ὡς καὶ τετελεσμένον ἔσται·
αἴ κέν μοι δώῃ Ζεύς τ' αἰγίοχος καὶ 'Αθήνη
'Ιλίου ἐξαλαπάξαι, ἐϋκτίμενον πτολίεθρον,
πρώτῳ τοι μετ' ἐμὲ πρεσβήϊον ἐν χερὶ θήσω,
ἢ τρίποδ' ἠὲ δύω ἵππους αὐτοῖσιν ὄχεσφιν   290
ἠὲ γυναῖχ', ἥ κέν τοι ὁμὸν λέχος εἰσαναβαίνοι."
    Τὸν δ' ἀπαμειβόμενος προσεφώνεε Τεῦκρος ἀμύμων·
"'Ατρείδη κύδιστε, τί με σπεύδοντα καὶ αὐτὸν
ὀτρύνεις; οὐ μέν τοι, ὅση δύναμίς γε πάρεστι,
παύομαι, ἀλλ' ἐξ οὗ προτὶ "Ιλιον ὠσάμεθ' αὐτούς,   295
ἐκ τοῦ δὴ τόξοισι δεδεγμένος ἄνδρας ἐναίρω.
ὀκτὼ δὴ προέηκα τανυγλώχινας ὀϊστούς,
πάντες δ' ἐν χροῒ πῆχθεν ἀρηϊθόων αἰζηῶν·
τοῦτον δ' οὐ δύναμαι βαλέειν κύνα λυσσητῆρα."
    'Η ῥα καὶ ἄλλον ὀϊστὸν ἀπὸ νευρῆφιν ἴαλλεν   300
'Εκτορος ἀντικρύ, βαλέειν δέ ἑ ἵετο θυμός·
καὶ τοῦ μέν ῥ' ἀφάμαρθ', ὁ δ' ἀμύμονα Γοργυθίωνα,
υἱὸν ἐῢν Πριάμοιο, κατὰ στῆθος βάλεν ἰῷ,

---

285. καὶ τηλόθ': 'even (though) far away' (Z., Y.3) | ἐπίβησον: 2 s. aor. imperat. act. ἐπιβαίνω
286. τετελεσμένον: nom. s. n. perf. part. pass. τελέω
287. δώῃ: 3 s. 2 aor. subjunc, act. δίδωμι; subjunc. after αἴ κεν in a fut. conditional (W.3a)
289. θήσω: fut. act. τίθημι
290. αὐτοῖσιν ὄχεσφιν: 'chariot and all' (K.4, E)
291. κεν εἰσαναβάινοι: potential conditional (W.4) – 'would climb into (if I had given her to you)'
293. καὶ αὐτὸν: 'even on my own' (Z,K.3)
294. μέν = μήν (Z) | τοι: 'let me tell you' (Z) | ὅση .. πάρεστι: supply something like 'using' – '(using) as much strength as there is (in me)'
295–6. παύομαι, ἐναίρω: pres. for perf. – 'I have been stopping, have been killing' | ἐξ οὗ .. ἐκ τοῦ: 'from the time when .. , from that time ..'
295. προτὶ = πρὸς (Y.9)
296. τόξοισι: pl. for s. | δεδεγμένος: perf. part. δέχομαι
297. προέηκα: 1 s. aor. act. προΐημι
298. πῆχθεν: 3 pl. aor. pass. πήγνυμι, –εν for –ησαν (L.5)
299. κύνα: acc. s. κύων; so 368
300. νευρῆφιν: for gen. s., νευρή (E)
301. ἑ: acc. s. 3 personal pronoun (H.2) | ἵετο: 3 s. imperf. mid. ἵημι

285 bastard son, took care of you in his house. Raise him to glory, even though he is far away. And I will declare (something) to you, and it will be accomplished. If Zeus who holds the aigis and Athene grant to me to sack Ilion, the well-built city, to you first after me I shall set the gift of

290 honour in your hand – either a tripod, or two horses with their chariot, or a woman who would climb into the bed that she would share with you."

And answering him the excellent Teukros said –

"Most glorious son of Atreus, why do you spur me on

295 when I am eager (enough) on my own? I tell you, I have not stopped labouring with all the strength that I have, but, from the moment that we drove them back towards Ilion, from that moment, indeed, I have been killing men, lying in wait for them with my bow. Eight long-pointed arrows I have shot forth, and every one of them has fixed itself in the flesh of men who are strong, and swift in war. But this mad dog I have not been able to hit."

300   He spoke, and shot another arrow from his bowstring straight at Hektor, and his heart was longing to hit him. And he missed him, and hit the excellent Gorguthion, the noble son of Priam, in the chest with his arrow –

τόν ῥ' ἐξ Αἰσύμηθεν ὀπυιομένη τέκε μήτηρ,
καλὴ Καστιάνειρα, δέμας ἐϊκυῖα θεῆσι.   305
μήκων δ' ὡς ἑτέρωσε κάρη βάλεν, ἥ τ' ἐνὶ κήπῳ,
καρπῷ βριθομένη νοτίῃσί τε εἰαρινῇσιν,
ὣς ἑτέρωσ' ἤμυσε κάρη πήληκι βαρυνθέν.

   Τεῦκρος δ' ἄλλον ὀϊστὸν ἀπὸ νευρῆφιν ἴαλλεν
Ἕκτορος ἀντικρύ, βαλέειν δέ ἑ ἵετο θυμός.   310
ἀλλ' ὅ γε καὶ τόθ' ἅμαρτε· παρέσφηλεν γὰρ Ἀπόλλων·
ἀλλ' Ἀρχεπτόλεμον, θρασὺν Ἕκτορος ἡνιοχῆα,
ἱέμενον πολεμόνδε βάλε στῆθος παρὰ μαζόν·
ἤριπε δ' ἐξ ὀχέων, ὑπερώησαν δέ οἱ ἵπποι
ὠκύποδες· τοῦ δ' αὖθι λύθη ψυχή τε μένος τε.   315
Ἕκτορα δ' αἰνὸν ἄχος πύκασε φρένας ἡνιόχοιο·
τὸν μὲν ἔπειτ' εἴασε καὶ ἀχνύμενός περ ἑταίρου,
Κεβριόνην δ' ἐκέλευσεν ἀδελφεὸν ἐγγὺς ἐόντα
ἵππων ἡνί' ἑλεῖν· ὁ δ' ἄρ' οὐκ ἀπίθησεν ἀκούσας.
αὐτὸς δ' ἐκ δίφροιο χαμαὶ θόρε παμφανόωντος   320
σμερδαλέα ἰάχων· ὁ δὲ χερμάδιον λάβε χειρί,
βῆ δ' ἰθὺς Τεύκρου, βαλέειν δέ ἑ θυμὸς ἀνώγει.
ἤτοι ὁ μὲν φαρέτρης ἐξείλετο πικρὸν ὀϊστόν,
θῆκε δ' ἐπὶ νευρῇ· τὸν δ' αὖ κορυθαίολος Ἕκτωρ
αὐερύοντα παρ' ὦμον, ὅθι κληῒς ἀποέργει   325
αὐχένα τε στῆθός τε, μάλιστα δὲ καίριόν ἐστι,

---

304. τέκε: 2 aor. act. τίκτω
305. δέμας: acc. of respect (G.1e) | ἐϊκυῖα = ἐοικυῖα, nom. s. f. of the part. of ἔοικα
306. ἑτέρωσε: 'to one side' (Y.1), as 308
307. εἰαρινῇσιν: εἰαρ– = ἐάρ–
308. ἤμυσε: aor. act. ἠμύω | πήληκι: dat. s. πήληξ | βαρυνθέν: nom. s. n. aor. part. pass.
βαρύνω, with κάρη
309–11. See on 300–2
311. παρέσφηλεν: aor. act. παρασφάλλω
312. ἡνιοχῆα: acc. s., –ηα for –εα (D.2b); ἡνιοχεύς = ἡνίοχος
313–7. See on 121–5
319–20. ὁ Kebriones, αὐτὸς Hektor (I.2, K.2). But at 321, 323, ὁ refers to Hektor
322. ἀνώγει: 3 s. plupf. act. ἄνωγα, with aor. sense
323–4. ἐξείλετο, θῆκε: both aor. with plupf. sense; ἐξείλετο 2 aor. mid. ἐξαιρέω, θῆκε aor. act.
τίθημι – 'had been taking out', 'had been placing' (Q.2)
325. αὐερύοντα: supply 'the string' as object | ἀποέργει = ἀποείργει

305 Gorguthion, whom his mother had borne, the beautiful
     Kastianeira, who was married from Aisume, in her body the
     equal of the goddesses. Like a poppy he dropped his head
     to one side – a poppy in a garden, when it is weighed down
     by its seed and the springtime showers. Thus his head
     drooped to one side, weighed down by his helmet.

     And Teukros shot another arrow from his bowstring
310 straight at Hektor, and his heart was longing to hit him. But
     he missed him then also, for Apollo diverted (the arrow),
     but he hit Arkheptolemos, the bold charioteer of Hektor, as
     he rushed into battle, in the chest by the nipple. He crashed
315 from his chariot, his swift-footed horses shied back, and his
     life and strength collapsed there and then. Bitter grief closed
     over Hektor's heart for his charioteer. Then he let him lie,
     even though he grieved for his companion, and he ordered
     Kebriones, his brother, who was nearby, to take the horses'
320 reins. And he, hearing, did not disobey. He himself
     jumped to the ground from the shining chariot, shouting
     terribly. He took a boulder in his hand, and went straight
     for Teukros, and his heart was urging him to hit him. He
     had taken out a bitter arrow from his quiver, and placed it on
325 the bowstring. But him Hektor of the flashing helmet, as he
     was drawing the string back to his shoulder, at the place
     where the collar-bone separates the neck from the chest –
     and it is a particularly vital spot – at that point

τῇ ῥ' ἐπὶ οἷ μεμαῶτα βάλεν λίθῳ ὀκριόεντι,
ῥῆξε δέ οἱ νευρήν· νάρκησε δὲ χεὶρ ἐπὶ καρπῷ,
στῆ δὲ γνὺξ ἐριπών, τόξον δέ οἱ ἔκπεσε χειρός.
Αἴας δ' οὐκ ἀμέλησε κασιγνήτοιο πεσόντος,   330
ἀλλὰ θέων περίβη καί οἱ σάκος ἀμφεκάλυψε.
τὸν μὲν ἔπειθ' ὑποδύντε δύω ἐρίηρες ἑταῖροι,
Μηκιστεὺς Ἐχίοιο πάϊς καὶ δῖος Ἀλάστωρ
νῆας ἔπι γλαφυρὰς φερέτην βαρέα στενάχοντα.

"Αψ δ' αὖτις Τρώεσσιν Ὀλύμπιος ἐν μένος ὦρσεν·   335
οἱ δ' ἰθὺς τάφροιο βαθείης ὦσαν Ἀχαιούς·
Ἕκτωρ δ' ἐν πρώτοισι κίε σθένεϊ βλεμεαίνων.
ὡς δ' ὅτε τίς τε κύων συὸς ἀγρίου ἠὲ λέοντος
ἅπτηται κατόπισθε, ποσὶν ταχέεσσι διώκων,
ἰσχία τε γλουτούς τε, ἑλισσόμενόν τε δοκεύει,   340
ὣς Ἕκτωρ ὤπαζε κάρη κομόωντας Ἀχαιούς,
αἰὲν ἀποκτείνων τὸν ὀπίστατον· οἱ δὲ φέβοντο.
αὐτὰρ ἐπεὶ διά τε σκόλοπας καὶ τάφρον ἔβησαν
φεύγοντες, πολλοὶ δὲ δάμεν Τρώων ὑπὸ χερσίν,
οἱ μὲν δὴ παρὰ νηυσὶν ἐρητύοντο μένοντες,   345

---

327. τῇ: 'there' (I.4 – likewise at 396), taking up ὅθι, 325 | οἷ: dat. s. 3 pers. pronoun, here with accent as it refers to Hektor, who is the subject of the verb (H.2)

328. ῥῆξε: aor. act. ῥήγνυμι

329. στῆ: here 'stayed', rather than 'stood', as the following words make clear | γνὺξ: 'on his knees', adv. from γόνυ | ἔκπεσε = ἐξέπεσε (R); 3 s. 2 aor. act. ἐκπίπτω; 2 aor. part in next line

331. θέων: pres. part. act. θέω ('of the gods' is θεῶν, with different accent) | ἀμφεκάλυψε: 3 s. aor. act. ἀμφικαλύπτω

332. ὑποδύντε: dual nom. ὑποδύς, pres. part. act. ὑποδύω (D.9)

334. στενάχοντα: acc. s. pres. part. act. στενάχω, going with τὸν, 332

335. Ὀλύμπιος: 'the Olumpian', i.e. Zeus | ἐν ... ὦρσεν: aor. act. ἐνόρνυμι

336. ὦσαν: aor. act. ὠθέω

338. συὸς: gen. s. σῦς, gen. with ἅπτηται

339. ἅπτηται: subjunc. after ὡς ὅτε – although δοκεύει, next line, is indic. | ποσὶν ταχέεσσι: both dat. pl., for πούσι ταχέσι (D.8) – ποσί again at 389, ποσσί at 443

340. ἰσχία, γλουτούς: these accs. are difficult to explain. Perhaps explanatory of κατόπισθε – 'from behind, i.e. by the haunches ..' | ἑλισσόμενον: acc. pres. part. mid., with 'the boar' understood

342. αἰὲν = ἀεί, as 361, etc. | ὀπίστατον: a superlative form, connected with ὄπισθε, 'behind'

344. δάμεν: 3 pl. aor. pass. δαμάζω, –εν for –ησαν (L.5)

Hektor struck him, as he was rushing at him, with the jagged stone, and smashed his bowstring. His hand went numb at the wrist, and falling on his knees he stayed there, 330 and his bow fell from his hand. But Aias did not neglect his fallen brother, but running up bestrode him, and covered him with his shield. Then, taking him up, his two loyal companions, Mekisteus the son of Ekhios and the godlike Alastor, carried him to the hollow ships, groaning heavily.

335 The Olumpian once more aroused strength in the Trojans, and they drove the Akhaians back straight towards the deep ditch. Hektor went among the first (of them), exulting in his strength. And as when a dog catches hold of a wild boar 340 or a lion from behind, pursuing it with swift feet, by its haunches and hind-quarters, and watches it closely as it turns about, so Hektor followed the long-haired Akhaians closely, always killing the one right at the rear, while they fled in terror. But when in their flight they passed the stakes and the ditch, and many had been subdued under the hands 345 of the Trojans, they halted by the ships, staying (there),

ἀλλήλοισί τε κεκλόμενοι καὶ πᾶσι θεοῖσι
χεῖρας ἀνίσχοντες μεγάλ' εὐχετόωντο ἕκαστος·
Ἕκτωρ δ' ἀμφιπεριστρώφα καλλίτριχας ἵππους
Γοργοῦς ὄμματ' ἔχων ἠὲ βροτολοιγοῦ Ἄρηος.

Τοὺς δὲ ἰδοῦσ' ἐλέησε θεὰ λευκώλενος Ἥρη,   350
αἶψα δ' Ἀθηναίην ἔπεα πτερόεντα προσηύδα·
"ὢ πόποι, αἰγιόχοιο Διὸς τέκος, οὐκέτι νῶϊ
ὀλλυμένων Δαναῶν κεκαδησόμεθ' ὑστάτιόν περ;
οἵ κεν δὴ κακὸν οἶτον ἀναπλήσαντες ὄλωνται
ἀνδρὸς ἑνὸς ῥιπῇ, ὁ δὲ μαίνεται οὐκέτ' ἀνεκτῶς   355
Ἕκτωρ Πριαμίδης, καὶ δὴ κακὰ πολλὰ ἔοργε."

Τὴν δ' αὖτε προσέειπε θεὰ γλαυκῶπις Ἀθήνη·
"καὶ λίην οὗτός γε μένος θυμόν τ' ὀλέσειε
χερσὶν ὑπ' Ἀργείων φθίμενος ἐν πατρίδι γαίῃ·
ἀλλὰ πατὴρ οὑμὸς φρεσὶ μαίνεται οὐκ ἀγαθῇσι,   360
σχέτλιος, αἰὲν ἀλιτρός, ἐμῶν μενέων ἀπερωεύς·
οὐδέ τι τῶν μέμνηται, ὅ οἱ μάλα πολλάκις υἱὸν
τειρόμενον σώεσκον ὑπ' Εὐρυσθῆος ἀέθλων.
ἤτοι ὁ μὲν κλαίεσκε πρὸς οὐρανόν, αὐτὰρ ἐμὲ Ζεὺς

---

346. τε: not with the καὶ in this line, but joining 346–7 to 345 – 'they halted ...., and, calling ...,
each one prayed ..'

347. ἀνίσχοντες: pres. part. of a form of ἀνέχω | εὐχετόωντο: 3 pl. imperf. εὐχετάομαι; it is
common for ἕκαστος, s., to take a pl. verb – e.g. 520–1

348. ἀμφιπερίστρωφα: 3 s. imperf. act. ἀμφι–περι–στρωφάω

349. Γοργοῦς, Ἄρηος: gen. s. Γοργώ, Ἄρης (D.3a)

350. ἰδοῦσ': nom. s. f. 2 aor. act. part. ὁράω

351. Ἀθηναίην = Ἀθήνην, as 384, etc.

352. νῶϊ: dual nom. 1 pers. – 'the two of us'; the same form as at 377, 458 (H.1)

353. κεκαδησόμεθ': fut. κήδομαι, here in a reduplicated form | ὑστάτιόν = ὕστατον, n. adj. as
adv. (G.1a)

354. See on 34

356. ἔοργε: 3 s. perf. act. ἔρδω; 'has done (and is doing)'

358. λίην = λίαν | ὀλέσειε: aor. opt. act. ὄλλυμι, opt. to express a wish

359. φθίμενος: 2 aor. part. mid. φθί(ν)ω

360. οὑμὸς = ὁ ἐμὸς

362. τῶν: demonstrative, 'these things' (I.2) – defined by the following ὅ, 'namely, that' (I.3),
clause | οἱ υἱὸν: 'his son' (H.3)

363–4. σώεσκον, κλαίεσκε: frequentatives (S) of σώζω and κλαίω; 'kept on saving', 'kept on
weeping'

363. ἀέθλων = ἄθλων

and, calling to one another and holding up their hands to all the gods, each one of them prayed in a loud voice. But Hektor kept wheeling his fine-maned horses this way and that, having the eyes of Gorgo, or of Ares, the plague of men.

350   Seeing them the white-armed goddess Here pitied them, and straight-away addressed winged words to Athene –

"Alas, child of aigis-bearing Zeus! Shall the two of us no longer care for the Danaans as they are being destroyed, even at this final hour? Are they to perish having fulfilled a 355 miserable fate, at the onset of a single man, while Hektor, the son of Priam, rages with a rage that can no longer be resisted, and does many, many deeds of evil?"

Then the grey-eyed goddess answered her –

"May he too surely lose his strength and his life, killed 360 under the hands of the Akhaians in his native land. But my father is raging with evil mind, hard-hearted that he is, ever wicked, the thwarter of my plans. And he has no thought at all for this, that many, many times I saved his son when he was being overwhelmed by the tasks of Eurustheus. He

τῷ ἐπαλεξήσουσαν ἀπ' οὐρανόθεν προΐαλλεν. 365
εἰ γὰρ ἐγὼ τάδε ᾔδε' ἐνὶ φρεσὶ πευκαλίμῃσιν,
εὖτέ μιν εἰς 'Αΐδαο πυλάρταο προὔπεμψεν
ἐξ 'Ερέβευς ἄξοντα κύνα στυγεροῦ 'Αΐδαο,
οὐκ ἂν ὑπεξέφυγε Στυγὸς ὕδατος αἰπὰ ῥέεθρα.
νῦν δ' ἐμὲ μὲν στυγέει, Θέτιδος δ' ἐξήνυσε βουλάς, 370
ἥ οἱ γούνατ' ἔκυσσε καὶ ἔλλαβε χειρὶ γενείου,
λισσομένη τιμῆσαι 'Αχιλλῆα πτολίπορθον.
ἔσται μάν, ὅτ' ἂν αὖτε φίλην γλαυκώπιδα εἴπῃ.
ἀλλὰ σὺ μὲν νῦν νῶϊν ἐπέντυε μώνυχας ἵππους,
ὄφρ' ἂν ἐγὼ καταδῦσα Διὸς δόμον αἰγιόχοιο 375
τεύχεσιν ἐς πόλεμον θωρήξομαι, ὄφρα ἴδωμαι
ἢ νῶϊ Πριάμοιο πάϊς κορυθαίολος 'Έκτωρ
γηθήσει προφανέντε ἀνὰ πτολέμοιο γεφύρας,
ἦ τις καὶ Τρώων κορέει κύνας ἠδ' οἰωνοὺς
δημῷ καὶ σάρκεσσι, πεσὼν ἐπὶ νηυσὶν 'Αχαιῶν." 380
   'Ὣς ἔφατ', οὐδ' ἀπίθησε θεὰ λευκώλενος 'Ήρη.
ἡ μὲν ἐποιχομένη χρυσάμπυκας ἔντυεν ἵππους
'Ήρη, πρέσβα θεά, θυγάτηρ μεγάλοιο Κρόνοιο·
αὐτὰρ 'Αθηναίη, κούρη Διὸς αἰγιόχοιο,

---

365. ἐπαλεξήσουσαν: acc. s. f. fut. part. act. ἐπαλέξω; fut. part. for purpose – 'sent me forth, to help'; likewise 368 (X.1b)

366. γὰρ: 'yes, for', developing what she said at 361–2 | ᾔδε': past tense οἶδα; 'if I had known' (W.2b)

367. μιν: Herakles | εἰς: supply δῶμα | 'Αΐδαο, πυλάρταο: both gen. s., –αο for –ου (B.6) | προὔπεμψεν: for προ–έπεμψεν, subject Eurustheus

368. 'Ερέβευς: gen. s. 'Έρεβος | κύνα: i.e. Kerberos

371. ἔλλαβε = ἔλαβε (N.2), as 452; followed by gen. in sense of 'took hold of'

373. μάν = μὴν (Z), as 512

374. μέν: not followed by δέ; she means, 'you do this, while I shall do that', but changes construction at 375 | νῶϊν: dat. dual 1 pers. pronoun (H.1)

375. καταδῦσα: nom. s. f. aor. part. act. καταδύ(ν)ω; so ἐνδῦσα, 387 (with different meaning)

376. θωρήξομαι: aor. subjunc. mid. θωρήσσω, –ομαι for –ωμαι (L.10) | ἴδωμαι: 1 s. 2 aor. subjunc. mid. ὁράω

378. προφανέντε: dual acc. προφανείς, aor. part. pass. προφαίνω; in m. form, although referring to Here and Athene. With νῶϊ, after γηθήσει – 'will rejoice at the two of us having appeared', i.e. 'that we have appeared'

379. κορέει: 3 s. fut. act. κορέννυμι (O.1)

365   kept on crying to heaven, and Zeus sent me forth from
heaven to help him. For if I had known this in my shrewd
mind, when he sent him forth to the house of Hades, the
fastener of the gate, to bring from Erebos the dog of hateful
Hades, he would not have got away from the headlong flow
370   of the water of Stux. But now he hates me, and has
accomplished the plans of Thetis, who kissed his knees and
took his chin in her hand, entreating him to honour
Akhilleus, the sacker of cities. The time will indeed come,
when he calls me his dear grey-eyed (daughter) again. But
do you now make ready the horses of uncloven hoof for us,
375   while I, going into the house of aigis-bearing Zeus, arm
myself with weapons for war, so that I may see whether the
son of Priam, Hektor of the flashing helmet, will be glad
that the two of us have appeared amid the spaces of the
battlefield, or whether one of the Trojans as well (as the
380   Akhaians) will glut the dogs and birds with his fat and flesh,
falling at the ships of the Akhaians."

Thus she spoke, and the white-armed goddess Here did
not disobey. Going about her work, she was harnessing the
horses, with their fillets of gold – Here, the august goddess,
the daughter of great Kronos. But Athene, the daughter of

πέπλον μὲν κατέχευεν ἑανὸν πατρὸς ἐπ' οὔδει, 385
ποικίλον, ὅν ῥ' αὐτὴ ποιήσατο καὶ κάμε χερσίν,
ἡ δὲ χιτῶν' ἐνδῦσα Διὸς νεφεληγερέταο
τεύχεσιν ἐς πόλεμον θωρήσσετο δακρυόεντα.
ἐς δ' ὄχεα φλόγεα ποσὶ βήσετο, λάζετο δ' ἔγχος
βριθὺ μέγα στιβαρόν, τῷ δάμνησι στίχας ἀνδρῶν 390
ἡρώων, τοῖσίν τε κοτέσσεται ὀβριμοπάτρη.
Ἥρη δὲ μάστιγι θοῶς ἐπεμαίετ' ἄρ' ἵππους·
αὐτόμαται δὲ πύλαι μύκον οὐρανοῦ, ἃς ἔχον Ὧραι,
τῆς ἐπιτέτραπται μέγας οὐρανὸς Οὔλυμπός τε
ἡμὲν ἀνακλῖναι πυκινὸν νέφος ἠδ' ἐπιθεῖναι. 395
τῇ ῥα δι' αὐτάων κεντρηνεκέας ἔχον ἵππους.
   Ζεὺς δὲ πατὴρ Ἴδηθεν ἐπεὶ ἴδε χώσατ' ἄρ' αἰνῶς,
Ἶριν δ' ὄτρυνε χρυσόπτερον ἀγγελέουσαν·
"βάσκ' ἴθι, Ἶρι ταχεῖα, πάλιν τρέπε μηδ' ἔα ἄντην
ἔρχεσθ'· οὐ γὰρ καλὰ συνοισόμεθα πτολεμόνδε. 400
ὧδε γὰρ ἐξερέω, τὸ δὲ καὶ τετελεσμένον ἔσται·
γυιώσω μέν σφωϊν ὑφ' ἅρμασιν ὠκέας ἵππους,
αὐτὰς δ' ἐκ δίφρου βαλέω κατά θ' ἅρματα ἄξω·
οὐδέ κεν ἐς δεκάτους περιτελλομένους ἐνιαυτοὺς
ἕλκε' ἀπαλθήσεσθον, ἅ κεν μάρπτῃσι κεραυνός· 405
ὄφρ' εἰδῇ γλαυκῶπις ὅτ' ἂν ᾧ πατρὶ μάχηται.

---

390. δάμνησι: 3 s. pres. act. δάμνημι, a verb connected with δαμνάω and δαμάζω
391. κοτέσσεται: aor. subjunc. mid. κοτέω, -εται for -ηται (L.10); 'with whomsoever she is angry' (W.8a)
393. μύκον: a 2 aor. act. form from μυκάομαι | ἔχον: imperf. ἔχω, as 396
394. ἐπιτέτραπται: 3 s. perf. pass. ἐπιτρέπω, s. although there are two subjects
395. ἐπιθεῖναι: aor. infin. act. ἐπιτίθημι
398. Ἶριν: acc. s.; voc. in next line (D.1, 2a) | ἀγγελέουσαν: acc. s. f. fut. part. act. ἀγγέλλω (O.1); fut. for purpose, 'to announce' (X.1b); so 409
399. βάσκ': 2 s. pres. imperat. act. of a frequentative (S) form of βαίνω | ἴθι: 2 s. imperat. εἶμι (U.5) | τρέπε, ἔα: supply 'them' (the goddesses) as object
400. καλὰ: adverbial | συνοισόμεθα: fut. mid. συμφέρω
402. σφῶϊν: dat. dual 3 pers. pronoun; note different accentuation from 2 pers. at 413, etc.(H.2,1); here possessive (H.3) – 'their chariot', 'their horses'
403. κατά .. ἄξω: fut. act. κατάγνυμι; fut. infin. at 417
404. κεν: with fut. (W.3a and 4) – 'they will not be fully healed (if I do this to them)'
405. ἕλκε' = ἕλκη, -εα for -η (D.5b) | ἀπαλθήσεσθον: 3 dual (2 at 419) fut. ἀπαλθαίνομαι | μάρπτῃσι: 3 s. pres. subjunc. act. μάρπτω, -ῃσι for -ῃ (L.9)
406. εἰδῇ: 3 s. subjunc. οἶδα (2 s. at 420); supply something like 'what happens' as the object

385 aigis-bearing Zeus, cast down on her father's floor the fine embroidered robe which she had made herself and worked with her hands; and putting on the tunic of Zeus the cloud-gatherer she armed herself with weapons for the fighting that brings tears. She stepped onto the chariot, which was

390 sparkling like fire, and grasped her spear, heavy, mighty, and strong, with which she tames the ranks of the heroes, whichever of them she, the daughter of a mighty father, is angry with. Here touched the horses sharply with her whip, and the gates of heaven groaned of their own accord – the gates which the Seasons were keeping, to whom great

395 heaven and Olumpos have been entrusted, both to open up the thick cloud and to close it. This way they held their horses, which endure the goad, through them.

When father Zeus saw from Ide he was very angry, and stirred golden-winged Iris to take a message –

"Be off, swift Iris, turn them back, and do not allow

400 them to come against me. For it will not be good for us to clash together in war. For thus I shall declare, and it will be accomplished. I shall lame their swift horses beneath their chariot, and hurl them from the chariot, and smash it. And

405 not even within the course of ten years will they be fully healed of the wounds which the thunderbolt inflicts, so that

Ἥρῃ δ' οὔ τι τόσον νεμεσίζομαι οὐδὲ χολοῦμαι·
αἰεὶ γάρ μοι ἔωθεν ἐνικλᾶν ὅττι κεν εἴπω."

  Ὣς ἔφατ', ὦρτο δὲ Ἶρις ἀελλόπος ἀγγελέουσα,
βῆ δὲ κατ' Ἰδαίων ὀρέων ἐς μακρὸν Ὄλυμπον.   410
πρώτῃσιν δὲ πύλῃσι πολυπτύχου Οὐλύμποιο
ἀντομένη κατέρυκε, Διὸς δέ σφ' ἔννεπε μῦθον·
"πῇ μέματον; τί σφῶϊν ἐνὶ φρεσὶ μαίνεται ἦτορ;
οὐκ ἐᾷ Κρονίδης ἐπαμυνέμεν Ἀργείοισιν.
ὧδε γὰρ ἠπείλησε Κρόνου πάϊς, ᾗ τελέει περ,   415
γυιώσειν μὲν σφῶϊν ὑφ' ἅρμασιν ὠκέας ἵππους,
αὐτὰς δ' ἐκ δίφρου βαλέειν κατά θ' ἅρματα ἄξειν·
οὐδέ κεν ἐς δεκάτους περιτελλομένους ἐνιαυτοὺς
ἕλκε' ἀπαλθήσεσθον, ἅ κεν μάρπτῃσι κεραυνός·
ὄφρ' εἰδῇς γλαυκῶπι, ὅτ' ἂν σῷ πατρὶ μάχηαι.   420
Ἥρῃ δ' οὔ τι τόσον νεμεσίζεται οὐδὲ χολοῦται·
αἰεὶ γάρ οἱ ἔωθεν ἐνικλᾶν ὅττι κεν εἴπῃ·
ἀλλὰ σύ γ' αἰνοτάτη, κύον ἀδεές, εἰ ἐτεόν γε
τολμήσεις Διὸς ἄντα πελώριον ἔγχος ἀεῖραι."

  Ἡ μὲν ἄρ' ὣς εἰποῦσ' ἀπέβη πόδας ὠκέα Ἶρις,   425
αὐτὰρ Ἀθηναίην Ἥρη πρὸς μῦθον ἔειπεν·
"ὦ πόποι, αἰγιόχοιο Διὸς τέκος, οὐκέτ' ἔγωγε
νῶϊ ἐῶ Διὸς ἄντα βροτῶν ἕνεκα πτολεμίζειν·
τῶν ἄλλος μὲν ἀποφθίσθω, ἄλλος δὲ βιώτω,

---

408. ἔωθεν = εἴωθεν, 3 s. perf. act. ἔθω | ὅττι: acc. n. s. ὅστις (A, J.3)

409. ὦρτο: 3 s. aor. mid. ὄρνυμι

412. σφ': dat. 3 pers. pl. pronoun (H.2)

413. μέματον: 2 dual μέμονα | σφῶϊν: dat. dual 2 pers. pronoun (H.1), as 416, 452, etc.

414. ἐᾷ for ἐᾷ (O.2a)

415. τελέει: 3 s. fut. act. τελέω (O.1) | περ: intensive (Z)

417–22. See on 403–8

420. μάχηαι: 2 s. pres. subjunc. μάχομαι; –ηαι for –ῃ (L.8)

423. σύ γ' αἰνοτάτη: supply 'are'

424. ἀεῖραι: aor. infin. act. ἀείρω, αἴρω

425. πόδας: acc. of respect (G.1e) – 'as far as her feet are concerned' | ὠκέα = ὠκεῖα, nom. s. f.

428. ἄντα, ἕνεκα: both after the word they govern

429. ἄλλος μὲν .. ἄλλος δὲ: 'one of them .., another ..' | ἀποφθίσθω: 3 s. 2 aor. imperat. mid. ἀποφθί(ν)ω | βιώτω: 3 s. pres. imperat. act. βιόω

the grey-eyed one may learn (what happens) when she fights with her father. But with Here I am not so much indignant and angry, for she is always in the habit of frustrating me, whatever I say."

Thus he spoke, and swift-footed Iris rushed to deliver the
410 message, and went down from the mountains of Ide to tall Olumpos. And meeting (the goddesses) at the front of the gates of Olumpos with its many valleys, she stopped (them), and told them of Zeus' words –

"Where are the two of you hurrying to? Why do your hearts rage within your breasts? The son of Kronos does
415 not allow you to help the Argives. For thus the child of Kronos threatened, even as he will fulfil it – that he will lame your swift horses beneath your chariot, and hurl you yourselves from the chariot, and smash it. And not even within the course of ten years will you be fully healed of the
420 wounds which the thunderbolt inflicts, so that you may know, grey-eyed one, (what happens) when you fight with your father. But with Here he is not so much indignant and angry, for she is always in the habit of frustrating him, whatever he says. But you (are) most terrible, you fearless dog, if you will truly dare to raise your monstrous spear against Zeus."

425 Speaking thus swift-footed Iris departed, and Here addressed a word to Athene –

"Alas, child of aigis-bearing Zeus! No longer do I permit the two of us to fight against Zeus on behalf of the mortals.
430 Let one of them die, let another live, as his fortune decides.

ὅς κε τύχῃ· κεῖνος δὲ τὰ ἃ φρονέων ἐνὶ θυμῷ   430
Τρωσί τε καὶ Δαναοῖσι δικαζέτω, ὡς ἐπιεικές."

   Ὣς ἄρα φωνήσασα πάλιν τρέπε μώνυχας ἵππους·
τῇσιν δ' Ὧραι μὲν λῦσαν καλλίτριχας ἵππους,
καὶ τοὺς μὲν κατέδησαν ἐπ' ἀμβροσίῃσι κάπῃσιν,
ἄρματα δ' ἔκλιναν πρὸς ἐνώπια παμφανόωντα·   435
αὐταὶ δὲ χρυσέοισιν ἐπὶ κλισμοῖσι καθῖζον
μίγδ' ἄλλοισι θεοῖσι, φίλον τετιημέναι ἦτορ.

   Ζεὺς δὲ πατὴρ Ἴδηθεν ἐύτροχον ἅρμα καὶ ἵππους
Οὔλυμπόνδε δίωκε, θεῶν δ' ἐξίκετο θώκους.
τῷ δὲ καὶ ἵππους μὲν λῦσε κλυτὸς ἐννοσίγαιος,   440
ἄρματα δ' ἂμ βωμοῖσι τίθει, κατὰ λῖτα πετάσσας·
αὐτὸς δὲ χρύσειον ἐπὶ θρόνον εὐρύοπα Ζεὺς
ἕζετο, τῷ δ' ὑπὸ ποσσὶ μέγας πελεμίζετ' Ὄλυμπος.
αἱ δ' οἶαι Διὸς ἀμφὶς Ἀθηναίη τε καὶ Ἥρη
ἥσθην, οὐδέ τί μιν προσεφώνεον οὐδ' ἐρέοντο·   445
αὐτὰρ ὁ ἔγνω ᾗσιν ἐνὶ φρεσὶ φώνησέν τε·
"τίφθ' οὕτω τετίησθον, Ἀθηναίη τε καὶ Ἥρη;
οὐ μέν θην κάμετόν γε μάχῃ ἔνι κυδιανείρῃ
ὀλλῦσαι Τρῶας, τοῖσιν κότον αἰνὸν ἔθεσθε.
πάντως, οἷον ἐμόν γε μένος καὶ χεῖρες ἄαπτοι,   450
οὐκ ἄν με τρέψειαν, ὅσοι θεοί εἰσ' ἐν Ὀλύμπῳ.

---

430. ὅς: antecedent ἄλλος; 'one of them, whosoever ..' | τύχῃ: 3 s. 2 aor. subjunc. τυγχάνω | τὰ ἃ: lit., 'those (things) of his'; τὰ demonstrative (I.2), ἃ 3 pers. possessive adj. (F)

431. δικαζέτω: 3 s. pres. imperat. act. δικάζω | ἐπιεικές: supply ἐστί

437. ἦτορ: acc. of the seat of the emotions, 'downcast *in* heart' (G.1c)

439. ἐξίκετο: 2 aor. ἐξικνέομαι, 'came *to*' (G.1b) | θώκους = θάκους

440. ἐννοσίγαιος: i.e. Poseidon, the god of earthquakes

441. ἂμ = ἀνὰ (Y.9) | βωμοῖσι: usually 'altar' (as 249), but here presumably 'stands' | κατὰ .. πετάσσας: nom. s. m. aor. part. act. καταπετάννυμι | λῖτα: clearly acc.; but the nom. of this word is not found, so that this could be m. or f. s. or n. pl.

444. ἀμφὶς = ἀμφὶ (Y.8 – so 481, though there it is an adv.) , here 'apart from', governing Διὸς

445. ἥσθην: 3 dual imperf. ἧμαι, as 458 (M.1)

446. ἔγνω: 3 s. 2 aor. act. γιγνώσκω

447. τίφθ' = τίπτε, a form of τί ποτε; 'why ever?' (J.2) | τετίησθον: 2 dual τετίημαι

448. θην: 'in truth' – sarcastic | κάμετόν: 2 dual 2 aor. act. κάμνω

449. ὀλλῦσαι: nom. pl. f. pres. part. act. ὄλλυμι; acc. s. m. of part. at 472 | ἔθεσθε: 2 pl. 2 aor. mid. τίθημι

450. οἷον: 'such (is)' | χεῖρες: supply εἰσί

451. τρέψειαν: 3 pl. aor. optat. act. τρέπω

And let him, thinking those thoughts of his in his heart, decide for the Trojans and the Danaans, in the way that is right."

Having spoken thus, she turned the horses of uncloven hoof back. The Seasons unyoked the lovely-maned horses 435 for them, and tied them to the ambrosial mangers, and leaned the chariot against the shining courtyard-walls. The goddesses sat on golden chairs, mingling with the other gods, and sorrowing in their hearts.

Father Zeus swiftly drove back his strong-wheeled chariot and horses from Ide to Olumpos, and he reached the 440 seats of the gods. The famous earth-shaker unyoked his horses for him, and set the chariot on its stand, putting cloth over it as a covering. The wide-seeing Zeus sat on his golden throne, and great Olumpos quaked beneath his feet. 445 Alone, apart from Zeus, sat Athene and Here, and they did not say anything at all to him, or ask him anything. But he understood in his mind, and he said –

"Why are you so sorrowful, Athene and Here? You have surely not exhausted yourselves in the battle where men gain glory, destroying the Trojans, on whom you have set your 450 terrible anger. Not even all the gods in Olumpos, such is my strength, and my invincible hands, would in any way at

σφῶιν δὲ πρίν περ τρόμος ἔλλαβε φαίδιμα γυῖα,
πρὶν πόλεμόν τε ἰδεῖν πολέμοιό τε μέρμερα ἔργα.
ὧδε γὰρ ἐξερέω, τὸ δέ κεν τετελεσμένον ἦεν·
οὐκ ἂν ἐφ' ὑμετέρων ὀχέων πληγέντε κεραυνῷ   455
ἂψ ἐς ᾿Ολυμπον ἵκεσθον, ἵν' ἀθανάτων ἕδος ἐστίν."

   ῝Ως ἔφαθ', αἱ δ' ἐπέμυξαν ᾿Αθηναίη τε καὶ ῝Ηρη·
πλησίαι αἵ γ' ἥσθην, κακὰ δὲ Τρώεσσι μεδέσθην.
ἤτοι ᾿Αθηναίη ἀκέων ἦν οὐδέ τι εἶπε,
σκυζομένη Διὶ πατρί, χόλος δέ μιν ἄγριος ᾕρει·   460
῝Ηρη δ' οὐκ ἔχαδε στῆθος χόλον, ἀλλὰ προσηύδα·
"αἰνότατε Κρονίδη, ποῖον τὸν μῦθον ἔειπες.
εὖ νυ καὶ ἡμεῖς ἴδμεν ὅ τοι σθένος οὐκ ἀλαπαδνόν·
ἀλλ' ἔμπης Δαναῶν ὀλοφυρόμεθ' αἰχμητάων,
οἵ κεν δὴ κακὸν οἶτον ἀναπλήσαντες ὄλωνται.   465
ἀλλ' ἤτοι πολέμου μὲν ἀφεξόμεθ', εἰ σὺ κελεύεις·
βουλὴν δ' ᾿Αργείοις ὑποθησόμεθ', ἥ τις ὀνήσει,
ὡς μὴ πάντες ὄλωνται ὀδυσσαμένοιο τεοῖο."

   Τὴν δ' ἀπαμειβόμενος προσέφη νεφεληγερέτα Ζεύς·
ἠοῦς δὴ καὶ μᾶλλον ὑπερμενέα Κρονίωνα   470
ὄψεαι, αἴ κ' ἐθέλησθα, βοῶπις πότνια ῝Ηρη,
ὀλλύντ' ᾿Αργείων πουλὺν στρατὸν αἰχμητάων·
οὐ γὰρ πρὶν πολέμου ἀποπαύσεται ὄβριμος ῝Εκτωρ,
πρὶν ὄρθαι παρὰ ναῦφι ποδώκεα Πηλεΐωνα,

452–3. πρίν: in 452 adv., pointing forward to the conjunction in 453; similarly at 473–4
453. ἰδεῖν: 2 aor. infin. act. ὁράω, infin. after πρὶν – 'before seeing'
454. τὸ .. ἦεν: 'it would have been fulfilled (if you had disobeyed me)' – W.4 | ἦεν: 3 s. imperf. εἰμί (U.4)
455. πληγέντε: dual nom. πληγείς (D.9), aor. part. pass. πλήσσω; m., although of Here and Athene, as προφανέντε, 378
456. ἵκεσθον: 2 dual 2 aor. ἱκνέομαι (M.1) | ἵν': 'where', and so followed by indic., as 479
457. ἐπέμυξαν: aor. act. ἐπιμύζω
458. μεδέσθην: 3 dual imperf. μέδομαι (M.2)
459. ἀκέων: here treated as indeclinable, and so –ων, although of Athene
461. ἔχαδε: 3 s. 2 aor. act. χανδάνω
463–8. See on 32–7
470. ἠοῦς: gen. s. ἠώς, as 508, 525; 'in the morning' (G.2a) | Κρονίωνα: 'son of Kronos', i.e. Zeus; so 474, Πηλεΐωνα, 'son of Peleus', i.e. Akhilleus
474. ὄρθαι: aor. infin. mid. ὄρνυμι, infin. after πρὶν | ναῦφι: for dat. pl. (E)

all divert me, whereas for you two trembling seized your shining limbs before you set eyes on war and the sorrowful deeds of war. For thus I shall speak, and it would have been accomplished. You, struck by my thunderbolt, would not have come back in your chariot to Olumpos, where the seat of the immortals is."

Thus he spoke, and Athene and Here muttered. They were sitting nearby, and planning evils for the Trojans. Athene was silent, and said nothing, being angry with her father Zeus, and wild rage was gripping her. But Here's breast did not contain her rage, and she said –

"Most terrible son of Kronos, what a word you have spoken. Well indeed do we know that your strength is not easily exhausted. But nevertheless we pity the Danaan spearmen, who are to perish having fulfilled a wretched fate. But we shall indeed keep ourselves away from the war, as you order. But we shall suggest a plan to the Argives, some one that will help them, so that they will not all perish because you are angry."

Answering her Zeus the cloud-gatherer said –

"In the morning you will even more see the mighty son of Kronos, if you want to, ox-eyed queen Here, destroying a great host of the Argive spearmen. For mighty Hektor will not cease from the war before the swift-footed son of

ἤματι τῷ ὅτ' ἂν οἱ μὲν ἐπὶ πρύμνῃσι μάχωνται　　　475
στείνει ἐν αἰνοτάτῳ περὶ Πατρόκλοιο θανόντος·
ὣς γὰρ θέσφατόν ἐστι· σέθεν δ' ἐγὼ οὐκ ἀλεγίζω
χωομένης, οὐδ' εἴ κε τὰ νείατα πείραθ' ἵκηαι
γαίης καὶ πόντοιο, ἵν' Ἰάπετός τε Κρόνος τε
ἥμενοι οὔτ' αὐγῆς Ὑπερίονος Ἠελίοιο　　　480
τέρποντ' οὔτ' ἀνέμοισι, βαθὺς δέ τε Τάρταρος ἀμφίς·
οὐδ' ἢν ἔνθ' ἀφίκηαι ἀλωμένη, οὔ σευ ἔγωγε
σκυζομένης ἀλέγω, ἐπεὶ οὐ σέο κύντερον ἄλλο."

　　"Ὣς φάτο, τὸν δ' οὔ τι προσέφη λευκώλενος Ἥρη.
ἐν δ' ἔπεσ' Ὠκεανῷ λαμπρὸν φάος ἠελίοιο　　　485
ἕλκον νύκτα μέλαιναν ἐπὶ ζείδωρον ἄρουραν.
Τρωσὶν μέν ῥ' ἀέκουσιν ἔδυ φάος, αὐτὰρ Ἀχαιοῖς
ἀσπασίη τρίλλιστος ἐπήλυθε νὺξ ἐρεβεννή.

　　Τρώων αὖτ' ἀγορὴν ποιήσατο φαίδιμος Ἕκτωρ,
νόσφι νεῶν ἀγαγὼν ποταμῷ ἔπι δινήεντι,　　　490
ἐν καθαρῷ, ὅθι δὴ νεκύων διεφαίνετο χῶρος.
ἐξ ἵππων δ' ἀποβάντες ἐπὶ χθόνα μῦθον ἄκουον,
τόν ῥ' Ἕκτωρ ἀγόρευε Διῒ φίλος· ἐν δ' ἄρα χειρὶ
ἔγχος ἔχ' ἐνδεκάπηχυ· πάροιθε δὲ λάμπετο δουρὸς
αἰχμὴ χαλκείη, περὶ δὲ χρύσεος θέε πόρκης·　　　495
τῷ ὅ γ' ἐρεισάμενος ἔπεα Τρώεσσι μετηύδα·
"κέκλυτέ μευ, Τρῶες καὶ Δάρδανοι ἠδ' ἐπίκουροι·
νῦν ἐφάμην νῆάς τ' ὀλέσας καὶ πάντας Ἀχαιοὺς
ἂψ ἀπονοστήσειν προτὶ Ἴλιον ἠνεμόεσσαν·

---

475. οἱ μὲν: 'they' (I.2), with μὲν not balanced by any succeeding particle

477. σέθεν: gen. s., 2 s. personal pronoun – so σευ, 482, σέο, 483 (H.1); gen. after ἀλεγίζω, in 482 after ἀλέγω

478. νείατα = νέατα, a superlative form ǀ πείραθ' = πείρατα, pl. of πεῖραρ ǀ ἵκηαι: 2 s. 2 aor. subjunc. ἱκνέομαι; so ἀφίκηαι, 482

481. Τάρταρος: supply ἐστί, as also after ἐπεὶ in 483

483. σέο: gen. of comparison with κύντερον – 'more shameless *than* you'

487. ἀέκουσιν = ἄκουσιν, dat. pl. ἄκων

490. ἀγαγὼν: nom. s. m. 2 aor. part. act. ἄγω; supply 'them' as object

492. ἀποβάντες: nom. pl. m. 2 aor. act. part. ἀποβαίνω

494. δουρὸς: gen. s. δόρυ

498. ἐφάμην: imperf. φημι, here, 'I was thinking', with fut. infin. in next line – 'that I would'

499. Ἴλιον: here f. – so ἠνεμόεσσαν. So 551, and elsewhere; but the word may also be n. – though it is often impossible to tell

ραι δὲ γυναῖκες ἐνὶ μεγάροισιν ἑκάστη   520
ἔγα καιόντων· φυλακὴ δέ τις ἔμπεδος ἔστω,
χος εἰσέλθῃσι πόλιν λαῶν ἀπεόντων.
τω, Τρῶες μεγαλήτορες, ὡς ἀγορεύω·
δ', ὃς μὲν νῦν ὑγιής, εἰρημένος ἔστω,
ἠοῦς Τρώεσσι μεθ' ἱπποδάμοις ἀγορεύσω.   525
αι εὐχόμενος Διί τ' ἄλλοισίν τε θεοῖσιν
ιν ἐνθένδε κύνας κηρεσσιφορήτους,
ῆρες φορέουσι μελαινάων ἐπὶ νηῶν.
ἤτοι ἐπὶ νυκτὶ φυλάξομεν ἡμέας αὐτούς,
δ' ὑπηοῖοι σὺν τεύχεσι θωρηχθέντες   530
ν ἔπι γλαφυρῇσιν ἐγείρομεν ὀξὺν Ἄρηα.
αι εἴ κέ μ' ὁ Τυδεΐδης κρατερὸς Διομήδης
νηῶν πρὸς τεῖχος ἀπώσεται, ἦ κεν ἐγὼ τὸν
ᾦ δῃώσας ἔναρα βροτόεντα φέρωμαι.
ν ἣν ἀρετὴν διαείσεται, εἴ κ' ἐμὸν ἔγχος   535
ᾗ ἐπερχόμενον· ἀλλ' ἐν πρώτοισιν ὀΐω
ται οὐτηθείς, πολέες δ' ἀμφ' αὐτὸν ἑταῖροι,
υ ἀνιόντος ἐς αὔριον· εἰ γὰρ ἐγὼν ὣς
ἀθάνατος καὶ ἀγήρως ἤματα πάντα,

ἔστω: 3 s. imperat. εἰμί; so 523 and 524 (U.5)

ἀπεόντων = ἀπόντων, gen. pl. pres. part. ἄπειμι (U.2); gen. absolute, 'while the army is
t'

ὃς: supply ἐστί | εἰρημένος ἔστω: 'let it have been spoken' (U.5), i.e. 'let what has been
n suffice'

τὸν δ': supply μῦθον; 'and another one ..'

ἐξελάαν: pres. infin. act. ἐξελάω, a form of ἐξελαύνω; –αα– for –α– (O.2d)

φυλάξομεν: jussive subjunc., as ἐγείρομεν, 532 (X.2)

ὑπηοῖοι: adj. for adv., 'in the morning' (Y.6)

εἴσομαι εἴ κε: 'I shall know whether'. Likewise 535 (W.6) | εἴσομαι: fut. οἶδα; fut. of
α at 535

τεῖχος: i.e. the wall of Troy | ἀπώσεται: aor. subjunc. mid. ἀπωθέω (L.10)

ἣν ἀρετὴν διαείσεται: 'he shall learn *about* his prowess, i.e. whether ...'

πολέες = πολλοί

ἀνιόντος: gen. s. pres. part. ἄνειμι (U.2) | εἰ γάρ: 'would that', with optat. (X.5) | ὣς
τως

εἴην: 1 s. optat. εἰμί (U.8) | ἤματα πάντα: 'for all my days' – acc. of duration of time
g); ἤματα acc. pl. ἦμαρ

Peleus arises by the ships, on that day when they fight at the
sterns in the direst crisis over the dead Patroklos. For so it   475
is divinely decreed. I do not care about you in your anger,
not even if you come to the lowermost limits of the earth and
the sea, where, seated, Iapetos and Kronos enjoy neither the   480
rays of Huperion the Sun nor the winds, and deep Tartaros
is round about. Not even if you come there in your
wandering do I care about you in your anger, since nothing
else is more shameless than you."

Thus he spoke, and white-armed Here said nothing at all
to him. The bright light of the sun fell into the Ocean,   485
drawing black night over the bountiful land. The Trojans
were sorry as the light set on them, but on the Akhaians the
dark night came welcome, and thrice prayed-for.

Now glorious Hektor held an assembly of the Trojans,
leading them away from the ships by the swirling river, on   490
an open spot, where space appeared between the corpses.
Dismounting from their horses to the ground, they listened
to the speech which Hektor, beloved of Zeus, made. In his
hand he held a spear eleven cubits long, and the bronze tip   495
of the spear gleamed in front, and a golden ring ran round it.
Leaning on this, he addressed words to the Trojans —

"Hear me, Trojans and Dardanians and allies. Just now I
was thinking that I should return again to windy Ilios having

ἀλλὰ πρὶν κνέφας ἦλθε, τὸ νῦν ἐσάωσε μάλιστα   500
'Αργείους καὶ νῆας ἐπὶ ῥηγμῖνι θαλάσσης.
ἀλλ' ἤτοι νῦν μὲν πειθώμεθα νυκτὶ μελαίνη
δόρπα τ' ἐφοπλισόμεσθα· ἀτὰρ καλλίτριχας ἵππους
λύσαθ' ὑπὲξ ὀχέων, παρὰ δέ σφισι βάλλετ' ἐδωδήν·
ἐκ πόλιος δ' ἄξεσθε βόας καὶ ἴφια μῆλα   505
καρπαλίμως, οἶνον δὲ μελίφρονα οἰνίζεσθε
σῖτόν τ' ἐκ μεγάρων, ἐπὶ δὲ ξύλα πολλὰ λέγεσθε,
ὥς κεν παννύχιοι μέσφ' ἠοῦς ἠριγενείης
καίωμεν πυρὰ πολλά, σέλας δ' εἰς οὐρανὸν ἵκη,
μή πως καὶ διὰ νύκτα κάρη κομόωντες 'Αχαιοὶ   510
φεύγειν ὁρμήσωνται ἐπ' εὐρέα νῶτα θαλάσσης.
μὴ μὰν ἀσπουδί γε νεῶν ἐπιβαῖεν ἔκηλοι,
ἀλλ' ὥς τις τούτων γε βέλος καὶ οἴκοθι πέσσοι,
βλήμενος ἢ ἰῷ ἢ ἔγχεϊ ὀξυόεντι
νηὸς ἐπιθρώσκων, ἵνα τις στυγέησι καὶ ἄλλος   515
Τρωσὶν ἐφ' ἱπποδάμοισι φέρειν πολύδακρυν "Αρηα.
κήρυκες δ' ἀνὰ ἄστυ Διὶ φίλοι ἀγγελλόντων
παῖδας πρωθήβας πολιοκροτάφους τε γέροντας
λέξασθαι περὶ ἄστυ θεοδμήτων ἐπὶ πύργων·

---

500. ἐσάωσε: aor. act. σαόω, a form of σῴζω
502. πειθώμεθα: 1 pl. pres. subjunc. mid. and pass. πείθω; jussive subjunc., as ἐφοπλισόμεσθα,
503 (X.2) – 'let us be persuaded by'
503. ἐφοπλισόμεσθα: 1 pl. pres. subjunc. mid., –ομεσθα for –ωμεθα (L.3, 10)
504. λύσαθ' = λύσατε: aor. imperat. act. | ὑπὲξ: ὑπό + ἐκ, 'out from under'
505. ἄξεσθε: imperat., from an unusual form of the 2 aor. mid. ἄγω, which recurs at 545
507. ἐπὶ: adv.
508. ὥς: 'in order that' (X.1a); κεν common in such clauses | μέσφ' = μέχρι', 'up until'
512. ἐπιβαῖεν: 2 aor. optat. ἐπιβαίνω, with gen., as often; optat. for wish for the future, as πέσσοι, 513 (X.5)
513. ὥς: 'in such a way that' | καὶ οἰκόθι: 'even at home' (Z, Y.3)
514. βλημένος: 2 aor. pass. part. βάλλω
515. ἐπιθρώσκων: pres. part. because referring to the same time as βλημένος | στυγέησι: 3 s. pres. subjunc. act. στυγέω (O.1, L.9)
516. "Αρηα: the god of war, here used for 'war', as 531, etc.
517. ἀγγελλόντων: 3 pl. pres. imperat. act. ἀγγέλλω; 'let them announce (X.2) So καιόντων, ἔστω, 521, 'let them burn .. let there be'
518. πρωθήβας: acc. pl.
519. λέξασθαι: aor. infin. λέχομαι; παῖδας ... λέξασθαι is a command after ἀγγελλόντων – 'announce that the boys .. are to bivouac'

500 destroyed the ships and all the Akhaians. But
darkness has come, which most of all has no
Argives and their ships on the shore where the
But let us now be persuaded by the black night,
our meal. So, loose your fair-maned horses fr
505 the chariots, and throw fodder among them.
from the city oxen and fat sheep quickly, fetc
wine and food from the houses, and gather m
besides, so that all night long up until dawn, the cl
morning, we may burn many fires, and their ligh
510 to the sky, in case somehow during the night the l
Akhaians set out to flee over the wide expanse o
May they indeed not board their ships free from c
ease, but in such a way that one of them may
wound even at home, having been struck by an ar
515 sharp spear as he leapt onto his ship, so that others
shrink from bringing tearful war on the hors
Trojans.

"And let the heralds, beloved of Zeus, bring the
through the city, that the boys in the prime of youth
old men growing grey at the temples are to bivouac

520 defences built by the gods round about the city. And let each one of the women burn a great fire in her home, and let there be a constant watch, in case a body of troops steals into the city while the army is away.

525 "Let it be so, great-hearted Trojans, as I say. Let my words, which are right for today, be sufficient, and in the morning I shall make another speech among the horse-taming Trojans. I hope, as I pray to Zeus and the other gods, to drive out from here the dogs who have been brought by the fates, whom the fates bring in the black

530 ships. But for the night let us guard ourselves; and early in the morning, armed with our weapons, let us arouse bitter war at the hollow ships. I shall know whether the son of Tudeus, the strong Diomedes, is to drive me back from the ships to the wall, or whether I, cutting him down with my

535 bronze, am to carry off the bloody spoils. Tomorrow he will learn his strength, whether he can withstand my spear as it comes at him; but among the first, I think, he will lie wounded, and many of his companions around him, as the sun rises for tomorrow. O, that I might as surely be

τιοίμην δ' ὡς τίετ' 'Αθηναίη καὶ 'Απόλλων,   540
ὡς νῦν ἡμέρη ἥδε κακὸν φέρει 'Αργείοισιν."
  Ὡς Ἕκτωρ ἀγόρευ', ἐπὶ δὲ Τρῶες κελάδησαν.
οἱ δ' ἵππους μὲν λῦσαν ὑπὸ ζυγοῦ ἰδρώοντας,
δῆσαν δ' ἱμάντεσσι παρ' ἅρμασιν οἷσιν ἕκαστος·
ἐκ πόλιος δ' ἄξοντο βόας καὶ ἴφια μῆλα   545
καρπαλίμως, οἶνον δὲ μελίφρονα οἰνίζοντο
σῖτόν τ' ἐκ μεγάρων, ἐπὶ δὲ ξύλα πολλὰ λέγοντο.
[ἔρδον δ' ἀθανάτοισι τεληέσσας ἑκατόμβας,]
κνίσην δ' ἐκ πεδίου ἄνεμοι φέρον οὐρανὸν εἴσω
[ἡδεῖαν· τῆς δ' οὔ τι θεοὶ μάκαρες δατέοντο,   550
οὐδ' ἔθελον· μαλὰ γάρ σφιν ἀπήχθετο Ἴλιος ἱρὴ
καὶ Πρίαμος καὶ λαὸς ἐϋμμελίω Πριάμοιο.]
  Οἱ δὲ μέγα φρονέοντες ἐπὶ πτολέμοιο γεφύρας
εἵατο παννύχιοι, πυρὰ δέ σφισι καίετο πολλά.
ὡς δ' ὅτ' ἐν οὐρανῷ ἄστρα φαεινὴν ἀμφὶ σελήνην   555
φαίνετ' ἀριπρεπέα, ὅτε τ' ἔπλετο νήνεμος αἰθήρ·
ἔκ τ' ἔφανεν πᾶσαι σκοπιαὶ καὶ πρώονες ἄκροι
καὶ νάπαι· οὐρανόθεν δ' ἄρ' ὑπερράγη ἄσπετος αἰθήρ,
πάντα δὲ εἴδεται ἄστρα, γέγηθε δέ τε φρένα ποιμήν·
τόσσα μεσηγὺ νεῶν ἠδὲ Ξάνθοιο ῥοάων   560

---

540. τιοίμην: optat. pass. | τίετ': pres. indic. pass.; and s. although there are two subjects
541. ὡς: picks up ὥς in 538; 'as surely immortal .. as surely as this day ..'
543. ἰδρώοντας = ἰδρῶντας, acc. pl. m. pres. part. ἰδρόω; –ωο– for –ω– (O.2b)
544. ἱμάντεσσι: dat. pl. ἱμάς (D.8) | παρ' .. ἕκαστος: 'each to his own chariot'
545. See on 505
548. τεληέσσας: acc. pl. f. τελήεις
549. εἴσω: normally the adv. from εἰς, but here with οὐρανὸν
550. τῆς: gen. with δατέοντο
551. ἀπήχθετο: 2 aor. ἀπεχθάνομαι
552. ἐϋμμελίω: gen. s., and with five syllables – ἐϋμμελίω
554. εἵατο = ἧντο, 3 pl. imperf. ἧμαι, with –ατο for –ντο (L.4); so 563
556. ἔπλετο: 2 aor. πέλομαι; gnomic aorist (Q.1), as also the verbs of the next two lines
557. ἐκ .. ἔφανεν: 3 pl. aor. pass. ἐκφαίνω, –εν for –ησαν (L.5)
558. ὑπερράγη: 3 s. aor. pass. ὑπορρήγνυμι
559. γέγηθε: perf. γηθέω, with pres. meaning | φρένα: acc. of part affected – 'rejoices *in* his heart' (G.1c)
560. νεῶν, ῥοάων: gen. after μεσηγὺ

540 deathless and ageless for all time, and honoured as Athene and Apollo are honoured, as this day surely brings disaster on the Argives."

      Thus Hektor addressed the assembly, and the Trojans shouted their applause. They loosed their sweating horses from beneath the yoke, and tethered them with straps, each

545 to his own chariot. They brought from the city oxen and fat sheep quickly, fetched cheering wine and food from the houses, and gathered much wood besides. [They performed full sacrifices to the immortals,] and the winds

550 carried the savour from the plain to the heavens – [a sweet savour, and yet the blessed gods did not take their share of it, and did not wish to; for sacred Ilios was very hateful to them, and Priam, and the people of Priam of the fine ashen spear]. In high confidence they sat all night long in the spaces of the battle, and their fires were burning in great

555 numbers. As when the stars appear brilliant in the sky around the shining moon, when the air is still: all the look-out places are clear, and the jutting ridges and the valleys: continual brightness pours forth from the sky, every star is

560 visible, and the shepherd rejoices in his heart. As many as

Τρώων καιόντων πυρὰ φαίνετο Ἰλιόθι πρό.
χίλι' ἄρ' ἐν πεδίῳ πυρὰ καίετο, πὰρ δὲ ἑκάστῳ
εἵατο πεντήκοντα σέλᾳ πυρὸς αἰθομένοιο.
ἵπποι δὲ κρῖ λευκὸν ἐρεπτόμενοι καὶ ὀλύρας,
ἑσταότες παρ' ὄχεσφιν, ἐΰθρονον Ἠῶ μίμνον.   565

---

561. Ἰλιόθι πρό: strictly, both adverbs (Y.3, 8) – 'at Ilion, in front'; but this amounts to 'in front of Ilion'

563. σέλᾳ: dat. s. σέλας

564. κρῖ: acc. s.

565. ἑσταότες = ἑστῶτες, nom. pl. m., perf. part. act. ἵστημι, intrans. | Ἠῶ: acc. s. Ἠώς

these between the ships and the stream of Xanthos the fires
of the Trojans appeared as they burned them in front of
Ilion. A thousand fires were alight in the plain, and beside
each of them sat fifty men in the gleam of the burning fire.
565   And the horses, munching white barley and spelt, standing
by the chariots, awaited Dawn of the beautiful throne.

ΙΛΙΑΔΟΣ Ι

Ὡς οἱ μὲν Τρῶες φυλακὰς ἔχον· αὐτὰρ Ἀχαιοὺς
θεσπεσίη ἔχε φύζα, φόβου κρυόεντος ἑταίρη,
πένθεϊ δ' ἀτλήτῳ βεβολήατο πάντες ἄριστοι.
ὡς δ' ἄνεμοι δύο πόντον ὀρίνετον ἰχθυόεντα,
Βορέης καὶ Ζέφυρος, τώ τε Θρήκηθεν ἄητον,   5
ἐλθόντ' ἐξαπίνης· ἄμυδις δέ τε κῦμα κελαινὸν
κορθύεται, πολλὸν δὲ παρὲξ ἅλα φῦκος ἔχευεν·
ὡς ἐδαΐζετο θυμὸς ἐνὶ στήθεσσιν Ἀχαιῶν.
   Ἀτρεΐδης δ' ἄχεϊ μεγάλῳ βεβολημένος ἦτορ
φοίτα κηρύκεσσι λιγυφθόγγοισι κελεύων   10
κλήδην εἰς ἀγορὴν κικλήσκειν ἄνδρα ἕκαστον,
μηδὲ βοᾶν· αὐτὸς δὲ μετὰ πρώτοισι πονεῖτο.

The following notes do not assume that Book VIII has been read, and so repeat some points that have already been made in the notes to VIII.

1. Ὡς: 'thus', as usually when accented (Y.5) | ἔχον: imperf. ἔχω, without augment (N), as ἔχε in 2

3. πένθεϊ = πένθει, dat. s. πένθος (D.4); so ἄχεϊ, 9, etc. | βεβολήατο = ἐβεβόληντο (L.1), 3 pl. plupf. pass. βολέω (= βάλλω)

4. ὀρίνετον: 3 dual pres. act. ὀρίνω; dual because the subject is *two* winds. So ἄητον (pres. ἄημι, 'blow') in 5 (M.1) | ἰχθυόεντα: acc. s. m. ἰχθυόεις

5. Βορέης: scan Βορ– long, and –εη– one syllable only, by synizesis (Scansion B5b) | τώ: nom. dual of the relative pronoun (I.1d), antecedent the two winds | τε: generalising, as in 6, etc. (Z) | Θρήκηθεν: –θεν 'from' (Y. 2)

6. ἐλθόντ': nom. dual 2 aor. part. ἔρχομαι (D.9)

7. πολλὸν: acc. s. n. πολύς, going with φῦκος | παρὲξ: preposition with acc. (παρά + ἐκ), here with ἅλα | ἅλα: acc. s. ἅλς | ἔχευεν: 3 s. aor. act. χεύω; gnomic aorist (Q.1)

8. ἐνὶ = ἐν (Y.9) | στήθεσσιν: dat. pl. στῆθος, –εσσιν for –εσιν (D.8)

9. Ἀτρεΐδης: 'son of Atreus' (B.8), i.e. Agamemnon | ἦτορ: '*in* his heart'; acc. of part affected (G.1d)

10. κηρύκεσσι = κήρυξι, dat. pl. κῆρυξ (D.8), dat. after κελεύω, which may take dat. or acc. | λιγυφθόγγοισι: dat. pl., –οισι for –οις (C.3)

11. ἀγορὴν = ἀγοράν (B.1) | κικλήσκειν: a reduplicated form of καλέω (T)

12. αὐτὸς: 'he himself', in contrast to the heralds (K.2)

ILIAD IX

So the Trojans kept guard. But dreadful Panic, the companion of chill Fear, possessed the Akhaians, and all the leaders had been struck with overpowering sorrow. Just as two winds arouse the sea that teems with fish, the north and the west winds, which blow from Thrace, having suddenly come forth; and the waves surge together darkly to a crest, and strew the seaweed thickly along the shore. So the hearts of the Akhaians were torn within their breasts.

The son of Atreus, his heart struck with great grief, was pacing up and down, telling the shrill-voiced heralds to call each man to the assembly by name, but without shouting;

ἷζον δ' εἰν ἀγορῇ τετιηότες· ἂν δ' 'Αγαμέμνων
ἵστατο δάκρυ χέων ὥς τε κρήνη μελάνυδρος,
ἥ τε κατ' αἰγίλιπος πέτρης δνοφερὸν χέει ὕδωρ·   15
ὣς ὁ βαρὺ στενάχων ἔπε' 'Αργείοισι μετηύδα·
"ὦ φίλοι, 'Αργείων ἡγήτορες ἠδὲ μέδοντες,
Ζεύς με μέγα Κρονίδης ἄτῃ ἐνέδησε βαρείῃ,
σχέτλιος, ὃς τότε μέν μοι ὑπέσχετο καὶ κατένευσεν
Ἴλιον ἐκπέρσαντ' εὐτείχεον ἀπονέεσθαι,   20
νῦν δὲ κακὴν ἀπάτην βουλεύσατο, καί με κελεύει
δυσκλέα "Αργος ἱκέσθαι, ἐπεὶ πολὺν ὤλεσα λαόν.
οὕτω που Διὶ μέλλει ὑπερμενέϊ φίλον εἶναι,
ὃς δὴ πολλάων πολίων κατέλυσε κάρηνα
ἠδ' ἔτι καὶ λύσει· τοῦ γὰρ κράτος ἐστὶ μέγιστον.   25
ἀλλ' ἄγεθ', ὡς ἂν ἐγὼ εἴπω, πειθώμεθα πάντες·
φεύγωμεν σὺν νηυσὶ φίλην ἐς πατρίδα γαῖαν·
οὐ γὰρ ἔτι Τροίην αἱρήσομεν εὐρυάγυιαν."
   'Ὣς ἔφαθ', οἱ δ' ἄρα πάντες ἀκὴν ἐγένοντο σιωπῇ.

---

13. εἰν = ἐν (Y.9) | τετιηότες: nom. pl. m. perf. part. act. in form; but the verb is otherwise only found in perf. mid. τετίημαι

13–14. ἂν .. ἵστατο = ἀνίστατο, with tmesis (R); 3 s. imperf. mid. ἀνίστημι; pres. part. mid. at 52

14. ὥς: 'like'. here accented (cf. on 1) because followed by an *enclitic* word (i.e. one that throws its accent back to the preceding one) | μελάνυδρος: a *two-termination* adj. – i.e. f. the same as m. throughout

15. χέει: second syllable scanned short, by *correption* (Scansion, B.5a), as φίλοι, 17, etc.

16 ὁ: 'he' (I.2) | βαρὺ: n. acc. s. adj. as adv. (Y.7), as μέγα, 18, etc. | ἔπε': acc. pl. ἔπος, –εα for –η (D.5) | μετηύδα: 'spoke' (V.3); imperf.

17. ἠδὲ: a Homeric word for 'and'

19. ὑπέσχετο: 2 aor. ὑπισχνέομαι

20. ἐκπέρσαντ': acc. s. m. aor. part. act. ἐκπέρθω. As it is subject of the following infin., ἀπονέεσθαι, it is acc., even though referring to μοι, dat.; 'promised to me that, when I had sacked .., I would return'. Likewise γήμαντα, 399 | ἀπονέεσθαι: uncontracted pres. infin. ἀπονέομαι (Q.1), with fut. meaning; initial ἀ– scanned long

22. δυσκλέα: acc. s. δυσκλέης, –εα for –εεα or –εῆ | "Αργος: n. acc. s. | ἱκέσθαι: 2 aor. infin. ἱκνέομαι; 'come *to* Argos' (G.1b) | ὤλεσα: 1 s. aor. act. ὄλλυμι

23. που: particle, 'I suppose' (Z) | Διὶ: dat. s. Ζεὺς (D.11)

24. πολλάων: gen. pl. f. πολύς (B.2) | πολίων: gen. pl. πόλις

25. τοῦ: 'of him', 'his' (I.2)

26. ἄγεθ' = ἄγετε, pres. imperat. ἄγω | ὡς ἂν: 'in whatever way', introducing an indefinite clause (W.8a) | εἴπω: 1 s. 2 aor. subjunc. | πειθώμεθα: pres. subjunc. mid. and pass.; jussive subjunc. (X.2). So φεύγωμεν, next line, πειθώμεθα again 65, etc.

27. νηυσὶ: dat. pl. ναῦς (D.11). Scanned as two syllables only, –ηυ– being a diphthong | ἐς = εἰς (Y.9)

29. ἔφαθ' = ἔφατο, 'he spoke' (V.3); so μετέειπε, 31 | ἀκὴν, σιωπῇ: 'silently, in silence' – a not infrequent tautology

and he was working among the first of them himself. The men sat downcast in assembly; and Agamemnon stood up, shedding a tear like a spring of black water which sends forth its dark stream down a sheer rock. So, groaning heavily, he addressed words to the Argives –

"O friends, lords and rulers of the Argives, Zeus, the son of Kronos, has encompassed me greatly with heavy delusion. Cruel god! Then he gave me promises and assurances that I should return home after sacking the strong-walled city of Ilion; but now he has devised an evil trickery, and orders me to go back to Argos discredited, when I have lost many of my people. This, I suppose, must be the pleasure of almighty Zeus, who has destroyed the crowns of very many cities, and will destroy still more; for his power is the greatest. But come, let us all follow what I say. Let us flee with our ships to the dear land of our fathers. For we shall not now take Troy with its broad streets."

So he spoke, and they all fell silent. For a long time the

δὴν δ' ἄνεῳ ἦσαν τετιηότες υἷες 'Αχαιῶν·   30
ὀψὲ δὲ δὴ μετέειπε βοὴν ἀγαθὸς Διομήδης·
"'Ατρεΐδη, σοὶ πρῶτα μαχήσομαι ἀφραδέοντι,
ἦ θέμις ἐστίν, ἄναξ, ἀγορῇ· σὺ δὲ μή τι χολωθῇς.
ἀλκὴν μέν μοι πρῶτον ὀνείδισας ἐν Δαναοῖσι,
φὰς ἔμεν ἀπτόλεμον καὶ ἀνάλκιδα· ταῦτα δὲ πάντα   35
ἴσασ' 'Αργείων ἠμὲν νέοι ἠδὲ γέροντες.
σοὶ δὲ διάνδιχα δῶκε Κρόνου πάϊς ἀγκυλομήτεω·
σκήπτρῳ μέν τοι δῶκε τετιμῆσθαι περὶ πάντων,
ἀλκὴν δ' οὔ τοι δῶκεν, ὅ τε κράτος ἐστὶ μέγιστον.
δαιμόνι', οὕτω που μάλα ἔλπεαι υἷας 'Αχαιῶν   40
ἀπτολέμους τ' ἔμεναι καὶ ἀνάλκιδας, ὡς ἀγορεύεις;
εἰ δέ τοι αὐτῷ θυμὸς ἐπέσσυται ὥς τε νέεσθαι,
ἔρχεο· πάρ τοι ὁδός, νῆες δέ τοι ἄγχι θαλάσσης
ἐστᾶσ', αἵ τοι ἕποντο Μυκήνηθεν μάλα πολλαί.

---

30. ἄνεῳ: written thus, this must be nom. pl. of an otherwise unknown irregular adj. ἄνεως | υἷες: nom. pl. υἱός; acc. pl. υἷας at 40

31. βοὴν: acc. of respect (G.1e); 'good *at* the shout'

32. 'Ατρεΐδη: voc. s. (B.5) | πρῶτα = πρῶτον | ἀφραδέοντι: dat. s. m. pres. part. act. ἀφραδέω, with σοὶ

33. ἦ: relative pronoun, 'something which', with ἦ in agreement with θέμις, as 134 | μή: 'don't', followed by subjunc. (X.4b) | τι: 'at all' (J.2) | χολωθῇς: 2 s. aor. subjunc. pass. χολόω

34. μοι: dat. s. ἐγώ (H.1) – 'made a reproach of my courage *against* me'; likewise τοι, 55 | ὀνείδισας: 2 s. aor. indic. act. ὀνειδίζω

35. φὰς: 'having said' (V.4), i.e. 'by saying' | ἔμεν: pres. infin. εἰμί, as ἔμεναι, 41 (U.3); supply με, 'saying that I was'

36. ἴσασ': 3 pl. οἶδα

37. δῶκε: 3 s. aor. act. δίδωμι, as 38, 39, etc. | ἀγκυλομητέω: gen. s., –εω for –ου (B.6); –εω scanned as a single syllable by *synizesis* (Scansion, B.5b)

38. τοι = σοι (H.1) as commonly | τετιμῆσθαι: perf. infin. pass. τιμάω; 'granted to you to be honoured' | περὶ: 'above', 'beyond' (Y.10)

39. ὅ: n., relative pronoun, attracted to the gender of κράτος following it, although its antecedent is ἀλκὴν

40. ἔλπεαι: 2 s. pres. ἔλπομαι, 'hope', 'expect'; –εαι for –ει (L.1)

42. ἐπέσσυται: perf. mid. and pass. ἐπισεύω (N.2) | ὥς τε: 'so as to'

43. ἔρχεο = ἔρχου, imperat. ἔρχομαι, –εο for –ου (L.2) | πάρ= παρά, here for πάρεστι, 'there is available to you'. So πάρα, 227

44. ἐστᾶσ': 3 pl. perf. act. ἵστημι | τοι: dat. with ἕποντο

ἀλλὰ πρὶν κνέφας ἦλθε, τὸ νῦν ἐσάωσε μάλιστα 500
'Αργείους καὶ νῆας ἐπὶ ῥηγμῖνι θαλάσσης.
ἀλλ' ἤτοι νῦν μὲν πειθώμεθα νυκτὶ μελαίνῃ
δόρπα τ' ἐφοπλισόμεσθα· ἀτὰρ καλλίτριχας ἵππους
λύσαθ' ὑπὲξ ὀχέων, παρὰ δέ σφισι βάλλετ' ἐδωδήν·
ἐκ πόλιος δ' ἄξεσθε βόας καὶ ἴφια μῆλα 505
καρπαλίμως, οἶνον δὲ μελίφρονα οἰνίζεσθε
σῖτόν τ' ἐκ μεγάρων, ἐπὶ δὲ ξύλα πολλὰ λέγεσθε,
ὥς κεν παννύχιοι μέσφ' ἠοῦς ἠριγενείης
καίωμεν πυρὰ πολλά, σέλας δ' εἰς οὐρανὸν ἵκῃ,
μή πως καὶ διὰ νύκτα κάρη κομόωντες 'Αχαιοὶ 510
φεύγειν ὁρμήσωνται ἐπ' εὐρέα νῶτα θαλάσσης.
μὴ μὰν ἀσπουδί γε νεῶν ἐπιβαῖεν ἕκηλοι,
ἀλλ' ὥς τις τούτων γε βέλος καὶ οἴκοθι πέσσοι,
βλήμενος ἢ ἰῷ ἢ ἔγχεϊ ὀξυόεντι
νηὸς ἐπιθρῴσκων, ἵνα τις στυγέῃσι καὶ ἄλλος 515
Τρωσὶν ἐφ' ἱπποδάμοισι φέρειν πολύδακρυν ῎Αρηα.
κήρυκες δ' ἀνὰ ἄστυ Διῒ φίλοι ἀγγελλόντων
παῖδας πρωθήβας πολιοκροτάφους τε γέροντας
λέξασθαι περὶ ἄστυ θεοδμήτων ἐπὶ πύργων·

---

500. ἐσάωσε: aor. act. σαόω, a form of σώζω

502. πειθώμεθα: 1 pl. pres. subjunc. mid. and pass. πείθω; jussive subjunc., as ἐφοπλισόμεσθα, 503 (X.2) – 'let us be persuaded by'

503. ἐφοπλισόμεσθα: 1 pl. pres. subjunc. mid., –ομεσθα for –ωμεθα (L.3, 10)

504. λύσαθ' = λύσατε: aor. imperat. act. | ὑπὲξ: ὑπὸ + ἐκ, 'out from under'

505. ἄξεσθε: imperat., from an unusual form of the 2 aor. mid. ἄγω, which recurs at 545

507. ἐπὶ: adv.

508. ὥς: 'in order that' (X.1a); κεν common in such clauses | μέσφ' = μέχρι', 'up until'

512. ἐπιβαῖεν: 2 aor. optat. ἐπιβαίνω, with gen., as often; optat. for wish for the future, as πέσσοι, 513 (X.5)

513. ὥς: 'in such a way that | καὶ οἰκόθι: 'even at home' (Z, Y.3)

514. βλημένος: 2 aor. pass. part. βάλλω

515. ἐπιθρῴσκων: pres. part. because referring to the same time as βλημένος | στυγέῃσι: 3 s. pres. subjunc. act. στυγέω (O.1, L.9)

516. ῎Αρηα: the god of war, here used for 'war', as 531, etc.

517. ἀγγελλόντων: 3 pl. pres. imperat. act. ἀγγέλλω; 'let them announce (X.2) So καιόντων, ἔστω, 521, 'let them burn .. let there be'

518. πρωθήβας: acc. pl.

519. λέξασθαι: aor. infin. λέχομαι; παῖδας ... λέξασθαι is a command after ἀγγελλόντων – 'announce that the boys .. are to bivouac'

475 Peleus arises by the ships, on that day when they fight at the
sterns in the direst crisis over the dead Patroklos. For so it
is divinely decreed. I do not care about you in your anger,
not even if you come to the lowermost limits of the earth and
480 the sea, where, seated, Iapetos and Kronos enjoy neither the
rays of Huperion the Sun nor the winds, and deep Tartaros
is round about.   Not even if you come there in your
wandering do I care about you in your anger, since nothing
else is more shameless than you."

Thus he spoke, and white-armed Here said nothing at all
485 to him. The bright light of the sun fell into the Ocean,
drawing black night over the bountiful land. The Trojans
were sorry as the light set on them, but on the Akhaians the
dark night came welcome, and thrice prayed-for.

Now glorious Hektor held an assembly of the Trojans,
490 leading them away from the ships by the swirling river, on
an open spot, where space appeared between the corpses.
Dismounting from their horses to the ground, they listened
to the speech which Hektor, beloved of Zeus, made. In his
495 hand he held a spear eleven cubits long, and the bronze tip
of the spear gleamed in front, and a golden ring ran round it.
Leaning on this, he addressed words to the Trojans –

"Hear me, Trojans and Dardanians and allies. Just now I
was thinking that I should return again to windy Ilios having

500 destroyed the ships and all the Akhaians. But before (that) darkness has come, which most of all has now saved the Argives and their ships on the shore where the sea breaks. But let us now be persuaded by the black night, and prepare our meal. So, loose your fair-maned horses from beneath 505 the chariots, and throw fodder among them. And bring from the city oxen and fat sheep quickly, fetch cheering wine and food from the houses, and gather much wood besides, so that all night long up until dawn, the child of the morning, we may burn many fires, and their light may rise 510 to the sky, in case somehow during the night the long-haired Akhaians set out to flee over the wide expanse of the sea. May they indeed not board their ships free from care and at ease, but in such a way that one of them may tend his wound even at home, having been struck by an arrow or a 515 sharp spear as he leapt onto his ship, so that others too may shrink from bringing tearful war on the horse-taming Trojans.

"And let the heralds, beloved of Zeus, bring the message through the city, that the boys in the prime of youth and the old men growing grey at the temples are to bivouac on the

θηλύτεραι δὲ γυναῖκες ἐνὶ μεγάροισιν ἑκάστη   520
πῦρ μέγα καιόντων· φυλακὴ δέ τις ἔμπεδος ἔστω,
μὴ λόχος εἰσέλθῃσι πόλιν λαῶν ἀπεόντων.
ὧδ' ἔστω, Τρῶες μεγαλήτορες, ὡς ἀγορεύω·
μῦθος δ', ὃς μὲν νῦν ὑγιής, εἰρημένος ἔστω,
τὸν δ' ἠοῦς Τρώεσσι μεθ' ἱπποδάμοις ἀγορεύσω.   525
ἔλπομαι εὐχόμενος Διί τ' ἄλλοισίν τε θεοῖσιν
ἐξελάαν ἐνθένδε κύνας κηρεσσιφορήτους,
οὓς κῆρες φορέουσι μελαινάων ἐπὶ νηῶν.
ἀλλ' ἤτοι ἐπὶ νυκτὶ φυλάξομεν ἡμέας αὐτούς,
πρῶϊ δ' ὑπηοῖοι σὺν τεύχεσι θωρηχθέντες   530
νηυσὶν ἔπι γλαφυρῇσιν ἐγείρομεν ὀξὺν Ἄρηα.
εἴσομαι εἴ κέ μ' ὁ Τυδείδης κρατερὸς Διομήδης
πὰρ νηῶν πρὸς τεῖχος ἀπώσεται, ἦ κεν ἐγὼ τὸν
χαλκῷ δῃώσας ἔναρα βροτόεντα φέρωμαι.
αὔριον ἣν ἀρετὴν διαείσεται, εἴ κ' ἐμὸν ἔγχος   535
μείνῃ ἐπερχόμενον· ἀλλ' ἐν πρώτοισιν ὀίω
κείσεται οὐτηθείς, πολέες δ' ἀμφ' αὐτὸν ἑταῖροι,
ἠελίου ἀνιόντος ἐς αὔριον· εἰ γὰρ ἐγὼν ὣς
εἴην ἀθάνατος καὶ ἀγήρως ἤματα πάντα,

---

521. ἔστω: 3 s. imperat. εἰμί; so 523 and 524 (U.5)

522. ἀπεόντων = ἀπόντων, gen. pl. pres. part. ἄπειμι (U.2); gen. absolute, 'while the army is absent'

524. ὅς: supply ἐστί | εἰρημένος ἔστω: 'let it have been spoken' (U.5), i.e. 'let what has been spoken suffice'

525. τὸν δ': supply μῦθον; 'and another one ..'

527. ἐξελάαν: pres. infin. act. ἐξελάω, a form of ἐξελαύνω; –αα– for –α– (O.2d)

529. φυλάξομεν: jussive subjunc., as ἐγείρομεν, 532 (X.2)

530. ὑπηοῖοι: adj. for adv., 'in the morning' (Y.6)

532. εἴσομαι εἴ κε: 'I shall know whether'. Likewise 535 (W.6) | εἴσομαι: fut. οἶδα; fut. of διοιδα at 535

533. τεῖχος: i.e. the wall of Troy | ἀπώσεται: aor. subjunc. mid. ἀπωθέω (L.10)

535. ἣν ἀρετὴν διαείσεται: 'he shall learn *about* his prowess, i.e. whether ... '

537. πολέες = πολλοί

538. ἀνιόντος: gen. s. pres. part. ἄνειμι (U.2) | εἰ γάρ: 'would that', with optat. (X.5) | ὣς = οὕτως

539. εἴην: 1 s. optat. εἰμί (U.8) | ἤματα πάντα: 'for all my days' – acc. of duration of time (G.1g); ἤματα acc. pl. ἦμαρ

sons of the Akhaians were despondent, and said nothing. But at last Diomedes, good at the shout, spoke –

"Son of Atreus, I will be the first to fight with you in your folly – this is the accepted practice, Sir, in assembly. And do not be angry. You first reproached my courage among the Danaans, saying that I was unwarlike and cowardly – the young and old alike of the Argives know all this. But the son of the devious Kronos has granted you gifts only by halves. He has granted you to be honoured with the sceptre above all men; but he has not granted you courage, which is the greatest power. Do you really suppose, good sir, that the sons of the Akhaians are such cowards and weaklings as you say? If your own heart is eager to return home, then go; the way is open for you, and the ships which have followed you in such numbers from

ἀλλ' ἄλλοι μενέουσι κάρη κομόωντες Ἀχαιοί,　　　　　　45
εἰς ὅ κέ περ Τροίην διαπέρσομεν. εἰ δὲ καὶ αὐτοὶ
φευγόντων σὺν νηυσὶ φίλην ἐς πατρίδα γαῖαν·
νῶι δ', ἐγὼ Σθένελός τε, μαχησόμεθ', εἰς ὅ κε τέκμωρ
Ἰλίου εὕρωμεν· σὺν γὰρ θεῷ εἰλήλουθμεν."

　Ὣς ἔφαθ', οἱ δ' ἄρα πάντες ἐπίαχον υἷες Ἀχαιῶν,　　　50
μῦθον ἀγασσάμενοι Διομήδεος ἱπποδάμοιο.
τοῖσι δ' ἀνιστάμενος μετεφώνεεν ἱππότα Νέστωρ·
"Τυδεΐδη, περὶ μὲν πολέμῳ ἔνι καρτερός ἐσσι,
καὶ βουλῇ μετὰ πάντας ὁμήλικας ἔπλευ ἄριστος.
οὔ τίς τοι τὸν μῦθον ὀνόσσεται, ὅσσοι Ἀχαιοί,　　　　55
οὐδὲ πάλιν ἐρέει· ἀτὰρ οὐ τέλος ἵκεο μύθων.
ἦ μὲν καὶ νέος ἐσσί, ἐμὸς δέ κε καὶ πάϊς εἴης
ὁπλότατος γενεῆφιν· ἀτὰρ πεπνυμένα βάζεις
Ἀργείων βασιλῆας, ἐπεὶ κατὰ μοῖραν ἔειπες.

---

45. μενέουσι: uncontracted fut. μένω (O.1) | κάρη: acc., s., κάρα; acc. of respect, 'as far as their heads are concerned' (G.1e) | κομόωντες: pres. part. κομάω, –οω – for – ω – (O.2c)

46. εἰς ὅ κε: 'up until that time when', as 48, etc. | περ: here intensive (Z); 'the very time when' | διαπέρσομεν: aor. subjunc. act. διαπέρθω, –ομεν for –ωμεν (L.10); subjunc. in an indefinite clause (W.8) | εἰ δὲ: 'but come'; an expression in which εἰ has no sense of 'if'; so 167, 262, etc. | αὐτοὶ: 'let *them*', in contrast with νῶι, 48

47. φευγόντων: 3 pl. pres. imperat. act. φεύγω, 'let them flee' (X.2)

48. νῶι: dual nom. 1 personal pronoun (H.1) – 'we two'

49. εὕρωμεν: 2 aor. subjunc. act. εὑρίσκω | εἰλήλουθμεν: 1 pl. perf. ἔρχομαι

51. ἀγασσάμενοι: aor. part. ἄγαμαι (Q.3) | Διομήδεος ἱπποδάμοιο: both gen. s., –εος for –ους, –οιο for –ου (D.3a, C.2)

52. τοῖσι: 'to them', dat. pl. ὁ (I.1c) | ἱππότα: nom. s. (B.4)

53. Τυδεΐδη: voc., 'son of Tudeus', i.e. Diomedes (B.5,8) | περὶ: adv., 'especially' (Y.4) | ἔνι = ἐν (Y.9,11) | ἐσσι: 2 s. pres. εἰμί, as 57, 69, etc. (U.1)

54. μετά: 'among' | ἔπλευ = ἔπλεο, 2 s. aor. πέλομαι; 'you have become', i.e. 'you are' | ἄριστος; superlative of ἀγαθός

55. ὀνόσσεται: fut. ὄνομαι | ὅσσοι = ὅσοι (A); supply εἰσί. With τις, 'anyone, as many as there are of the Akhaians', i.e. 'anyone of the Akhaians'. Cf. 642

56. πάλιν ἐρέει: 'will speak in contradiction' (V.2) | ἵκεο = ἵκου, 2 s. 2 aor. ἱκνέομαι, –εο for – ου (L.2)

57. εἴης: 2 s. optat. εἰμί (U.8). *Potential* conditional (W.4) – 'You could be my son (if one judged by your youth)'

58. γενεῆφιν: for dat. s. γενέη (E), 'youngest in age'

59. βασιλῆας: acc. pl. βασιλεύς, –ῆας for –εῖς (D.6). A second object of βάζεις, 'you speak appropriate words to the chieftains' | ἔειπες = εἶπες, 'you spoke' (A, Y.3)

45 Mukenai are standing by the sea. But the rest of the long-haired Akhaians will stay until we sack Troy. Or, let them too flee with their ships to the dear land of their fathers. Yet the two of us, I and Sthenelos, will fight until we achieve our object in Ilios; for we have come with god's guidance."

50 Such were his words, and the sons of the Akhaians all applauded, full of admiration for the speech of Diomedes, the tamer of horses. Standing up, the horseman Nestor spoke among them –

"Son of Tudeus, you are outstandingly strong in war, and in council too you have proved best among all the men
55 of your own age. No one among all the Akhaians will find fault with what you say, or contradict you. And yet, you did not take your argument the whole way. You are, to be sure, a young man, and you could even be my son, my youngest-born; but you speak appropriately to the chiefs of

ἀλλ' ἄγ' ἐγών, ὃς σεῖο γεραίτερος εὔχομαι εἶναι,　　60
ἐξείπω καὶ πάντα διίξομαι· οὐδέ κέ τίς μοι
μῦθον ἀτιμήσει', οὐδὲ κρείων 'Αγαμέμνων.
ἀφρήτωρ ἀθέμιστος ἀνέστιός ἐστιν ἐκεῖνος
ὃς πολέμου ἔραται ἐπιδημίου ὀκρυόεντος.
ἀλλ' ἤτοι νῦν μὲν πειθώμεθα νυκτὶ μελαίνῃ　　65
δόρπά τ' ἐφοπλισόμεσθα· φυλακτῆρες δὲ ἕκαστοι
λεξάσθων παρὰ τάφρον ὀρυκτὴν τείχεος ἐκτός.
κούροισιν μὲν ταῦτ' ἐπιτέλλομαι· αὐτὰρ ἔπειτα,
'Ατρεΐδη, σὺ μὲν ἄρχε· σὺ γὰρ βασιλεύτατός ἐσσι.
δαίνυ δαῖτα γέρουσιν· ἔοικέ τοι, οὔ τοι ἀεικές.　　70
πλεῖαί τοι οἴνου κλισίαι, τὸν νῆες 'Αχαιῶν
ἡμάτιαι Θρήκηθεν ἐπ' εὐρέα πόντον ἄγουσι·
πᾶσά τοί ἐσθ' ὑποδεξίη, πολέεσσι δ' ἀνάσσεις.
πολλῶν δ' ἀγρομένων τῷ πείσεαι ὅς κεν ἀρίστην
βουλὴν βουλεύσῃ· μάλα δὲ χρεὼ πάντας 'Αχαιοὺς　　75
ἐσθλῆς καὶ πυκινῆς, ὅτι δήϊοι ἐγγύθι νηῶν

---

60. ἀλλ' ἄγ' ἐγών: 'But come, let me'; ἐγών = ἐγώ (H.1) | σεῖο: gen. 2 s. personal pronoun (H.1); gen. of comparison after γεραίτερος, 'older *than* you' | εὔχομαι εἶναι: literally, 'claim to be'; but often little more than 'am'

61. ἐξείπω: 1 s. subjunc. ἐξεῖπον, jussive (X.2) | διίξομαι: fut. διικνέομαι | οὐδέ τίς: 'and nobody'

62. ἀτιμήσει': 3 s. aor. optat. act. ἀτιμάω. Potential conditional (W.4) – 'Nobody would disrespect my words (if the matter was opened for debate)' | οὐδὲ: 'not even'

64. πολέμου: gen. with ἔραται

65. ἤτοι: 'indeed' (Z) | νυκτὶ: dat. after πειθώμεθα

66. τ': 'and' | ἐφοπλισόμεσθα: aor. subjunc. mid., –όμεσθα for –ώμεθα (L.10)

67. λεξάσθων: 3 pl. aor. imperat. λέχομαι – 'let them camp out' (X.2) | τείχεος: gen. s. τεῖχος, –εος for –ους (D.3b), as 87, etc.; gen. with ἐκτός

70. δαίνυ: 2 s. imperat. δαίνυμι | δαῖτα: acc. s. δαίς | ἀεικές: supply ἐστί

71. πλεῖαι: supply εἰσί | τοι: possessive (H.3); 'your tents' | τὸν: relative pronoun, antecedent οἴνου

72. εὐρέα: acc. s. m., –έα for –ύν

73. ἐσθ' = ἐστί | πολέεσσι: dat. (with ἀνάσσεις) pl. πολύς

74. πολλῶν ἀγρομένων: gen. absolute, 'when many are gathered together' | ἀγρομένων: 2. aor. mid. part. ἀγείρω | τῷ ὅς κεν 'that man whosoever'; τῷ dat. with πείσεαι | πείσεαι: 2 s. fut. mid. πείθω, –εαι for –ει (L.1)

75. βουλεύσῃ: 3 s. aor. subjunc. act. βουλεύω | χρεὼ: nom. s., and scanned as a single syllable, as at 197, etc. Supply ἐστί ; 'there is need to the Akhaians of counsel'

76. ἐσθλῆς: supply βουλῆς from βουλὴν in the previous line | νηῶν: gen. pl. ναῦς (D.11)

60 the Argives, for you have spoken as you should. But come, let me speak, as I can claim to be older than you, and I will go over the whole matter. No one would be disrespectful of what I say, not even lord Agamemnon. That man who pursues the horrors of war against his own people is banished from his tribe, outside the laws, and cast from his

65 home. But now we should certainly give in to the darkness of night, and make ready our meal, while the guards one and all take up position by the ditch that has been dug outside the wall. Those are my instructions to the young men; and then you, son of Atreus, must take the lead, for

70 you are the most royal man. Give a banquet to the elders – this is the right thing for you, it is not unfitting. Your huts are full of wine, which the ships of the Akhaians bring over the wide sea from Thrace every day. All hospitality is in your hands, and you rule over many. When many are

75 gathered together, you will follow that man who gives the best council. And all the Akhaians certainly stand in need of good, sound, council, now that the enemy are burning many

καίουσιν πυρὰ πολλά· τίς ἂν τάδε γηθήσειε;
νὺξ δ᾽ ἥδ᾽ ἠὲ διαρραίσει στρατὸν ἠὲ σαώσει."
    Ὣς ἔφαθ᾽, οἱ δ᾽ ἄρα τοῦ μάλα μὲν κλύον ἠδὲ πίθοντο.
ἐκ δὲ φυλακτῆρες σὺν τεύχεσιν ἐσσεύοντο   80
ἀμφί τε Νεστορίδην Θρασυμήδεα, ποιμένα λαῶν,
ἠδ᾽ ἀμφ᾽ Ἀσκάλαφον καὶ Ἰάλμενον, υἷας Ἄρηος,
ἀμφί τε Μηριόνην Ἀφαρῆά τε Δηΐπυρόν τε,
ἠδ᾽ ἀμφὶ Κρείοντος υἱὸν Λυκομήδεα δῖον.
ἕπτ᾽ ἔσαν ἡγεμόνες φυλάκων, ἑκατὸν δὲ ἑκάστῳ   85
κοῦροι ἅμα στεῖχον δολίχ᾽ ἔγχεα χερσὶν ἔχοντες·
κὰδ δὲ μέσον τάφρου καὶ τείχεος ἷζον ἰόντες·
ἔνθα δὲ πῦρ κήαντο, τίθεντο δὲ δόρπα ἕκαστος.
    Ἀτρεΐδης δὲ γέροντας ἀολλέας ἦγεν Ἀχαιῶν
ἐς κλισίην, παρὰ δέ σφι τίθει μενοεικέα δαῖτα.   90
οἱ δ᾽ ἐπ᾽ ὀνείαθ᾽ ἑτοῖμα προκείμενα χεῖρας ἴαλλον.
αὐτὰρ ἐπεὶ πόσιος καὶ ἐδητύος ἐξ ἔρον ἔντο,
τοῖς ὁ γέρων πάμπρωτος ὑφαίνειν ἤρχετο μῆτιν
Νέστωρ, οὗ καὶ πρόσθεν ἀρίστη φαίνετο βουλή·
ὅ σφιν ἐϋφρονέων ἀγορήσατο καὶ μετέειπεν·   95
"Ἀτρεΐδη κύδιστε, ἄναξ ἀνδρῶν Ἀγάμεμνον
ἐν σοὶ μὲν λήξω, σέο δ᾽ ἄρξομαι, οὕνεκα πολλῶν
λαῶν ἔσσι ἄναξ καί τοι Ζεὺς ἐγγυάλιξε

---

77. γηθήσειε: aor. opt. act. γηθέω; 'Who would be glad of this (if he were in his right senses)?'
78. σαώσει: fut indic. σαόω, a form of σῴζω
79. τοῦ: 'him' (I.2); gen. with κλύον
80. ἐκ .. ἐσσεύοντο: imperf. mid.
85. ἔσαν: 3 pl. imperf. εἰμί (U.4)
86. ἔγχεα: acc. pl., –εα for –η (D.5b)
87. κὰδ = κατά (Y.9); with μέσον, – 'in the space between' | ἰόντες: pres. part. εἶμι (U.2)
88. κήαντο: 3 pl. aor. mid. καίω | τίθεντο: 3 pl. imperf. mid. τίθημι; a pl. verb with ἕκαστος, s., is common, e.g. 656
89. ἀολλέας: acc. pl. m., –έας for –εῖς (D.6)
90. σφι: dat. (after παρά) 3 pl. personal pronoun (H.2), as 95, etc. | τίθει: 3 s. imperf. act. τίθημι | μενοεικέα: acc. s. f., –εα for –ῆ (D.2c)
91. ὀνείαθ᾽ = ὀνείατα, acc. pl. ὄνειαρ, 'food'
92. πόσιος, ἐδητύος: gen. s. πόσις, ἐδητύς | ἐξ .. ἔντο: 3 pl. 2 aor. mid. ἐξίημι
94. οὗ: gen. s. relative pronoun. 'whose' | καὶ πρόσθεν: 'beforehand as well'
97. σέο: gen. 2 s. pronoun (H.1), as 102, etc.; gen. with ἄρξομαι

fires near to our ships. Who could be glad about that? This
night will either break our army, or preserve it."

80   These were his words; and they heard him well, and
obeyed him. The guards hastened off in their armour,
around Thrasumedes, the son of Nestor and shepherd of his
people, and around Askalaphos and Ialmenos, the sons of
Ares, and around Meriones and Aphareus and Deipuros,
and around the son of Kreion, the godlike Lukomedes.
85   There were seven commanders of the guard, and a hundred
young men went with each of them, with long spears in
their hands. They went, and took up their positions
between the ditch and the wall. There they lit fires, and each
man made his meal.

      But the son of Atreus was leading the councillors of the
90   Akhaians all together to his hut, and he set before them a
pleasing meal. They put their hands to the good things that
lay ready; and when they had put away their desire for food
and drink, the aged Nestor, the man whose advice had
proved best before this too, first of all began to weave his
95   plan to them. Full of good will, he counselled them and
spoke –

      "Most glorious son of Atreus, Agamemnon, lord of men,
with you I will end, and with you I will begin, since you are
the master of many people, and Zeus has conferred on you

σκῆπτρόν τ' ἠδὲ θέμιστας, ἵνα σφίσι βουλεύῃσθα.
τῶ σε χρὴ περὶ μὲν φάσθαι ἔπος ἠδ' ἐπακοῦσαι, 100
κρηῆναι δὲ καὶ ἄλλῳ, ὅτ' ἄν τινα θυμὸς ἀνώγῃ
εἰπεῖν εἰς ἀγαθόν· σέο δ' ἕξεται ὅττι κεν ἄρχῃ.
αὐτὰρ ἐγὼν ἐρέω ὥς μοι δοκεῖ εἶναι ἄριστα.
οὐ γάρ τις νόον ἄλλος ἀμείνονα τοῦδε νοήσει
οἷον ἐγὼ νοέω, ἠμὲν πάλαι ἠδ' ἔτι καὶ νῦν, 105
ἐξ ἔτι τοῦ ὅτε, διογενές, Βρισηΐδα κούρην
χωομένου Ἀχιλῆος ἔβης κλισίηθεν ἀπούρας
οὔ τι καθ' ἡμέτερόν γε νόον· μάλα γάρ τοι ἔγωγε
πόλλ' ἀπεμυθεόμην· σὺ δὲ σῷ μεγαλήτορι θυμῷ
εἴξας ἄνδρα φέριστον, ὃν ἀθάνατοί περ ἔτισαν, 110
ἠτίμησας· ἑλὼν γὰρ ἔχεις γέρας· ἀλλ' ἔτι καὶ νῦν
φραζώμεσθ' ὥς κέν μιν ἀρεσσάμενοι πεπίθωμεν

---

99. σφίσι: dat. 3 pl. personal pronoun (H.2) | βουλεύῃσθα: 2 s. pres. subjunc. mid. βουλεύω (L.7)

100. τῶ: 'therefore' (I.4) | φάσθαι: aor. infin. mid. φημί

101. κρηῆναι: aor. infin. act. of the verb that later established itself as κραίνω. But Hom. more commonly uses the form κραιαίνω. Supply as object here something like 'this same thing' | ὅτ' ἄν: 'whenever' | ἀνώγῃ: subjunc. of ἄνωγα, a perf. form with pres. sense

102. σέο: gen. with ἕξεται | ἕξεται: fut. mid. ἔχω, with the meaning 'be held to the credit of' | ὅττι = ὅτι, 'whatever' (A, J.3)

104. νόον = νοῦν (C.1) | ἀμείνονα: acc. s. m. ἀμείνων, comparative of ἀγαθός | τοῦδε: gen. of comparison, 'better *than* this one'

105. νοέω: pres., but here to be translated 'I have been thinking'

106. ἐξ ἔτι τοῦ ὅτε: 'from that time when' | διογενές: first syllable always long in Homer | Βρισηΐδα: acc. s. Βρισηΐς, 'Briseis', 'daughter of Briseus'

107. χωομένου: either gen. absolute; or, the usual interpretation, with κλισίηθεν, 'from the tent of the angry A.'; or gen. of separation (G.2e) with ἀπούρας, 'took from the angry A.' | κλισίηθεν: with ἀπούρας, 'having taken from the tent' | ἀπούρας: aor. part. act. of a verb that lacks most of the usual forms. At 131 it appears in the 1 s. imperf. act.

108. ἔγωγε = ἐγώ; so acc. ἔμεγ' at 315

109. πόλλ': adverbial, 'repeatedly' (Y.7) | ἀπεμυθεόμην: *conative* imperf. – 'was *trying to* dissuade'

110. εἴξας: aor. part. act. εἴκω | περ: intensive (Z) – '*even* the gods', supporting the contrast ἔτισαν/ἠτίμησας

111. ἑλὼν: 2 aor. part. act. αἱρέω. So ἕλεν, 2 aor. indic., 129, ἐξελόμην, 2 aor. mid., 130, etc.

112. μιν: acc. 3 s. personal pronoun (H.2), as 142, etc. | ἀρεσσάμενοι: aor. mid. part. ἀρέσκω; aor. infin. act. at 120 | πεπίθωμεν: subjunc. of a reduplicated form of the aor. of πείθω (T)

the sceptre and the institutions of law, so that you may guide
them. You, therefore, more than anyone else, must speak
and must listen, and you must complete matters for another
man, too, whenever someone is prompted by his heart to
speak for our good. Whatever he begins, the credit for it
will go to you. But I shall now speak as seems to me best.
For no one will conceive a better idea than this one that I
have had, both long ago and still today, since that time
when, child of a god, you went off, taking away the girl
Briseis from the tent of the furious Akhilleus – something
that went right against our own feelings. For over and over
again I was trying to dissuade you. But you, giving in to
your proud heart, dishonoured the best of men, whom even
the immortals honoured. For you have taken his prize, and
you keep it. But let us even now consider how we may
please him, and win him over with fine gifts and soothing
words."

δώροισίν τ' ἀγανοῖσιν ἔπεσσί τε μειλιχίοισι."

   Τὸν δ' αὖτε προσέειπεν ἄναξ ἀνδρῶν 'Αγαμέμνων·
"ὦ γέρον, οὔ τι ψεῦδος ἐμὰς ἄτας κατέλεξας·   115
ἀασάμην, οὐδ' αὐτὸς ἀναίνομαι. ἀντί νυ πολλῶν
λαῶν ἐστὶν ἀνὴρ ὅν τε Ζεὺς κῆρι φιλήσῃ,
ὡς νῦν τοῦτον ἔτισε, δάμασσε δὲ λαὸν 'Αχαιῶν.
ἀλλ' ἐπεὶ ἀασάμην φρεσὶ λευγαλέῃσι πιθήσας,
ἂψ ἐθέλω ἀρέσαι δόμεναί τ' ἀπερείσι' ἄποινα.   120
ὑμῖν δ' ἐν πάντεσσι περικλυτὰ δῶρ' ὀνομήνω,
ἕπτ' ἀπύρους τρίποδας, δέκα δὲ χρυσοῖο τάλαντα,
αἴθωνας δὲ λέβητας ἐείκοσι, δώδεκα δ' ἵππους
πηγοὺς ἀθλοφόρους, οἳ ἀέθλια ποσσὶν ἄροντο.
οὔ κεν ἀλήϊος εἴη ἀνὴρ ᾧ τόσσα γένοιτο,   125
οὐδέ κεν ἀκτήμων ἐριτίμοιο χρυσοῖο,
ὅσσα μοι ἠνείκαντο ἀέθλια μώνυχες ἵπποι.
δώσω δ' ἑπτὰ γυναῖκας ἀμύμονα ἔργα ἰδυίας
Λεσβίδας, ἃς ὅτε Λέσβον ἐϋκτιμένην ἕλεν αὐτὸς
ἐξελόμην, αἳ κάλλει ἐνίκων φῦλα γυναικῶν.   130
τὰς μέν οἱ δώσω, μετὰ δ' ἔσσεται ἣν τότ' ἀπηύρων

---

115. ψεῦδος: acc. s. – 'You have not called my delusions a lie'

116. ἀντί: 'as good as', with λαῶν | νυ: particle, 'indeed'

118. ἔτισε, δάμασσε: 'He has honoured him, and has tamed ..', i.e. 'has honoured him by   taming ..'

119. λευγαλέῃσι: dat. pl. f. λευγάλεος (B.3) | πιθήσας: 'trusting in', with dat.; in form, an aor. part. act., nom. s. m., as though from a verb πιθέω – though this form is not in fact found

120. ἂψ: 'in return' | δόμεναί: aor. infin. act. δίδωμι (P)

121. ἐν: 'among' | πάντεσσι: dat. pl. m. πᾶς (D.8) | ὀνομήνω: aor. subjunc. (jussive) act. ὀνομαίνω

123. ἐείκοσι = εἴκοσι (A), also 139, etc.

124. ἀέθλια = ἆθλα, as 127 | ποσσὶν: dat. pl. πούς | ἄροντο: 2 aor. ἄρνυμαι

125. γένοιτο: 2 aor. optat. γίγνομαι. Optat. as though this were the protasis of a conditional clause. 'That man would not be without booty, to *whom* so many things came', i.e. '*if* so many things came to him'

127. ἠνείκαντο: aor. mid. φέρω, meaning 'win' in mid.

128. ἰδυίας: acc. pl. f. of the part. of οἶδα

129. Λεσβίδας: the –ις, gen. –ιδος, ending denotes Lesbian *women*. So Τρωϊάδας, 139 | αὐτὸς: subject of ἕλεν, not ἐξελόμην

131. μετὰ: here adverbial, as ἐπί, 132, ἐν, 154, etc. | ἔσσεται: fut. εἰμί(U.6);so παρέσσεται,135 | ἣν: '(the one) whom'

And in his turn Agamemnon, the lord of men, addressed him:–

115   "O sir, you said nothing at all untrue about my folly. I was deluded, and I do not deny it. Worth many a warrior, indeed, is the man whom Zeus loves in his heart as he has now honoured that man, and he has subdued the army of the Akhaians. But since I have been deluded, giving way to the
120   wretched counsels of my heart, I want to make things good again, and to give unlimited reparation.

    "Let me now before you all name my magnificent gifts – Seven tripods untouched by fire, ten talents of gold, twenty sparkling cauldrons, and twelve strong champion horses
125   who have won prizes in the races. The man who had so much would not be short of booty nor without priceless gold, so much as the prizes that my horses with uncloven hoof have won for me. And I will give seven women,
130   excellent in their handiwork, from Lesbos, whom I picked out when he himself took well-built Lesbos, women who excelled all others in their beauty. These I will give to him, and among them will be the one whom I then took from

κούρη Βρισῆος· ἐπὶ δὲ μέγαν ὅρκον ὀμοῦμαι
μή ποτε τῆς εὐνῆς ἐπιβήμεναι ἠδὲ μιγῆναι,
ἢ θέμις ἀνθρώπων πέλει ἀνδρῶν ἠδὲ γυναικῶν.
ταῦτα μὲν αὐτίκα πάντα παρέσσεται· εἰ δέ κεν αὖτε 135
ἄστυ μέγα Πριάμοιο θεοὶ δώωσ' ἀλαπάξαι,
νῆα ἅλις χρυσοῦ καὶ χαλκοῦ νηησάσθω
εἰσελθών, ὅτε κεν δατεώμεθα ληΐδ' Ἀχαιοί,
Τρωϊάδας δὲ γυναῖκας ἐείκοσιν αὐτὸς ἑλέσθω,
αἵ κε μετ' Ἀργείην Ἑλένην κάλλισται ἔωσιν. 140
εἰ δέ κεν Ἄργος ἱκοίμεθ' Ἀχαιϊκόν, οὖθαρ ἀρούρης,
γαμβρός κέν μοι ἔοι· τίσω δέ μιν ἶσον Ὀρέστῃ,
ὅς μοι τηλύγετος τρέφεται θαλίῃ ἔνι πολλῇ.
τρεῖς δέ μοί εἰσι θύγατρες ἐνὶ μεγάρῳ εὐπήκτῳ,
Χρυσόθεμις καὶ Λαοδίκη καὶ Ἰφιάνασσα, 145
τάων ἥν κ' ἐθέλῃσι φίλην ἀνάεδνον ἀγέσθω
πρὸς οἶκον Πηλῆος· ἐγὼ δ' ἐπὶ μείλια δώσω
πολλὰ μάλ', ὅσσ' οὔ πώ τις ἑῇ ἐπέδωκε θυγατρί.
ἑπτὰ δέ οἱ δώσω εὖ ναιόμενα πτολίεθρα,

---

132. Βρισῆος: final syllable long, as sometimes happens when a syllable that would otherwise be short comes immediately before the caesura and coincides with a pause in the sense | ὀμοῦμαι: fut. ὄμνυμι

133. μή: introduces the content of the oath. 'that I never ..', followed by infin. | τῆς: 'of her', 'her' | ἐπιβήμεναι: aor. infin. ἐπιβαίνω (P), 'mounted her bed' | μιγῆναι: aor. infin. pass. μ(ε)ίγνυμι; so προμιγῆναι, 452

135. εἰ .. κεν: with subjunc. for future conditional (W.3a) – 'if the gods (shall) grant, then let him heap up'

136. δώωσ': 3 pl. aor. subjunc. act. δίδωμι | ἀλαπάξαι: aor. infin. act. ἀλαπάζω

137. νῆα: acc. s. ναῦς (D.11) | χρυσοῦ, χαλκοῦ: gen. with νηησάσθω | νηησάσθω: 3 s. aor. imperat. mid. νέω

139. ἑλέσθω: 3 s. 2 aor. imperat. mid. αἱρέω

140. ἔωσιν: 3 pl. subjunc. εἰμί (U.7)

141. εἰ .. κεν: with optat., for future (W.3b) – 'if we come .., .. he will be ..' Cf. 135–6 | ἱκοίμεθ': 2 aor. optat. ἱκνέομαι | οὖθαρ: acc., in apposition to Ἄργος

142. ἔοι: 3 s. optat. εἰμί (U.8) | τίσω: fut. τίνω; the fut. now displaces the optat.

146. τάων: gen. pl. f. ὁ ἡ τό (I.1b); 'of these' | ἐθέλῃσι: lengthened form of 3 s. pres. subjunc. act. ἐθέλω (L.9) | φίλην: 'as his dear one', i.e. his wife | ἀγέσθω: 3 s. pres. imperat. mid. ἄγω (X.2)

147–8. ἐπὶ .. δώσω, ἐπέδωκε: fut. act., aor. act. ἐπιδίδωμι, 'give besides'

148. ἑῇ: dat. s. f. ἑός, 'his own' (F)

149. πτολίεθρα: for πολίεθρα, as 402, etc.; ππ – causes the –α at the end of the previous word to be lengthened (Scansion, B.2)

him, the daughter of Briseus. And I will swear a mighty oath into the bargain that I have never mounted her bed or lain with her, something that is natural for people, for men and women.

135   "All this will be his immediately. And if the gods later grant that we sack Priam's great city, let him, having entered it, heap his ship high with plenty of gold and bronze, whenever we Akhaians divide up the spoil. And let him

140 choose twenty Trojan women for himself, whichever ones are the most beautiful after Argive Helen. And if we reach the fertile soil of Akhaian Argos, he will be my son-in-law, and I will honour him exactly as I honour Orestes, my beloved son, who is growing up there in great prosperity. I

145 have three daughters in my strong palace, Khrusothemis, Laodike, and Iphianassa. Whichever of these he wishes, let him take her as his own dear wife to the house of Peleus, without paying a bride-price. And I will add a great abundance of soothing things besides, more than any man has ever yet given to his daughter. I will give him seven

Καρδαμύλην Ἐνόπην τε καὶ Ἱρὴν ποιήεσσαν,   150
Φηράς τε ζαθέας ἠδ' Ἄνθειαν βαθύλειμον,
καλήν τ' Αἴπειαν καὶ Πήδασον ἀμπελόεσσαν.
πᾶσαι δ' ἐγγὺς ἁλός, νέαται Πύλου ἠμαθόεντος·
ἐν δ' ἄνδρες ναίουσι πολύρρηνες πολυβοῦται,
οἵ κέ ἑ δωτίνῃσι θεὸν ὣς τιμήσουσι   155
καί οἱ ὑπὸ σκήπτρῳ λιπαρὰς τελέουσι θέμιστας.
ταῦτά κέ οἱ τελέσαιμι μεταλλήξαντι χόλοιο.
δμηθήτω· Ἀΐδης τοι ἀμείλιχος ἠδ' ἀδάμαστος.
τοὔνεκα καί τε βροτοῖσι θεῶν ἔχθιστος ἁπάντων·
καί μοι ὑποστήτω ὅσσον βασιλεύτερός εἰμι   160
ἠδ' ὅσσον γενεῇ προγενέστερος εὔχομαι εἶναι."

   Τὸν δ' ἠμείβετ' ἔπειτα Γερήνιος ἱππότα Νέστωρ·
"Ἀτρεΐδη κύδιστε, ἄναξ ἀνδρῶν Ἀγάμεμνον,
δῶρα μὲν οὐκέτ' ὀνοστὰ διδοῖς Ἀχιλῆϊ ἄνακτι·
ἀλλ' ἄγετε, κλητοὺς ὀτρύνομεν, οἵ κε τάχιστα   165
ἔλθωσ' ἐς κλισίην Πηληϊάδεω Ἀχιλῆος.
εἰ δ' ἄγε, τοὺς ἂν ἐγὼ ἐπιόψομαι, οἱ δὲ πιθέσθων.

---

150. ποιήεσσαν: acc. s. f. ποιήεις. So ἀμπελόεσσαν, 152

153. νέαται = νείαται. Nom. pl. f. of a superlative form. Literally, 'outermost' (as VIII 478), 'at the bottom of'. But the sense here seems to require, 'just beyond the borders of' | ἠμαθόεντος: gen. s. m. ἠμαθόεις; Πύλος can be either m. or f.

154. ἐν: 'in them'

155. ἑ: acc. 3 s. personal pronoun (H.1)

156. τελέουσι: 3 pl. fut. act. τελέω(O.1); aor. optat. act. in next line

157. τελέσαιμι: for fut., as 141–2 | μεταλλήξαντι: dat. s. m. aor. part. act. μεταλήγω, with the – λ – reduplicated. The participle is used conditionally – literally, 'I will pay this to him having stopped ..', – i.e. 'I will pay this if he stops' | χόλοιο: 'from his anger' (G.2e)

158. δμηθήτω: 3 s. aor. pass. imperat. δαμάζω; lit. 'let him be tamed' | τοι: particle, 'let me tell you' (Z)

159. τοὔνεκα: 'and that is the reason why' | ἔχθιστος: superlative of ἐχθρός

160. ὑποστήτω: 3 s. 2 aor. imperat. act. ὑφίστημι; 'let him submit' | ὅσσον = ὅσον (A); 'inasmuch as'

164. διδοῖς: 2 s. pres. act. δίδωμι

165. ὀτρύνομεν: pres. subjunc. act. (L.10) ὀτρύνω

166. ἔλθωσ': 3 pl. 2 aor. subjunc. ἔρχομαι | Πηληϊάδεω: 'son of Peleus', i.e. Akhilleus. Gen. s. (B.6), with –εω scanned as one syllable by synizesis (Scansion, B.5b)

167. ἐπιόψομαι: fut. indic. (unusually in an indefinite clause – W.8a) ἐφοράω | δὲ: the *apodotic* δέ, not to be translated | πιθέσθων: 3 pl. 2 aor. imperat. mid. πείθω

150 well-settled cities – Kardamule, Enope, and grassy Hire, sacred Pherae and Antheia with its deep meadows, beautiful Aipeia, and Pedasos with its vineyards. All of these are close to the sea, just beyond the borders of sandy Pulos, and in them dwell men who are rich in sheep and rich in

155 cattle, who will honour him with their gifts like a god, and will pay him rich dues under his sceptre. This I will give to him if he gives up his anger.

"Let him give in – it is Hades who is indeed unyielding and implacable, and for that reason he is the most hateful of

160 all the gods to men as well. And let him place himself under me, as I am the more kingly, and claim to be the more distinguished in ancestry."

Then the Gerenian horseman Nestor answered him –

"Most glorious son of Atreus, Agamemnon, lord of men, you now offer gifts to lord Akhilleus that cannot be

165 criticised. But come, let us hasten our chosen men on their way, that they may go with all speed to the hut of Akhilleus, the son of Peleus. Come then – Whomsoever I shall

Φοῖνιξ μὲν πρώτιστα Διῒ φίλος ἡγησάσθω,
αὐτὰρ ἔπειτ' Αἴας τε μέγας καὶ δῖος Ὀδυσσεύς·
κηρύκων δ' Ὀδίος τε καὶ Εὐρυβάτης ἅμ' ἑπέσθων.　　　170
φέρτε δὲ χερσὶν ὕδωρ, εὐφημῆσαί τε κέλεσθε,
ὄφρα Διὶ Κρονίδῃ ἀρησόμεθ', αἴ κ' ἐλεήσῃ."

"Ὣς φάτο, τοῖσι δὲ πᾶσιν ἑαδότα μῦθον ἔειπεν.
αὐτίκα κήρυκες μὲν ὕδωρ ἐπὶ χεῖρας ἔχευαν,
κοῦροι δὲ κρητῆρας ἐπεστέψαντο ποτοῖο,　　　175
νώμησαν δ' ἄρα πᾶσιν ἐπαρξάμενοι δεπάεσσιν.
αὐτὰρ ἐπεὶ σπεῖσάν τ' ἔπιόν θ' ὅσον ἤθελε θυμός,
ὁρμῶντ' ἐκ κλισίης Ἀγαμέμνονος Ἀτρεΐδαο.
τοῖσι δὲ πόλλ' ἐπέτελλε Γερήνιος ἱππότα Νέστωρ,
δενδίλλων ἐς ἕκαστον, Ὀδυσσῆϊ δὲ μάλιστα,　　　180
πειρᾶν ὡς πεπίθοιεν ἀμύμονα Πηλεΐωνα.

Τὼ δὲ βάτην παρὰ θῖνα πολυφλοίσβοιο θαλάσσης
πολλὰ μάλ' εὐχομένω γαιηόχῳ ἐννοσιγαίῳ
ῥηϊδίως πεπιθεῖν μεγάλας φρένας Αἰακίδαο.
Μυρμιδόνων δ' ἐπί τε κλισίας καὶ νῆας ἱκέσθην,　　　185

---

168. Διῒ: dat. s. Ζεύς (D.11); so Διΐ, 172.　|　ἡγησάσθω: 3 s. aor. imperat. ἡγέομαι

170. ἑπέσθων: 3 pl. imperat. ἕπομαι

171. φέρτε = φέρετε, pres. imperat. act. φέρω　|　κέλεσθε: pres. imperat. κέλομαι, a form of κελεύω

172. ἀρησόμεθ': aor. subjunc. ἀράομαι (L.10)　|　αἴ κ': 'in the hope that' (W.5)

173. ἑαδότα: acc. s. m. perf. part. act. ἁνδάνω

175. ἐπεστέψαντο: aor. ἐπιστέφομαι　|　ποτοῖο: 'with drink' (G.2d)

176. νώμησαν: supply 'the drink' as object

177. σπεῖσαν: 3 pl. aor. act. σπένδω; aor. part at 657, 712　|　ἔπιον: 3 pl. 2 aor. act. πίνω

181. πειρᾶν: pres. infin. πειράω; infin. as if δενδίλλων were introducing an indirect command – 'glancing at each man to (i.e. that he should) try'　|　ὡς πεπίθοιεν: 'that they should persuade', i.e. 'to persuade'　|　πεπίθοιεν: 3 pl. optat. – see on 112　|　Πηλεΐωνα: 'son of Peleus', i.e. Akhilleus

182. Τὼ: dual nom., 'the two of them'. Acc. at 196 (I.1d)　|　βάτην: 3 dual. aor. βαίνω, as 192

183. εὐχομένω: pres. part. εὔχομαι, dual nom　|　γαιηόχῳ ἐννοσιγαίῳ: i.e. Poseidon, who as god of the sea 'holds' – i.e. surrounds – the earth, and is also god of earthquakes

184. ῥηϊδίως = ῥᾳδίως　|　πεπιθεῖν: 'to persuade', i.e. 'that they may persuade'　|　Αἰακιδάο: gen. (B.6); 'descendant of Aiakos', i.e. Akhilleus, A.'s grandson

185. ἱκέσθην: 3 dual 2 aor. ἱκνέομαι

choose, let them be prevailed upon. First of all, let Phoinix, beloved of Zeus, lead the way, and then mighty Aias and
170   godlike Odusseus.   And of the heralds let Odios and Eurubates go along with them. Bring water for their hands, and order a ritual silence, so that we may pray to Zeus the son of Kronos for his pity."

Thus he spoke, and the words that he uttered were pleasing to them all. Assistants immediately poured water
175   over their hands, and young men filled the mixing-bowls to the brim with wine, and they distributed the cups to everyone, after putting a libation into each. Then, when they had made their libation and drunk as much as their hearts wanted, they were setting forth from the hut of Agamemnon, the son of Atreus. The Gerenian horseman Nestor was giving them many a word of instruction,
180   glancing at each of them, and especially at Odusseus, that they should try to win over the excellent son of Peleus.

The two of them went along the shore of the resounding sea, making prayer after prayer to the god who holds and shakes the earth, that they might easily persuade the great
185   heart of the child of Aiakos. They came to the tents and the

τὸν δ' εὗρον φρένα τερπόμενον φόρμιγγι λιγείῃ,
καλῇ δαιδαλέῃ, ἐπὶ δ' ἀργύρεον ζυγὸν ἦεν,
τὴν ἄρετ' ἐξ ἐνάρων πόλιν Ἠετίωνος ὀλέσσας·
τῇ ὅ γε θυμὸν ἔτερπεν, ἄειδε δ' ἄρα κλέα ἀνδρῶν.
Πάτροκλος δέ οἱ οἶος ἐναντίος ἧστο σιωπῇ,　　　　　　190
δέγμενος Αἰακίδην ὁπότε λήξειεν ἀείδων.
τὼ δὲ βάτην προτέρω, ἡγεῖτο δὲ δῖος Ὀδυσσεύς,
στὰν δὲ πρόσθ' αὐτοῖο· ταφὼν δ' ἀνόρουσεν Ἀχιλλεὺς
αὐτῇ σὺν φόρμιγγι, λιπὼν ἕδος ἔνθα θάασσεν.
ὣς δ' αὔτως Πάτροκλος, ἐπεὶ ἴδε φῶτας, ἀνέστη.　　　　195
τὼ καὶ δεικνύμενος προσέφη πόδας ὠκὺς Ἀχιλλεύς·
"χαίρετον· ἦ φίλοι ἄνδρες ἱκάνετον· ἦ τι μάλα χρεώ,
οἵ μοι σκυζομένῳ περ Ἀχαιῶν φίλτατοί ἐστον."
　　Ὣς ἄρα φωνήσας προτέρω ἄγε δῖος Ἀχιλλεύς,
εἷσεν δ' ἐν κλισμοῖσι τάπησί τε πορφυρέοισιν.　　　　　200
αἶψα δὲ Πάτροκλον προσεφώνεεν ἐγγὺς ἐόντα·
"μείζονα δὴ κρητῆρα, Μενοιτίου υἱέ, καθίστα,

---

186. εὗρον: 3 pl. 2 aor. act. εὑρίσκω; 2 aor. infin. at 250
187. καλῇ: first syllable always long in Hom. (Scansion, B.3d) | ἐπὶ .. ἦεν: 3 s. imperf. ἔπειμι (U.4)
188. ὀλέσσας: nom. s. m. aor. part. act. ὄλλυμι, with doubled σ (Q.3)
190. ἧστο: 3 s. imperf. ἧμαι
191. δέγμενος: clearly 'waiting for', and connected with δέχομαι. Thought to be from a form δέγμαι, although this form does not survive. Likewise ποτιδέγμενοι, 628 | λήξειεν: 3 s. aor. optat. act. λήγω
193. στὰν: 3 pl. 2 aor. act. ἵστημι | πρόσθ': preposition, with gen.
194. αὐτῇ σὺν φόρμιγγι: 'with lyre and all' (K.4) | λιπὼν: nom. s. m. 2 aor. act. part. λείπω | θάασσεν = ἔθασσεν, imperf. act. θάσσω
195. ἴδε = εἶδε, 3 s. 2 aor. act. ὁράω | φῶτας: acc. pl. φώς | ἀνέστη: 3 s. 2 aor. act. ἀνίστημι
196. δεικνύμενος: could be pres. part. mid. δείκνυμι, normally 'show'. But the meaning here must be something like 'welcoming', and so it is thought to be associated with δειδίσκομαι, 'greet' | πόδας ὠκὺς: acc. of respect (G.1e); 'swift as to his feet', i.e. 'swift-footed'
197. χαίρετον: 2 dual pres. imperat. act. χαίρω | ἱκάνετον: 2 dual pres. act. ἱκάνω
198. ἐστον: 2 dual pres. εἰμί (U.1)
200. εἷσεν: aor. act. ἵζω
201. ἐόντα: acc. s. m. pres. part. εἰμί (U.2)
202. καθίστα: 2 s. pres. imperat. act. καθίστημι

ships of the Murmidons, and they found him delighting his
heart with a clear-sounding lyre, a fine, well-wrought one,
with a crosspiece of silver on it, a lyre which he had won
from the spoils when he destroyed the city of Eetion. With
this he was delighting his heart, and he was singing of the
190   famous deeds of men. And Patroklos was sitting opposite
him, alone and in silence, waiting for the moment when the
child of Aiakos would cease from his singing. The two of
them went forward, and the godlike Odusseus led the way,
and they stood in front of him. Astonished, Akhilleus leapt
up, still holding his lyre, and leaving the seat where he was
195   sitting. And likewise Patroklos stood up when he saw the
men. And, extending his hand in welcome to the pair, the
swift-footed Akhilleus said –

"Welcome! You are certainly dear friends who have
come. There is indeed much need – you who are the dearest
of the Akhaians to me, even in my anger."

200   Speaking thus, godlike Akhilleus led them forward, and
placed them on chairs and purple coverlets. And
straightaway he addressed Patroklos, who was nearby –

"Set up a larger mixing-bowl, son of Menoitios, and mix

ζωρότερον δὲ κέραιε, δέπας δ' ἔντυνον ἑκάστῳ·
οἱ γὰρ φίλτατοι ἄνδρες ἐμῷ ὑπέασι μελάθρῳ."
    Ὣς φάτο, Πάτροκλος δὲ φίλῳ ἐπεπείθεθ' ἑταίρῳ.   205
αὐτὰρ ὅ γε κρεῖον μέγα κάββαλεν ἐν πυρὸς αὐγῇ,
ἐν δ' ἄρα νῶτον ἔθηκ' ὄϊος καὶ πίονος αἰγός,
ἐν δὲ συὸς σιάλοιο ῥάχιν τεθαλυῖαν ἀλοιφῇ.
τῷ δ' ἔχεν Αὐτομέδων, τάμνεν δ' ἄρα δῖος 'Αχιλλεύς.
καὶ τὰ μὲν εὖ μίστυλλε καὶ ἀμφ' ὀβελοῖσιν ἔπειρε,   210
πῦρ δὲ Μενοιτιάδης δαῖεν μέγα, ἰσόθεος φώς.
αὐτὰρ ἐπεὶ κατὰ πῦρ ἐκάη καὶ φλὸξ ἐμαράνθη,
ἀνθρακιὴν στορέσας ὀβελοὺς ἐφύπερθε τάνυσσε,
πάσσε δ' ἁλὸς θείοιο κρατευτάων ἐπαείρας.
αὐτὰρ ἐπεί ῥ' ὤπτησε καὶ εἰν ἐλεοῖσιν ἔχευε,   215
Πάτροκλος μὲν σῖτον ἑλὼν ἐπένειμε τραπέζῃ
καλοῖς ἐν κανέοισιν, ἀτὰρ κρέα νεῖμεν 'Αχιλλεύς.
αὐτὸς δ' ἀντίον ἷζεν 'Οδυσσῆος θείοιο
τοίχου τοῦ ἑτέροιο, θεοῖσι δὲ θῦσαι ἀνώγει
Πάτροκλον ὃν ἑταῖρον· ὁ δ' ἐν πυρὶ βάλλε θυηλάς.   220
οἱ δ' ἐπ' ὀνείαθ' ἑτοῖμα προκείμενα χεῖρας ἴαλλον.
αὐτὰρ ἐπεὶ πόσιος καὶ ἐδητύος ἐξ ἔρον ἕντο,
νεῦσ' Αἴας Φοίνικι· νόησε δὲ δῖος 'Οδυσσεύς,
πλησάμενος δ' οἴνοιο δέπας δείδεκτ' 'Αχιλῆα·

---

203. ζωρότερον: comparative adv., 'more strongly' | ἔντυνον: 2 s. aor. imperat. act. ἐντύνω
204. οἱ: 'these' (I.2) | ὑπέασι: 3 pl. pres. ὕπειμι (U.1)
205. ἐπεπείθεθ' = ἐπεπείθετο, 3 s. imperf. ἐπι-πείθομαι
206. κάββαλεν = κατέβαλεν, 3 s. 2 aor. act. καταβάλλω (N.1)
207–8. ὄϊος, αἰγός, συὸς: gen. s. ὄϊς, αἴξ, σῦς
208. τεθαλυῖαν: acc. s. f. perf. part. act. θάλλω
212. κατὰ .. ἐκάη: 3 s. aor. pass. κατακαίω
213. στορέσας: nom. s. m. aor. part. act. στόρνυμι; aor. infin. act. at 621 and 659, aor. indic. act. at 660
214. ἁλὸς: gen. with πάσσε; 'sprinkled *with* salt' | κρατευτάων: gen. with ἐπαείρας, 'raising *on* the rests' | ἐπαείρας: nom. s. m. aor. part. act. ἐπ-αιρω
219. τοίχου: gen. of place; '*at* the wall' | ἀνώγει: from ἄνωγα; plupf. in form, aor. in meaning
221–2. See on 91–2
224. πλησάμενος: aor. part. mid. πίμπλημι | οἴνοιο: '*with* wine' (G.2d) | δείδεκτ': 3 s. as though from a perf. mid. and pass. δείδεγμαι. Thought to be connected with δείκνυμι – see on 196, also 671

the wine stronger, and prepare a cup for each of them. For these men who are under my roof are my dearest friends."

205   So he spoke, and Patroklos obeyed his dear companion. Then he laid down a large carving-block in the light of the fire, and on it he placed the backs of a sheep and a fat goat, and the chine of a fat hog, rich in lard. Automedon held the
210   meat for him, and the godlike Akhilleus cut it. He cut it up well, and stuck the pieces on spits, and the son of Menoitios, a man who was the equal of the gods, made the fire into a great blaze. Then, when the fire had burned down and the flames had died away, scattering the embers he laid the spits over them, and sprinkled the meat with holy
215   salt, putting the spits on the fire-rests. Then, when he had roasted it and spread it on the side-tables, Patroklos, taking the bread, put it out on the table in fine baskets, and Akhilleus served the meat. He himself sat facing the godlike
220   Odusseus by the wall opposite, and he ordered Patroklos his companion to sacrifice to the gods; and Patroklos cast the sacrificial parts of the meat into the fire.

They put their hands to the good things that lay ready. Then, when they had put away their desire for food and drink, Aias gave a nod to Phoinix. But godlike Odusseus spotted it, and, filling his cup with wine, he toasted Akhilleus.

"χαῖρ', Ἀχιλεῦ· δαιτὸς μὲν ἐΐσης οὐκ ἐπιδευεῖς　　　　　225
ἠμὲν ἐνὶ κλισίῃ Ἀγαμέμνονος Ἀτρεΐδαο
ἠδὲ καὶ ἐνθάδε νῦν, πάρα γὰρ μενοεικέα πολλὰ
δαίνυσθ'· ἀλλ' οὐ δαιτὸς ἐπηράτου ἔργα μέμηλεν,
ἀλλὰ λίην μέγα πῆμα, διοτρεφές, εἰσορόωντες
δείδιμεν· ἐν δοιῇ δὲ σαωσέμεν ἢ ἀπολέσθαι　　　　　230
νῆας ἐϋσσέλμους, εἰ μὴ σύ γε δύσεαι ἀλκήν.
ἐγγὺς γὰρ νηῶν καὶ τείχεος αὖλιν ἔθεντο
Τρῶες ὑπέρθυμοι τηλεκλειτοί τ' ἐπίκουροι,
κηάμενοι πυρὰ πολλὰ κατὰ στρατόν, οὐδ' ἔτι φασὶ
σχήσεσθ', ἀλλ' ἐν νηυσὶ μελαίνῃσιν πεσέεσθαι.　　　　　235
Ζεὺς δέ σφι Κρονίδης ἐνδέξια σήματα φαίνων
ἀστράπτει· Ἕκτωρ δὲ μέγα σθένεϊ βλεμεαίνων
μαίνεται ἐκπάγλως πίσυνος Διί, οὐδέ τι τίει
ἀνέρας οὐδὲ θεούς· κρατερὴ δέ ἑ λύσσα δέδυκεν.
ἀρᾶται δὲ τάχιστα φανήμεναι Ἠῶ δῖαν·　　　　　240
στεῦται γὰρ νηῶν ἀποκόψειν ἄκρα κόρυμβα
αὐτάς τ' ἐμπρήσειν μαλεροῦ πυρός, αὐτὰρ Ἀχαιοὺς
δηώσειν παρὰ τῇσιν ὀρινομένους ὑπὸ καπνοῦ.
ταῦτ' αἰνῶς δείδοικα κατὰ φρένα, μή οἱ ἀπειλὰς

---

225. δαιτὸς: gen. with ἐπιδευεῖς | ἐπιδευεῖς: supply ἐσμέν
226–7. ἠμὲν .. ἠδὲ: 'both .. and', as 258, etc.
228. δαίνυσθ': pres. infin. mid. δαίνυμι | μέμηλεν: perf. μέλω
229. λίην = λίαν | εἰσορόωντες: pres. part. εἰσοράω, – οω – for – ω – (O.2c)
230. δείδιμεν: 2 pl. perf., with pres. sense, δείδω | ἐν δοιῇ: supply ἐσμέν | σαωσέμεν: aor.
infin. act. σαόω (P), object νῆας, 231 | ἀπολέσθαι: 2 aor. infin. mid. ἀπόλλυμι ; 'whether we are
to save our ships or to be destroyed'
231. δύσεαι: 2 s. fut. mid. δύ(ψ)ω (L.1)
234. κηάμενοι: aor. part. mid. καίω | φασὶ: 'they think', 3 pl. pres. φημί; so φησιν, 'he thinks',
305
235. σχήσεσθ': fut. infin. mid. ἔχω, here with pass. meaning, as 655. The Trojans are the subject
of both this infin. and πεσέεσθαι – 'they do not think that they will be checked, but that they will
fall upon' | πεσέεσθαι: fut. infin. mid. πίπτω (O.1)
239. ἀνέρας = ἄνδρας; first syllable always scanned long in Hom. in three-syllable forms of ἀνήρ
240. φανήμεναι: aor. infin. pass. φαίνω (P) | Ἠῶ: acc. s. Ἠώς
242. ἐμπρήσειν: fut. infin. act. ἐμπίμπρημι | πυρός: gen. with ἐμπρήσειν; 'burn them *with* fire'
244. δείδοικα = δέδοικα, 1 s. perf. δείδω, with pres. meaning; followed by μή and subjunc. (X.3)

225   "Hail, Akhilleus! We do not go short of a feast shared between all, both in the tent of Agamemnon the son of Atreus and also now here; for there are many fine things here to feast on. But our concern is not with a delightful feast, but as we look, child of a god, upon a sorrow that is

230   all too great, we are afraid, and it is in doubt whether we save our ships with their fine benches, or whether we perish, unless you put on your martial spirit. For the high-spirited Trojans and their far-famed allies have made their camp close to the ships and the wall, lighting many fires

235   amid their army, and they do not now expect to be stopped, but to fall upon our black ships. And Zeus, son of Kronos, showing them favourable signs, hurls down lightning; and Hektor, exulting greatly in his strength, rages terribly, trusting in Zeus, and he has no respect at all for men or for

240   gods; a mighty madness has come upon him. He is praying that holy Dawn may come with all speed, for he is threatening to hack away the tips of our ships' stern-posts, and to burn the ships with consuming fire, and then to destroy the Akhaians beside them as they are bewildered by the smoke. I am dreadfully afraid of this in my heart, that

ἐκτελέσωσι θεοί, ἡμῖν δὲ δὴ αἴσιμον εἴη   245
φθίσθαι ἐνὶ Τροίῃ ἑκὰς Ἄργεος ἱπποβότοιο.
ἀλλ' ἄνα, εἰ μέμονάς γε καὶ ὀψέ περ υἷας Ἀχαιῶν
τειρομένους ἐρύεσθαι ὑπὸ Τρώων ὀρυμαγδοῦ.
αὐτῷ τοι μετόπισθ' ἄχος ἔσσεται, οὐδέ τι μῆχος
ῥεχθέντος κακοῦ ἔστ' ἄκος εὑρεῖν· ἀλλὰ πολὺ πρὶν   250
φράζευ ὅπως Δαναοῖσιν ἀλεξήσεις κακὸν ἦμαρ.
ὦ πέπον, ἦ μὲν σοί γε πατὴρ ἐπετέλλετο Πηλεὺς
ἤματι τῷ ὅτε σ' ἐκ Φθίης Ἀγαμέμνονι πέμπε·
'τέκνον ἐμόν, κάρτος μὲν Ἀθηναίη τε καὶ Ἥρη
δώσουσ' αἴ κ' ἐθέλωσι, σὺ δὲ μεγαλήτορα θυμὸν   255
ἴσχειν ἐν στήθεσσι· φιλοφροσύνη γὰρ ἀμείνων·
ληγέμεναι δ' ἔριδος κακομηχάνου, ὄφρά σε μᾶλλον
τίωσ' Ἀργείων ἠμὲν νέοι ἠδὲ γέροντες.'
ὣς ἐπέτελλ' ὁ γέρων, σὺ δὲ λήθεαι· ἀλλ' ἔτι καὶ νῦν
παύε', ἔα δὲ χόλον θυμαλγέα· σοὶ δ' Ἀγαμέμνων   260
ἄξια δῶρα δίδωσι μεταλλήξαντι χόλοιο.
εἰ δὲ σὺ μέν μευ ἄκουσον, ἐγὼ δέ κέ τοι καταλέξω
ὅσσά τοι ἐν κλισίῃσιν ὑπέσχετο δῶρ' Ἀγαμέμνων·
ἕπτ' ἀπύρους τρίποδας, δέκα δὲ χρυσοῖο τάλαντα,
αἴθωνας δὲ λέβητας ἐείκοσι, δώδεκα δ' ἵππους   265
πηγοὺς ἀθλοφόρους, οἳ ἀέθλια ποσσὶν ἄροντο.
οὔ κεν ἀλήϊος εἴη ἀνὴρ ᾧ τόσσα γένοιτο

---

245. ἐκτελέσωσι: aor. subjunc. act. ἐκτελέω | εἴη: optat. εἰμί (U.8) – 'fear that the gods may accomplish, and that it would (then) be our fate'

246. φθίσθαι: aor. infin. mid. φθί(ν)ω

247. καὶ ὀψέ περ: 'even though it is late' (Z)

248. ἐρύεσθαι ὑπὸ: 'to rescue from'

250. ῥεχθέντος: gen. s. n. aor. part. pass. ῥέζω | ἔστ' = ἔσται

251. φράζευ: 2 s. pres. imperat. mid. φράζω; –ευ for –ου | Δαναοῖσιν: 'from the Danaans'; so again with ἀλέξω, 347, and with ἀμύνω, 435, etc. | ἀλεξήσεις: fut. ἀλέξω | ἦμαρ: a common alternative to ἡμέρα; dat. s. at 253, acc. pl. at 326, etc.

256. ἴσχειν: infin. of a form of ἔχω (Hom. uses this form only for 'restrain', as 352, etc.); infin. for imperat., as ληγέμεναι, 257

257. ληγέμεναι: pres. infin. act. λήγω (P)

259. λήθεαι: 2 s. pres. mid. λήθω (L.1); 'you forget'

261. μεταλλήξαντι χόλοιο: see on 157

262. μευ: gen. 1 s. personal pronoun (H.1) | ἄκουσον: 2 s. aor. act. imperat. ἀκούω

264–298. Deduct 142 to get the corresponding line of Agamemnon's speech

245   the gods will fulfil his threats for him, and that it would be
our fate to be destroyed at Troy, far from Argos where
horses are grazed. But up, if you are minded, even though
it is late, to rescue the beleaguered sons of the Akhaians
from the clamour of the Trojans. For you yourself there
250   will be grief hereafter, and there will be no means of finding
a cure once harm has been done. But long before that
consider how you will ward off the evil day from the
Danaans.

"Good sir, your father gave you instructions on that day
when he sent you from Phthie to Agamemnon: 'My child,
255   Athene and Here will give you strength, if they are so
willing, but do you keep your proud heart in check within
your breast – for good feelings between friends are better –
and cease from strife which brings evil, so that young and
old alike of the Argives will honour you the more.' These
were the old man's instructions, but you forget them. But
260   cease even now, and relinquish the anger that grieves men's
hearts. Agamemnon is offering you full recompense if you
give up your anger. Come, hear me, and I will spell out to
you all the gifts that Agamemnon has promised to you in the
tents –

265   "Seven tripods untouched by fire, ten talents of gold, twenty
sparkling cauldrons, and twelve strong champion horses
who have won prizes in the races. The man who had so
much would not be short of booty nor without priceless

οὐδέ κεν ἀκτήμων ἐριτίμοιο χρυσοῖο,
ὅσσ' Ἀγαμέμνονος ἵπποι ἀέθλια ποσσὶν ἄροντο.
δώσει δ' ἑπτὰ γυναῖκας ἀμύμονα ἔργα ἰδυίας   270
Λεσβίδας, ἃς ὅτε Λέσβον ἐϋκτιμένην ἕλες αὐτὸς
ἐξέλεθ', αἳ τότε κάλλει ἐνίκων φῦλα γυναικῶν.
τὰς μέν τοι δώσει, μετὰ δ' ἔσσεται ἣν τότ' ἀπηύρα
κούρη Βρισῆος· ἐπὶ δὲ μέγαν ὅρκον ὀμεῖται
μή ποτε τῆς εὐνῆς ἐπιβήμεναι ἠδὲ μιγῆναι,   275
ἣ θέμις ἐστίν, ἄναξ, ἤ τ' ἀνδρῶν ἤ τε γυναικῶν.
ταῦτα μὲν αὐτίκα πάντα παρέσσεται· εἰ δέ κεν αὖτε
ἄστυ μέγα Πριάμοιο θεοὶ δώωσ' ἀλαπάξαι,
νῆα ἅλις χρυσοῦ καὶ χαλκοῦ νηήσασθαι
εἰσελθών, ὅτε κεν δατεώμεθα ληΐδ' Ἀχαιοί,   280
Τρωϊάδας δὲ γυναῖκας ἐείκοσιν αὐτὸς ἑλέσθαι,
αἵ κε μετ' Ἀργείην Ἑλένην κάλλισται ἔωσιν.
εἰ δέ κεν Ἄργος ἱκοίμεθ' Ἀχαιϊκόν, οὖθαρ ἀρούρης,
γαμβρός κέν οἱ ἔοις· τίσει δέ σε ἶσον Ὀρέστῃ,
ὅς· οἱ τηλύγετος τρέφεται θαλίῃ ἔνι πολλῇ.   285
τρεῖς δέ οἱ εἰσι θύγατρες ἐνὶ μεγάρῳ εὐπήκτῳ
Χρυσόθεμις καὶ Λαοδίκη καὶ Ἰφιάνασσα,
τάων ἥν κ' ἐθέλησθα φίλην ἀνάεδνον ἄγεσθαι
πρὸς οἶκον Πηλῆος· ὁ δ' αὖτ' ἐπὶ μείλια δώσει
πολλὰ μάλ', ὅσσ' οὔ πώ τις ἑῇ ἐπέδωκε θυγατρί.   290
ἑπτὰ δέ τοι δώσει εὖ ναιόμενα πτολίεθρα
Καρδαμύλην Ἐνόπην τε καὶ Ἱρὴν ποιήεσσαν,
Φηράς τε ζαθέας ἠδ' Ἄνθειαν βαθύλειμον,
καλήν τ' Αἴπειαν καὶ Πήδασον ἀμπελόεσσαν.
πᾶσαι δ' ἐγγὺς ἁλός, νέαται Πύλου ἠμαθόεντος·   295
ἐν δ' ἄνδρες ναίουσι πολύρρηνες πολυβοῦται,
οἵ κέ σε δωτίνῃσι θεὸν ὣς τιμήσουσι
καί τοι ὑπὸ σκήπτρῳ λιπαρὰς τελέουσι θέμιστας.
ταῦτά κέ τοι τελέσειε μεταλλήξαντι χόλοιο.
εἰ δέ τοι Ἀτρείδης μὲν ἀπήχθετο κηρόθι μᾶλλον,   300
αὐτὸς καὶ τοῦ δῶρα, σὺ δ' ἄλλους περ Παναχαιοὺς

---

300. ἀπήχθετο: 2 αοr. ἀπεχθάνομαι | κηρόθι: 'in your heart' (Y.3)
301. σὺ δ': 'yet do you'; δ' apodotic, as 167, etc.

gold, so much as the prizes that the horses of Agamemnon have won in the races. And he will give seven women, excellent in their handiwork, from Lesbos, whom he picked out when you yourself took well-built Lesbos, women who then excelled all others in their beauty. These he will give to you, and among them will be the one whom he then took, the daughter of Briseus. And he will swear a mighty oath into the bargain that he has never mounted her bed or lain with her, something that is the custom, Sir, for men and women.

"All this will be yours immediately. And if the gods later grant that we sack Priam's great city, then having entered it, heap your ship high with plenty of gold and bronze, whenever we Akhaians divide up the spoil. And choose twenty Trojan women for yourself, whichever ones are the most beautiful after Argive Helen. And if we reach the fertile soil of Akhaian Argos, you will be his son-in-law, and he will honour you exactly as he honours Orestes, his beloved son, who is growing up there in great prosperity. He has three daughters in his strong palace, Khrusothemis, Laodike, and Iphianassa. Whichever of these you wish, take her as your own dear wife to the house of Peleus, without paying a bride-price. And he will add a great abundance of soothing things besides, more than any man has ever yet given to his daughter. He will give you seven well-settled cities – Kardamule, Enope, and grassy Hire, sacred Pherae and Antheia with its deep meadows, beautiful Aipeia, and Pedasos with its vineyards. All of these are close to the sea, just beyond the borders of sandy Pulos, and in them dwell men who are rich in sheep and rich in cattle, who will honour you with their gifts like a god, and will pay you rich dues under your sceptre. This he will give to you if you give up your anger.

"But if the son of Atreus is hateful to you in your heart more (than anyone else), he and his gifts, yet have pity on

τειρομένους ἐλέαιρε κατὰ στρατόν, οἵ σε θεὸν ὣς
τίσουσ'· ἦ γάρ κέ σφι μάλα μέγα κῦδος ἄροιο·
νῦν γάρ χ' Ἕκτορ' ἕλοις, ἐπεὶ ἂν μάλα τοι σχεδὸν ἔλθοι
λύσσαν ἔχων ὀλοήν, ἐπεὶ οὔ τινά φησιν ὁμοῖον   305
οἳ ἔμεναι Δαναῶν οὓς ἐνθάδε νῆες ἔνεικαν."
    Τὸν δ' ἀπαμειβόμενος προσέφη πόδας ὠκὺς Ἀχιλλεύς·
"διογενὲς Λαερτιάδη, πολυμήχαν' Ὀδυσσεῦ,
χρὴ μὲν δὴ τὸν μῦθον ἀπηλεγέως ἀποειπεῖν,
ᾗ περ δὴ φρονέω τε καὶ ὡς τετελεσμένον ἔσται,   310
ὡς μή μοι τρύζητε παρήμενοι ἄλλοθεν ἄλλος.
ἐχθρὸς γάρ μοι κεῖνος ὁμῶς Ἀΐδαο πύλῃσιν
ὅς χ' ἕτερον μὲν κεύθῃ ἐνὶ φρεσίν, ἄλλο δὲ εἴπῃ.
αὐτὰρ ἐγὼν ἐρέω ὥς μοι δοκεῖ εἶναι ἄριστα·
οὔτ' ἔμεγ' Ἀτρείδην Ἀγαμέμνονα πεισέμεν οἴω   315
οὔτ' ἄλλους Δαναούς, ἐπεὶ οὐκ ἄρα τις χάρις ἦεν
μάρνασθαι δηΐοισιν ἐπ' ἀνδράσι νωλεμὲς αἰεί.
ἴση μοῖρα μένοντι καὶ εἰ μάλα τις πολεμίζοι·
ἐν δὲ ἰῇ τιμῇ ἠμὲν κακὸς ἠδὲ καὶ ἐσθλός·
κάτθαν' ὁμῶς ὅ τ' ἀεργὸς ἀνὴρ ὅ τε πολλὰ ἐοργώς.   320
οὐδέ τί μοι περίκειται, ἐπεὶ πάθον ἄλγεα θυμῷ
αἰεὶ ἐμὴν ψυχὴν παραβαλλόμενος πολεμίζειν,
ὡς δ' ὄρνις ἀπτῆσι νεοσσοῖσι προφέρῃσι
μάστακ' ἐπεί κε λάβῃσι, κακῶς δ' ἄρα οἱ πέλει αὐτῇ,
ὡς καὶ ἐγὼ πολλὰς μὲν ἀΰπνους νύκτας ἴαυον,   325
ἤματα δ' αἱματόεντα διέπρησσον πολεμίζων

---

303. σφι: 'in their eyes' | ἄροιο: 2 s. 2 aor. optat. ἄρνυμαι
304. ἕλοις, ἔλθοι: 2 aor. optat., 2 s. act. αἱρέω, 3 s. ἔρχομαι
306. οἳ: 'to him', accented because referring to Hektor, who is the subject of the verb of this clause
(H.2) | ἔνεικαν: 3 pl. aor. act. φέρω
311. ἄλλοθεν ἄλλος: 'one on one side, and one on another'; with pl. verb
312. ὁμῶς: adv. from ὁμοῖος; 'similarly to'; so 320, etc.
313. ἕτερον μὲν .. ἄλλο δὲ: 'one thing .. another thing / something else'
316. ἄρα: 'so it seems', with imperf., where Eng. uses pres.
317. νωλεμὲς: neut. adj. for adv. (Y.7)
320. κάτθαν' = κατέθανε, 2 aor. καταθνήσκω; gnomic aor. (Q.1) | ἐοργώς: perf. part. act. ἔρδω
323. προφέρῃσι: subjunc. is common in similes (though πέλει, 324, is indic.)
324. ἐπεί κε: 'whenever' | λάβῃσι: 3 s. 2 aor. subjunc. act. λαμβάνω (L.9) | κακῶς πέλει: 'it
goes badly'; so κακῶς ἦν, 551

all the other Akhaians in the army in their distress, and they
will honour you like a god; for you would indeed win very
great glory in their eyes.   For now you could destroy
305   Hektor, since he in his deadly madness would come up very
close to you, as he believes that there is no one equal to him
among the Danaans whom the ships have brought here."

Akhilleus, swift of foot, spoke to him in reply –

"Child of a god and son of Laertes, resourceful
310   Odusseus, I must be forthright in declaring my words, how
I think and how things will be accomplished, so that you,
sitting by my side, do not croak away at me one after the
other. For that man is as hateful to me as the doors of Hell
who conceals one thing in his heart and says something
different. But I shall speak as seems to me best.

315   "I do not think that Agamemnon the son of Atreus will
persuade me, nor the other Danaans either, since there are
no thanks, so it seems, in fighting on relentlessly day after
day against the enemy. There is (just) the same share to the
man who stays at home and if one fights very hard.
320   Coward and hero stand in equal honour.   The man who
does nothing and the man who does much both alike die.
And there is no advantage at all to me when I have suffered
pains in my heart, forever risking my life in battle. But as a
bird brings morsels, whenever she gets them, to her
325   unfledged chicks, but for herself things go badly, just so I
have spent many nights in sleeplessness, and I have spent

ἀνδράσι μαρνάμενος ὀάρων ἕνεκα σφετεράων.
δώδεκα δὴ σὺν νηυσὶ πόλεις ἀλάπαξ᾽ ἀνθρώπων,
πεζὸς δ᾽ ἕνδεκά φημι κατὰ Τροίην ἐρίβωλον·
τάων ἐκ πασέων κειμήλια πολλὰ καὶ ἐσθλὰ   330
ἐξελόμην, καὶ πάντα φέρων Ἀγαμέμνονι δόσκον
Ἀτρείδῃ· ὁ δ᾽ ὄπισθε μένων παρὰ νηυσὶ θοῇσι
δεξάμενος διὰ παῦρα δασάσκετο, πολλὰ δ᾽ ἔχεσκεν.
ἄλλα δ᾽ ἀριστήεσσι δίδου γέρα καὶ βασιλεῦσι·
τοῖσι μὲν ἔμπεδα κεῖται, ἐμεῦ δ᾽ ἀπὸ μούνου Ἀχαιῶν   335
εἵλετ᾽, ἔχει δ᾽ ἄλοχον θυμαρέα· τῇ παριαύων
τερπέσθω. τί δὲ δεῖ πολεμιζέμεναι Τρώεσσιν
Ἀργείους; τί δὲ λαὸν ἀνήγαγεν ἐνθάδ᾽ ἀγείρας
Ἀτρείδης; ἦ οὐχ Ἑλένης ἕνεκ᾽ ἠϋκόμοιο;
ἦ μοῦνοι φιλέουσ᾽ ἀλόχους μερόπων ἀνθρώπων   340
Ἀτρεΐδαι; ἐπεὶ ὅς τις ἀνὴρ ἀγαθὸς καὶ ἐχέφρων
τὴν αὑτοῦ φιλέει καὶ κήδεται, ὡς καὶ ἐγὼ τὴν
ἐκ θυμοῦ φίλεον, δουρικτητήν περ ἐοῦσαν.
νῦν δ᾽ ἐπεὶ ἐκ χειρῶν γέρας εἵλετο καί μ᾽ ἀπάτησε
μή μευ πειράτω εὖ εἰδότος· οὐδέ με πείσει.   345
ἀλλ᾽, Ὀδυσεῦ, σὺν σοί τε καὶ ἄλλοισιν βασιλεῦσι
φραζέσθω νήεσσιν ἀλεξέμεναι δήϊον πῦρ.
ἦ μὲν δὴ μάλα πολλὰ πονήσατο νόσφιν ἐμεῖο,
καὶ δὴ τεῖχος ἔδειμε, καὶ ἤλασε τάφρον ἐπ᾽ αὐτῷ
εὐρεῖαν μεγάλην, ἐν δὲ σκόλοπας κατέπηξεν·   350
ἀλλ᾽ οὐδ᾽ ὧς δύναται σθένος Ἕκτορος ἀνδροφόνοιο
ἴσχειν· ὄφρα δ᾽ ἐγὼ μετ᾽ Ἀχαιοῖσιν πολέμιζον

---

329. πεζὸς δ᾽: supply ἀλαπάξαι from the previous line
330. πασέων: gen. pl. f. πᾶς (B.2)
331. δόσκον: frequentative (S) form from δίδωμι; so διὰ .. δασάσκετο, ἔχεσκεν, from διαδατέομαι, ἔχω, 333
337. τερπέσθω: 3 s. pres. imperat. mid. and pass. τέρπω (X.2)
341. ἐπεὶ: 'for' | ὅς τις: supply 'is'
345. εἰδότος: gen. s. m. part. οἶδα, with μευ; 'as I know him well'
348. ἐμεῖο: gen. 1 s. personal pronoun (H.1)
349. ἔδειμε, ἤλασε: aor. act. δέμω, ἐλαύνω
350. κατέπηξεν: aor. act. καταπήγνυμι

bloody days in fighting, battling with men for the sake of their wives. I have sacked twelve cities of men with my ships, and on foot I claim to have sacked (another) eleven around fertile Troy. From all of these I took many fine treasures, and I used to bring them all to Agamemnon the son of Atreus and give them to him. But he, staying behind by the swift ships and receiving them, divided them out in small portions, and kept most of them (for himself). The other prizes he gave to the lords and the chieftains, and they stayed safe with them; but from me alone of the Akhaians he has taken away (my prize), and he keeps the bride who is my heart's love. Let him lie with her and enjoy himself. Why must the Argives fight with the Trojans? Why did the son of Atreus gather the host and lead them here? Was it not for the sake of the fair-haired Helen? Do the sons of Atreus alone among men love their wives? No! – Any good, sensible man loves his wife and cares for her, just as I loved this girl with all my heart, even though she was won by the spear. But now, since he has taken my prize from my hands and cheated me, let him not try me out – for I know him well. He will not persuade me.

"But, Odusseus, let him consider with you and with the other chieftains how to keep the consuming fire from the ships. He has certainly worked very hard in my absence – he has built a wall, and added a ditch to it, a broad and wide one, and fixed stakes in it. But not even like that can he check the strength of the murderous Hektor. While I was fighting with the Akhaians, Hektor was not prepared to

οὐκ ἐθέλεσκε μάχην ἀπὸ τείχεος ὀρνύμεν Ἕκτωρ,
ἀλλ' ὅσον ἐς Σκαιάς τε πύλας καὶ φηγὸν ἵκανεν·
ἔνθα ποτ' οἷον ἔμιμνε, μόγις δέ μευ ἔκφυγεν ὁρμήν.   355
νῦν δ' ἐπεὶ οὐκ ἐθέλω πολεμιζέμεν Ἕκτορι δίῳ,
αὔριον ἱρὰ Διὶ ῥέξας καὶ πᾶσι θεοῖσι,
νηήσας εὖ νῆας, ἐπὴν ἅλαδε προερύσσω,
ὄψεαι, αἴ κ' ἐθέλησθα καὶ αἴ κέν τοι τὰ μεμήλῃ,
ἦρι μάλ' Ἑλλήσποντον ἐπ' ἰχθυόεντα πλεούσας   360
νῆας ἐμάς, ἐν δ' ἄνδρας ἐρεσσέμεναι μεμαῶτας·
εἰ δέ κεν εὐπλοίην δώῃ κλυτὸς ἐννοσίγαιος,
ἤματί κε τριτάτῳ Φθίην ἐρίβωλον ἱκοίμην.
ἔστι δέ μοι μάλα πολλά, τὰ κάλλιπον ἐνθάδε ἔρρων·
ἄλλον δ' ἐνθένδε χρυσὸν καὶ χαλκὸν ἐρυθρὸν   365
ἠδὲ γυναῖκας ἐϋζώνους πολιόν τε σίδηρον
ἄξομαι, ἄσσ' ἔλαχόν γε· γέρας δέ μοι, ὅς περ ἔδωκεν,
αὖτις ἐφυβρίζων ἕλετο κρείων Ἀγαμέμνων
Ἀτρεΐδης· τῷ πάντ' ἀγορευέμεν ὡς ἐπιτέλλω
ἀμφαδόν, ὄφρα καὶ ἄλλοι ἐπισκύζωνται Ἀχαιοὶ   370
εἴ τινά που Δαναῶν ἔτι ἔλπεται ἐξαπατήσειν,
αἰὲν ἀναιδείην ἐπιειμένος· οὐδ' ἂν ἔμοιγε
τετλαίη κύνεός περ ἐὼν εἰς ὦπα ἰδέσθαι·
οὐδέ τί οἱ βουλὰς συμφράσσομαι, οὐδὲ μὲν ἔργον·
ἐκ γὰρ δή μ' ἀπάτησε καὶ ἤλιτεν· οὐδ' ἂν ἔτ' αὖτις   375
ἐξαπάφοιτ' ἐπέεσσιν· ἅλις δέ οἱ· ἀλλὰ ἔκηλος

---

354. ὅσον: 'as much as (and no more)' – 'only as far as'

355. οἷον: supply ἐμέ

359. ὄψεαι: 2 s. fut. mid. ὁράω (L.1). The subject changes in mid-sentence, and 'you will see' here leaves ῥέξας and νηήσας, both referring to Akhilleus, hanging in mid-air ! μεμήλῃ: 3 s. subjunc. μέλω, perf. in form, pres. in meaning

361. μεμαῶτας: acc. pl. m. μεμαώς, part. from a form of μέμονα; so 532, etc., and indic., μέμαμεν, 641

364. κάλλιπον = κατέλιπον, 2 aor. act. καταλείπω (N.1)

367. ἄσσ': n. pl. ὅστις | ὅς περ: 'even though he' (Z)

372. ἐπιειμένος: perf. part. mid. and pass. ἐπιέννυμι

373. τετλαίη: perf. (for pres.) optat. τλάω

374. ἔργον: like βουλάς, but quite inappropriately at a literal level, governed by συμφράσσομαι – a *zeugma*

375. ἤλιτεν: 2 aor. act. ἀλιταίνω

376. ἐξαπάφοιτ': 3 s. 2 aor. optat. mid. ἐξαπαφίσκω | ἐπέεσσιν: dat. pl. ἔπος (D.8) | ἅλις δέ οἱ: supply ἐστί; 'it (i.e. the trickery that he's perpetrated already) is (quite) enough for him'

make battle away from the wall, but he came (only) as far as
355   the Skaian gate and the oak-tree. There he did once face me
alone, and only with difficulty did he escape my onrush.
But as I do not now want to fight the godlike Hektor,
tomorrow, having sacrificed to Zeus and all the gods, and
having loaded my ships well, when I draw them to the sea,
you will see, if you care to, and if that is of concern to you,
360   my ships sailing out very early in the morning over the
Hellespont that teems with fish, and in them the men eager
to row.   And if the famous Earthshaker grants a good
voyage, I shall reach fertile Phthie on the third day. I have
plenty of possessions there, which I left behind when I
365   made my way here. And from here I shall take other gold,
and red bronze, and beautifully girdled women, and grey
iron, all that I have been assigned as my portion. But as for
my special prize, the man who gave it, lord Agamemnon,
the son of Atreus – he has insultingly taken it. Tell him
370   everything as I command you, openly, so that the rest of the
Akhaians may also feel indignant, if he is still perhaps
hoping to cheat one of the Danaans, clothed in
shamelessness as he always is. But, cur though he is, he
would not dare to look me in the face. I will not join with
375   him in any counsel, nor in any action. For he has cheated
me and wronged me. But he will cheat me with his words

ἐρρέτω· ἐκ γάρ εὖ φρένας εἵλετο μητίετα Ζεύς.
ἐχθρὰ δέ μοι τοῦ δῶρα, τίω δέ μιν ἐν καρὸς αἴσῃ.
οὐδ' εἴ μοι δεκάκις τε καὶ εἰκοσάκις τόσα δοίη
ὅσσα τέ οἱ νῦν ἔστι, καὶ εἴ ποθεν ἄλλα γένοιτο,	380
οὐδ' ὅσ' ἐς Ὀρχομενὸν ποτινίσεται, οὐδ' ὅσα Θήβας
Αἰγυπτίας, ὅθι πλεῖστα δόμοις ἐν κτήματα κεῖται,
αἵ θ' ἑκατόμπυλοί εἰσι, διηκόσιοι δ' ἀν' ἑκάστας
ἀνέρες ἐξοιχνεῦσι σὺν ἵπποισιν καὶ ὄχεσφιν·
οὐδ' εἴ μοι τόσα δοίη ὅσα ψάμαθός τε κόνις τε,	385
οὐδέ κεν ὥς ἔτι θυμὸν ἐμὸν πείσει' Ἀγαμέμνων,
πρίν γ' ἀπὸ πᾶσαν ἐμοὶ δόμεναι θυμαλγέα λώβην.
κούρην δ' οὐ γαμέω Ἀγαμέμνονος Ἀτρεΐδαο,
οὐδ' εἰ χρυσείῃ Ἀφροδίτῃ κάλλος ἐρίζοι,
ἔργα δ' Ἀθηναίῃ γλαυκώπιδι ἰσοφαρίζοι·	390
οὐδέ μιν ὥς γαμέω· ὁ δ' Ἀχαιῶν ἄλλον ἑλέσθω,
ὅς τις οἷ τ' ἐπέοικε καὶ ὃς βασιλεύτερός ἐστιν.
ἢν γὰρ δή με σαῶσι θεοὶ καὶ οἴκαδ' ἵκωμαι,
Πηλεύς θήν μοι ἔπειτα γυναῖκά γε μάσσεται αὐτός.
πολλαὶ Ἀχαιΐδες εἰσὶν ἀν' Ἑλλάδα τε Φθίην τε	395
κοῦραι ἀριστήων, οἵ τε πτολίεθρα ῥύονται.
τάων ἥν κ' ἐθέλωμι φίλην ποιήσομ' ἄκοιτιν.
ἔνθα δέ μοι μάλα πολλὸν ἐπέσσυτο θυμὸς ἀγήνωρ
γήμαντα μνηστὴν ἄλοχον, ἐϊκυῖαν ἄκοιτιν,
κτήμασι τέρπεσθαι τὰ γέρων ἐκτήσατο Πηλεύς·	400
οὐ γὰρ ἐμοὶ ψυχῆς ἀντάξιον οὐδ' ὅσα φασὶν

---

377. εὖ: gen. 3 s. pronoun (H.2)
378. ἐν καρὸς αἴσῃ: an obscure expression. καρός does not occur elsewhere; αἴσῃ literally, 'portion' (cf. 608). But clearly equivalent to 'not one scrap'
381. ποτινίσεται: ποτι- = προσ- (Y.9)
382. Αἰγυπτίας : -ίας scanned as one syllable only
383. ἑκάστας: supply πύλας, '200 to each gate'; Hom. does not use the s. πύλη, so that the pl. must sometimes be translated as s.
384. ὄχεσφιν: for dat. pl. ὄχος (E)
388. γαμέω: fut. act., as 391 (O.1)
389–90. κάλλος, ἔργα: accs. of respect (G.1e); '*in* her beauty, deeds'
392. ὅς τις: 'someone who'
394. μάσσεται: fut. μαίομαι
397. ἐθέλωμι: lengthened form of pres. subjunc. act. ἐθέλω; so ἵκωμι, 414 (L.6)
399. γήμαντα: acc. s. m. aor. part. act. γαμέω

no more. He has done enough. But let him please himself and go to Hell. For Zeus the counsellor has robbed him of his wits.

"I hate his gifts, and I have not a scrap of respect for
380 him. Not even if he gave me ten or twenty times what he now has, and if there were other things from elsewhere, not even everything that comes into Orkhomenos, and into Thebes, Egyptian Thebes, where many, many possessions lie in the houses, and it has one hundred gates, and two hundred men go forth through each of them with their
385 horses and chariots, not even if he gave me as many gifts as there are grains of sand and specks of dust – not even thus would Agamemnon now turn my mind, before he pays me back in full for the dishonour that grieves my heart. I shall not marry a daughter of Agamemnon the son of Atreus, not
390 even if she rivalled golden Aphrodite in her beauty and equalled bright-eyed Athene in her accomplishments. Not even so will I marry her. Let him choose another of the Akhaians, someone who is suitable for him, and more royal.

"If the gods save me and I reach home, then for sure
395 Peleus himself will search out a wife for me. There are many Akhaian women in Hellas and Phthie, daughters of noblemen who protect cities, and whichever of these I want I shall make my own wife. My proud heart over and over again urges me to take a wife in marriage there, a fitting
400 partner, and to enjoy the possessions which the aged Peleus has gained. For to me it is not as valuable as life, not even

Ἴλιον ἐκτῆσθαι, εὖ ναιόμενον πτολίεθρον,
τὸ πρὶν ἐπ' εἰρήνης, πρὶν ἐλθεῖν υἷας 'Αχαιῶν,
οὐδ' ὅσα λάϊνος οὐδὸς ἀφήτορος ἐντὸς ἐέργει
Φοίβου 'Απόλλωνος Πυθοῖ ἔνι πετρηέσσῃ.　　　　　　405
ληϊστοὶ μὲν γάρ τε βόες καὶ ἴφια μῆλα,
κτητοὶ δὲ τρίποδές τε καὶ ἵππων ξανθὰ κάρηνα,
ἀνδρὸς δὲ ψυχὴ πάλιν ἐλθεῖν οὔτε λεϊστὴ
οὔθ' ἑλετή, ἐπεὶ ἄρ κεν ἀμείψεται ἕρκος ὀδόντων.
μήτηρ γάρ τέ μέ φησι θεὰ Θέτις ἀργυρόπεζα　　　　410
διχθαδίας κῆρας φερέμεν θανάτοιο τέλοσδε.
εἰ μέν κ' αὖθι μένων Τρώων πόλιν ἀμφιμάχωμαι,
ὤλετο μέν μοι νόστος, ἀτὰρ κλέος ἄφθιτον ἔσται·
εἰ δέ κεν οἴκαδ' ἵκωμι φίλην ἐς πατρίδα γαῖαν,
ὤλετό μοι κλέος ἐσθλόν, ἐπὶ δηρὸν δέ μοι αἰὼν　　　415
ἔσσεται, οὐδέ κέ μ' ὦκα τέλος θανάτοιο κιχείη.
καὶ δ' ἂν τοῖς ἄλλοισιν ἐγὼ παραμυθησαίμην
οἴκαδ' ἀποπλείειν, ἐπεὶ οὐκέτι δήετε τέκμωρ
Ἰλίου αἰπεινῆς· μάλα γάρ ἔθεν εὐρύοπα Ζεὺς
χεῖρα ἑὴν ὑπερέσχε, τεθαρσήκασι δὲ λαοί.　　　　420
ἀλλ' ὑμεῖς μὲν ἰόντες ἀριστήεσσιν 'Αχαιῶν
ἀγγελίην ἀπόφασθε ‒ τὸ γὰρ γέρας ἐστὶ γερόντων ‒
ὄφρ' ἄλλην φράζωνται ἐνὶ φρεσὶ μῆτιν ἀμείνω,
ἥ κέ σφιν νῆάς τε σαῷ καὶ λαὸν 'Αχαιῶν
νηυσὶν ἔπι γλαφυρῇς, ἐπεὶ οὔ σφισιν ἥδε γ' ἑτοίμη　　425

---

402. ἐκτῆσθαι: perf. infin. κτάομαι, with imperf. meaning; 'they say that Ilion used to possess'
404. ἐέργει = εἴργει
405. Πυθοῖ: dat. Πυθώ
408. ἐλθεῖν: consecutive infin.; 'so that it may come back'
409. ἀμείψεται: aor. subjunc. mid. ἀμείβω, (L.10)
414. ἵκωμι: the short first syllable here is quite irregular
416. κιχείη: 3 s. 2 aor. optat. κιγχάνω
418. ἀποπλείειν: pres. infin. act. ἀποπλέω | δήετε: pres. with fut. sense, as 685
419. Ἰλίου: the following αἰπεινῆς shows that it is here f., 'Ilios'; but often n., 'Ilion' – though it is sometimes impossible to tell | ἔθεν: gen. of 3 s. personal pronoun (H.2); gen. with ὑπερέσχε
420. ὑπερέσχε: 3 s. 2 aor. act. ὑπερέχω
422. ἀπόφασθε: aor. imperat. mid.
423. ἀμείνω: acc. s. f. ἀμείνων
424. ἥ κε .. σαῷ: 'whatever one may save'; σαῷ 3 s. pres. subjunc. act. σαόω
425. ἥδε: i.e. the μῆτις of 423

all that men say that the well-founded city of Ilion used to possess before, in the time of peace, before the sons of the Akhaians arrived, not even all that the stone entrance of the Archer God, Phoibos Apollo, guards within, in rocky Putho. Cattle and fine sheep can be rustled, tripods and tawny horses can be acquired. But a man's life cannot be rustled or acquired so that it comes back again, when once it crosses the barrier of the teeth. For my mother, the silver-footed goddess Thetis, says that two different fates are bringing me to death's end. If, staying here, I fight around the city of the Trojans, my return home is lost, but my glory will be everlasting. But if I go home to my dear native land, my good fame is lost, but a long life will remain for me, and death's end will not come upon me quickly.

"And I would advise the others too to sail off home, since you will not now reach your goal in steep Ilios. For the far-seeing Zeus has extended his hand firmly over it, and its people are confident. But you, going on your way, declare a message to the chiefs of the Akhaians – for that is the privilege of elders – so that they may think out in their minds another, better, plan which may save their ships and the host of the Akhaians by their hollow ships, since this one

ἣν νῦν ἐφράσσαντο ἐμεῦ ἀπομηνίσαντος·
Φοῖνιξ δ' αὖθι παρ' ἄμμι μένων κατακοιμηθήτω,
ὄφρα μοι ἐν νήεσσι φίλην ἐς πατρίδ' ἕπηται
αὔριον ἢν ἐθέλησιν· ἀνάγκῃ δ' οὔ τί μιν ἄξω."

   'Ὡς ἔφαθ', οἱ δ' ἄρα πάντες ἀκὴν ἐγένοντο σιωπῇ   430
μῦθον ἀγασσάμενοι· μάλα γὰρ κρατερῶς ἀπέειπεν·
ὀψὲ δὲ δὴ μετέειπε γέρων ἱππηλάτα Φοῖνιξ
δάκρυ' ἀναπρήσας· περὶ γὰρ δίε νηυσὶν Ἀχαιῶν·
"εἰ μὲν δὴ νόστον γε μετὰ φρεσί, φαίδιμ' Ἀχιλλεῦ,
βάλλεαι, οὐδέ τι πάμπαν ἀμύνειν νηυσὶ θοῇσι   435
πῦρ ἐθέλεις ἀΐδηλον, ἐπεὶ χόλος ἔμπεσε θυμῷ,
πῶς ἂν ἔπειτ' ἀπὸ σεῖο, φίλον τέκος, αὖθι λιποίμην
οἶος; σοὶ δέ μ' ἔπεμπε γέρων ἱππηλάτα Πηλεὺς
ἤματι τῷ ὅτε σ' ἐκ Φθίης Ἀγαμέμνονι πέμπε
νήπιον, οὔ πω εἰδόθ' ὁμοιΐου πολέμοιο   440
οὐδ' ἀγορέων, ἵνα τ' ἄνδρες ἀριπρεπέες τελέθουσι.
τοὔνεκά με προέηκε διδασκέμεναι τάδε πάντα,
μύθων τε ῥητῆρ' ἔμεναι πρηκτῆρά τε ἔργων.
ὡς ἂν ἔπειτ' ἀπὸ σεῖο, φίλον τέκος, οὐκ ἐθέλοιμι
λείπεσθ', οὐδ' εἰ κέν μοι ὑποσταίη θεὸς αὐτὸς   445
γῆρας ἀποξύσας θήσειν νέον ἡβώοντα,
οἷον ὅτε πρῶτον λίπον Ἑλλάδα καλλιγύναικα
φεύγων νείκεα πατρὸς Ἀμύντορος Ὀρμενίδαο,
ὅς μοι παλλακίδος περιχώσατο καλλικόμοιο,
τὴν αὐτὸς φιλέεσκεν, ἀτιμάζεσκε δ' ἄκοιτιν,   450
μητέρ' ἐμήν· ἣ δ' αἰὲν ἐμὲ λισσέσκετο γούνων

---

427. ἄμμι = ἡμῖν (H.1) | κατακοιμηθήτω: 3 s. aor. imperat. pass. κατακοιμάω
433. ἀναπρήσας: aor. part. act. ἀναπρήθω | περί: 'for' | δίε: 2 aor. act. δείδω
437. λιποίμην: 2 aor. optat. mid. λείπω, here with pass. sense
440. εἰδόθ' = εἰδότα: acc. s. m. part. of οἶδα | ὁμοιΐου: meaning obscure; perhaps 'the same for all'
442. προέηκε: 3 s. aor. act. προΐημι; so ἐπιπροέηκεν, 520 | διδασκέμεναι: purpose, 'to teach', with σε to be supplied as object
445. ὑποσταίη: 2 aor. optat. act. ὑφίστημι; 2 aor. indic. at 519
446. ἡβώοντα: acc. s. m. pres. part. act. ἡβάω, – ωο – for – ω – (O.2b)
447. οἷον: 'such as I was', attracted into the case of νέον
449. παλλακίδος: '*for* his mistress' (G.2c)
451. γούνων: understand something like 'clasping me by'

is no good for them, the one they have thought out now, when I have been consumed with anger. But let Phoinix stay here with us and lie down, so that he may follow me in the ships to our dear homeland tomorrow, if he wants to. But I will not compel him to."

430   So he spoke, and they all fell silent, stunned by his speech – for he had spoken very forcefully. But at last Phoinix, the aged driver of horses, addressed him, his tears bursting forth; for he feared for the ships of the Akhaians –

435   "If indeed, glorious Akhilleus, you are contemplating in your mind your return home, and you have no wish at all to ward off the consuming fire from the swift ships, since anger has fallen on your heart, then how, dear child, could I be left here apart from you, alone? The aged driver of horses Peleus was sending me as a companion to you on the

440   day when he sent you from Phthie to Agamemnon as a little child who did not yet know of war which is the same for both sides, nor of assemblies, where men become distinguished. For this reason he sent me forth to teach all these things, for you to be both a speaker of words and a

445   doer of deeds. So then, dear child, I should not want to be left apart from you, not even if the god himself promised to me that he would strip away my old age and make me a vigorous young man, such as I was when I first left Hellas with its beautiful women, fleeing away from the reproaches of my father Amuntor, the son of Ormenos.

"He was very angry with me over his mistress with the

450   beautiful hair, whom he was loving, and dishonouring his wife, my mother. And she was always entreating me,

παλλακίδι προμιγῆναι, ἵν' ἐχθήρειε γέροντα.
τῇ πιθόμην καὶ ἔρεξα· πατὴρ δ' ἐμὸς αὐτίκ' ὀϊσθεὶς
πολλὰ κατηρᾶτο, στυγερὰς δ' ἐπεκέκλετ' Ἐρινῦς,
μή ποτε γούνασιν οἷσιν ἐφέσσεσθαι φίλον υἱὸν   455
ἐξ ἐμέθεν γεγαῶτα· θεοὶ δ' ἐτέλειον ἐπαράς,
Ζεύς τε καταχθόνιος καὶ ἐπαινὴ Περσεφόνεια.
[τὸν μὲν ἐγὼ βούλευσα κατακτάμεν ὀξέϊ χαλκῷ·
ἀλλά τις ἀθανάτων παῦσεν χόλον, ὅς ῥ' ἐνὶ θυμῷ
δήμου θῆκε φάτιν καὶ ὀνείδεα πόλλ' ἀνθρώπων,   460
ὡς μὴ πατροφόνος μετ' Ἀχαιοῖσιν καλεοίμην.]
ἔνθ' ἐμοὶ οὐκέτι πάμπαν ἐρητύετ' ἐν φρεσὶ θυμὸς
πατρὸς χωομένοιο κατὰ μέγαρα στρωφᾶσθαι.
ἦ μὲν πολλὰ ἔται καὶ ἀνεψιοὶ ἀμφὶς ἐόντες
αὐτοῦ λισσόμενοι κατερήτυον ἐν μεγάροισι,   465
πολλὰ δὲ ἴφια μῆλα καὶ εἰλίποδας ἕλικας βοῦς
ἔσφαζον, πολλοὶ δὲ σύες θαλέθοντες ἀλοιφῇ
εὑόμενοι τανύοντο διὰ φλογὸς Ἡφαίστοιο,
πολλὸν δ' ἐκ κεράμων μέθυ πίνετο τοῖο γέροντος.
εἰνάνυχες δέ μοι ἀμφ' αὐτῷ παρὰ νύκτας ἴαυον·   470
οἱ μὲν ἀμειβόμενοι φυλακὰς ἔχον, οὐδέ ποτ' ἔσβη
πῦρ, ἕτερον μὲν ὑπ' αἰθούσῃ εὐερκέος αὐλῆς,
ἄλλο δ' ἐνὶ προδόμῳ, πρόσθεν θαλάμοιο θυράων.
ἀλλ' ὅτε δὴ δεκάτη μοι ἐπήλυθε νὺξ ἐρεβεννή,
καὶ τότ' ἐγὼ θαλάμοιο θύρας πυκινῶς ἀραρυίας   475
ῥήξας ἐξῆλθον, καὶ ὑπέρθορον ἑρκίον αὐλῆς
ῥεῖα, λαθὼν φύλακάς τ' ἄνδρας δμῳάς τε γυναῖκας.
φεῦγον ἔπειτ' ἀπάνευθε δι' Ἑλλάδος εὐρυχόροιο,

---

452. ἐχθήρειε: aor. optat. act. ἐχθαίρω
453. ὀϊσθείς: aor. part., pass. in form, οἴομαι; 'suspecting'
454. ἐπεκέκλετ': reduplicated 2 aor. ἐπικέλομαι | Ἐρινῦς: acc. pl.
455. ἐφέσσεσθαι: fut. infin. mid. ἐφίζω
456. γεγαῶτα: acc. s. m. of a perf. part. of γίγνομαι
457. Ζεὺς καταχθόνιος: 'Zeus beneath the earth', i.e. Hades
468. Ἡφαίστοιο: the god of fire, hence 'fire'; so Ares for 'war', 532, etc.
471. ἔσβη: 2 aor. σβέννυμι, intrans.
475. ἀραρυίας: acc. pl. f. perf. part. act. ἀραρίσκω, intrans.
476. ῥήξας: aor. part. act. ῥήγνυμι | ὑπέρθορον: 2 aor. act. ὑπερθρῴσκω
477. λαθών: 2 aor. act. part. λανθάνω; 2 aor. indic. mid. at 537

(clasping me) by the knees, to lie with his mistress first, so
that she would hate the old man. I obeyed her, and did so.
And my father, immediately suspecting (this), called down
many curses, and invoked the hateful Erinues, that he
should never set on his knees a dear son born of me. And
the gods were fulfilling his curses, Zeus beneath the earth,
and dread Persephone. [I planned to kill him with my sharp
bronze. But one of the immortals checked my rage; he put
into my heart the talk of the people and the many reproaches
of men, so that I should not be called the murderer of my
father among the Akhaians.] Then the heart within my
breast was no longer constrained to go up and down in the
halls of my father while he was angry with me. Indeed, my
cousins and my kinsmen who were round about entreated
me time after time, and tried to keep me there in the palace.
They were slaughtering many strong sheep and oxen with
crooked horns and shambling gait, and many pigs, rich in
fat, were being stretched, singed, over the flame of the fire,
and much of the old man's wine was being drunk from jars.

"Nine nights they spent close beside me. They kept
watch in turn, and the fires never went out, one of them
beneath the colonnade of the well-walled courtyard, the
other in the porch, in front of the bedroom-doors. But
when the tenth dark night came upon me, then I, breaking
open the closely fitting doors of the bedroom, went out, and
leapt swiftly over the courtyard-wall, unobserved by the
men on guard and the maidservants. Then I fled far off

Φθίην δ' ἐξικόμην ἐριβώλακα, μητέρα μήλων,
ἐς Πηλῆα ἄναχθ'· ὁ δέ με πρόφρων ὑπέδεκτο,　　　　　480
καί μ' ἐφίλησ' ὡς εἴ τε πατὴρ ὃν παῖδα φιλήσῃ
μοῦνον τηλύγετον πολλοῖσιν ἐπὶ κτεάτεσσι,
καί μ' ἀφνειὸν ἔθηκε, πολὺν δέ μοι ὤπασε λαόν·
ναῖον δ' ἐσχατιὴν Φθίης Δολόπεσσιν ἀνάσσων.
καί σε τοσοῦτον ἔθηκα, θεοῖς ἐπιείκελ' Ἀχιλλεῦ,　　　485
ἐκ θυμοῦ φιλέων, ἐπεὶ οὐκ ἐθέλεσκες ἅμ' ἄλλῳ
οὔτ' ἐς δαῖτ' ἰέναι οὔτ' ἐν μεγάροισι πάσασθαι,
πρίν γ' ὅτε δή σ' ἐπ' ἐμοῖσιν ἐγὼ γούνεσσι καθίσσας
ὄψου τ' ἄσαιμι προταμὼν καὶ οἶνον ἐπισχών.
πολλάκι μοι κατέδευσας ἐπὶ στήθεσσι χιτῶνα　　　　490
οἴνου ἀποβλύζων ἐν νηπιέῃ ἀλεγεινῇ.
ὣς ἐπὶ σοὶ μάλα πολλὰ πάθον καὶ πολλὰ μόγησα,
τὰ φρονέων, ὅ μοι οὔ τι θεοὶ γόνον ἐξετέλειον
ἐξ ἐμεῦ· ἀλλὰ σὲ παῖδα, θεοῖς ἐπιείκελ' Ἀχιλλεῦ,
ποιεύμην, ἵνα μοί ποτ' ἀεικέα λοιγὸν ἀμύνῃς.　　　　495
ἀλλ', Ἀχιλεῦ, δάμασον θυμὸν μέγαν· οὐδέ τί σε χρὴ
νηλεὲς ἦτορ ἔχειν· στρεπτοὶ δέ τε καὶ θεοὶ αὐτοί,
τῶν περ καὶ μείζων ἀρετὴ τιμή τε βίη τε.
καὶ μὲν τοὺς θυέεσσι καὶ εὐχωλῆς ἀγανῇσι
λοιβῇ τε κνίσῃ τε παρατρωπῶσ' ἄνθρωποι　　　　　500
λισσόμενοι, ὅτε κέν τις ὑπερβήῃ καὶ ἁμάρτῃ.
καὶ γάρ τε λιταί εἰσι Διὸς κοῦραι μεγάλοιο,

---

480. ἄναχθ' = ἄνακτα ǀ ὑπέδεκτο: 2 aor. ὑποδέχομαι

482. ἐπὶ: 'as the heir to' ǀ κτεάτεσσι: dat. pl. κτέαρ (D.8)

485. τοσοῦτον: 'as great as you are now'

487. πάσασθαι: aor. infin. πατέομαι

488. πρίν γ' ὅτε: 'until the time when', as 588 ǀ καθίσσας: aor. part. act. καθίζω (Q.3)

489. προταμὼν, ἐπισχών: 2 aor. act. part. προτέμνω, ἐπέχω

491. οἴνου: partitive gen.; 'some of the wine'

493. τὰ .. ὅ : 'this, namely that' (I.3)

495. ποιεύμην = ἐποιούμην, imperf. mid. ποιέομαι ǀ ἀμύνῃς: subjunc., although the main verb is imperf.; 'that you might defend, and may do so still'

496. δάμασον: 2 s. aor. imperat. act. δαμάζω

498. τῶν περ: 'even though their' (Z)

501. ὑπερβήῃ, ἁμάρτῃ: aor. subjunc. ὑπερβαίνω, ἁμαρτάνω; 'whenever someone *has* overstepped and transgressed'

through the wide spaces of Hellas, and I reached fertile
480 Phthie, the mother of flocks, and lord Peleus. He received
me graciously, and loved me as a father loves his son, an
only child who is especially cherished, the heir to many
possessions. He made me rich, and the lord over many
people, and I was living on the border of Phthie, ruling over
485 the Dolopes. And I made you as great (as you now are),
Akhilleus like to the gods, loving you from the heart, since
you did not want to go to the banquet with anyone else, nor
to feast in the palace, before I, setting you on my knees,
filled you with food, cutting the first slice for you and
490 putting wine to your lips. Many times you wetted the shirt
on my chest, dribbling out some of the wine in your childish
helplessness. Thus I suffered much and laboured much
over you, thinking on this, that the gods would not bring to
birth any child of mine. But you, Akhilleus like to the gods,
495 I was making my child, so that you may one day save me
from shameful ruin.

"But, Akhilleus, tame your mighty passion. It is not at
all right that you should have a pitiless heart. Even the gods
themselves can be swayed, greater though their majesty and
500 honour and strength are. And yet men move them by
sacrifices and humble prayers and libations and burnt
offerings, entreating them when someone has stepped too
far and transgressed.

"For there are Apologies, daughters of great Zeus, lame

χωλαί τε ῥυσαί τε παραβλῶπές τ᾿ ὀφθαλμώ,
αἵ ῥά τε καὶ μετόπισθ᾿ ἄτης ἀλέγουσι κιοῦσαι.
ἡ δ᾿ ἄτη σθεναρή τε καὶ ἀρτίπος, οὕνεκα πάσας   505
πολλὸν ὑπεκπροθέει, φθάνει δέ τε πᾶσαν ἐπ᾿ αἶαν
βλάπτουσ᾿ ἀνθρώπους· αἱ δ᾿ ἐξακέονται ὀπίσσω.
ὃς μέν τ᾿ αἰδέσεται κούρας Διὸς ἆσσον ἰούσας,
τὸν δὲ μέγ᾿ ὤνησαν καί τ᾿ ἔκλυον εὐχομένοιο·
ὃς δέ κ᾿ ἀνήνηται καί τε στερεῶς ἀποείπῃ,   510
λίσσονται δ᾿ ἄρα ταί γε Δία Κρονίωνα κιοῦσαι
τῷ ἄτην ἅμ᾿ ἕπεσθαι, ἵνα βλαφθεὶς ἀποτίσῃ.
ἀλλ᾿, Ἀχιλεῦ, πόρε καὶ σὺ Διὸς κούρῃσιν ἕπεσθαι
τιμήν, ἥ τ᾿ ἄλλων περ ἐπιγνάμπτει νόον ἐσθλῶν.
εἰ μὲν γὰρ μὴ δῶρα φέροι τὰ δ᾿ ὄπισθ᾿ ὀνομάζοι   515
Ἀτρεΐδης, ἀλλ᾿ αἰὲν ἐπιζαφελῶς χαλεπαίνοι,
οὐκ ἂν ἔγωγέ σε μῆνιν ἀπορρίψαντα κελοίμην
Ἀργείοισιν ἀμυνέμεναι χατέουσί περ ἔμπης·
νῦν δ᾿ ἅμα τ᾿ αὐτίκα πολλὰ διδοῖ τὰ δ᾿ ὄπισθεν ὑπέστη,
ἄνδρας δὲ λίσσεσθαι ἐπιπροέηκεν ἀρίστους   520
κρινάμενος κατὰ λαὸν Ἀχαιϊκόν, οἵ τε σοὶ αὐτῷ
φίλτατοι Ἀργείων· τῶν μὴ σύ γε μῦθον ἐλέγξῃς
μηδὲ πόδας· πρὶν δ᾿ οὔ τι νεμεσσητὸν κεχολῶσθαι.
οὕτω καὶ τῶν πρόσθεν ἐπευθόμεθα κλέα ἀνδρῶν
ἡρώων, ὅτε κέν τιν᾿ ἐπιζάφελος χόλος ἵκοι·   525

---

503. ὀφθαλμώ: dual acc. (C.4), acc. of respect (G.1e); 'squinting as to their eyes', i.e. 'squint-eyed'

504. ἀλέγουσι κιοῦσαι: 'make it their business to go'

505. οὕνεκα: 'for which reason'

506. φθάνει: first syllable scanned long in Hom.

508. μέν: balanced by the δέ of 510 | αἰδέσεται: aor. subjunc. αἰδέομαι (L.10)

509. δὲ: *apodotic*, i.e. not to be translated; so 511 | ὤνησαν, ἔκλυον: gnomic aorists (Q.1), from ὀνίνημι, κλύω

510. ἀνήνηται: aor. subjunc. ἀναίνομαι

512. ἀποτίσῃ: aor. subjunc. act. ἀποτίνω

513. πόρε: imperat. from a 2 aor. ἔπορον, which occurs at 667; 'do you furnish honour, so that it may follow'

515. τὰ δ᾿ ὄπισθ᾿: 'and others to come'; so 519

523. πόδας: literally, 'feet', so here 'journey' | κεχολῶσθαι: perf. infin. mid. and pass. χολόω; perf. part. at 566

524. ἐπευθόμεθα: from πεύθομαι, a form of πυνθάνομαι

and wrinkled and squint-eyed, who make it their business to
go behind Ruin. Ruin is strong, and sure-footed, and she
therefore far outstrips all the Apologies, and she first does
harm to men over all the earth. But the Apologies bring
healing in her wake. Whoever respects the daughters of
Zeus as they come near, him they help greatly, and listen to
him as he prays. But whenever someone rejects them and
stubbornly denies them, then they go to Zeus the son of
Kronos and entreat him that Ruin should follow that man,
that he may be injured and so make full requital. But do you
too, Akhilleus, provide that honour shall attend the
daughters of Zeus, honour which bends the minds of men,
even of the great ones. For if the son of Atreus were not
bringing gifts, and naming others that are to come, but was
forever raging terribly, I should not be asking you to cast
aside your anger and help the Argives, even though they are
in need. But now he is offering many gifts straightaway,
and has promised others to come later, and he has sent forth
the best men to entreat you, choosing them from the
Akhaian host, the men who are the dearest of the Argives to
yourself. Do not scorn their words, or their journey –
though previously there was no fault at all to be found in
your anger.

"Even so have we heard of the famous deeds of the
heroes of previous times, whenever mighty rage came upon

δωρητοί τε πέλοντο παράρρητοί τ' ἐπέεσσι.
μέμνημαι τόδε ἔργον ἐγὼ πάλαι, οὔ τι νέον γε,
ὡς ἦν· ἐν δ' ὑμῖν ἐρέω πάντεσσι φίλοισι.
Κουρῆτές τ' ἐμάχοντο καὶ Αἰτωλοὶ μενεχάρμαι
ἀμφὶ πόλιν Καλυδῶνα καὶ ἀλλήλους ἐνάριζον,   530
Αἰτωλοὶ μὲν ἀμυνόμενοι Καλυδῶνος ἐραννῆς,
Κουρῆτες δὲ διαπραθέειν μεμαῶτες Ἄρηϊ.
καὶ γὰρ τοῖσι κακὸν χρυσόθρονος Ἄρτεμις ὦρσε,
χωσαμένη ὅ οἱ οὔ τι θαλύσια γουνῷ ἀλωῆς
Οἰνεὺς ῥέξ'· ἄλλοι δὲ θεοὶ δαίνυνθ' ἑκατόμβας,   535
οἴη δ' οὐκ ἔρρεξε Διὸς κούρῃ μεγάλοιο.
ἢ λάθετ' ἢ οὐκ ἐνόησεν· ἀάσατο δὲ μέγα θυμῷ.
ἡ δὲ χολωσαμένη δῖον γένος ἰοχέαιρα
ὦρσεν ἔπι χλούνην σῦν ἄγριον ἀργιόδοντα,
ὃς κακὰ πόλλ' ἔρδεσκεν ἔθων Οἰνῆος ἀλωήν·   540
πολλὰ δ' ὅ γε προθέλυμνα χαμαὶ βάλε δένδρεα μακρὰ
αὐτῇσιν ῥίζῃσι καὶ αὐτοῖς ἄνθεσι μήλων.
τὸν δ' υἱὸς Οἰνῆος ἀπέκτεινεν Μελέαγρος
πολλέων ἐκ πολίων θηρήτορας ἄνδρας ἀγείρας
καὶ κύνας· οὐ μὲν γάρ κε δάμη παύροισι βροτοῖσι·   545
τόσσος ἔην, πολλοὺς δὲ πυρῆς ἐπέβησ' ἀλεγεινῆς.
ἡ δ' ἀμφ' αὐτῷ θῆκε πολὺν κέλαδον καὶ ἀϋτὴν
ἀμφὶ συὸς κεφαλῇ καὶ δέρματι λαχνήεντι,
Κουρήτων τε μεσηγὺ καὶ Αἰτωλῶν μεγαθύμων.
ὄφρα μὲν οὖν Μελέαγρος ἀρηΐφιλος πολέμιζε,   550

---

531. Καλυδῶνος: gen. after ἀμυνόμενοι; 'warding off danger *from*'

532. διαπραθέειν: 2 aor. infin. διαπέρθω

534. ὅ: 'because' (I.3) | γουνῷ ἀλωῆς: meaning uncertain; γουνῷ perhaps connected with γόνυ, 'knee', and so 'rising ground'

535. δαίνυνθ' = ἐδαίνυντο; 3 pl. imperf. mid. δαίνυμι

537. ἢ οὐκ: scanned as a single syllable by synizesis (Scansion, B.5b)

538. δῖον γένος: in apposition to ἡ

539. ὦρσεν ἔπι = ἐπῶρσεν (R) | χλούνην: meaning quite uncertain

540. ἔθων: part. of ἔθω; 'being accustomed to', so 'in his usual way'

545. δάμη: 3 s. aor. pass. δαμάζω

546. ἐπέβησ': 1 s. aor. act. ἐπιβαίνω, transitive

547. ἡ: Artemis

550. μὲν: balanced by ἀλλ', 553; the δὲ of 551 is apodotic (see on 509)

one of them – they were open to gifts, and could be persuaded by words. I remember how this action of old was, – it's certainly nothing new – and I will tell it among you all, who are my friends.

"The Kouretes and the Aitolians, stout in the battle, were
530   fighting around the city of Kaludon, and killing one another, the Aitolians defending lovely Kaludon, and the Kouretes furious to sack it in war. For Artemis of the golden throne
535   had driven evil on them, enraged that Oineus had not offered to her the first fruits from the high ground in his garden. The other gods were feasting on hecatombs, and only to the daughter of great Zeus had he made no offering. Either he forgot, or he did not think of her; but he made a dreadful mistake in his heart. But she, the daughter of Zeus and shooter of arrows, enraged, sent against him a fierce wild
540   boar, foaming at the mouth, and with white tusks, which in its usual way wrought havoc time and time again on Oineus' orchard. It uprooted many tall trees and hurled them to the ground, roots and ripe fruit and all. Meleagros, the son of
545   Oineus, killed it, having gathered huntsmen and hounds from many cities, for it would not have been overcome by just a handful of men – it was so enormous, and had brought many men to the sorrowful funeral-pyre. But Artemis aroused much din and shouting of battle over it, over the head of the boar and its shaggy hide, between the Kouretes and the stout-hearted Aitolians.

550   "As long as Meleagros, the favourite of Ares, was

τόφρα δὲ Κουρήτεσσι κακῶς ἦν, οὐδὲ δύναντο
τείχεος ἔκτοσθεν μίμνειν πολέες περ ἐόντες·
ἀλλ' ὅτε δὴ Μελέαγρον ἔδυ χόλος, ὅς τε καὶ ἄλλων
οἰδάνει ἐν στήθεσσι νόον πύκα περ φρονεόντων,
ἤτοι ὁ μητρὶ φίλῃ 'Αλθαίῃ χωόμενος κῆρ   555
κεῖτο παρὰ μνηστῇ ἀλόχῳ καλῇ Κλεοπάτρῃ
κούρῃ Μαρπήσσης καλλισφύρου Εὐηνίνης
"Ιδεώ θ', ὃς κάρτιστος ἐπιχθονίων γένετ' ἀνδρῶν
τῶν τότε· καί ῥα ἄνακτος ἐναντίον εἵλετο τόξον
Φοίβου 'Απόλλωνος καλλισφύρου εἵνεκα νύμφης,   560
τὴν δὲ τότ' ἐν μεγάροισι πατὴρ καὶ πότνια μήτηρ
'Αλκυόνην καλέεσκον ἐπώνυμον, οὕνεκ' ἄρ' αὐτῆς
μήτηρ ἀλκυόνος πολυπενθέος οἶτον ἔχουσα
κλαῖεν ὅ μιν ἐκάεργος ἀνήρπασε Φοῖβος 'Απόλλων·
τῇ ὅ γε παρκατέλεκτο χόλον θυμαλγέα πέσσων   565
ἐξ ἀρέων μητρὸς κεχολωμένος, ἥ ῥα θεοῖσι .
πόλλ' ἀχέουσ' ἠρᾶτο κασιγνήτοιο φόνοιο,
πολλὰ δὲ καὶ γαῖαν πολυφόρβην χερσὶν ἀλοία
κικλήσκουσ' 'Αΐδην καὶ ἐπαινὴν Περσεφόνειαν
πρόχνυ καθεζομένη, δεύοντο δὲ δάκρυσι κόλποι,   570
παιδὶ δόμεν θάνατον· τῆς δ' ἠεροφοῖτις Ἐρινὺς
ἔκλυεν ἐξ Ἐρέβεσφιν ἀμείλιχον ἦτορ ἔχουσα.
τῶν δὲ τάχ' ἀμφὶ πύλας ὅμαδος καὶ δοῦπος ὀρώρει
πύργων βαλλομένων· τὸν δὲ λίσσοντο γέροντες
Αἰτωλῶν, πέμπον δὲ θεῶν ἱερῆας ἀρίστους,   575
ἐξελθεῖν καὶ ἀμῦναι ὑποσχόμενοι μέγα δῶρον·
ὁππόθι πιότατον πεδίον Καλυδῶνος ἐραννῆς,

---

555. κῆρ: acc. of seat of the emotions (G.1c); 'in his heart'
557. Εὐηνίνης: 'daughter of Euenos'
558. "Ιδεω: gen. s. (B.6); with –εω scanned as one syllable only (Scansion, B.5b)
559. ἐναντίον: preposition, governing ἄνακτος
561. τὴν: Kleopatre
565. παρκατέλεκτο: aor. παρακαταλέχομαι; so 664, and κατέλεκτο, 662
567. φόνοιο: causal gen.; 'because of the killing'
572. Ἐρέβεσφιν: for gen. s. (E)
573. τῶν: the Kouretes | ὀρώρει: plupf. act. ὄρνυμι, here intrans; perf. subjunc. at 610
577. ὁππόθι: supply 'was'

fighting, so long things went badly for the Kouretes, and for all their numbers they were unable to make a stand outside the wall. But when anger came upon Meleagros, anger which swells the heart in the breast of other men too,

555   even men of excellent sense, then he, angry in his heart with his own mother Althaie, lay beside his wedded wife, the beautiful Kleopatre, the daughter of Marpesse of the beautiful ankles. She was the daughter of Euenos and of Idas, who was the strongest of earthly men of that time – he

560   even took his bow against the lord Phoibos Apollo for the sake of his bride of the beautiful ankles. (Kleopatre's) father and royal mother used to call her in their house by the name of Alkuone, because·her mother, sharing the fate of the mournful kingfisher, was weeping that Phoibos Apollo who works from afar had snatched her away.

" – Meleagros lay beside Kleopatre, brooding over the

565   anger which grieved his heart, enraged by the curses of his mother. She was making many prayers to the gods in her grief over the death of her brother, and was striking the bountiful earth many times with her hands, calling on Hades and dread Persephone as she crouched on her knees,

570   wetting her lap with her tears, that they should bring death to her son. And the Erinus that walks in darkness, and has an implacable heart, heard her from Erebos. Soon the din and crash of the Kouretes arose around the gates as the towers were being battered. The elders of the Aitolians

575   were imploring Meleagros, and sending the best priests of the gods, that he should come forth and help, promising him a great gift. Wherever was the richest ground of lovely Kaludon, there they bade him choose for himself a very

ἔνθα μιν ἤνωγον τέμενος περικαλλὲς ἑλέσθαι
πεντηκοντόγυον, τὸ μὲν ἥμισυ οἰνοπέδοιο,
ἥμισυ δὲ ψιλὴν ἄροσιν πεδίοιο ταμέσθαι.   580
πολλὰ δέ μιν λιτάνευε γέρων ἱππηλάτα Οἰνεὺς
οὐδοῦ ἐπεμβεβαὼς ὑψηρεφέος θαλάμοιο,
σείων κολλητὰς σανίδας γουνούμενος υἱόν·
πολλὰ δὲ τόν γε κασίγνηται καὶ πότνια μήτηρ
ἐλλίσσονθ'· ὁ δὲ μᾶλλον ἀναίνετο· πολλὰ δ' ἑταῖροι,   585
οἵ οἱ κεδνότατοι καὶ φίλτατοι ἦσαν ἁπάντων·
ἀλλ' οὐδ' ὣς τοῦ θυμὸν ἐνὶ στήθεσσιν ἔπειθον,
πρίν γ' ὅτε δὴ θάλαμος πύκ' ἐβάλλετο, τοὶ δ' ἐπὶ πύργων
βαῖνον Κουρῆτες καὶ ἐνέπρηθον μέγα ἄστυ.
καὶ τότε δὴ Μελέαγρον ἐΰζωνος παράκοιτις   590
λίσσετ' ὀδυρομένη, καί οἱ κατέλεξεν ἅπαντα
κήδε', ὅσ' ἀνθρώποισι πέλει τῶν ἄστυ ἁλώῃ·
ἄνδρας μὲν κτείνουσι, πόλιν δέ τε πῦρ ἀμαθύνει,
τέκνα δέ τ' ἄλλοι ἄγουσι βαθυζώνους τε γυναῖκας.
τοῦ δ' ὠρίνετο θυμὸς ἀκούοντος κακὰ ἔργα,   595
βῆ δ' ἰέναι, χροῒ δ' ἔντε' ἐδύσετο παμφανόωντα.
ὣς ὁ μὲν Αἰτωλοῖσιν ἀπήμυνεν κακὸν ἦμαρ
εἴξας ᾧ θυμῷ· τῷ δ' οὐκέτι δῶρα τέλεσσαν
πολλά τε καὶ χαρίεντα, κακὸν δ' ἤμυνε καὶ αὔτως.
ἀλλὰ σὺ μή μοι ταῦτα νόει φρεσί, μηδέ σε δαίμων   600
ἐνταῦθα τρέψειε, φίλος· κάκιον δέ κεν εἴη
νηυσὶν καιομένῃσιν ἀμυνέμεν· ἀλλ' ἐπὶ δώροις
ἔρχεο· ἶσον γάρ σε θεῷ τίσουσιν Ἀχαιοί.
εἰ δέ κ' ἄτερ δώρων πόλεμον φθισήνορα δύῃς
οὐκέθ' ὁμῶς τιμῆς ἔσεαι πόλεμόν περ ἀλαλκών."   605
    Τὸν δ' ἀπαμειβόμενος προσέφη πόδας ὠκὺς Ἀχιλλεύς·

---

580. ταμέσθαι: 2 aor. infin. mid. τέμνω; repeat ἤνωγον with it
582. ἐπεμβεβαώς: perf. part. act. ἐπεμβαίνω
589. βαῖνον, ἐνέπρηθον: *inceptive* imperfs.; 'were beginning to'
592. ἁλώῃ: 3 's. aor. subjunc. ἁλίσκομαι
600. μοι: 'I beg you'
601. τρέψειε: 3 s. aor. optat. act. τρέπω; wish for the future (X.5) – 'may the god not turn you'
602. ἐπί: 'in response to'
605. τιμῆς = τιμήεις, 'honoured' (but at 608 and 616 it is gen. s. τιμή)

beautiful estate of fifty acres, marking off half of it from the
580 vineyards, and half from the plain as open ploughland. And
the aged driver of horses Oineus begged him many times,
standing at the threshold of his high-roofed bedroom,
shaking the closely-fitted doors, imploring his son. And his
585 sisters and royal mother entreated him many times. But he
refused all the more. And his companions (entreated him)
many times, who were the closest to him and the dearest of
all. But not even so did they persuade the heart in his
breast, before even his bedroom was being bombarded with
missiles, and the Kouretes were climbing up the towers and
590 setting fire to the great city. And then his fair-girdled wife
implored Meleagros in tears, and told him of all the sorrows
which come to men whose city has been captured – they kill
the men, fire levels the city, and others lead off the children
595 and the deep-girdled women. As he heard of these evil
deeds, his heart was stirred, and he set forth, and put the
shining armour over his body. Thus he warded off the evil
day from the Aitolians, giving way to his feelings. But they
no longer gave him the many fine gifts, and he warded off
the evil for nothing.

600 "But, I beg you, do not think these things in your mind,
and may a god not turn you in that direction, my friend. It
would be worse to defend the ships when they were ablaze.
But come in response to the gifts, for the Akhaians will
honour you equal to a god. But if you enter the war that
605 destroys men without the gifts, you will no longer be
equally honoured, even though you ward off the war."

Answering him the swift-footed Akhilleus said –

Φοῖνιξ, ἄττα γεραιὲ διοτρεφές, οὔ τί με ταύτης
χρεὼ τιμῆς· φρονέω δὲ τετιμῆσθαι Διὸς αἴσῃ,
ἥ μ' ἕξει παρὰ νηυσὶ κορωνίσιν εἰς ὅ κ' ἀϋτμὴ
ἐν στήθεσσι μένῃ καί μοι φίλα γούνατ' ὀρώρῃ.   610
ἄλλο δέ τοι ἐρέω, σὺ δ' ἐνὶ φρεσὶ βάλλεο σῇσι·
μή μοι σύγχει θυμὸν ὀδυρόμενος καὶ ἀχεύων,
Ἀτρεΐδῃ ἥρωϊ φέρων χάριν· οὐδέ τί σε χρὴ
τὸν φιλέειν, ἵνα μή μοι ἀπέχθηαι φιλέοντι.
καλόν τοι σὺν ἐμοὶ τὸν κήδειν ὅς κ' ἐμὲ κήδῃ·   615
ἶσον ἐμοὶ βασίλευε καὶ ἥμισυ μείρεο τιμῆς.
οὗτοι δ' ἀγγελέουσι, σὺ δ' αὐτόθι λέξεο μίμνων
εὐνῇ ἔνι μαλακῇ· ἅμα δ' ἠοῖ φαινομένηφι
φρασσόμεθ' ἤ κε νεώμεθ' ἐφ' ἡμέτερ' ἦ κε μένωμεν."

῍Η καὶ Πατρόκλῳ ὅ γ' ἐπ' ὀφρύσι νεῦσε σιωπῇ   620
Φοίνικι στορέσαι πυκινὸν λέχος, ὄφρα τάχιστα
ἐκ κλισίης νόστοιο μεδοίατο· τοῖσι δ' ἄρ' Αἴας
ἀντίθεος Τελαμωνιάδης μετὰ μῦθον ἔειπε·
"διογενὲς Λαερτιάδη, πολυμήχαν' Ὀδυσσεῦ,
ἴομεν· οὐ γάρ μοι δοκέει μύθοιο τελευτὴ   625
τῇδέ γ' ὁδῷ κρανέεσθαι· ἀπαγγεῖλαι δὲ τάχιστα
χρὴ μῦθον Δαναοῖσι, καὶ οὐκ ἀγαθόν περ ἐόντα,
οἵ που νῦν ἕαται ποτιδέγμενοι. αὐτὰρ Ἀχιλλεὺς
ἄγριον ἐν στήθεσσι θέτο μεγαλήτορα θυμόν,
σχέτλιος, οὐδὲ μετατρέπεται φιλότητος ἑταίρων   630

---

608. τετιμῆσθαι Διὸς αἴσῃ: 'that I have been (and am) honoured by the portion (i.e. dispensation) of Zeus'

609. μ' ἕξει: 'will remain with me'; ἕξει fut. ἔχω

611. βάλλεο = βάλλου; 2 s. pres. imperat. mid. βάλλω (L.2); so μείρεο, for 2 s. imperat. μείρομαι, 616, and λέξεο, aor. imperat. λέχομαι, 617

614. ἀπέχθηαι: 2 s. 2 aor. subjunc. ἀπεχθάνομαι (L.8)

618. ἅμα ἠοῖ φαινομένηφι: literally, 'as soon as dawn appearing'; ἠοῖ dat. s. ἠώς, φαινομένηφι for φαινομένη (E); so 682

619. φρασσόμεθ': aor. subjunc. mid. (L.10, Q.3)

620. ῍Η: 'he spoke' (V.3)

622. μεδοίατο = μέδοιντο (L.4); 3 pl. pres. optat. μέδομαι; the subject is the other ambassadors

625. ἴομεν: pres. subjunc. εἶμι (L.10, U.7)

626. κρανέεσθαι: fut. infin. mid. κραίνω (O.1), with pass. sense

628. ἕαται = ἧνται, 3 pl. pres. ἧμαι (L.4) | ποτιδέγμενοι: ποτι- for προσ-; see on 191

"Phoinix, aged father, child of a god, I have no need of this honour. I believe that I am honoured by the providence of Zeus, which will remain with me by the beaked ships as long as breath remains in my breast and my own knees uphold me. But I will tell you something else, and do you plant it in your mind. Do not confuse my heart by weeping and sorrowing, doing a favour to the hero son of Atreus. It is not right that you should love him, lest you become hateful to me, although I love you. It is a good thing for you that with me you should give pain to whoever gives pain to me. Be king equally with me, and take half of the honour as your share. These men will take the message, but you, staying here, lie on a soft bed. As soon as dawn appears, let us consider whether we are to go to our homes, or to stay here."

He spoke, and silently nodded to Patroklos with his brows to make up a thick bed for Phoinix, so that they should very quickly think of return from the tent. And to them Aias, the godlike son of Telamon, spoke a word –

"Child of a god and son of Laertes, resourceful Odusseus, let us go. For it does not seem to me that an end of words will be accomplished, at least by this journey. We must very quickly report the news back to the Danaans, even though it is not good – I imagine they are now sitting waiting for it. But Akhilleus has made savage the mighty heart in his breast – hard man that he is, and he cares

τῆς ᾗ μιν παρὰ νηυσὶν ἐτίομεν ἔξοχον ἄλλων,
νηλής· καὶ μέν τίς τε κασιγνήτοιο φονῆος
ποινὴν ἢ οὗ παιδὸς ἐδέξατο τεθνηῶτος·
καί ῥ᾽ ὁ μὲν ἐν δήμῳ μένει αὐτοῦ πόλλ᾽ ἀποτίσας,
τοῦ δέ τ᾽ ἐρητύεται κραδίη καὶ θυμὸς ἀγήνωρ   635
ποινὴν δεξαμένῳ· σοὶ δ᾽ ἄλληκτόν τε κακόν τε
θυμὸν ἐνὶ στήθεσσι θεοὶ θέσαν εἵνεκα κούρης
οἵης· νῦν δέ τοι ἑπτὰ παρίσχομεν ἔξοχ᾽ ἀρίστας,
ἄλλα τε πόλλ᾽ ἐπὶ τῇσι· σὺ δ᾽ ἵλαον ἔνθεο θυμόν,
αἴδεσσαι δὲ μέλαθρον· ὑπωρόφιοι δέ τοί εἰμεν   640
πληθύος ἐκ Δαναῶν, μέμαμεν δέ τοι ἔξοχον ἄλλων
κήδιστοί τ᾽ ἔμεναι καὶ φίλτατοι ὅσσοι Ἀχαιοί."
    Τὸν δ᾽ ἀπαμειβόμενος προσέφη πόδας ὠκὺς Ἀχιλλεύς·
"Αἶαν διογενὲς Τελαμώνιε, κοίρανε λαῶν,
πάντα τί μοι κατὰ θυμὸν ἐείσαο μυθήσασθαι·   645
ἀλλά μοι οἰδάνεται κραδίη χόλῳ ὁππότε κείνων
μνήσομαι, ὥς μ᾽ ἀσύφηλον ἐν Ἀργείοισιν ἔρεξεν
Ἀτρεΐδης ὡς εἴ τιν᾽ ἀτίμητον μετανάστην.
ἀλλ᾽ ὑμεῖς ἔρχεσθε καὶ ἀγγελίην ἀπόφασθε·
οὐ γὰρ πρὶν πολέμοιο μεδήσομαι αἱματόεντος   650
πρίν γ᾽ υἱὸν Πριάμοιο δαΐφρονος, Ἕκτορα δῖον,
Μυρμιδόνων ἐπί τε κλισίας καὶ νῆας ἱκέσθαι
κτείνοντ᾽ Ἀργείους, κατά τε σμῦξαι πυρὶ νῆας.
ἀμφὶ δέ τοι τῇ ἐμῇ κλισίῃ καὶ νηῒ μελαίνῃ
Ἕκτορα καὶ μεμαῶτα μάχης σχήσεσθαι ὀίω."   655
    Ὣς ἔφαθ᾽, οἱ δὲ ἕκαστος ἑλὼν δέπας ἀμφικύπελλον

---

631. τῆς ᾗ: 'that friendship with which'
632. φονῆος: '*from* the murderer'
633. ἐδέξατο: gnomic aorist (Q.1)
636. δεξαμένῳ: the dat. is natural with ἐρητύεται κραδίη, 'his heart ....., when he has received';
and it overrides the gen. τοῦ at the beginning of 635
638. παρίσχομεν = παρέχομεν
639–40. ἔνθεο, αἴδεσσαι: 2 s. aor. imperat. mid. ἐντίθημι (L.2), αἰδέομαι
645. ἐείσαο: 2 s. aor. εἴδομαι
647. μνήσομαι: aor. subjunc. mid. μιμνήσκω (L.10) | ἔρεξεν: with two accs.; 'did me harm'
648. ὡς εἴ: 'as though I were'; but acc. retained after μ᾽, 647

nothing for the friendship of his comrades, the friendship with which we honoured him at the ships above the others. Pitiless man! – And yet a man accepts recompense for his brother or his dead son from the murderer, who, having made much repayment, stays there among the people, and the heart and high anger of the other is checked when he has received the recompense. But for you the gods have placed in your breast an implacable and bad spirit, (just) for a single girl. We are now offering you seven outstandingly excellent girls, and many other things as well as them. Do you adopt a gracious spirit, and respect your house. We, from the host of the Danaans, are under the same roof as you, and we are eager beyond the rest to be closest and dearest to you of all the Akhaians."

Answering him the swift-footed Akhilleus said –

"Aias, child of a god and son of Telamon, ruler of people, you seemed to say everything in accordance with my feelings. But my heart swells with anger whenever I remember those things, how the son of Atreus did me insult among the Argives, as if I were a refugee with no rights. But you, go, and declare the message. For I shall not think of bloody war until the son of the wise Priam, the godlike Hektor, by killing Argives has reached the tents and ships of the Murmidons, and set the ships aflame with fire. But around my tent and black ship I think that Hektor will be stopped, eager though he is for battle."

So he spoke, and each of them took a two-handled cup,

σπείσαντες παρὰ νῆας ἴσαν πάλιν· ἦρχε δ' Ὀδυσσεύς.
Πάτροκλος δ' ἐτάροισιν ἰδὲ δμωῇσι κέλευσε
Φοίνικι στορέσαι πυκινὸν λέχος ὅττι τάχιστα.
αἱ δ' ἐπιπειθόμεναι στόρεσαν λέχος ὡς ἐκέλευσε, 660
κώεά τε ῥῆγός τε λίνοιό τε λεπτὸν ἄωτον.
ἔνθ' ὁ γέρων κατέλεκτο καὶ ἠῶ δῖαν ἔμιμνεν.
αὐτὰρ Ἀχιλλεὺς εὗδε μυχῷ κλισίης εὐπήκτου·
τῷ δ' ἄρα παρκατέλεκτο γυνή, τὴν Λεσβόθεν ἦγε,
Φόρβαντος θυγάτηρ, Διομήδη καλλιπάρῃος. 665
Πάτροκλος δ' ἐτέρωθεν ἐλέξατο· πὰρ δ' ἄρα καὶ τῷ
Ἶφις ἐΰζωνος, τήν οἱ πόρε δῖος Ἀχιλλεὺς
Σκῦρον ἑλὼν αἰπεῖαν, Ἐνυῆος πτολίεθρον.
    Οἱ δ' ὅτε δὴ κλισίῃσιν ἐν Ἀτρείδαο γένοντο,
τοὺς μὲν ἄρα χρυσέοισι κυπέλλοις υἷες Ἀχαιῶν 670
δειδέχατ' ἄλλοθεν ἄλλος ἀνασταδόν, ἔκ τ' ἐρέοντο·
πρῶτος δ' ἐξερέεινεν ἄναξ ἀνδρῶν Ἀγαμέμνων·
"εἴπ' ἄγε μ', ὦ πολύαιν' Ὀδυσεῦ, μέγα κῦδος Ἀχαιῶν,
ἦ ῥ' ἐθέλει νήεσσιν ἀλεξέμεναι δήϊον πῦρ,
ἦ ἀπέειπε, χόλος δ' ἔτ' ἔχει μεγαλήτορα θυμόν;" 675
    Τὸν δ' αὖτε προσέειπε πολύτλας δῖος Ὀδυσσεύς·
"Ἀτρείδη κύδιστε, ἄναξ ἀνδρῶν Ἀγάμεμνον,
κεῖνός γ' οὐκ ἐθέλει σβέσσαι χόλον, ἀλλ' ἔτι μᾶλλον
πιμπλάνεται μένεος, σὲ δ' ἀναίνεται ἠδὲ σὰ δῶρα.
αὐτόν σε φράζεσθαι ἐν Ἀργείοισιν ἄνωγεν 680
ὅππως κεν νῆάς τε σαῷς καὶ λαὸν Ἀχαιῶν·
αὐτὸς δ' ἠπείλησεν ἅμ' ἠοῖ φαινομένηφι
νῆας ἐϋσσέλμους ἅλαδ' ἑλκέμεν ἀμφιελίσσας.

---

657. ἴσαν: imperf. εἶμι (U.4)
671. δειδέχατ': 3 pl. (L.4), from δειδίσκομαι, 'pledged'. Cf. on 196 and 224
673. μ' = μοι
678. σβέσσαι: aor. infin. act. σβέννυμι

and making a libation, they went back past the ships, and Odusseus led the way. Patroklos ordered his companions and the maidservants to make up a thick bed for Patroklos as
660 quickly as possible. And they, obeying, made up a bed as he had ordered, with fleeces and a rug, and a fine nap of linen. Then the old man lay down, and awaited the fair Dawn. And Akhilleus slept in the corner of his well-made tent, and beside him lay a woman whom he brought from
665 Lesbos, the daughter of Phorbas, Diomede of the fair cheeks. Patroklos lay on the opposite side, and beside him the fair-girdled Iphis, whom the godlike Akhilleus gave to him after taking steep Skuros, the city of Enueus.

670 And when they were in the tents of the son of Atreus, the sons of the Akhaians, standing up, from all sides drank a welcome to them from golden cups, and questioned them. And first Agamemnon, the lord of men, asked –

"Come, tell me, much-celebrated Odusseus, great glory of the Akhaians, is he willing to keep off the consuming fire
675 from the ships, or has he refused, and does rage still possess his mighty heart?"

The much-enduring godlike Odusseus answered him –

"Most glorious son of Atreus, Agamemnon lord of men, he is not willing to quench his anger, but he is filled with
680 rage still more, and he rejects you and your gifts. He orders you to consider for yourself among the Argives how you may save the ships and the host of the Akhaians, and he threatened as soon as dawn appears to drag his well-

καὶ δ' ἂν τοῖς ἄλλοισιν ἔφη παραμυθήσασθαι
οἴκαδ' ἀποπλείειν, ἐπεὶ οὐκέτι δήετε τέκμωρ 685
Ἰλίου αἰπεινῆς· μάλα γὰρ ἔθεν εὐρύοπα Ζεὺς
χεῖρα ἑὴν ὑπερέσχε, τεθαρσήκασι δὲ λαοί.
ὣς ἔφατ'· εἰσὶ καὶ οἵδε τάδ' εἰπέμεν, οἵ μοι ἔποντο,
Αἴας καὶ κήρυκε δύω πεπνυμένω ἄμφω.
Φοῖνιξ δ' αὖθ' ὁ γέρων κατελέξατο, ὣς γὰρ ἀνώγει, 690
ὄφρα οἱ ἐν νήεσσι φίλην ἐς πατρίδ' ἔπηται
αὔριον, ἢν ἐθέλησιν· ἀνάγκῃ δ' οὔ τί μιν ἄξει."
    Ὣς ἔφαθ', οἱ δ' ἄρα πάντες ἀκὴν ἐγένοντο σιωπῇ
μῦθον ἀγασσάμενοι· μάλα γὰρ κρατερῶς ἀγόρευσε.
δὴν δ' ἄνεῳ ἦσαν τετιηότες υἷες Ἀχαιῶν· 695
ὀψὲ δὲ δὴ μετέειπε βοὴν ἀγαθὸς Διομήδης·
"Ἀτρεΐδη κύδιστε, ἄναξ ἀνδρῶν Ἀγάμεμνον,
μὴ ὄφελες λίσσεσθαι ἀμύμονα Πηλεΐωνα
μυρία δῶρα διδούς· ὁ δ' ἀγήνωρ ἐστὶ καὶ ἄλλως·
νῦν αὖ μιν πολὺ μᾶλλον ἀγηνορίῃσιν ἐνῆκας. 700
ἀλλ' ἤτοι κεῖνον μὲν ἐάσομεν ἤ κεν ἴῃσιν
ἤ κε μένῃ· τότε δ' αὖτε μαχήσεται ὁππότε κέν μιν
θυμὸς ἐνὶ στήθεσσιν ἀνώγῃ καὶ θεὸς ὄρσῃ.
ἀλλ' ἄγεθ', ὡς ἂν ἐγὼ εἴπω, πειθώμεθα πάντες·
νῦν μὲν κοιμήσασθε τεταρπόμενοι φίλον ἦτορ 705
σίτου καὶ οἴνοιο· τὸ γὰρ μένος ἐστὶ καὶ ἀλκή·
αὐτὰρ ἐπεί κε φανῇ καλὴ ῥοδοδάκτυλος Ἠώς,
καρπαλίμως πρὸ νεῶν ἐχέμεν λαόν τε καὶ ἵππους
ὀτρύνων, καὶ δ' αὐτὸς ἐνὶ πρώτοισι μάχεσθαι."

684–7. See on 417–20

688. εἰσὶ .. εἰπέμεν: 'these men are (here) to say (i.e. confirm) this'

694. μάλα .. ἀγόρευσε: The subject has sometimes been taken to be Akhilleus (cf. 431); but it seems unlikely that it is not the same as for ἔφαθ' in 693, i.e. Odusseus. Cf. VIII 28–9; and Introduction, p. 9

698. μὴ ὄφελες: 'you should not have'; ὄφελες 2 aor. ὀφείλω

701. ἐάσομεν: aor. subjunc. ἐάω (L.10) | ἴῃσιν: 3 s. subjunc. εἶμι (U.7)

705. τεταρπόμενοι: reduplicated 2 aor. mid. τέρπω | ἦτορ: acc. of part affected (G.1d)

benched ships, curved at both ends, to the sea. And he said
685 that he would advise the others too to sail home, since you
will not now reach your goal in steep Ilios. For the far-
seeing Zeus has extended his hand firmly over it, and the
people are confident. Thus he spoke, and these men who
followed me are here to confirm this, Aias and the two
690 heralds, both of them wise men. But the aged Phoinix lay
down there, for that was what he ordered, so that he could
follow him in the ships to his dear homeland tomorrow, if
he wants to. But he will not compel him to."

Thus he spoke, and they all fell silent, stunned by his
695 words; for he had spoken very strongly. For a long time the
sons of the Akhaians were despondent, and said nothing;
but at last Diomedes, good at the shout, spoke –

"Most glorious son of Atreus, Agamemnon lord of men,
you should not have entreated the excellent son of Peleus,
offering countless gifts. He is a proud man at the best of
700 times, and now you have driven him into his pride much
more. But let us leave him, either to go or to stay. Then he
will fight again, whenever his heart in his breast bids him
and the god arouses him. But come, let us all do as I say.
705 Go now to bed, having gladdened your dear hearts with
food and wine, for that is (the source of) strength and
courage. But when beautiful rosy-fingered Dawn appears,
quickly array the army and the horses in front of the ships,
urging them on, and you yourself fight among the
foremost."

Ὥς ἔφαθ', οἱ δ' ἄρα πάντες ἐπήνησαν βασιλῆες,   710
μῦθον ἀγασσάμενοι Διομήδεος ἱπποδάμοιο.
καὶ τότε δὴ σπείσαντες ἔβαν κλισίηνδε ἕκαστος,
ἔνθα δὲ κοιμήσαντο καὶ ὕπνου δῶρον ἕλοντο.

710 So he spoke, and the chieftains all approved, admiring the speech of Diomedes, the tamer of horses. And then, making a libation, each of them went to his tent, and there they lay down, and took the gift of sleep.

Commentary

BOOK VIII

1 – 52 Zeus forbids the gods to intervene further in the fighting at Troy, at which Athene protests, and he then takes up position on Mount Ide.

The *Iliad*'s first day of fighting had begun at IV 446 and lasted until VII 57, with heavy casualties on both sides, and no clear advantage to either the Akhaians or the Trojans. That was followed by two days in which the dead were collected and cremated, after which the Akhaians hurriedly built their wall and ditch. The new day that now begins is therefore the second day of fighting, and it lasts until VIII 484, by which time the Trojans have established a firm advantage, so that they can prepare for the first time to encamp outside their city.

The day begins with the extended family of the gods and goddesses gathered in council on Olumpos, and the ensuing scene is one of those which 'present intensely human divinities whose adventures are entertaining, undignified, and often comic' (Edwards 1987, 125). See Introduction, **6d**, on the relationship of this opening scene to the remainder of the book.

1–3   **Yellow-robed Dawn ... many-ridged Olumpos:** 'Yellow-robed' is a formulaic epithet (likewise 'who delights in thunderbolts' in 2) – see Introduction, 4; there is no necessary suggestion that Dawn is more, or more significantly, yellow-robed now than on other occasions. There is striking variety in Homer's descriptions of the appearance of Dawn; they 'illustrate both Homer's art of variation and his ability to use such variation for a deeper purpose' (Macleod, 45–6). Here, with successive lines beginning Ἠώς μὲν ... Ζεὺς δέ, Homer prefaces his god-scene with a brief contrasting, general, reference to what is happening on earth.

2   **made an assembly:** It is perhaps not accidental that this book begins with the leader of the gods calling an assembly, and IX with the leader of the Akhaians doing so. On the human level the ἀγορή is open to all, whereas the βουλή is for the leaders only; and so here all the gods, female no less than male, are present (28), although Athene is the only one to respond to Zeus' words.

3   **Olumpos:** Homer regularly envisages the gods as living on Mount Olumpos, the highest mountain in Greece, in the north-east of the country, on the border of Thessaly and Macedonia. But as 23–5 make clear, he does not think of Olumpos as a precise, earthbound, location.

5–9   **Listen to me ... end these actions:** Zeus makes his stern tone unmistakeably clear with his first two sentences, beginning with one imperative for his first word, and with two more at the beginnings of 8 and 9, and in each sentence making it explicit that his commands are addressed to the whole of the company. In his previous address to the gods at IV 14 he had suggested, 'Let us consider how such things shall be'; but after his rebuff then, he is in no mood for half-measures now.

7   **female god:** Zeus begins with the goddesses, no doubt because it is from Here and Athene that he most anticipates opposition. Zeus' brother Poseidon turns down Here's suggestion of defiance at 198–211, but at 351ff. Here finds a more willing accomplice in Athene.

11   **Danaans:** This is one of Homer's words for the Greeks – he does not use the classical word Ἕλληνες. His other words are Ἀργεῖοι and, much the commonest, Ἀχαιοί. The origin of 'Danaans' is not certain; it is probably connected with a mythological figure, either Danaos, the king who took refuge in Argos with his daughters the Danaids, or with Danae, the mother of Perseus.

13–26   **I shall hurl ... in mid-air:** Zeus' anger at the prospect of his will again being crossed reaches a crescendo. He regularly resorts to physical violence when he has been disobeyed. He hurled the god Hephaistos down to Lemnos (I 590–4), and at XV 18–24 he gloatingly recalls how he hung Here up with anvils tied to her feet, and then threw anyone who tried to help her down to earth.

13   **Tartaros:** Elsewhere in Greek Tartaros is synonymous with Hades. But here and at 481, the only other place where it occurs in Homer, the context makes clear that it must be an abyss below Hades.

17   **he will come .. all the gods:** For Zeus the present issue is entirely his superiority to the other gods – as he says again in his last sentence, 27. The effect of his edict on the human action appears to be of less account to him. The ensuing action does have the effect of establishing Zeus' authority. The pro-Akhaian goddesses Here and Athene are cowed into submission by him, Hektor prays to him in confidence at 526–8, and in the next book Agamemnon acknowledges that he has now been completely defeated at the hands of Zeus – IX 17–22.

22   **Zeus, the supreme master:** Zeus is so possessed now by the idea of his own authority that he refers to himself with the third, rather than the first, person.

23–26   **whenever I wanted ... be in mid-air:** Zeus seems to be guilty of some inconsistency here. Hitherto, the cord has been stretched from the sky to the earth, with Zeus tugging at it from above and the other gods from below. But now he says that he would pull up the gods with the land and sea as well, and would *then* tie the cord around Olumpos, and leave everything hanging in mid-air – as though Olumpos was somewhere midway between the earth and the sky. But it would be wrong to make too much of this; the whole picture of the tug-of-war is clearly not meant to be taken seriously.

27   **So much ... to men:** Zeus ends in appropriately resounding style. The repeated περί τ' εἰμί, and the four long syllables, εἴμ' ἀνθρώπων (giving the less common spondee in the fifth foot), make a thundering final line. One might expect that his words, and the tone in which he has expressed them, would admit of no argument – but this would very much overrate the concord that exists within the family of the gods.

28–30   **Thus he spoke ... Athene spoke:** These three lines are entirely made up of elements that appear elsewhere. See, for instance, IX 29, 430–2, and 693–4 – respectively, the Akhaians' reaction to the speech of Agamemnon, the ambassadors' reaction to the speech of Akhilleus, and the Akhaians' reaction to that speech as it has been reported to them by Odusseus. And 'the grey-eyed goddess Athene' is a recurrent phrase filling up the second half of the line where the first half has contained a verb of which Athene is the subject. See Introduction, **4**. The various phrases here are all part of the oral poet's stock-in-trade, which he has at his disposal whenever the situation in the narrative calls for them. As Lord 1960, 37, wrote of the contemporary oral poetry that he studied in the then Yugoslavia, 'Each singer has a group of formulas which form the basis of his style. These change but seldom; on them he patterns others'.

In fact 28–40 are entirely composed of lines that are found elsewhere (for the details, see Leaf on 28); and on these grounds they were athetised – that is, marked as in his opinion not properly belonging here – by Aristarkhos, who further commented that Zeus' giving way to Athene at 39–40 is inappropriate to this context. On the latter point, see Introduction, **6f**. Zeus' change of heart is certainly unexpected; but it has a clear, and perhaps intentional, parallel in the ensuing action when Zeus gives heed to the desperate prayer of Agamemnon at 245–52. On the former, Aristarkhos has been followed by some modern scholars, who may – or may not – be right in their assertions that on the other occasions where these lines appear they are more appropriate than they are here; but it is going too far to rule out the possibility that the oral poet draws on his stock of traditional material, and uses it more appropriately on one occasion, and less so on another. See Willcock 1990, 1–4.

30   **Athene:** After the god-scene in IV, we might have expected that if anyone would now challenge Zeus, it would be Here. But Zeus has shown that he is in no mood for the thoroughly confrontational approach that is Here's usual style. An appeal from his daughter has much better chances of success. **Grey-eyed** is the regular epithet of Athene; with her name, it completes the line after the caesura in the fourth foot (Introduction, **4.**).

31–33   **O father ... But nevertheless:** Athene's approach is subtle. She wants to win a concession from Zeus; and so she begins in the most fulsome terms, explicitly acknowledging the point of view that he has just expressed so forcibly. But that done she comes immediately to her point.

34   **who are to perish:** See Introduction, **6d**. Athene takes Zeus' apparently impartial decree to spell total disaster for the Akhaians; and this viewpoint is maintained throughout the book. Zeus had seen his edict entirely as a matter of his asserting his authority over the other gods; and now Athene sees it entirely in the light of its likely consequences for the Akhaians. Neither displays any concern for the long-term consequences of the war and the fate of Troy.

39–40   **take heart ... kind to you:** Zeus responds to his daughter in the most affectionate terms. He has been totally won over by her appeal, at least for the moment. The repetition of πρόφρων from 23 helps to underline the extent of his volte-face. The etymology of **Tritogeneia**, an epithet that is also used of Athene elsewhere, is not clear. There was a sea-deity Triton, and the ancient commentators suggested that the epithet was connected with him; but Athene is not otherwise associated with the sea. Chantraine, s. v. Τριτογένεια, suggests a connection with τρίτος, 'third' – Athene was third-born, or born on the third day of the month. If this is right, then the short first syllable of τρίτος has somehow become lengthened in the derivative. But these suggestions are hardly persuasive, and it is best to acknowledge our complete uncertainty.

40   **kind to you:** Not actually what Athene had asked! Zeus is anxious to make peace with his daughter, but he does not commit himself over her expectation of the imminent destruction of the Akhaians.

41–44   **gold, golden:** The horses' golden manes, and Zeus' golden clothing and whip, can scarcely be taken literally, but they suitably portray the splendour of his appearance and equipment, and are one of the means by which Homer distances the gods from mortals. The permanence of gold reflects the immortality of the gods; no human would be equipped like this.

46   **between earth and starry heaven:** A journey by air presents no problems to the horses of Zeus.

47–48   **Ide, Gargaros:** Burkert 1985, 398, n. 8, remarks, 'The real Mount Ida – Kaz Dagi (1767 metres) – is 60 kilometres from Troy and anything but impressive from there: the Weather god has brought his mountain with him as it were'. Gargaros (or Gargaron; the gender of the word is not certain) is the highest peak of Ida, the range south-east of Troy.

48   **precinct:** The *temenos* is a special piece of land, separated off from the rest, and sacred to the god. So Sarpedon to Glaukos at XII 312–3, 'Everyone looks on us as gods, and we possess a great *temenos*' – though the idea here (and at IX 578) that a *temenos* may be granted to a great warrior as a royal estate, as well as to a god, is not found later than Homer.

51–52   **He himself ... the Akhaians:** Zeus is again represented by the emphatic αὐτός, as when he began to speak at 4. But now he is in calmer mood; and his lofty survey of the human action from above marks both the significance of that action and his own superiority to it. Griffin 1982, 82, comments, 'The gods find nothing so enthralling as the spectacle of human heroism and suffering; their attention marks its importance, but equally their superiority marks its smallness in another perspective'.

53 – 129 The fighting resumes – at first inconclusively, but then Zeus weighs the scales and throws his thunderbolt, and the Akhaian leaders take to their heels. Diomedes rescues the isolated Nestor, kills Hektor's charioteer, and restores the Akhaian fortunes.

The description of the fighting begins with a long-range, general, view, with no individuals mentioned by name; but after Zeus weighs the scales, Homer uses what Edwards 1987, 86, calls 'zoom'-technique, and focusses on the individual combatants. He leaves it to the reader to conclude that the fortunes of the individual represent the fortunes of the side for which he is fighting. See Introduction, **6e**.

53–65   **The flowing-haired ... flowed with blood:** The description of the resumption of fighting is, like the previous section, largely made up of elements that are found elsewhere in the *Iliad* – 58–9 = II 809–10, and 60–65 = IV 446–51; and notice also the identical line-ending at 59 and 63. See on 28–30.

53   **The flowing-haired Akhaians:** A formulaic expression, which fills the second half of the line after the caesura following the second syllable of the third foot. 'Akhaians' attracts formulaic epithets much more frequently than Homer's other two words for the Greeks, 'Argives' and 'Danaans', do. The expression distinguishes the Greeks from peoples such as the Abantes (II 542) and the Threikes (IV 533), who apparently shave their hair. Page 1959, 245, connected the epithet with the long-haired figures that we find on some Mycenaean monuments; but it has also been observed, e.g. by Pinsent 1984, 147, that in Homer's own day aristocrats apparently wore their hair long, short hair being a mark of inferior social status.

their meal: At the end of the previous book, the Akhaians had spent most of the night in feasting; but they nevertheless take another meal now before the day's fighting begins. When the occasion demands it, a meal is taken regardless of when the participants last ate; so in IX Akhilleus feasts the ambassadors immediately on their arrival, although they had already eaten before setting forth. The δεῖπνον is the main meal of the day, without necessary reference to the time at which it is taken.

55   **in the city:** At present the Trojans are still penned within the city; but the present day's fighting will allow them for the first time to encamp outside it.

56   **fewer in number:** It is not possible to form a precise picture of the numbers of the opposing forces, and such indications as Homer gives are sometimes clearly exaggerated – e.g. 562–3, which taken literally would mean that the Trojans numbered 50,000, and IX 85. At II 129–33 Agamemnon says that the Trojans are far outnumbered by the Greeks, but that their numbers are made up by the allies who have come to help them.

58   **The whole gate:** The Greek expression is plural; but Homer does not use πύλαι in the singular, and he is probably thinking of the Trojans streaming forth from the double doors of a single gate. The main gate of Troy was the Skaian gate, and whether Homer envisaged any other gate besides this is a matter of some doubt – see Kirk 1985 on III 145.

60–65   **And when, coming ... flowed with blood:** The repeated use of enjambment in these lines helps to convey the breathlessness and confusion of the mêlée. The fighting assumes no clear pattern until the Greek leaders take to their heels at 77–8. On the methods of fighting portrayed in the *Iliad*, see Willcock 1976, Appendix B.

62   **bronze breastplates:** The equipment of the Homeric heroes is regularly of bronze (but note the 'ox-hide shields' at 61) – a faithful picture of conditions at the end of the Mycenaean age, and a clear distinction from Homer's own day. Bronze was so highly esteemed by the Mycenaeans that bronze-smiths were granted a tax rebate – Taylour, 132.

64–65   **Then there were ... flowed with blood:** The introductory general picture of battle is rounded off by two fine sonorous lines. Note the three long syllables of οἰμωγή and εὐχωλή, the recurring –ων in ἀνδρῶν, ὀλλύντων and ὀλλυμένων, the switch from active to passive in ὀλλύντων τε καὶ ὀλλυμένων, an expression that overrides the caesura that one would expect in the third foot, and the brief but effective concluding ῥέε δ' αἵματι γαῖα.

66–67   **While it was ... men were falling:** These lines recur at XI 84–5, in the following day's fighting, when battle again remains evenly poised until midday.

68   **had crossed:** The daily course of the sun follows a path across the sky, so that its arrival at the mid-point of the sky signifies midday.

69–77   then indeed the Father ... seized them all: Up until now the fighting has been inconclusive; and Zeus balances the scales to find out what course events are to take. Having found this out, he launches his lightning-flash among the Akhaians, and they in terror take to flight. But there is no suggestion at all that the weighing of the scales in itself represents any partisanship on Zeus' part; it is simply a visual representation of the moment when the ill-fortune of the Akhaians becomes inevitable.

The scales give no indication of how long the superiority of the Trojans is to last. At 470–7 Zeus gives a much more precise picture of the course that the war is to take, saying that this is θέσφατον, 'divinely decreed'. We should perhaps conclude that his uncertainty is only over the immediate course of events, and that he is in no doubt about the long-term pattern of the war.

Zeus again balances the scales at XXII 209–12, before the final stage of the duel between Akhilleus and Hektor which forms the climax of the fighting in the poem, when the scales confirm the inevitable doom of Hektor. In that passage lines 209–10 exactly repeat 69–70 here, and 212 repeats 72, except for Ἕκτορος instead of Ἀχαιῶν.

71   horse-taming: This is much the most common single epithet of the Trojans, and in the plural is used almost exclusively of them. It is especially used, as here, in the genitive, but in the singular, ἱπποδάμοιο, the Akhaian Diomedes receives it as often as the Trojan leader, Hektor.

72   down sank: The losers' fate is the heavier of the two, and so it sinks downwards. At XXII 213 it is made clear that the sinking-down of the scale portends the loser's journey to Hades. There is an appropriate air of finality about this line. The five successive dactyls are noteworthy, as also are the two clauses placed side-by-side, or *paratactically*, divided from each other by the caesura, and both beginning with the verb, and ending with the same heavy sound, –ων.

73–74   The fates of the Akhaians ... broad sky: The dual form ἐζέσθην in 74 makes it clear that there are *two* fates of the Akhaians; this is not vitiated by the plural, rather than dual, ἄερθεν, of the Trojan fates, as the plural is freely used for two, as well as more than two. But from 70 we would have assumed that there was *one* fate for each army. For this reason Aristarkhos regarded these lines as spurious. They could certainly be removed without prejudicing the sense of the passage; and it has been suspected that they were a later addition to the text, made with the intention of amplifying what is said in 72. At XXII 213, the sinking of Hektor's scale is followed by no more than 'and it went towards Hades'.

75–76   blazing flash: I.e. a flash of lightning. The meaning of the flash is unmistakeable to the Greeks.

78–79   Then neither ... servants of Ares: After its inconclusive beginning, the fighting now turns into a rout of the Akhaians, in consequence, clearly, of Zeus' weighing of the scales. From the fact that the Akhaian leaders can no longer stand their ground we are left to infer that the rout was general.

The men named here are, in the absence of Akhilleus, the leading warriors on the Greek side, along with Diomedes and Odusseus, who appear at 91–92. Idomeneus, the king of Knossos in Crete, had a brief success at the beginning of the fighting (V 43–7), and he will play a more prolonged part at XIII 361–515. Of the two Aiantes, the son of Oileus, who led the Lokrians from northern Greece, was the first major hero to be named in the so-called Catalogue of Ships, the passage in which Homer surveys the contingents, and their leaders, which make up the Akhaian force (II 527); his particular distinction is in the rapid pursuit of the enemy when they are in flight (XIV 450–2). His unrelated namesake is the son of Telamon. This Aias was the clear choice of his men for the duel with Hektor in VII which ended inconclusively, and he will be one of the three ambassadors to Akhilleus in IX.

80   **Nestor:** The aged king of Pulos, in the south-west of the Peloponnese, is one of Homer's favourite characters; and, as befits a man of his age, he excels in the giving of wise advice. He was the first to attempt to mediate in the quarrel of Agamemnon and Akhilleus in I, and although on that occasion he was unsuccessful his qualities will show to great advantage in the following book. But Diomedes' judgement at 102–4 that he is now too old for fighting is one that he has himself already expressed at VII 133ff.; both there and in his long speech to Patroklos at XI 656–803 he combines this acknowledgement of his present incapacity for fighting with fond and extended memories of his achievements in battle in the past.

Gerenian is a regular epithet of Nestor at this position in the line, i.e. from the weak caesura to the end of the fourth foot. But the meaning of the epithet is quite unclear. The ancient commentators connected it with an otherwise unknown place Gerenia (or Gerenon), at which Nestor had allegedly spent his childhood, or with γέρων, 'old man'. But both of these explanations look like no more than guesses.

See Introduction, **2** on this episode of Nestor being rescued by Diomedes, and a later, non-Homeric, episode in which Nestor is again saved in battle, this time by his son Antilokhos.

81–82   **the godlike Alexandros ... struck with an arrow:** Alexandros is another name of Paris, the son of the Trojan king Priam, who judged the contest between the goddesses for the golden apple, and who later took Helen back with him to Troy from Sparta – the action which gave rise to the Trojan war. He is regularly described, as here, as the husband of Helen. The arrow is his usual weapon, the one with which he later killed Akhilleus, as is foreshadowed at XXII 359.

87   **the traces:** This is the first indication that the horse that has been hit is the third, trace-, horse, rather than one of the two who pulled the chariot. The point of a third horse for a chariot in battle is quite obscure; such knowledge as we have of the use of the trace-horse comes from chariot-racing, and in battle a trace-horse on a war-chariot would surely have been a liability. But it is convenient for the narrative that the chariot-team should contain a third horse, which, when wounded, can be cut free without disabling the whole team. The trace-horse reappears in the fighting at XVI 152–4 and 467–75, and the latter passage is the only one apart from this when a chariot-horse is killed in battle.

These appearances of the trace-horse are one of a number of suggestions that Homer did not fully understand chariot-fighting, but is inserting into his narrative of heroic battle conditions of fighting that no longer existed in his own day. See Greenhalgh, 17. Men rarely fight from their chariots in the *Iliad*; more commonly, the chariot is a method of transport, from which they jump down when they are ready to fight. It is noticeable that most of the figures who are associated with chariots in the *Iliad* are, like Nestor, old men – although the possession of horses is still an important symbol of status, and is freely ascribed to younger men as well, notably Diomedes (see on 71).

88–90   **Hektor's swift horses ... master, Hektor:** Hektor's arrival in the battle is described through the arrival of his horses and chariot, with his own name not in the nominative, but first genitive and then accusative. Since Hektor's team do not in the event achieve their object of finishing off Nestor, there is little to be made of their arrival. θρασύν is a regular epithet of Hektor at this position in the line. The ἡνίοχος, literally, 'he who holds (ἔχω) the reins (ἡνία)', is usually, e.g. at 119, used of the driver of the chariot; but Hektor's charioteer is now Eniopeus (120), so the word here must be translated 'master' or 'warrior'.

91   **Diomedes:** Diomedes, the leader from Argos, and a particular favourite of the goddess Athene, had, in the absence of Akhilleus, emerged as the leading fighter on the Akhaian side when battle was resumed, and Book V is largely an account of his *aristeia*, in which he fights successfully not only with humans, but even with the gods Aphrodite and Ares. He was the son of Tudeus, who played a prominent part in the campaigning at Thebes in the previous generation. Diomedes continues to distinguish himself in the following day's fighting; but he is then wounded, and there is little room left for him once Akhilleus returns to the fight. As both the beginning and the end of the following book will show, his straightforward good sense and resolution also enable him to distinguish himself at the conference-table, on the basis of which he is often contrasted, by modern scholars, with Akhilleus. Taplin, 135, says of him, 'Diomedes is Achilleus without the complications, and his stature in the *Iliad* is to a large extent made possible by the vacuum left by Achilleus'.

93–96   **Child of a god ... old man:** Odusseus and Diomedes are also found working together elsewhere, e.g at XI 396ff., when Odusseus helps Diomedes after he has been wounded by Paris. But, while it is common for one hero to tax another one in the heat of the battle, this speech is nevertheless a curious one. It has no sequel in the narrative; and Diomedes' assertion that Odusseus is acting like a coward is a very serious one indeed (cf. what Diomedes says at 147–50, and Nestor's response to him, 152–6), which it is hardly possible to parallel from anywhere else in the *Iliad*. Odusseus is doing no more than what Idomeneus, Agamemnon, and the other leaders are already doing. Perhaps Diomedes has been carried away into extravagant language by the urgency of the present situation.

93   **Child ... Odusseus:** This full-line address of Odusseus appears 7 times altogether in the *Iliad* (e.g. at IX 308, the beginning of Akhilleus' speech), and 15 times in the *Odyssey*. It is a common mark of respect to address a hero as 'child of a god', but in fact Odusseus' descent from the gods is not particularly prominent on the side of either his father Laertes or his mother Antikleia.

96   **wild fellow:** I.e. Hektor. Hektor's wildness, and even madness, are common themes on the lips of his Akhaian opponents, e.g. VIII 299, IX 238, XIII 53, but there is not much confirmation for them in Homer's narrative, except when he goes berserk after breaking through to the Greek ships at XV 605ff.

97   **did not hear:** ἐσακούω does not occur elsewhere in Homer, but from what we know of the root, ἀκούω, we may be confident that the meaning here could also be 'did not listen', i.e that Odusseus chose not to hear. This would fit with the view that Diomedes has taken of Odusseus' retreat at 94–5; but that Homer is imputing rank cowardice to Odusseus, and that he does so in an episode that has no sequel, seems improbable, and hardly matches the view that he takes of Odusseus elsewhere.

Odusseus is above all the man to call on when a job needs to be done properly. He restores Khruseis to her father, the priest Khruses, at I 311, and is chosen by Athene to retrieve the situation after Agamemnon's disastrous suggestion of withdrawal at II 169; it is he who delivers Agamemnon's offer of recompense to Akhilleus in IX; and he is prominent in the eventual reconciliation between Agamemnon and Akhilleus in XIX. But he can also cut a formidable figure as a warrior, e.g. at XI 396ff., where he does debate with himself the possibility of flight, but only to reject it.

99   **on his own:** αὐτός is not often used in this sense. Homer perhaps wishes to reinforce the picture of Diomedes having been abandoned by Odusseus.

100   **son of Neleus:** I.e. Nestor. Neleus was the previous king of Pulos, and had been attacked there by Herakles, who killed all his sons except for Nestor. See XI 690ff.

102–105   **indeed ... my chariot:** ἦ μάλα δή is most emphatic, and in his first three lines Diomedes give a staccato outline of no less than five different aspects of Nestor's present predicament. But he relaxes this tone somewhat at 105, when he turns from what the situation is to what is to be done about it.

105–108   **But come ... from Aineias:** 105–7 have already been spoken by Aineias to Pandaros at V 221–3, just before his horses are captured by Sthenelos, the lieutenant of Diomedes. These horses had originally been given by Zeus to Tros, a prince of Troy, three generations ago; and Diomedes wins the chariot-race with them in the funeral-games for Patroklos at XXIII 291ff.

Aineias, the son of the goddess Aphrodite by a mortal father Ankhises, was named at II 819–21 in the Trojan Catalogue, the review of the Trojan forces which follows the Akhaian Catalogue of Ships (see on 78–79). He is related to the royal family of Troy, and is à leading, but not especially prominent, fighter on the Trojan side. Aphrodite intervenes on his behalf at V 311ff.. At XX 307–8 there is a hint of the story which was later made famous by Virgil in his *Aeneid*, of how Aineias just escaped when the Greeks sacked Troy and ultimately established himself in Italy at the place that was afterwards to become the site of Rome.

109–110   **the two of us steer:** Diomedes is not content with rescuing Nestor, but intends to launch an attack on the Trojans as well. Diomedes is a consistently resolute character. In the following book he is the first to challenge Agamemnon's counsel of despair at the beginning of the book, and at the end of it he is again the first man with practical proposals to make after the grim news that Akhilleus still refuses to fight. Diomedes' lieutenant is Sthenelos (114).

111   **my spear too rages:** Such metaphorical language is common in Homer; it is not, of course, the spear that rages, but Diomedes rages as he uses it. Similarly elsewhere, arrows and spearheads are said to proceed eagerly to their targets. The vividness of Homer's metaphors was a favourite subject of the ancient critics, beginning with Aristotle (*Poetics* 1459a6, *Rhetoric* 1405a8). See Moulton, 279–93.

113   **Nestor's horses:** The ending Νεστορέας shows that the horses are here envisaged as feminine, i.e. mares. But at 104 they are βραδέες, and so masculine, as they are also when Nestor's son Antilokhos uses them in the chariot-race at XXIII 408–9. It appears that Homer has here made some mistake. See Introduction, **6f**.

114   **Sthenelos ... Eurumedon:** Sthenelos is the second-in-command of the contingent from Argos and Diomedes' charioteer, and Eurumedon must be Nestor's. A charioteer of Agamemnon has the same name at IV 228. Eurumedon's epithet

ἀγαπήνωρ, 'manly', comes interestingly after Diomedes has just referred to him as
ἠπεδανός, 'weakling', at 104.

117   **whipped on:**   Nestor has now taken over the reins of Diomedes' chariot, while
Diomedes is presumably aiming at the oncoming chariot of Hektor.

119–129   **He missed ... in his hands:**   The description of Eniopeus' death at 119–26 is verbally
very close to that of the death of his successor, Arkheptolemos, at 311–319. The
death itself occupies less than a line in 123, but the search for his successor, and his
instalment in Hektor's chariot, occupies almost four. The course of events is too
rapid to allow Homer to linger over Eniopeus. To be the charioteer of Hektor is a
dangerous vocation. After Eniopeus and Arkheptolemos, the third charioteer,
Kebriones, succumbs at XVI 737–743 – a fine passage.

The episode of Nestor and his chariot has occupied 50 lines, a treatment that may
seem excessively generous. But the importance of the episode lies less in the story
of Nestor's difficulties and rescue, than in the reversal that this causes in the fortunes
of the battle as a whole. It begins as the Akhaian leaders are in flight (78–9); but
with his rescue of Nestor Diomedes seizes the initiative, and his success becomes
apparent through his killing of Hektor's charioteer. This leads – although 129–30 are
the only explicit indication to this effect – to a renewed onset by the Akhaian forces,
and the withdrawal of the Trojans.

*130 – 197 Zeus sends thunder and lightning and stops Diomedes in his tracks. Nestor, despite
protests from Diomedes, realises that the time has come to withdraw. Hektor exultantly
addresses first the Trojans, and then his horses.*

At 75–7 Zeus sent thunder and lightning to turn what had been an even mêlée into a rout of the
Akhaians, and now he uses the same means to check the onrush of Diomedes. Similarly at
335, after Teukros has once more restored the Akhaians' fortunes, the Trojan recovery is only
made possible by Zeus' action in arousing their spirits. The impression is maintained
throughout the book that but for the interventions of Zeus the Akhaians would have been more
than a match for the Trojans.

The bulk of the present episode is in the form of speech – 45 lines out of 68. It is from
Nestor's exchange with Diomedes and Hektor's addresses to his men and horses that we can
infer that the tide of battle is once more turning firmly in favour of the Trojans. Not until 213–
5 are we explicitly told that the Akhaians have been forced back behind their wall.

130–131   **Then there would ... in Ilion like lambs:**   The narrative is elliptical. Diomedes'
success in halting Hektor must have led to a revival of the Akhaians, which threatens
to pen the Trojans within their walls, and so to frustrate Zeus' weighing of the scales
at 69–72. Hence, 'disaster and deeds beyond control'. The comparison of the
Trojans to lambs suggests the vulnerability of the Trojans; they have little hope of
success without the intervention of Zeus.

133–134   **Thundering terribly ... Diomedes' horses:**   Zeus this time directs his thunder and
lightning at Diomedes alone; at 75–6 he had sent it on the Akhaian force generally.
But what follows makes it clear that by checking Diomedes and forcing Nestor to
withdraw he effectively halts the whole Akhaian advance.

139–156 Son of Tudeus ... in the dust: Nestor's exchange with Diomedes well illustrates the great difference in their ages. Nestor is content to accept that for the moment Zeus has turned against the Akhaians, firm in the hope that in due course he will reverse his intentions; and the prospect of withdrawal therefore presents no difficulty to him. But for Diomedes the needs of the present moment, and of his own personal standing, are all-important.

141 **glory:** For Nestor 'glory', *kudos*, is synonymous with success in battle. This view is at the heart of his counter-argument to Diomedes at 154–6: 'If you retreat from the Trojans this time, yet they will remember the number of times that you overcame them, and so will not be inclined to call into question your *kudos*'.

144 **he is ... more powerful:** Diomedes had received much the same admonition in the heat of battle at V 442–3, when Apollo reminded him, 'Never is the race of immortal gods like that of earthbound men'. But this is something which he did himself acknowledge when he addressed the Trojan Glaukos at VI 128–9 with, 'If you are one of the immortals come down from the sky, then I would not fight with the gods of the heavens'.

147–150 **But this deep sorrow ... gape open for me:** Diomedes cannot bear to lose face, even before his enemies; whatever prudence may suggest, the sense of shame makes retreat unthinkable. Other heroes advance the same argument elsewhere, e.g. Hektor to his wife Andromakhe at VI 441–3.

154 **descendants of Dardanos:** I.e. The Dardanians, who originally came from the foothills of Mount Ide. Dardanos was the first king of Troy, whose line is now represented by Aineias, not by Priam. The two lines of descent are kept separate in the Trojan Catalogue, but little, if any, distinction between them is intended here, or at 173. See Kirk 1985, on II 819–20, and Edwards 1991, on XX 215–40.

155 **great-hearted:** Epithets referring to a person's character are much more common with the Trojans than the Akhaians. By 'great-hearted', Homer wishes to show the Trojans as worthy adversaries of the Akhaians; but it is perhaps going too far to say, as Blegen, 17, does, that the epithet represents the Trojans as 'a proud, arrogant people'.

161–197 Son of Tudeus ... this very night: Hektor's three speeches grow in length as his self-confidence grows. In the next day's fighting we shall see sure signs of Hektor's dangerous tendency towards excessive self-confidence; see Edwards 1991, 61, and on XVII 194–209. But here we must allow that Hektor's exultancy has some basis in fact, that he is correct in recognising that Zeus is now on his side (175–6), and that the Akhaian rout is more extensive than 157–9 might suggest. Hektor makes his confidence clear by expressing his hopes for the future, first that he will overcome Diomedes (166), then that he will overrun the Akhaian ditch, set fire to their ships and kill the men (177–83), and thirdly that by seizing the special armour of Nestor and Diomedes he will cause the Akhaians to board their ships – i.e. to abandon their campaign and return home. The second and third of these are inconsistent with each other; and in the event it is only the overrunning of the Akhaian ditch and the setting fire to their ships that comes anywhere near fulfilment. Hektor returns to the prospect of forcing the Akhaians to return to Greece in his speech at 526–31.

161–166 Son of Tudeus ... fate to you: With colourful language, and short, incisive, phrases, Hektor insults Diomedes in very much the way that Diomedes had anticipated to

Nestor at 146–50 – although he perhaps surprisingly says nothing along the lines of, 'You are giving way before a better man'.

162   **your seat ... full cups:** Diomedes is honoured at the feast, which is a central feature of Homer's aristocratic society. See Murray 1978, 47f., with evidence chiefly from the *Odyssey*. For examples from the *Iliad*, note Agamemnon's fulsome address to Idomeneus at IV 257–64, and the important speech of Sarpedon to Glaukos at XII 310–28.

165–6   **lead off our womenfolk:** This is just what the Greeks did do after their victory, when their captives included Hektor's wife Andromakhe, queen Hekabe, and Hekabe's daughter Kassandra.

167–171   **the son of Tudeus ... in the fight:** Consistently with his character as so far represented, Diomedes still hesitates before following Nestor in flight, and even the further sign from Zeus and Nestor's withdrawal leave him unpersuaded.

169–170   **Three times ... three times:** The contrast τρὶς μέν ... τρὶς δέ is common in Homer at moments of high importance – e.g. Patroklos' attack on Troy at XVI 702–3. See Janko 1992, on XVI 702–6. But this is the only time when the expression is used of a mental act such as pondering.

171   **a sign to ... that changes sides:** It is not made clear how the thunder-claps promise victory to the Trojans; but throughout the book the humans have no difficulty in making the correct interpretation of Zeus' signs. See here Hektor at 175–6.

173   **Lukians:** The Lukians are the last of the allies of Troy to be mentioned in the Trojan Catalogue, at II 876–7 – a surprisingly short notice. Their leaders were Glaukos and Sarpedon, who play the leading parts after Hektor on the Trojan side. Lukia is in the south-west corner of Asia Minor, in the fertile valley of the river Xanthos.

177   **walls:** Hektor refers to the defensive wall which the Akhaians had built around their camp the previous day, VII 436–41, and which will figure prominently in the following day's fighting in Books XI–XV.

180–183   **And when I am ... bewildered by the smoke:** Cf. IX 241–3, where in his speech to Akhilleus Odusseus gives every sign of having heard what Hektor says here. This is of course not possible; but Homer sometimes allows his characters to 'know' items from the preceding narrative which strictly they could not have been aware of. The 'consuming fire' anticipates Hektor's cry, 'bring fire', at the height of his success at XV 718.

Hektor's words here may be compared with Zeus' prediction at 473–4. There is irony in Hektor's perceiving correctly some, but not all, of what lies ahead.

185   **Xanthos ... noble Lampos:** Like Hektor here, Akhilleus also addresses his horses at XIX 400ff. (as does Antilokhos at XXIII 402–17); both scenes give insights into the hero's frame of mind. Hektor's horses have typical names – 'Bay' (also of a horse of Akhilleus at XVI 148), 'Fleet of Foot' (of a horse of Menelaos at XXIII 295, where Aithe is the name of a horse of Agamemnon), 'Fiery', and 'Bright' (of a horse of Dawn at *Od.* XXIII 246). It is curious that Hektor should address four horses here, both in view of the following duals, as though he there has only two in mind, at 186 and 191, and also because the four-horse chariot is not otherwise found (except in chariot-racing, rather than warfare, at XI 699) in the *Iliad*. It has been suggested that originally 185 may have contained the names of only two horses, to which the further two names were added by someone afterwards, in replacement of whatever it was that had previously made up the line. But this is only speculation.

187   **Andromakhe ... Eetion:**   The sack of Thebe, south of Troy, was one of Akhilleus' exploits in the earlier years of the war, to which Agamemnon refers at IX 129–30; for the extent of Akhilleus' operations, see Hainsworth 1993, ad loc. On that occasion Andromakhe's father Eetion, and all her brothers, were killed. Hektor and his wife Andromakhe have already been seen together in the powerful scene at VI 395ff. – the only time that they meet before Hektor's death.

189   **mixed in wine:**   Aristarkhos took exception to the horses drinking wine, and accordingly athetised this line, and in this he has been followed by a number of modern scholars. This may be right; but we should bear in mind the possibility that the horses of a hero may have unexpected capacities.

191–197 But come on ... this very night: Hektor reaches a climax, not just to this speech, but to the sequence of three speeches that he began at 161. He has now so worked himself up that he wildly supposes, both that he will force the Akhaians back to Greece, and that to do so no more is necessary than to secure the special armour of Nestor and Diomedes. He follows the same lines as the narrative has done in identifying the Akhaian resistance principally with Nestor and Diomedes.

  Neither Nestor's golden shield nor the breastplate that the blacksmith-god Hephaistos made for Diomedes is heard of elsewhere; they are doubtless introduced to give special weight to Hektor's address. The **staves**, κανόνας, of Nestor's shield appear elsewhere only on the shield of Idomeneus at XIII 407, and it is uncertain whether they are hand-grips, or struts to keep the shield in shape. See Lorimer, 192–4, and Snodgrass 1964, 46, 65.

  At 197 the ships of the Akhaians are 'swift', as they commonly are, even though they are stationary on the Trojan shore.

198 – 252 Here tries to persuade Poseidon to intervene with her on the Akhaians' behalf, but Poseidon refuses, and Here will not intervene on her own. Hektor's successes continue. Agamemnon sternly reproaches his men for their feebleness, and adds a prayer to Zeus. Zeus responds with a sign to the Akhaians, and they take heart again.

The extent of the present success of the Trojans has so far been made clear only by the somewhat wild words of Hektor. But it now receives sure confirmation from both Here's protest and Poseidon's firm refusal to help; and when the scene switches from Olumpos back to Troy we find Agamemnon as gloomy as Hektor has just been exultant. But Zeus receives Agamemnon's prayer kindly – an unexpected departure from the firm resolution that he expressed at the beginning of the book, which recalls his equally surprising volte-face to Athene at 38–40.

198–199 queen Here ... to quake: Here has so far kept silence in this book; but her implacable hostility to the Trojans is already a well-established factor of the narrative, that has been made clear especially in the god-scene at the beginning of IV. Her causing her throne, and then the whole of Olumpos, to shake is one of several comical aspects of the god-scenes of this book. Olumpos again shakes, this time under the feet of Zeus, at 443.

200   **Poseidon:** He is the brother of Zeus, although, as he acknowledges at 211, he is not Zeus' equal. He is the god of the sea, and also of earthquakes – hence his epithet ἐννοσίγαιος (201), 'shaker of the earth'. His hostility to Troy, which Here reminds him of at 205, originated long ago, when Laomedon, the Trojan king, got his help in building Troy's walls, and then cheated him of his pay. See VII 452–3, XXI 441–58. But he became angry towards the Akhaians at VII 446–53, when the wall that they had built at Troy appeared to challenge the original wall built by him and Apollo.

201–202 **does not even ... being destroyed?:** Here's language is similar to that which Athene had used in her appeal to Zeus at 33–4.

203   **gifts:** These would include, as well as the sacrifice of animals, the 'first fruits' – a portion of what the worshippers had derived from agriculture, hunting and fishing, which they would bring as an offering to the god's altar. Spoils from war might also be included – Hektor promises at VII 81 to dedicate the armour of his opponent to Apollo, and Odusseus at X 459–64 hands over Dolon's cap, bow and spear to Athene. That mortals bring gifts to a god does not by any means ensure the god's favour to them; see especially Zeus and Here at IV 44–54.

Helike, Aigai: Centres of the worship of Poseidon, both in Akhaia, on the northern coast of the Peloponnese .

206   **to drive back the Trojans:** Here shows no misgivings at all at the prospect of contravening the solemn ban that Zeus issued at the beginning of the book. Her brevity shows that for her it is the natural thing to do.

211   **he is certainly much stronger:** Poseidon recognises the superiority of Zeus exactly as Zeus had declared it at the beginning of the book, and in doing so he brings the god-scene to an inconsequential end. But his own attitude has reminded us of Zeus' authority, while the attitude of Here, from whom we have not hitherto heard in this book, both recalls Athene at the opening scene, and also points the way to the more extended god-scene that begins at 350. The scene is therefore valuable in keeping the divine action of the book going.

At attitude Poseidon will not take action for the Akhaians now, he does do so at the beginning of XIII – even though Zeus' interdict is supposedly still in force there.

213   **And as much ... from the wall:** The meaning is not entirely clear. We should assume that there was a space between the wall that the Akhaians have built around their ships and the ditch outside it, and that the Akhaians have now been beaten back into this space. This has not been explained by the preceding narrative; and the difficulties that the ditch presents to both attackers and defenders in the fighting is less clear than in Books XI–XVI. 'Beyond the ships' is an unnecessary extra detail.

215   **hemmed in ... was hemming:** The run-over of εἰλομένων from the nouns with which it goes in the previous line, and the repetition, εἰλομένων εἶλει, effectively introduce the change from the general picture to the eager onrush of Hektor, as does the enjambment in two successive lines, 214 and 215.

the equal of rapid Ares: As he has been represented already in this book, Hektor may indeed seem the equal of the god of war; but elsewhere in the *Iliad* he is not the equal of the best of the Akhaian warriors. He has already had the worse of things against Aias in VII, he does poorly against both Agamemnon and Diomedes in XI, and he proves no match at all for Akhilleus when they finally confront each other in XXII.

218   **queen Here ... mind of Agamemnon:** Here does finally manage to do something to retrieve the Akhaians' situation, although this can hardly have been what was in her mind when she addressed Poseidon. It is a common feature of the *Iliad* that the deities put ideas into men's minds. Sometimes a sort of double process takes place, whereby the deity inspires an idea that the mortal was anyhow thinking of, e.g. IX 702–3, where Diomedes says of Akhilleus, 'He will fight again, whenever his heart in his breast bids him, and the god arouses him'. This is not explicitly the case here – although one might well expect that Agamemnon would think of spurring on his men on his own, without the prompting of Here.

221   **great purple cloak:** Agamemnon wishes to draw attention to himself. There is no device comparable to this elsewhere in the poem.

223–225 in the middle ... at the extreme ends: From hints elsewhere in the poem, it is possible to draw up a picture of the positions of all of the different Akhaian contingents, not just those of Akhilleus and Aias at the ends and Odusseus in the centre. See Willcock 1978, 225. In the present passage, the fact that Agamemnon is within earshot of the positions of Akhilleus and Aias is hardly to the point, as he is directing his words at his men between the ditch and the wall. And how is he to make himself both heard and seen over the wall?

228–244 Shame, Argives, ... Trojans like this: Agamemnon's speech to his men contrasts sharply with that which Hektor has just delivered at 173–83. Hektor was all exuberance and energy, confident in Zeus, in himself, and in his men. Agamemnon begins by insulting his men, and excusing himself from their boasting, and he then addresses Zeus in self-pity and self-righteousness, and seeks from him only that the Akhaian force should somehow escape from the present crisis, not that they should redeem it by their fighting prowess. We shall see the same despairing reaction to adversity on his part at the beginning of the next book. This is one of Agamemnon's few contributions to the action of this book, and it does nothing to dispel the impression of a maladroit and self-centred leader that we have already received from the previous books. But Agamemnon's prayer to Zeus does nevertheless have the desired effect.

229–230 we said ... you vainly uttered: Agamemnon begins by tactfully acknowledging his own part in the bravado on Lemnos, but he then loses no time in switching from 'we' to 'you'.

230   **Lemnos:** The island directly west of Troy, where the Akhaians had stopped on their voyage to Troy (II 722), and which was now a source of supplies to them (VII 467–8). But this feasting there is not otherwise recorded.

232   **bowls:** The κρητήρ, or κρατήρ, is the mixing-bowl, in which the wine is mixed with water before it is distributed for drinking. See Luke 1994. The idea of drinking directly from the mixing-bowl is a strange one. At *Od.* II 431 we have a line ending with the same three words as here, but there the first word, στήσαντο, 'they set up', fits better than πίνοντες does here.

235   **who will quickly ... blazing fire:** Agamemnon is no less assured of Hektor's impending success than Hektor himself had been at 177–83. And he goes on at 242–4 to pray that Hektor's hope at 196–7 that the Akhaians should board their ships again will be fulfilled.

236–238 Father Zeus ... I declare that: The emphatic beginnings to Agamemnon's first two
sentences to Zeus, ἦ ῥά τιν' and οὐ μὲν (here for μήν) δή ποτέ, show that
desperation has now replaced the contempt with which he initially addressed his
men. His tone here re-appears in the speech that he makes to his men at the
beginning of the next book.

237   **deluded ... delusion:** *Atē* is a delusion, usually sent by Zeus, that momentarily robs
a man of his judgement and causes him to behave in an uncharacteristic way, and
with disastrous results. It is an important idea in Homer, which is illuminatingly
discussed by Dodds, chap. 1. Elsewhere it is particularly used by Agamemnon of his
treatment of Akhilleus at the quarrel in I – see II 111, IX 18, XIX 86ff. This could
be the meaning here – 'If only I had not mistreated Akhilleus, the present crisis
would not have arisen'. But Agamemnon's quarrel with Akhilleus does not otherwise
appear in this book; and in view of what he next says, the *atē* here is perhaps rather
Agamemnon's former expectation that he would sack Troy and thereby gain great
kudos. At II 37, Agamemnon, after receiving the false Dream from Zeus, had
expected to take Troy that very day.

239   **came on my journey:** ἔρρω is normally used in somewhat colloquial expressions
(Richardson on XXIII 440), and it has been so used by Hektor at 164. Agamemnon
may now be regretting that he ever came to Troy – 'when I made my miserable way
here'.

242–243 at least ... at least: The repeated περ in successive lines makes clear how low
Agamemnon's spirits have sunk. Survival and escape are the most that can be prayed
for now.

245   **pouring forth a tear:** Agamemnon again weeps at IX 14, as does Phoinix at IX
433, when he has heard Akhilleus' devastating rejection of Agamemnon's offer, and
Patroklos at XVI 3 – where Akhilleus compares him to a 'poor little girl'. The heroes
are reduced to tears more easily than we might expect. Akhilleus weeps at I 349,
where one of the ancient commentators remarks, 'The heroic temperament inclines
easily to tears'. In the *Odyssey* Odusseus is in tears on his very first appearance at V
151–8.

246   **that his army ... not destroyed:** Zeus again appears to go back on his original
words, as he has already done to Athene at 39–40. At this point his apparent changes
of mind may seem arbitrary. But he makes his ultimate intentions clear at 473–6,
and again, and more fully, at XV 59–77 – the Trojans are to prosper up until the
moment that Hektor kills Patroklos (this occurs in XVI), but ultimately the Akhaians
are to prevail. So now, while he must fulfil his promise to Thetis, the disaster that
this is to cause to the Akhaians must be kept within bounds.

247   **eagle:** The eagle is the especial portent of Zeus. This is made clear again at XII 209,
where, like the Akhaians here (251), the Trojans unerringly recognise that a portent
of an eagle and a snake has come from Zeus. It is for this reason that the eagle is a
source of unique authority – τελειότατον.

249   **the most beatiful altar of Zeus:** This is presumably in the Akhaian camp, although
we do not hear of it elsewhere. The depositing of the fawn at *Zeus*' altar makes the
source of the portent doubly clear.

250   **god of all omens:** The ὀμφή is the voice of the god; at II 41 it is 'poured over'
Agamemnon as he awakes from the sleep in which he had been visited by the

deceitful Dream that had been sent to him by Zeus. πανομφαῖος is not otherwise used by Homer as an epithet of Zeus, but it is perhaps used here to contrast Zeus' speaking through the omen of the eagle and the fawn with his earlier pronouncements (75–6, 133–4) through thunder and lightning.

252   **rushed more ... fighting spirit:** The portent again has immediate effect. It is understandable that it is not Agamemnon's speech, but the omen from Zeus, that restores the Akhaians' spirits. Their revival now lasts until 335, when Zeus once more turns the tables.

253 – 334 In response to the sign from Zeus, the Akhaians revive, and first Diomedes, and then Teukros with his archery, restore their ascendancy.

The sign from Zeus is clear. This is not the time for deliberation or doubt, but Diomedes, who has been the focus of the Akhaian war-effort in the book up to now, immediately springs into action, to be followed without delay by the other Akhaian leaders. This new phase of the fighting is represented almost entirely by the *aristeia* of Teukros – an unexpected episode, both because Teukros is not otherwise a particularly prominent figure among the Akhaian warriors, and because this is the only *aristeia* in the poem which is conducted by the bow, rather than by hand-to-hand fighting.

256–260 but ... clattered over on him: Homer rapidly switches the subject back and forth from Diomedes to Agelaos, thereby indicating the speed with which the events are taking place – D. ἔλεν, A. ἔτραπεν, D. πῆξεν and ἔλασσεν, A. ἤριπε, and finally A.'s armour ἀράβησε. Agelaos, like so many of the recorded victims of the fighting, is not heard of elsewhere, but his flight and death introduces a general rout of the Trojans. But this is the sole action of Diomedes in this new phase of the fighting; once he has restored the Akhaian initiative, Homer's focus switches to the other leaders.

258   **Diomedes fixed ... between his shoulders:** Diomedes wounds Agelaos in exactly the way that he had feared that Odusseus might be wounded at 95. μεταστρεφθέντι, 'having wheeled about', indicates that Agelaos has already turned his chariot.

261–264 the sons of Atreus ... Meriones: The Akhaian warriors who now take up the fight include the four who 'did not dare to stand firm' at 78–9, to whom, as well as Diomedes, are added Agamemnon's brother Menelaos, Idomeneus' comrade Meriones, Eurupulos, and Teukros. There has already been a list of nine of the Akhaian leaders at VII 162–8, the response to Hektor's open challenge to a duel. The most interesting change in this list is the replacement of Odusseus by Teukros. Perhaps Odusseus is not present after his untimely withdrawal at 97–8. He plays no further part in this book, but he does distinguish himself in the fighting on the following day at XI 310ff.

264   **Meriones ... Enualios:** This line, with the remarkable effect of prosody in the last two words, has already appeared at II 651 and VII 166. 'Enualios' is a very old word, which Homer uses interchangeably with Ares (Burkert 1985, 43f.), so that Meriones is now being described as Hektor was at 215. Meriones inflicts gruesome wounds on his opponents at V 66–7 and XIII 567–9 and 651–2, and he is one of the more prominent of the junior officers on the Akhaian side, distinguished especially, as Kretans commonly are, for his archery.

266 **Teukros:** He is the brother of Telamonian Aias, or more strictly, half-brother, although 284 is the *Iliad*'s only mention of this. He regularly fights with the bow.

267 **shield:** Aias' huge body-shield, 'like a tower', has appeared at VII 219, and will do so again at XI 485 and XVII 128. It is quite unlike the round shield which is the normal equipment of the warriors of the *Iliad*, but it effectively contributes to the interesting picture here of Teukros now sheltering under it, and now darting forth from under it to shoot an opponent, and then scampering back under it again. Sherratt, 151, shows how the archaeological evidence makes it clear that a shield such as Aias' comes from the *early* Mycenaean period, and had fallen out of use well before any probable date for a historical Trojan war.

271 **as a child ... of his mother:** As Nilsson 1933, 276f., observed, Homer's similes commonly take us momentarily away from the heroic world and the heat of battle to peaceful scenes of everyday domestic life. We have already seen this at 131, where the representation of the Trojans as lambs is as vivid and simple as that of Teukros as a little child is here.

273 **Which then of the Trojans:** Homer does not say to whom he is addressing this question, but it must presumably be to his Muse, on whom he called at the outset of the poem (I 1, with Willcock 1978, ad loc.). The alternative explanation is that he is addressing his audience, but this seems unlikely, as the audience can hardly know more about Teukros' victims than Homer does himself; see de Jong, 49f. The Muse is the daughter of Zeus and of Memory, and is the authoritative source of Homer's information about the past, and about the actions of the gods. The address to the Muse gives importance to what is taking place; it occurs particularly commonly where, as here, Homer introduces a catalogue of victims – V 703, XI 299, XVI 692.

274–276 **Orsilokhos ... Melanippos:** Teukros, presumably using the method of attack that has just been described, shoots down eight Trojans. All are quite obscure, and have Greek-looking names (e.g. Lukophontes 'Wolf-slayer', Melanippos 'Black horse'), which occur elewhere either not at all, or only as the names of further victims. Homer has a stock of common names for the minor warriors on each side, which he draws on as the occasion requires. That the obscure Lukophontes should be 'godlike' shows that the epithet is not restricted to especially significant characters. Here both the epithet and the following patronymic for Amopaon introduce variety into the list.

278 **lord of men:** A regular description of Agamemnon. *anax* is a very old word, and was apparently originally the title of the king, whereas the *basileus* – which later became the word for 'king' – was subordinate to the *anax*. See Murray, chaps. 3 and 4, especially 37–8. *anax* is not applied exclusively among mortals to Agamemnon, nor among gods to Zeus; but its use here, and at passages such as I 7, is doubtless intended to hint at Agamemnon's superior rank.

279 **ranks:** The *phalanges* are simply the rows or lines of troops abreast. The phalanx as a specialised military formation is certainly later than Mycenaean times, and may, though the matter is a controversial one, be later than Homer.

281–291 **Teukros, dear man, ... share with you:** Agamemnon's spirits fluctuate wildly, and his mood is very different from that of his speech to the army at large at 228–44. He begins with the hope that Teukros will bring 'light' – i. e. relief – to the Greeks, but thereafter concentrates on the prospect of glory for Teukros, and so for his father, and then on the promise of material reward. Such a prospect could reasonably be expected to carry weight with the Homeric heroes. When Akhilleus in the following book renounces it, that is quite unexpected and exceptional.

281–282 Teukros, dear man, ... in case you may: Agamemnon begins with a line of five dactyls and three vocative nouns, giving his words an air of imploring urgency. In his next line, as he makes his request, he uses a solemn run of long syllables up to the main caesura of the line.

287   the aigis: The aigis is a divine piece of equipment, commonly supposed to have been a shield of goat-skin (αἴξ = 'goat'), although in classical art it is represented as more of a shawl thrown over the shoulders. But the idea of the aigis seems likely to have come originally from the human view of the dark underside of a stormcloud, and from that to have been developed into a sort of shield which the divinities wear – Willcock 1976, 198, on XVII 593–4. It is particularly associated with Athene (e.g. line 384 of this book); at V 738–742 her aigis is decorated with horrifying emblems designed to fill her enemies with terror.

289   first after me: It is in keeping with Agamemnon's character as represented elsewhere that he should think of himself first, and only secondly of his men.

290   tripod: A three-legged (τρίς, πούς) metal implement, sometimes on wheels, on which a cauldron was placed, which was then heated over the fire for cooking or to boil water. The tripod was highly esteemed as a prize; seven of them are included in Agamemnon's promised recompense to Akhilleus at IX 122, and they appear again in Priam's offer to Akhilleus at XXIV 274–7; see also *Od.* IV 128–35. In a list of prizes at the funeral-games for Patroklos at XXIII 702–5, a tripod is a higher prize than a woman.

293–299 Most glorious ... to hit: Teukros' reply to Agamemnon is brief and to the point. He is more concerned with action than with words. But at 295 he gives a timely reminder that the tide of battle is now running in favour of the Akhaians.

297   eight: ὀκτώ gains emphasis from its position at the beginning of the line and the sentence, and the emphasis is continued by the following δή. The number of Teukros' arrows exactly matches the number of his victims at 274–6.

299   this mad dog: Teukros does not name Hektor, but follows the common assumption of both the narrative and the speeches of the Akhaians that he is the centre of the Trojan war-effort. In the next book Odusseus refers to Hektor's supposed madness at 239 and 305, as does Poseidon at XIII 53, and this is an aspect of him which Hektor does much to confirm by his wild behaviour when he succeeds in breaking through to the Akhaian ships at XV 603–612. He will shortly again be likened to a dog in the simile at 338–40.

302–303 And he missed ... excellent Gorguthion: Similarly at 119–20 Diomedes missed Hektor, and hit and killed Hektor's charioteer Eniopeus; and the same thing will happen with Arkheptolemos at 309–313.

302–304 Gorguthion, the noble son ... married from Aisume: Gorguthion is not found elsewhere. Priam was reputed to have had fifty sons altogether; in the *Iliad* we learn the names of twenty-two of them, of whom eleven are killed. Priam's regular wife was Hekabe; but he is represented as polygamous, in deliberate contrast to Greek practice. See XXI 85–8, where his wives include Laothoe 'and many others'.

Aisume was said to be in Thrace, on the other side of the Dardanelles from Troy. Like the following simile, these genealogical details give a sudden and unexpected importance to Gorguthion, and his death assumes a different character from that of Teukros' eight victims at 274–5.

306–307 Like a poppy ... springtime showers: No more than the fact of their deaths was recorded of Teukros' earlier victims; but Gorguthion is enriched by this beautiful simile. It is a characteristic feature of Homer's technique to invest the death of an otherwise completely obscure character with an arrestingly touching simile; cf. IV 482–7, where the equally obscure Simoeisios is likened to a fallen poplar tree when he is killed immediately on the resumption of hostilities; and see Griffin 1976. The connection of the simile with the narrative is worth noting. We have heard only that Gorguthion has been hit when the simile tells us at 306 that the poppy-head drooped to one side; then at 308, with ὡς ἑτέρωσ' repeated from 306 – an example of ring-composition that is common in the similes – we learn that Gorguthion's head did likewise – i.e. that his wound was fatal.

309–317 And Teukros ... his companion: These lines are very largely made up of elements that have appeared already; 309–10 = 300–1, and 314–7 = 122–5. Teukros' shooting is almost mechanical; Hektor's second charioteer dies as his first had done; and Hektor's initial reaction is just the same. But the sequel is quite different. After Eniopeus' death Hektor had confined himself to finding another charioteer; now, after appointing Kebriones, he succeeds in stopping Teukros in his tracks.

311 Apollo: It is natural that Apollo should divert Teukros' shot, both because he is the god of archery, and because he consistently champions the Trojans and Hektor throughout the *Iliad.* Homer does not account for this attitude; but elsewhere we hear that it arose from Apollo's anger with Akhilleus for slaughtering Priam's son Troilos in his temple in one of the earliest episodes of the war. Does Apollo actually intervene to divert Teukros' shot (thereby contravening Zeus' edict at the beginning of the book)? Homer appears to say so. But it is possible that no more is meant than that Teukros' arrow missed its target, and that this is ascribed to Apollo's agency simply because he is the god of archery. See Willcock 1970.

318 Kebriones: He too is eventually killed at XVI 733–76, a passage which leads directly to the death of his killer Patroklos at the hands of Hektor.

321 a boulder: It is not uncommon for heroes to be wounded, but not fatally, by a stone-throw – e. g. Aineias by Diomedes at V 305–10.

323–329 He had taken out ... fell from his hand: The way in which Homeric archers took their stance was a matter of dispute in ancient times; but the picture here seems a clear one. Teukros stands sideways to his target, with the bow in his left hand; and as he draws the string past his left shoulder with his right hand, Hektor's stone hits, and presumably breaks, both his collar-bone and the string – whereupon his left wrist goes numb, and the bow falls from his hand.

333 Mekisteus, Alastor: Minor figures, although they reappear when lines 331–4 are repeated at XIII 420–3, an incident from the fighting on the day following the present one. With Teukros' withdrawal, another phase in the fighting is now over.

335 – 484 Heartened by Zeus, the Trojans recover the initiative, and drive the Akhaians back towards their ships. Here and Athene take pity on the Akhaians, and prepare to intervene on their behalf. But Zeus sends a stern message by Iris calling them off, and Here, taunted by her husband, admits defeat.

No more than 15 lines, 335–349, are necessary to show the Akhaian rout, which comes about as Hektor builds on his success in checking Teukros. This brief episode concludes the fighting in this book, and it therefore comes as something of a surprise to find the Trojans completely in the ascendant at 485ff. – such a drastic change of fortune on the battlefield might have been prepared for with a fuller description of the fighting that led to it. That the Akhaians are routed Homer makes clear enough, with φέβοντο at the end of 342 and φεύγοντες at the beginning of 344, but this hardly prepares us for the consequences that we find at 485ff.; why should this phase of the fighting be more decisive than the previous ones have been? It is necessary to see the Trojan ascendancy as arising, not only out of Hektor's success, but also out of Zeus' overruling Here and Athene in the scenes which follow. These scenes repeat the picture of wayward and warring divinities with which the book opened, but what happens on Olumpos, difficult though some of it is to take seriously, is again of the utmost importance for the action on the human level. Once Here admits defeat, the Akhaian position is indeed desperate. See Introduction, **6d**.

335   **The Olumpian:** I. e. Zeus. The deities regularly give strength to their human favourites – e.g. Athene to Diomedes at the beginning of his *aristeia* at V 1–2, where, as here, the intervention of the deity marks a new stage in the fighting. Zeus' intervention also helps to prepare for the Trojans' single success in halting Teukros leading to the full-scale rout of the Akhaians.

336   **the deep ditch:** See on 213. In the present sequence, there is no explicit mention of the Akhaian wall; but the Akhaians are clearly being driven back over the ditch and towards their camp.

337   **Hektor:** In his usual manner, Homer concentrates his scene of battle on a single figure, and allows Hektor's success to stand for the success of the whole Trojan army.

338–342 **as when ... in terror:** Teukros had described Hektor as a maddened dog at 299. But, as Coffey, 119, points out, this simile is not about Hektor's appearance; it is only in his movements that he resembles a dog.

343   **the stakes:** From XII 54–7 it appears that these stakes were not in the trench, but immediately behind it on the Akhaian side. See also VII 441, with Willcock 1978, ad loc.

348   **Hektor kept wheeling:** At 320 Hektor had dismounted from his chariot to hurl the boulder at Teukros. Presumably that success has caused him to remount, so that he can press home the advantage that the wounding of Teukros has secured.

349   **Gorgo:** Gorgo, or Medusa, was a terrifying monster in Greek mythology, her face so terrible that anyone who looked on it was turned to stone. To escape this fate, the hero Perseus was given a mirror by Athene, and with this help he killed her. This subject is a popular one in Greek art from the 7th. century onwards (Kirk 1962, 186); but in the *Iliad* the Gorgo appears elsewhere only at V 741 and XI 36, where her face is a terrifying emblem on the shields of Athene and Agamemnon.

       Ares: Hektor has already been likened to the god of war at 215, and he will be so again as he makes his assault on the Akhaian ships at XV 605.

350–437 Seeing them ... their hearts: The scenes of the goddesses' departure and return are neatly balanced – 47 lines (350–96) for the one, and 41 (397–437) for the other.

352–356 Alas, child ... deeds of evil?: Here is moved by the same pity for the Akhaians as had moved Athene to address Zeus at 31–7, with 354 identical to 34. Here does no more for the moment than sketch the present desperate situation of the Akhaians, and in doing so she adds force to the picture of the Akhaian rout that has just been given. But it is Athene who makes the explicit suggestion that she and Here should take a hand in the fighting themselves.

355   a single man: Here confirms the clear impression that this book has given so far, that the Trojan war-effort depends overwhelmingly on Hektor. He is the only Trojan to have been named in the fighting, other than the victims of Tudeus. Elsewhere, Aineias, Sarpedon and Glaukos are prominent among the individual Trojan warriors.

358–380 May he ... ships of the Akhaians: Athene's grievances against her father contrast strongly with the warmth of her exchange with him at 28–40; and the length to which she pursues them perhaps arises out of uneasiness over the proposal she makes at the end of her speech, that Here and she should now intervene, and so, though she does not say so, contravene Zeus' edict. Herakles was a son of Zeus, not by Here, but by the mortal Alkmene – hence Zeus' concern for him, and his despatch of Athene to his aid. Athene's present reference to Herakles is surprising, in that elsewhere one of the main features of Homer's representation of Herakles is Here's unremitting hostility to him – V 392–4, XIV 250–5, XV 25–30, XVIII 117–9.

358–359 May he ... native land: Athene's prophecy is fulfilled when Hektor is killed by Akhilleus in XXII, the climax of the fighting in the poem.

362–369 his son ... water of Stux: Herakles belongs to a generation previous to that of the action of the *Iliad*. It was for Eurustheus, a king of Tiryns, that, by the contrivance of Here, who was resentful of a child of Zeus by a mortal, he performed his celebrated labours; but the capture of Kerberos, the watchdog of the Underworld, is the only one of the twelve labours to be mentioned in the *Iliad*. The later tradition represents Athene as his constant supporter throughout his labours.

368   Erebos: Erebos is the subterranean darkness where the spirits of the dead live. From references in the *Odyssey* – XI 37 and 564, XX 356 – it seems to be envisaged as a sort of passageway between Earth and Hades.

368–370 hateful ... he hates: the root of στυγεροῦ is repeated in Στυγός and στυγέει in the next two lines. The Stux is the most important of the rivers of the Underworld.

370–372 Thetis ... Akhilleus: Akhilleus' mother made her appeal to Zeus at I 500–10, asking that Zeus put strength into the Trojans in return for Agamemnon's having dishonoured Akhilleus by taking Briseis from him; the Akhaians' discomfiture in the absence of Akhilleus will bring honour to him. At I 500–1, Thetis took the normal position of a suppliant as she addressed Zeus, clasping his knees with one hand while she reached for his chin with the other. That she *kissed* Zeus' knees seems to be an elaboration of Athene's.

sacker of cities: For Akhilleus' exploits in the earlier years of the war, see on 187. πτολίπορθος is an epithet which Akhilleus shares with Odusseus, of whom alone the epithet is used in the *Odyssey* (and also *Il.* II 278) – on the basis of his part in the sack of Troy.

373   **The time ... (daughter) again:** Athene is convinced that Zeus is angry with her now, no doubt on the score of the proposal that she is about to make to disobey him; but she is confident that his anger will not last for ever. Zeus has already called Athene 'dear child' at 39.

374–376 **But do you ... weapons of war:** Athene is to do the fighting, while Here acts as charioteer. These were also the roles of the two when they intervened at V 720ff., a scene that shares many elements with the forthcoming one.

375   **going into the house:** The present whereabouts of the goddesses is not clear. They had been with Zeus on Olumpos at the beginning of this book, and it would have been within their power to watch the action at Troy from there. But καταδῦσα suggests that they are now somewhere else – possibly on Mount Ide with Zeus.

378   **spaces of the battlefield:** The expression γεφύρας πτολέμοιο also occurs elsewhere, and is thought to refer to the spaces between the ranks of the combatants – though it could also be the space between the two armies. The meaning 'bridge' for γέφυρα is post-Homeric.

380   **at the ships of the Akhaians:** Athene seems to assume that the Trojans cannot now be stopped before they reach the Akhaian ships. This assumption is hardly justified by the narrative so far, or by what is to come. The Trojans spend much of the following day fighting their way through to the ships.

381–396 Thus she spoke ... through them: The scene of the goddesses' preparations and departure repeats elements that have already appeared in the similar scene in Book V. Thus, 382–3 = V 720–1; 384–8 = V 733–7; 389–96 = V 745–52; and, just as here, the scene in V has been introduced by Here's protests to Athene about the current success of the Trojans. But the earlier scene also includes the preparation of the chariot by Hebe, the goddess of youth, and much fuller details of Athene arming herself. That these are omitted here is perhaps because the present scene, in that it does not in the event lead to intervention in the fighting, is in less need of amplification. But the most important difference between the two scenes is that in V the goddesses seek, and obtain, Zeus' permission for their intervention in the human action, whereas here they act in calculated defiance of Zeus.

383   **daughter of great Kronos:** Being the daughter of Kronos, Here is the sister, as well as the wife, of Zeus.

384–391 But Athene ... is angry with: Homer juxtaposes Athene's function as goddess of handicrafts, who has made her robe herself, with the particular association that she always has with war. The exact nature of women's dress in Mycenaean and Homeric times is difficult to determine; see Lorimer, chap. VI, especially 377–391. But from representations in later art, we know that the πέπλος was a long tunic made from a single rectangle of wool which was draped around the body and held at the shoulders by long pins, while the χιτών, which could be held without pins, was a linen garment, and fell over the body in lighter, more delicate, folds. The πέπλος was worn by women only, the χιτών by men and women alike. The three adjectives at 390 for Athene's spear are used together elsewhere only of Akhilleus' special 'Pelian ash-spear'; the absence of connective words with them adds to the impressiveness of the picture, and helps to explain why Iris at 424 describes the spear as 'monstrous'. The suggestion at 390–1 that Athene regularly intervenes in war herself is scarcely borne out by the *Iliad,* where her role is much more that of inspiring the human warriors with martial spirit; see especially II 446–54 and XX 48–50 (Akhilleus' re-entry into battle). The Boiotian poet Hesiod, probably working a little later than Homer, describes Athene as 'dread rouser of the battle-strife, unwearied leader of the host, the mistress who delights in the clamorous cry of war and battle and slaughter' (*Theogony*, 925f.). She does physically help her human favourite Diomedes at V 835ff., but this is in a fight with another deity, Ares.

393–395 the gates of heaven ... to close it: The gates are formed by the clouds, so that it is natural that the Seasons should be their guardians. The Seasons reappear at 433 to take care of the horses and chariot when the goddesses' expedition has been called off. That gates formed by clouds should be capable of groaning is an imaginative touch. The precise relationship between heaven, οὐρανός, and Olumpos here is not clear; the verb, ἐπιτέτραπται, is singular, and this perhaps suggests that οὐρανός and Olumpos are being thought of as one and the same. So Burkert 1985, 126.

397 from Ide: Zeus is still in the position he took up at 51, and from there has no difficulty in seeing what is happening across the Aegean sea on Olumpos. The narrative now diverges sharply from the similar passage at V 719ff., where the goddesses, having prepared themselves, seek Zeus' permission to intervene, and receive it.

398 Iris: She is regularly the messenger of the gods throughout the *Iliad* (in the *Odyssey*, the gods' messenger is Hermes), and is the only winged deity to appear in it. Whether she has been with Zeus on Ide, or has come to him from Olumpos, Homer does not make clear. For anyone but a deity, gold would, of course, be the most unnatural material from which to make wings.

402–405 I shall lame ... thunderbolt inflicts: Zeus now enlarges on the threats that he had made to the deities at line 12, and in very much the same stern, exaggerated, tone. For Zeus, who is the god of the sky and of weather, the thunderbolt, κεραυνός, is a natural weapon (and 'cloud-gatherer', νεφεληγερέτης, a natural epithet – e.g. 387), one which he alone commands, and before which his opponents are powerless.

406–408 so that the grey-eyed ... whatever I say: Athene has had much more to say than Here about the present situation, and it was she who made the proposal to intervene in it. Now Zeus directs his wrath chiefly at her, perhaps because it is she, so the goddesses' intention is, who is to do the fighting, whereas Here will do no more than drive the chariot, but perhaps also because Zeus is normally more affectionate towards his daughter (cf. 30–40) than his chronically recalcitrant wife.

408 for she is always ... whatever I say: Here in fact belies this assessment of her at 427–8; but it is amply justified by her behaviour elsewhere – e.g. IV 51–67, where she will have nothing to do with Zeus' suggestion that Troy should after all be saved.

411–412 meeting ... gates of Olumpos: The journey from Ide to Olumpos seems to take Iris no time at all.

412 told them of Zeus' words: It is usual in Homer for ambassadors, messengers, etc., to deliver their messages in exactly the words in which they have received them; e.g. Odusseus in the next book repeats almost verbatim the offer to Akhilleus that Agamemnon had set forth at the *boulē* of the Greek leaders. Iris does this here at 415–22, but then makes a stinging addition of her own in her last two lines.

413 rage: With μαίνεται Iris levels at Athene and Here the word that Athene had herself used of Zeus at 360.

423–424 But you (are) ... against Zeus: As messenger of Zeus Iris has no need to stand in awe before his wife and daughter. The violence of her words to them here resembles the abuse which the deities exchange with each other in the Battle of the Gods, or Theomakhy, at XXI 388–513. Iris' words have their effect. Athene is stunned into silence, and Here into submission.

427–431 Alas, child ... that is right: Here begins by addressing Athene in exactly the same words as in her defiant speech at 352, but immediately thereafter gives in to Zeus. Zeus has referred to Here's chronic recalcitrance at 407–8, but defying him in words is quite different from embarking on actions against his will 'on behalf of mortals' (428); there are strict limits to the gods' concern for the mortals. And Athene, who is to maintain her stunned silence throughout the remainder of this episode, has been cowed into forgetting the concern for the Akhaians that she had expressed to Zeus after his interdict at the beginning of the book. The remarkable completeness of Here's surrender is made clear by her last three lines. The fates of the mortals are no longer of any concern to her at all – cf. 352–6!; it is even 'right', ἐπιεικές, that these should be decided by Zeus. The goddesses have tasted disobedience, but now they renounce it.

433–435 The Seasons ... courtyard-walls: The Seasons have already appeared as the keepers of the gate at 393. Now their function is extended to receiving and tending the horses and carriage of the goddesses.

435   courtyard-walls: The ἐνώπια (the word appears elsewhere in the *Iliad* only at XIII 261) appear strictly to be the façades of plaster on the bricks by the entrance to the palace – Lorimer, 428.

436   chairs: The deities normally sit on a θρόνος; the κλισμοί, although still golden, are presumably something less exalted. At IX 200 it is on κλισμοί that Akhilleus seats the ambassadors from Agamemnon when he has received them into his tent.

438–439 Father Zeus ... seats of the gods: Zeus had taken up his seat on Ide to watch the fighting that was to ensue at 51–2. His withdrawal now is a sign that the fighting is over for the day – although enough of the day must still be remaining for Here and Athene to have intervened in the fighting had Zeus not prevented them.

440   The famous earth-shaker: The Seasons had received the goddesses' carriage; but the more important carriage of Zeus is received by his brother Poseidon.

441   as a covering: The chariots are protected from the dust while they are not in use, as at II 777 and V 194–5.

443   quaked: At 199 Here had caused Olumpos to shake by her anger; now Zeus does so simply by sitting down.

447–456 Why are you ... seat of the immortals is: Zeus is exultant at his success in frustrating his wife and daughter. He levels sarcasm on them with κάμετον (448), φαίδιμα (452), and the repeated πόλεμος in 453, and ends by repeating the threats that he had made in his first speech in this book. There he had declared that his supreme authority would prevail; now he is assured that it has done so. Despite the lack of dignity in the present section, the episode of the goddesses' frustrated intervention has had more significance than at first appears. The supreme authority of Zeus on which he had insisted at the beginning has now finally been confirmed.

457–468 Thus he spoke ... you are angry: Lines 457–62 repeat IV 20–5, where Zeus addresses an *agorē* of the gods, airs the possibilty that Troy might after all be saved from eventual destruction, and is met, as here, by an indignant response from Here; and 463–8 very largely repeat Athene's protest to Zeus at 32–7 of this book. Such repetitions are a feature of oral poetry, and Homer uses them freely when similar situations recur. Examples have already been provided by the deaths of Hektor's charioteers at 119–26 and 314–9. See Introduction, **4**.

467   **a plan ... one that will help them:** Here's undertaking here is hardly fulfilled in the ensuing narrative, any more than Athene's at 36 is. In each case the goddesses are giving generalised notice of their unwavering support for the Akhaians.

470–483 In the morning ... shameless than you: Zeus' reply is uncompromising. This resumes the stance that he had taken at the beginning of the book, but diverges from the sequence at the beginning of IV, and from his reply to Athene at 39–40, the passages that have been suggested by the verbal repetitions in the previous lines.

472   **destroying:** With ὀλλύντ' Zeus repeats, no doubt deliberately, the verb that Here had used at 468.

473–477 For mighty Hektor ... divinely decreed: On the foreshadowing of the future in Books VIII and IX, see Introduction, **5d**. In the case of Zeus' present prophecy, some difficulty has been felt over 'on that day when they fight', which seems a curious way of referring to what will in fact happen on the next day, and over 'at the sterns', since the fighting over Patroklos' corpse takes place not at the ships, but on the plain between the ships and Troy. But one should not make too much of this. Although Patroklos' death is no more than one day off, yet it does not occur until Book XVI, which is still a long way on from the present passage; and it is a feature of the prophecies of the *Iliad* that they often do not *exactly* foreshadow what is to come.

By 'For so it is divinely decreed', Zeus is doing no more than give the pattern that in his higher wisdom he can see that events are to take. As with the earlier balancing of the scales one should not think of Zeus taking sides, or of some predetermined course of events which has the human participants helplessly in its grip.

478–482 not even if you come ... in your wandering: Why should Here make such a journey? Zeus means that his position will remain unchanged whatever lengths Here goes to; but by working in the reference to his already defeated enemies he deftly turns his statement into a threat that Here is in danger of sharing their fate, and thereby repeats his threat of 13–16.

479   **Iapetos and Kronos:** Zeus is referring to his defeat of the Titans, including his own father, which was the prelude to his accession to his present position. Iapetos was the father of Prometheus, the god who gave fire to mortals. Zeus' struggle with the Titans was a popular subject in Greek art. Homer nowhere outlines it systematically (but see XIV 203–4, with Janko ad loc.), but it is to be found in the *Theogony* of Hesiod.

480–481 Huperion, Tartaros: Huperion is no more than a name for the Sun, both here and at its only other appearance in the *Iliad* at XIX 398. On Tartaros, see on 13.

483   **more shameless:** With κύντερον, a comparative adjective from κύων, Zeus echoes the disparaging reference to Athene as a dog that Iris had made at 423. Zeus' address to his wife repeats the scorn and anger that he had vented on her in her absence at

407–8. It is in marked contrast to the conciliatory tone he had adopted to Athene at 39–40.

484 – 565 Night ends the fighting. Hektor gives a rousing speech to his men assembled in the plain, and prepares to encamp there. Countless fires burn as the Trojans, confident of success, await the dawn.

The defeat of the goddesses leads to a calm that contrasts sharply with all the confusion that has gone on before on both the human and the divine levels. Homer allows Hektor to speak for the ascendancy that the Trojans have now established, as he specifies the preparations necessary to allow them for the first time to encamp outside the city. The book ends with the celebrated description of the Trojan watch-fires.

484–488 Thus he spoke ... and thrice prayed-for: In no more than five lines, Homer interweaves Here's wordless submission, the end of the day, and the overwhelming superiority that the Trojans now enjoy. This superiority may appear hardly to have been established in the narrative so far; but it is the principal concern of the remainder of the book, which thereby produces a satisfactory context for the despondency in the Akhaian camp with which the following book opens.

485–486 The bright light ... bountiful land: At the end of the day the sun sinks into the Ocean. Homer visualises the earth as a flat disk, surrounded by the river Okeanos. See V 6, with Kirk 1990, ad loc. The night that is now beginning continues until the beginning of Book XI.

489ff. The human narrative is resumed from 349. It is now clear, which it hardly was then, that the fighting has left the Trojans with a firm position on the plain outside Troy, within range (490) of the Greek ships.

489 **an assembly:** The *agorē* is a gathering of the full Trojan force, which is followed at the start of the next book by a similar gathering of the Greeks. The *boulē* is the gathering that is restricted to the leaders alone. Taplin, 10, contrasts this gathering of the Trojans with the one at XVIII 243ff., where they respond to the terrifying news that Akhilleus is to rejoin the fighting.

490 **away from the ships:** But not all that far away, as appears from IX 76 and 232.
the swirling river: I.e. the Skamandros, or Xanthos (560), the river which runs northwards over the plain of Troy, to be joined north of Troy by the Simois from the east, from where it runs out into the Hellespont.

491 **space appeared between the corpses:** Hitherto the descriptions of the fighting have been largely concerned with individual warriors, and this is the first indication that casualties on both sides have been heavy since the introductory passage at 65.

492–496 the speech which Hektor ... words to the Trojans: As Edwards 1970, 23, observes, the two introductions to Hektor's speech, separated from each other by the description of his splendid weaponry, are a fitting prelude to its triumphant tone.

493 **beloved of Zeus:** 'The epithets which belong to them (sc. Homer's heroes) as heroes contrast poignantly with their human fate' – Griffin 1980, 83. Griffin goes on to show how 'beloved of a god' is an epithet that is particularly applied to the most tragic figures in the poem – as well as Hektor, Zeus' son Sarpedon and Patroklos, both of whom are killed in battle in XVI, and, above all, Akhilleus.

494   **a spear eleven cubits long:** The cubit is the length from the elbow to the finger-tip
– so that Hektor's spear is more than four metres long. Homeric warriors have two
sorts of spear, a long thrusting-spear and a much shorter throwing one; this spear
must be of the former type. Sherratt, 150–1, maintains on the basis of the
archaeological evidence that the two types of spear come from different periods, the
thrusting-spear from the thirteenth century or earlier, the throwing-spear from the
twelfth century at the earliest and from then on until Homer's own day. The
thrusting-spear, that is, may have already become obsolete before any likely date for
a Trojan war. Hektor here holds his spear, not for fighting – the fighting is over for
the day – but as a symbol of his military authority. The downcast Agamemnon has
no such symbol as he addresses his men at the beginning of the next book.

495   **a golden ring:** The πόρκης is the ring that fixes the socket of the spearhead onto the
shaft – Lorimer, 260. That it is golden is a further sign of Hektor's authority.

497–541 Hear me, ... disaster on the Argives: Hektor resumes the confident and belligerent
tone of his earlier speech at 185–97 (where, as here, he identifies Diomedes as the
Trojans' principal opponent); 'he turns the anticipation of dawn into a rallying-cry',
Taplin, 23. Fault has sometimes been found with this speech on the grounds of its
alleged excessive length and rambling and repetitive nature. But Homer is thinking
of his own audience, as well as Hektor's. Zeus has already established the
expectation of immediate Trojan success (473–7), and it is through Hektor's speech
that Homer conveys the new situation, with the Trojans now firmly in control. His
principal means of doing so is to get Hektor to outline in full the preparations that are
necessary for the Trojans to take up position on the plain, rather than to continue
being penned up in the city; and the generous space that Homer allocates to the
speech is a means of underlining the importance of what is being expressed. See also
on 528, 532–41 and 538–41. The relation of Hektor's speech to narrative is thus
similar to what it was at 173–97, where it was again through Hektor's words that
Homer clarified the present situation on the ground.

502–511 But let us ... expanse of the sea: Both the length of this sentence, and its repeated
use of enjambment, are remarkable. Hektor has outlined the situation in his first
sentence, and now he rattles off a list of measures which the situation calls for. He is
confident and excited, and feels in complete control; and this is conveyed by the
breathlessness of these lines.

507   **the houses:** The *megaron* is the chief room of the Homeric palace; examples have
been found on the Greek mainland at Mykenai, Tiryns, and at 'Nestor's palace' at
Ano Englianos, near to the present-day Pylos. But Homer uses the word in the plural
for 'palace' or 'house'; so 520.

512–516 May they indeed ... horse-taming Trojans: Hektor is now well and truly into his
stride, and, having previously envisaged no more than that the Akhaians should not
be allowed to slip away during the night, he now envisages their total annihilation.
There is a strain of gathering, and excessive, self-confidence – a characteristic that
Hektor also displays elsewhere – throughout the remainder of his speech. Homer
makes the most of the irony of the situation; we have heard Zeus set firm limits to
the Trojan success at 474–6, but Hektor of course has not.

519   **defences built by the gods:** This is the great wall of Troy that had been built by
Poseidon and Apollo for Laomedon, the father of Priam – VII 452–3, XXI 441–57.

520–521 And let each ... in her home: The women too have their part to play in affirming the present success of the Trojans. The light of their fires will expose any Akhaians who steal into the city, as well as reinforcing the picture of Trojan alertness that the Akhaians will receive from the activities in the Trojan camp.

525   another speech: Hektor fulfils this undertaking at XI 286–90, but hardly in the way that he must here be anticipating._ By that time Agamemnon has by his *aristeia* partially restored the Akhaian fortunes, and Hektor has on instructions from Zeus kept out of the fighting until Agamemnon is wounded and forced to withdraw.

528   whom the fates ... black ships: A curious line, which, as the Alexandrian critics observed, could be omitted without damage to the sense of the passage. The present tense of φορέουσι is surprising; Hektor is not thinking of Akhaians who may be coming over the sea at this moment, but of those who have already come, and/or perhaps others who may come in the future. It looks as though the line may have been inserted into the *Iliad* by someone who was anxious to explain the unusual word κηρεσσιφορήτους. We find similar examples elsewhere of phrases and lines which are detachable from the text, and which may perhaps be explanations of something that has been felt to be difficult in what has just been said, or is about to be said. IX 124 is perhaps an example; horses are there described as ἀθλοφόρους, 'prize-winning', and the line is then completed with οἳ ἀέθλια ποσσὶν ἄροντο, 'who have won prizes with their racing' – tautologically, and perhaps in explanation of ἀθλοφόρους.

532–541 I shall know ... disaster on the Argives: The last ten lines of Hektor's speech have received much critical attention, and from Alexandrian times scholars have suspected that some of these lines may be later additions to Homer's original. (See also on 528 and 538–41.) 535–7 are perhaps the most suspicious, as apparently adding little or nothing to 532–4; but 538–41, although they were apparently questioned by Aristarkhos, are surely necessary as the finale to the speech. Willcock 1978, on 523–41, suggests that 'the repetitiveness of (Hektor's) remarks' may be a piece of characterisation; Hektor 'is blustering and trying to convince himself'.

532   Diomedes: In the absence of Akhilleus, Hektor identifies Diomedes as the Trojans' principal opponent – a justified interpretation of the action both of this book and of V, which is largely an account of the *aristeia* of Diomedes. In VII it was Aias, a senior man to Diomedes, who undertook what ultimately proved an abortive duel with Hektor; but the selection of an opponent for Hektor was done by the random process of lot.

538–541 O, that I might ... disaster on the Argives: With this sentence, Hektor is not entertaining the possibility that he *will* become the equal of Athene and Apollo; but his wish to become so is nevertheless a dangerous presumption on his part. 541 is another curious line. Unless we arbitrarily suppose that φέρει here has the unique meaning 'portends', then by ἡμέρη ἥδε Hektor must mean 'tomorrow' rather than 'today', and by φέρει he must mean 'will bring' rather than 'brings'. Hektor repeats 540–1 at XIII 827–8, where, however, the second line is not open to the same objections that it is here.

543–547 They loosed ... much wood besides: Homer leaves it to us to infer that with Hektor's address completed the *agorē* breaks up; likewise after the Akhaian *agorē* at

IX 79–80. The ensuing narrative sticks closely to the language of the instructions of Hektor at 505–7 that are now carried out, with the repetition of the unusual form of the 2 aor. mid. of ἄγω, and the *zeugma* in the use of οἰνίζομαι, whereby it is followed not only by the natural οἶνον, but by σῖτον as well. This close repetition of the language of the instructions at the point where they are carried out is common; see on 412.

548–552 [They performed ... ashen spear]: 549 is the only one of these lines to appear in the vulgate; the other four are cited in the dialogue *Alcibiades II*, 149D, which is included in the mss. of Plato, although it is probably not by him. In this passage a paraphrase of 549 is also given, and it is stated that the lines are Homeric, and refer to the Trojans camping out, although no precise reference is given as to where they are supposed to occur. The lines were accepted into the text here by the earliest of Homer's modern editors, but nowadays they are generally excised. 548, which has already appeared at I 315 and II 306, does seem necessary to explain the origin of the κνίσην at 549; but against 550–2 it has been objected that both this conception of sacrifice, and the suggestion of *all* the gods being hostile to Troy, are inconsistent with the remainder of the *Iliad*. On sacrifice in Homer, see Kirk 1990, 9–13, who maintains that Homer's gods do not feed on sacrifices, but merely savour the smoke that arises from them. (This view appears to be contradicted at IX 535, but that, as Kirk points out, is an episode earlier than the action of the *Iliad*.) As for the gods' hostility, little has so far been seen in this book of those gods – principally Aphrodite, Apollo, Ares and Artemis – who are normally pro-Trojan, so that Homer's lapse, if it is one, is understandable. The lines surely do go well here, with the reminder of the gods' hostility to Troy an ironic counter-weight to the present picture of the Trojans' success and confidence. ἑκατόμβη is derived from ἑκατὸν βοῦς – i.e a sacrifice of a hundred oxen. But elsewhere sheep and goats may be involved, and the number may be less than a hundred (e.g. I 66, VI 115 with 93); the word is used of any large sacrifice. What is here meant by the adjective τεληέσσας is not clear. The word comes from τέλος, 'fulfilment', and it has been suggested, e.g. by LSJ., s.v., that it may mean 'to the full number'. But 'capable of fulfilment' seems a plausible alternative.

553–565 In high confidence ... the beautiful throne: The conclusion of the book, and especially the clarity and simplicity of the simile of the stars and the final picture of the horses munching their fodder, is a much-praised passage. The scene has been illuminatingly discussed by Edwards 1987, 86–7, who emphasises that it is not merely decorative, but serves to underline the extent of the Trojan success; and he also sees the scene as an example of what he calls Homer's '"zoom" technique' – from the first, general, view of the camp-fires Homer narrows down to the close-up pictures of the men sitting round the fires and the horses chomping at their fodder. The first four lines are predominantly dactylic, to introduce the calmness and serenity of the scene; but Homer brings the passage to a close with a single spondaic word, Ἠώ, unusually occupying the fifth foot of 565. The overall effect is to end the book in a *pianissimo* mood which contrasts sharply both with the incessant hustle and bustle that has reigned on both the divine and the human levels since Zeus first declared his intentions and with the desperation and discord in the Akhaian camp with which the next book opens.

553   **spaces of the battle:** For the πτολέμοιο γεφύρας, see on 378.

555–561 As when ... in front of Ilion: A justly celebrated simile; it is thought that similes of
this length and elaboration may be an innovation by Homer on the epic tradition as
he found it – see Coffey, 115, and Kirk 1962, 327f. The explicit point of comparison
is between the number of the stars and the number of the Trojan watchfires, but it is
the details of the simile that are apparently superfluous to this, rather than the
surrounding narrative, that establish the mood of calmness and confidence within the
Trojan camp, and the fine picture of the joyous shepherd momentarily takes us away,
as Homer's similes often do, from the wars of the heroes to the ordinary life of
everyday people. See Edwards 1991, 31–33. The Trojan watchfires provide the
point of departure for the simile at 554, and they re-appear, by the common device of
ring-composition, immediately the simile is over at 562–3.

557–558 All the look-out places ... from the sky: The authenticity of these lines also has
been called into question. They recur exactly at XVI 299–300, in a simile of Zeus
moving a cloud from a mountain-top, and it is maintained that from there a post-
Homeric writer has inappropriately introduced them here, where the visibility of the
surrounding features seems unexceptionable, but the brightness bursting forth from
the sky hardly fits the scene of a calm night. But Willcock 1978, ad loc., suggests
that the general context may have suggested the lines to Homer at this point,
whatever inappropriateness the details of them may have to this particular situation.

BOOK IX

1 – 88   After the day's setbacks, panic reigns among the Akhaians. Agamemnon calls a gathering of the full force, and proposes that the expedition be abandoned forthwith. Diomedes demurs, and insists that he at least will stay and fight on. Nestor counters this, suggesting that guards be posted for the night, while the senior leaders take counsel with Agamemnon. The suggestion is accepted, and the guards take their positions.

The present scene is to be thought of as taking place simultaneously with the scene of the Trojans preparing to encamp outside their walls with which the previous book had ended. It is entirely in Homer's manner that, once having begun on a scene, he takes this scene through to its end before beginning on another one, even if this second scene is in fact simultaneous with the first one – see Janko to XIV 1–152. While there is the sharpest possible contrast in the tone of the two scenes, yet the thematic similarities between them are firmly set forth, with the similes of 4–8 and 14–15 balancing the simile of the Trojan watchfires at VIII 555–560, and the *agorē* of the Akhaians and the speech of Agamemnon balancing the Trojan *agorē* and the speech of Hektor at VIII 489–551. The role played by Diomedes here is significantly recalled at the end of the book, when it is he once again who has practical suggestions to offer in the face of the new crisis that has arisen out of Akhilleus' dismissal of the embassy.

1   **The Trojans ... the Akhaians:** No time is lost in making the contrast between the two sides, with the buoyant Trojans in the nominative case and the subdued Akhaians in the accusative. The contrast is intensified by the positioning of Τρῶες immediately before the main caesura of the line, and 'Αχαιούς at the end. On Homer's words for the Akhaians, see on VIII 11. Hellas, the classical word for Greece, will appear in its restricted sense of an area of Thessaly, in northern Greece, at 447.

2   **Panic, Fear:** Qualities such as Panic and Fear are regularly personified by Homer – e.g. when Fear and Terror accompany Ares, the god of war, to the battlefield at IV 440, and when Death and Sleep carry away the corpse of Sarpedon at XVI 681–3. There is no difficulty in understanding such personifications here; they 'simply underline what is visibly happening at the human level' – Griffin 1977, 48. But Phoinix's personification of the *Litai* and *Atē* at 502ff. is less straightforward. φόβος commonly connotes flight in Homer.

3   **leaders:** Literally, 'best men'; but Homer regularly uses both the superlative adjective ἄριστος and the noun ἀριστεύς for 'leader'.

4–7   **Just as ... along the shore:** The narrative has reached a critical point, and so Homer, as often, marks the occasion with the introduction of a simile, with another one to follow at 14–15. But similes are a device of the narrative rather than speech, and so in this book, where speech predominates over narrative, the only further one is at 323–4, in Akhilleus' great speech. These two similes have a strongly narrative function; they are almost all that Homer needs to represent the despondency of the Akhaians generally and of Agamemnon before allowing the despondency to express itself in the words of the Akhaian leaders. This simile arises from the narrative, 'the leaders were in confusion'; but, a little unexpectedly, it develops the idea of confusion (caused by the winds), not that of the leaders.

5   **Thrace:**   The area which forms the eastern half of the Balkan peninsula. This passage, which represents the north and west winds as blowing from Thrace, is commonly cited in support of the view that Homer came, not from mainland Greece, but from the area of Asia Minor or the islands of the eastern Aegean. See also II 394ff. and IV 422ff.; and Introduction, **3b**.

8   **So the hearts ... their breasts:** Homer returns to the point from which he had departed at line 3 to introduce his simile. An example of ring-composition, the function of which 'is to resume the narrative of a given sequence of themes at the correct point' – Hainsworth 1966, 160.

9   **The son of Atreus:** In itself, Ἀτρείδης can refer to either of Atreus' sons, Agamemnon or Menelaos. But when only one of these is referred to without further explanation, it is Agamemnon, the commander-in-chief, and so a more important man than his brother.

    struck: Homer repeats the word that he has used of the Akhaian leaders generally at 3. As his speech makes clear, Agamemnon is in no mood to give his men the positive leadership that the present crisis requires.

11   **the assembly:** For the *agorē* and the *boulē*, see on VIII 489. The calling of an assembly is regularly the beginning of a fresh sequence of the narrative, e.g. I 54, II 250, XIX 46.

12   **without shouting:** Agamemnon is all too well aware that the Trojans are now within earshot of his own men.

14   **shedding a tear:** On Agamemnon's tears, see on VIII 245.

14–15   **like a spring ... sheer rock:** Unusually for Homer's similes (Edwards 1991, 24), this one is repeated at XVI 3–4, where Akhilleus' faithful friend Patroklos is reduced to tears by the desperate situation of the Akhaians in the fighting on the day following the present night. That passage is followed by Patroklos' request to Akhilleus that he (P.) should enter the fighting himself, his *aristeia*, and the events that lead to his death – a turning-point in the action of the *Iliad*, in that it is Patroklos' death that finally impels Akhilleus to resume fighting. Some scholars have seen especial significance in this repetition of the simile – here it begins a book which will show Akhilleus refusing to re-enter battle; in XVI it occurs when Akhilleus' continued absence has produced the emergency in which Patroklos enters battle, and dies, and so provides the occasion for Akhilleus to resume fighting. But others argue that this is only another example of the repetitions that are basic to the oral method of composition. See Macleod, 45; and Introduction, **4**.

17–78   **O friends ... preserve it:** The three speeches of the *agorē* sharply characterise the speakers, and contrast them with each other – Agamemnon haunted by failure and, one supposes, by developing uneasiness over his treatment of Akhilleus, Diomedes provoked by his leader's failure of nerve into a unilateral act of defiance, and Nestor, with more concern for the army as a whole than the other two, delicately finding a middle way between them. Diomedes' speech is a little longer than Agamemnon's, Nestor's a little longer than Diomedes'; Homer gradually and carefully develops the situation until the time is ripe for the proposal to appeal to Akhilleus. Lohmann, 214, observes how the three speeches here foreshadow the three speeches in the ensuing

boulē, the three pairs of speeches in Akhilleus' tent, and the three speeches at the end
of the book.

17–28   O friends ... broad streets: Agamemnon is no less despondent now than he had
been in his speech at VIII 228–44, and again turns towards thoughts of abandoning the
expedition forthwith. That Zeus then responded favourably to his prayer he has now forgotten
under the stress of the subsequent setbacks that the Akhaians have suffered. He does not now
put forward alternative policies for debate; and his speech is hardly that of a leader, and shows
little concern for his men –δυσκλέα, the first word of 22, makes clear that it is personal loss of
face that concerns him. As Taplin, 91, observes, Agamemnon's addresses to his men are
consistently maladroit and ill-timed throughout the poem. But he does, at least implicitly,
discard the counsel of despair that he puts forward here, first when at the *boulē* he accepts
Nestor's proposal that reconciliation be sought with Akhilleus, and again at the end of the book
when he acquiesces in the suggestion of Diomedes that the Akhaians prepare for battle again
on the following day. But he resumes his present proposal at XIV 74–81, when he is once
more over-ruled.

Agamemnon's speech exactly reproduces his words at II 111–118 and 139–141.
There, a False Dream sent by Zeus had prompted Agamemnon to take the battle to the Trojans
immediately, and his speech was a ruse – one which recoiled on him disastrously – which was
designed by its apparent faint-heartedness to stir his men to action. But this time Agamemnon
is in earnest. On Agamemnon's part, the repetition here can only be accidental; but Homer
could perhaps be using the repetition purposefully, to exploit the irony of Agamemnon now
being forced into repeating his vain proposal, but this time for real.

17   **lords and rulers:** Agamemnon had at 11 called *all* his men to the assembly, and so
          his address here to the leaders only is curious – he speaks as though addressing a
          boulē rather than an *agorē*. It looks as though either Homer or Agamemnon is
          forgetting himself; or has Agamemnon called the army at large, not so that they may
          participate in debate themselves, but only that they should hear their leaders doing
          so, which in the event is all that they do do?

18   **delusion:** On *atē*, see on VIII 237. Agamemnon seems here to have in mind the
          assurance that the False Dream from Zeus gave him at II 28–30 that he would take
          Troy. But see next note.

19   **Then:** Here, and at II 112, the mss. read πρίν, 'previously', which the early
          commentators on Homer took to refer to an omen that the Akhaians received at
          Aulis, before setting sail from Greece, of a serpent devouring a sparrow and its
          young, an omen which was interpreted as portending the eventual success of the
          Akhaian expedition, as Odusseus recalls at II 299–330. τότε was introduced into
          Homer's text by Aristarkhos, and is thought to be a more precise reference to the
          False Dream. This hardly seems sufficient grounds for rejecting the mss. reading.
          As Willcock 1978, ad loc, writes, 'The whole principle of formulaic repetition ...
          argues against this sort of tinkering with the individual words in a repeated line'.

22   **Argos:** Homer uses Argos in four different ways – for the town of Argos, for the
          neighbourhood around the town (the Argolid), for the Peloponnese as a whole, and
          for Greece as a whole – hence 'Αργεῖοι for the Greeks. Agamemnon here
          presumably means the Peloponnese, where his own home at Mukenai lay.

I have lost ... my people: ὤλεσα could also mean 'I have destroyed', and there may, as Griffin 1980, 163–4, suggests, be something of both meanings here – in his present mood Agamemnon accepts that by his undertaking he has brought disaster on the whole force. The λαός is the people as a whole, who support their leader, and for whom the leader is responsible. At I 117, it is his wish that the λαός shall be safe that prompts Agamemnon to give Khruseis back to her father; and at XXII 107, Hektor feels obliged to face Akhilleus by the prospect that he will be reproached with having destroyed his λαός if he does not do so.

26–28 **But come ... broad streets:** Faint-hearted though it is, there is no lack of clarity or authority in the proposal that Agamemnon now puts forward. The three successive lines each comprising an entire sense-unit on its own, and ended by heavy punctuation ('end-stopping'), give his words an imperious air.

29–31 **So he spoke ... shout, spoke:** Three formulaic lines – see on VIII 28–30, and for reappearances in this book, 430–1 and 693–6. For a solemn speech followed by a long silence, see elsewhere at, e.g., VII 398, X 218. See Introduction, **4**.

31 **Diomedes:** For Diomedes, see on VIII 91. It is in this book, with his speeches here and at 697–709, that his qualities in council first emerge clearly, and so point the contrast between him and Akhilleus. See Griffin 1980, 74–7.

32–49 **Son of Atreus ... god's guidance:** Diomedes addresses Agamemnon – rather than the whole assembly – out of the brooding resentment, that he has so far kept concealed, over the insult that Agamemnon delivered him in IV. He uses the same devices of abuse, sarcasm, and throwing Agamemnon's words back in his face, that Akhilleus had used in the quarrel in I; but his position is the exact opposite of Akhilleus' – he will not withdraw, but stay and fight – with only Sthenelos for company if necessary. His flat opposition to Agamemnon leaves it open to Nestor to propose a middle way.

34 **reproached my courage:** This was at IV 370–400, during the *Epipōlēsis,* Agamemnon's review of the troops before they went into battle, when he reminded Diomedes at some length of the exploits of his father Tudeus in the campaign of the Seven against Thebes. By 'first', Diomedes presumably means 'You began it (and I am now reciprocating)'. That Diomedes assesses Agamemnon's courage exactly as Agamemnon has assessed his is made clear when ἀλκήν is again the first word of the line at 39. Diomedes raises the subject of ἀλκή again in his later speech at 706.

38 **sceptre:** The sceptre is the outward symbol of kingly power; see especially the 'genealogy' of Agamemnon's sceptre at II 101–8. Diomedes' point is that it is *only* the sceptre that gives Agamemnon authority, whereas his lack of ἀλκή disqualifies him from it. There is much in what Diomedes is now saying with which Akhilleus would heartily agree.

40 **good sir:** Of δαιμόνιε Griffin 1986, 40, writes that it 'hardly seems to have what properly ought to be called a meaning; its use conveys an attitude of shock or rebuke on the part of the speaker towards the person addressed'. Both shock and rebuke underlie Diomedes' use of the word here.

44 **in such numbers:** The Catalogue of Ships (II 576) gives 100 as the number of ships from Mukenai, under the command of Agamemnon, that were supplied to the Akhaian expedition – the largest single contingent. This line was athetised by Aristarkhos, as lines that can be discarded without prejudice to the passage in which they occur often are; but there seems no good reason why it should not be accepted. See the note on VIII 528.

45   **long-haired:** On this epithet see on VIII 53.

46   **let them too ..:** It has sometimes been thought that there has been ellipsis of a verb here to complete the conditional clause with εἰ; and so editors have printed a comma after αὐτοί – 'if they too (are resolved on flight), then let them flee ...'. This is not necessary. εἰ is used with the imperative without any conditional sense, but rather 'interjectionally' – 'well, then'. So at lines 167 and 262 of this book, and in other places, such as I 302.

48   **Sthenelos:** The faithful charioteer of Diomedes, and jointly with him commander of the Argive contingent. Their fathers, Kapaneus and Tudeus, had fought together at Thebes; and Sthenelos answers Agamemnon's insult on Diomedes' behalf at IV 404–10, and is at his side throughout his *aristeia* in V, and again at the rescue of Nestor at VIII 114.

48–49   **our object in Ilios:** Literally, 'the aim (τέκμωρ) of Ilios'. Homer uses the form *Ilios* much more commonly than *Ilion*. The latter was the name given to the settlement on the site of ancient Troy that was made in the seventh century B. C., and is the form regularly used after that.

49   **with god's guidance:** Diomedes may have in mind the portent at Aulis (see on 19) – so Taplin, 49; or he may share the confidence of the Akhaians at such passages as IV 163–5 and VII 401–2 that the crime of the Trojan Paris in abducting Helen from her marital home in Sparta with Menelaos ensures the support of the gods and the ultimate success of the Akhaian cause. His words certainly give his speech a resounding ending, especially the four-syllable word εἰλήλουθμεν, with its first three syllables all long, filling the two final feet of the line.

50–51   **Such were ... of horses:** Diomedes' forthright speech produces a more immediate response than Agamemnon's had done at 29–30. These two lines have already appeared at VII 404, where Diomedes firmly rejected Paris' offer of handsome payment to the Greeks provided that he was allowed to retain Helen, and 51 is used again for the reception of his speech at the end of this book, 711. Where a similar situation recurs, Homer uses similar words to describe it.

53–78   **Son of Tudeus ... preserve it:** Like Agamemnon and Diomedes, Nestor does not address the assembly at large, but begins with Diomedes and at 69 turns to Agamemnon. Nestor was out of his depth in the fighting at VIII 80–158; but he is the supreme mediator and counsellor, introduced as venerable, lucid, and well-intentioned when he took the initiative in trying, albeit unsuccessfully, to mediate in the quarrel between Agamemnon and Akhilleus at I 248–252, and the first to speak after Agamemnon has divulged the contents of the False Dream at II 79–83. The present occasion, when the grave military situation has been exacerbated by the rift that has appeared within the high command, finds him at his very best. His practical proposals for meeting the present crisis occupy no more than three lines, 65–67, and the bulk of his speech is concerned with ensuring that these proposals, which represent a middle way between the extreme views so far expressed, should find disfavour neither with Diomedes nor with Agamemnon. His method is masterly. He painstakingly avoids explicit criticism of either man (in this respect, his speech is different from the one he had made at the quarrel at I 254–284), and instead shows himself deeply sensitive to the feelings of both. When he begins by fulsomely acknowledging Diomedes' prowess in war, he is responding to what Diomedes had said about Agamemnon's criticisms of his ἀλκή; and he brings in the subject of Diomedes' youth with extreme delicacy, presenting this only as a contrast to his own greater age and, therefore, authority. (There is again a contrast here with how he presented the matter of his own seniority to Agamemnon and Akhilleus at the quarrel.) When he comes to Agamemnon, the very first thing that he does is to acknowledge Agamemnon's authority, a matter on which Agamemnon always shows himself extremely sensitive, especially when, as here, this authority is under challenge. It is in keeping with this shrewd approach that Nestor's proposals for the present situation are modest ones. We cannot tell whether he already has in mind the grand idea that he successfully presents to the ensuing *boulē*, that approaches be made to Akhilleus. But what is clear is that Nestor recognises that in the heat of the present moment it is only the immediate situation that can be dealt with. The challenge of the watch-fires that the Trojans have now lit *outside* the city walls must be met; and discussions among the Akhaian leaders must be continued among themselves alone, where there is a better chance than there is in the present *agorē* of the whole force that Agamemnon will be prepared to give ground.

53–54   **war, council:** The two crucial areas for the Homeric hero to display his prowess in. See especially 443, Peleus' instruction to Phoinix that he was to teach Akhilleus to be 'a speaker of words and doer of deeds', and such passages elsewhere as I 258 and 490 and II 202. In commending Diomedes on both counts, Nestor confers the highest praise on him; and he may perhaps also have in mind a contrast with Akhilleus, who does not likewise show equal prowess in words as well as deeds.

54   **men of your own age:** Nestor unobtrusively brings in the subject of Diomedes' youth, the subject to which he will return when he says that his own seniority gives him more authority to speak. Nestor goes on to declare that no one will contradict Diomedes, at the moment when he is about to do exactly that.

57   **to be sure:** Having clearly established his deep respect for Diomedes, Nestor can afford not to mince words on the subject of Diomedes' youthfulness; ἦ μέν is a very strong expression – cf. Akhilleus' use of it at 348, and Denniston, 389. The point must be made, as it is his own seniority that privileges Nestor's advice above Diomedes'. But with his usual tact Nestor immediately modifies his message with what he says about Diomedes' skill in addressing the chiefs of staff.

58   **youngest-born:** At I 250–252 Nestor is represented as having lived through three generations, which would make him about 70 years of age by now.

58–59   **speak appropriately ... spoken as you should:** πεπνυμένος 'denotes one who observes the courtesies of life, especially in speech. It is seldom used of great heroes, but is a regular description of youthful or subordinate characters' – Hainsworth, in Heubeck, etc., on *Od.* VIII 388. Nestor commends Diomedes' awareness of his rank, and seeks to undo the effect of Diomedes' attack on Agamemnon by pretending that it has not happened. And Diomedes has spoken κατὰ μοῖραν, literally 'according to his portion', – thus here, in a manner that suits his years and stature. This again hardly seems appropriate of the abuse that Diomedes has just levelled at his commander; but by passing over that Nestor says what not only Diomedes, but also Agamemnon, would like to hear.

59   **chiefs:** βασιλεύς is not a very precise word in the *Iliad*. The usual meaning is 'person of rank', and XI 46 is the only passage where it means the king of a particular place. The translation 'monarch' is generally inappropriate; the position of the βασιλεύς vis-à-vis the rest of the force is far from clear. At 69 below, Nestor acknowledges Agamemnon's authority with the superlative adjective βασιλεύτατος, and at 160 Agamemnon uses the comparative, βασιλεύτερος, of himself, which might perhaps suggest that there were degrees of βασίλεια. But the question is a very vexed one. See Taplin, 47–49, and Hainsworth on XI 46. When Nestor addresses Agamemnon at the *boulē*, he calls him, not βασιλεύς, but ἄναξ, twice in 96–98, and Homer uses the same word of him when Agamemnon begins his speech at 114, and repeatedly elsewhere. See also on ἄναξ at VIII 278; and Murray, 38.

60   **can claim:** Besides 'pray', εὔχομαι can also mean both 'claim', as here, and 'boast'; when Agamemnon uses it at 161 both these meanings are probably present. The word is often used by speakers to establish and confirm the sense of their own value.

62   **what I say ... lord Agamemnon:** μῦθος is no more than 'speech', as again at 431 and 443; the connection of the word with 'fiction' and 'myth' only comes later – Dowden, 4f. Nestor then cleverly works in a first, glancing, reference to Agamemnon's authority, a subject on which he will have more to say in due course.

63–64   **That man ... his home:** Nestor makes a thundering outburst against discord, beginning with three consecutive α– adjectives (the *privative* α), with no connecting word between them (*asyndeton*). He has been more powerfully affected than he has hitherto shown by the quarrel between Agamemnon and Akhilleus in I; what he here says goes well beyond the present disagreement between Diomedes and Agamemnon. ἀφρήτωρ is literally 'without phratry'. The phratry, which Nestor also refers to at II 362–3, was a social grouping, or 'brotherhood', which, as Andrewes shows, Homer seems to have transferred from his own times to the Mycenaean age. The word provides the root for the Latin *frater*, and so German *Bruder*, French *frère*, and English *brother*.

66   **meal:** A dinner is often the occasion for discussion among the chieftains; cf. Nestor's addresses at II 432–40 and VII 327–343.

67   **ditch:** For the ditch, or trench, see 87, and VIII 213–6. It appears to have been dug at some distance *outside* the defensive wall; but this has sometimes been felt inconsistent with VII 341–2 and 440–1, where, so it is maintained, the ditch seems more like a moat, adjacent to the wall. See Page, 315–324, but also Hainsworth 1993, on the present verse.

69   **take the lead:** Nestor now turns to Agamemnon, and loses no time in acknowledging his authority, recognising that this is the necessary condition of any solution being found to the present impasse. To be recognised as βασιλεύτατος is exactly what Agamemnon likes to hear; cf. his own words at 160. Nestor's respectful address gains emphasis from the repeated personal pronoun, σὺ μὲν ἄρχε· σὺ γάρ ..., and the effect is continued by τοι, 'to you' three times in the next four lines.

71–72 **wine, which ... every day:** One of the very few insights we are given into the Akhaian lines of supply. At VII 467–471 we hear of wine coming to them also from the island of Lemnos, and of special wine from there for Agamemnon and Menelaos alone.

73   **All hospitality ... over many:** Nestor enlarges on the idea of Agamemnon's royalty, and puts it to practical use. This line is an example of *parataxis*, a common device in Homer – 'all hospitality is yours, and (i.e. since) you rule over many'. Nestor means that Agamemnon's position gives him the responsibility to summon the chiefs and give them hospitality, a point illustrated by Agamemnon's invitations at, e.g., II 402–8, VII 313–302.

74   **that man:** Nestor presumably means himself, but it would be tactless to say so, and so he makes an indefinite clause out of it, 'that man whosoever..'

77   **many fires:** Homer gives Nestor language that recalls the Trojan watchfires at the end of the previous book, VIII 555–9, with γηθέω both here and at VIII 559. The Trojan fires, revealing their presence encamped outside the city, are the visible symbol of their present success, and of the dangers that the Akhaians now face, as again at 234. Things were very different while Akhilleus was still in action, and the Trojans were kept penned within their walls.

78   **This night ... preserve it:** Nestor brings his speech to an end no less resoundingly than Diomedes had done; but in the event his prediction that the present night will either make or break the Akhaians is not fulfilled.

79–88   **These were ... his meal:** The *agorē* now breaks up, although Homer says no more than that Nestor's advice was followed; and the first part of that advice, the posting of the guards, follows immediately as an appendix to the *agorē* scene. The guards know what they are to do; Nestor's practical proposal has gone some way towards abating the universal despondency in the Akhaian camp with which the book opened.

81–84   **Thrasumedes ... Lukomedes:** These men are the κοῦροι, literally 'young men', to whom Nestor addressed his instructions at 68; the leading officers in the Akhaian army, apart from Agamemnon and Akhilleus, are the seven γέροντας ἀριστῆας Παναχαιῶν who are named at II 404–8. The commanders of the guard have made little or no appearance in the action so far, but all of them except Ialmenos have some part to play in the fighting in Books XIII–XVII, where Meriones, the second-in-command of Idomeneus' contingent from Crete, performs with some distinction, e.g. XIII 244–329. The title 'sons of Ares' is sometimes an honorific one, but Askalaphos and his brother Ialmenos really are the sons of Ares, the god of war – II 512–5, XV 111–2.

85   **a hundred:** Making a force of 7 leaders and 700 men altogether – which is, strictly, an implausibly high figure. On the numbers of the Akhaian and Trojan forces, see on VIII 56. On the long spears of 86, see on VIII 494.

89 – 181 The Akhaian leaders meet in Agamemnon's tent. After a meal, Nestor suggests that an approach be made to Akhilleus. Agamemnon readily agrees, and sets forth a magnificent list of reparations that he will pay to Akhilleus if he will return to battle. Nestor speaks again, appointing Phoinix, Aias and Odusseus to take Agamemnon's offer to Akhilleus, and after the due ceremonies have been performed, the embassy departs.

89   **councillors:** γέροντας is literally 'old men', but the word is commonly used of councillors, regardless of their age. Cf. what Nestor has just said to Diomedes about their respective ages. Diomedes is in fact present at this council, 697–709.

90–92   **set before them ... and drink:** The eating occupies less than 3 lines. The discussion that is to follow is much more important; but a meal is a necessary first step on such an occasion. Lines 91–2 are formulaic, and used repeatedly elsewhere, e.g. at 221–2. But the meal which is there concluded, that by which Akhilleus receives the ambassadors from Agamemnon, is a more momentous one than this one is, and so is narrated at correspondingly greater length.

94   **before this too:** This may refer to Nestor's performance at the *agorē*, or it may be general. The following line has already been used to introduce Nestor at the quarrel at I 253.

96–113 **Most glorious ... soothing words:** Nestor builds on his success at the assembly, and once again exercises the greatest sensitivity in advancing his crucial proposal that an approach be made to Akhilleus. He begins with 7 lines of fulsome acknowledgement of Agaamemnon's authority; and when he comes, as he now has to, to the delicate issue of Agamemnon's seizure of Briseis from Akhilleus, he says no more about it than he has to, introducing it as unobtrusively as he can within a subordinate clause (106), and making it an issue, not between Agamemnon and himself, but for the whole of the high command – 'Let *us* consider'. And he also goes no further than he has to. The matter of Briseis raised, Nestor leaves it to Agamemnon to propose restitution and reparation. As Redfield, 12f., observes, Nestor is a much shrewder judge than Akhilleus of how to make Agamemnon retract.

96   **Most glorious:** Nestor appropriately begins with a full-line address to Agamemnon. At the assembly he had used no more than a one-word patronymic for both Agamemnon and Diomedes; but the council is a more patrician occasion.

97–98 **with you ... on you:** Nestor again deploys the repetition of the personal pronoun, as he had done at 69–70, to convey intense respect for Agamemnon and his authority. The authority of Homer's leaders is regularly represented as deriving from Zeus – e.g. II 102–8.

106   **child of a god:** Not literally true of Agamemnon, whose father was Atreus – any more than it is of Odusseus (father Laertes) whom Akhilleus addresses as διογενές at 308. But Nestor is careful to slip in an honorific epithet as he comes to the sensitive issue of Briseis.

    the girl Briseis: κούρη may be used for 'young woman', 'unmarried girl' (so 396), or 'daughter' (so 132 and 557 – of a woman who is now married). In some passages it is difficult to decide which meaning is the right one; but here 'young woman' seems the most likely. Briseis had once been married, but her husband was killed in battle – XIX 291–2.

107   **Akhilleus:** Perhaps out of regard for Agamemnon's feelings, Nestor does not elsewhere use Akhilleus' name. Agamemnon has a pronounced distaste for using it; he does so not once in the ensuing speech, nor at 673–5.

    taking away: This assertion is out of step with the narrative of the crucial incident at I 327–47, where it is not Agamemnon himself, but heralds sent on his orders, who go to Akhilleus' tent to take away Briseis. The same inconsistency has already appeared at I 356 and II 240, when Akhilleus and Thersites respectively maintain that Agamemnon took away Briseis αὐτός, ' himself'. That is indeed what Agamemnon threatened to do, at I 137 and 185; and it looks as though it is this threat, rather than what actually happened, that has now taken hold of the characters' memories. See Kirk 1985, on I 185.

109   **was trying to dissuade:** This was in his speech at I 254–84, especially 274–6. But Nestor was less blunt then than he is now, and his use here of πόλλ', 'repeatedly', hardly fits the facts. Reinhardt, 79–81, suggests that Nestor is now giving an *interpretation* of his earlier speech, representing what he had been trying, but without success, to convey then.

your proud heart: Nestor uses of Agamemnon an expression which Agamemnon uses of Akhilleus at 675, as does Odusseus, to Akhilleus' face, at 255.

110   **best of men:** In describing Akhilleus with the superlative, φέριστον, here, Nestor may have in mind the language of the quarrel. So Lohmann, 226. Agamemnon there said (I 184–7) that by taking Briseis he would teach Akhilleus that he, Agamemnon, was φέρτερος, comparative; and when Nestor came to speak, he maintained that, though Akhilleus was καρτερός, 'strong' (not a comparative), yet it was Agamemnon who was φέρτερος, 'because he rules over more people' (I 280–1). If that is right, then Nestor is now being more forthright in his criticism of Agamemnon's conduct than would at first appear.

the immortals honoured: Nestor perhaps has no particular occasion in mind, and is simply thinking of Akhilleus as a man on whom the gods have looked particularly kindly. Or is he somehow aware that the Akhaians' present misfortunes are Zeus' way of bringing recompense to Akhilleus for Agamemnon's insult? – i.e. is Homer supposing that Nestor has heard, or heard of, Akhilleus' appeal to his mother Thetis in I, and Thetis' transmission of it to Zeus? The point he makes here is taken up by Agamemnon at 118, with the same verb, ἔτεισε, but in a quite different spirit.

111   **you have taken ... keep it:** Four words are all that Nestor needs to present Akhilleus' case against Agamemnon. It is not the loss of Briseis as a person that hurts (although at 342–3 Akhilleus maintains that this did hurt too), but the loss of the *geras*, the prize which, alone of the leaders, Akhilleus has been obliged to relinquish. What Nestor here says repeats, with verbal similarities, some of what Akhilleus has already said at the quarrel at I 161–8 and in his prayer to his mother Thetis at I 356. The line has unusual metrical features which give additional force to Nestor's point. It is uncommon to find the first caesura in the line after the second syllable of the second foot; and to have the complete sense-unit, ἑλὼν ... γέρας, contained within the line is also unusual, although this device is employed, again at moments of high tension, by Akhilleus at 197 and 376.

112–113 **let us even ... soothing words:** Nestor has set the agenda, and his own proposals can now be made in little more than two lines. With 'let us consider' he invites the involvement of the whole council, but in the event only Agamemnon responds, and this is no doubt just what Nestor has intended.

113   **soothing words:** This part of Nestor's advice Agamemnon disregards altogether. See the conclusion of his speech, 158–61.

114   **And in his turn ... addressed him:** At the assembly Homer briefly indicated how the speeches were received generally, but now he does so only after Nestor's second speech (173) – as though the debate were between Nestor and Agamemnon alone. Agamemnon's speech is itself the response to Nestor's first speech, as is Nestor's second to Agamemnon's. On Agamemnon's title 'lord of men', see on VIII 278. Here too the title is used where Agamemnon's rank is a factor in the present situation.

115–161 **O sir, ... in ancestry:** Nestor's shrewd approach has struck home; and Agamemnon responds royally to it. He begins by accepting fully Nestor's criticisms of his behaviour over Briseis, and openly acknowledges that he has been led astray by *atē*. What he here says builds on what he had already said in response to Nestor at II 375–8, where he also admitted that he had been misled by Zeus (though he did not there bring *atē* explicitly into it), and had started the quarrel. But that passage was followed by a call to arms, with no thought for the absent Akhilleus, whereas the present one leads into the enumeration of the magnificent reparations that Agamemnon will now provide. The enumeration is given clearly and confidently, with each item plainly directed by its magnificence to glorifying Akhilleus. The reparations include the restitution of Briseis; but they include a great deal else besides. It is not Akhilleus' loss of Briseis alone that demands compensation, but also, and much more, Akhilleus' loss of his *geras* and so of his standing with the army; and Agamemnon's response is as clear and as handsome as it could be.

No fault can be found with the scale of Agamemnon's proposed reparations – that is, indeed, the first thing that Nestor says after hearing them at 164. But the speech nevertheless contains hints that point forward to Akhilleus' flat rejection of the reparations. From start to finish Agamemnon does not mention Akhilleus by name (so too in his speech at the final reconciliation, XIX 78–124); and he overlooks altogether Nestor's final words, that Akhilleus should be placated by 'soothing words'. The acknowledgement of *atē* is followed immediately by a decidedly grudging statement that Akhilleus has found more favour with Zeus than he has found himself; and in the catalogue of reparations that follows, while their grand scale is a fitting tribute to the stature of Akhilleus, it says something also about the stature of Agamemnon. As no one but Akhilleus is worthy to receive recompense on this scale, so no one but Agamemnon is capable of offering it. This is not well-judged; 'by his very act of recompense, Agamemnon asserts his superiority over Akhilleus' – Redfield, 14. Throughout this speech, Agamemnon is still preoccupied, as he had been in I, with his own rank; and nothing could be clearer, or more ominous, than his final four lines (158–161), in which he makes Akhilleus' abandoning of his anger into a matter of his recognising Agamemnon's superior standing. He is blind to the part that his rank has played in the quarrel; and this speech builds well on the picture of Agamemnon, and of his obsessive concern for his own status, that the poem has already presented. The issues that had surfaced so disastrously in I remain unresolved. See Introduction, **7b**.

115   **folly:** On *atē*, see on VIII 237. Agamemnon develops at some length the theme of his delusion by Zeus in his speech at the final reconciliation-scene, XIX 85–138, where he ends with exactly the same words as at 120 here. Neither there nor here does he offer any other explanation than this for his treatment of Akhilleus in I. There is something distasteful about Agamemnon's recourse to citing the agency of *atē*, as though he were thereby exculpating himself.

118   **honoured ... subdued:** Nestor had voiced at 110 the honour that the gods have paid to Akhilleus, and Agamemnon repeats the point here, but less generously – 'Zeus has loaded me with *atē*, Akhilleus with honour'. This line is another example of parataxis; literally, 'Zeus has honoured that man, *and* he has subdued..', hence, 'honoured .., by subduing'. The chastening defeats that the day's fighting have brought are sufficient proof that Zeus is against the Akhaians – and, therefore, for Akhilleus. Akhilleus' wishes when he appealed to his mother in I are now fulfilled; and Agamemnon again overlooks Zeus' favourable response to his prayer at VIII 245–52.

121-156 Let me now ... under his sceptre: This list of reparations is repeated almost verbatim by Odusseus when he conveys Agamemnon's offer to Akhilleus at 264-98. Agamemnon spares no detail to make his list persuasive – the horses have won prizes, the gold will make Akhilleus rich, the women are especially attractive ones. The list is divided by the times when the different gifts will be made – Immediately, 122-135: when Troy is sacked, 135-140: when we return home, 141-156. But it could also be divided – Recompense for Akhilleus, 119-140: honours that will be paid to him, 141-156.

121   **before you all:** Agamemnon declares his offer openly before the whole *boulē* as a way of giving it especial solemnity.

122   **tripods untouched by fire:** I.e. ones that have not been used. For the tripod, see on VIII 290. The value of the tripod as a gift is confirmed by a number of passages in the *Odyssey*, e.g. XIII 13f.; and Lorimer, 68f., records the modern discovery of some particularly elaborate ones.

From here to 134 the gifts are immediately available, and so presumably all with Agamemnon at Troy. The richness of the gifts is in keeping with Homer's picture of Agamemnon's capital, Mukenai, of which he commonly uses the epithet 'golden' – a picture that was confirmed by Schliemann's discoveries at the site. Neither Agamemnon nor Akhilleus (who does not mention them at all) anticipates that the tripods or other objects will be of practical use; it is the wealth that they represent that is important.

talents: The weight of Homer's talent is not known; it was certainly much less than it became in classical times. At XXIII 269 two talents of gold are no more than the fourth prize in the chariot race, and this is inferior to a cauldron in mint condition.

124   **prizes:** These prizes would probably be the ones on offer in funeral games, as at the games for Patroklos at XXIII 164-5. Prizes simply for sport are mentioned only at XI 699-701, an episode earlier than the action of the *Iliad*. The second half of this line is no more than an explanation of the unusual word ἀθλοφόρους. See on VIII 528.

128-132 women ... Briseus: Agamemnon sets great store by Akhilleus' appetite for women. Besides these seven from Lesbos, he is also to receive Briseis (131), twenty Trojan women (139), and one of Agamemnon's own daughters (146) – 29 in all! Apart from Briseis, these women do not in fact move Akhilleus, the only ones he mentions being Agamemnon's daughters, and them only in scornful rejection. Akhilleus' raids on the land and islands around Troy are one of the few items that Homer gives us from the earlier years of the war; both Briseis and Agamemnon's original prize, Khruseis, had been among the spoils from these operations, and at VI 414-2; Hektor's wife Andromakhe recalls how all her family but she were killed when Akhilleus raided their home-town of Thebe. Akhilleus mentions these operations himself at 328-33. Now he is to be recompensed with spoils that he had won himself! Of Briseis' father (132) we know nothing beyond his name.

141   **Akhaian Argos:** See on 22. Agamemnon must here mean the Peloponnese, where his own kingdom of Mukenai lay. But in classical times Akhaia and Argos were distinct areas of the Peloponnese.

142-143 Orestes, my beloved son: The only mention of Orestes in the *Iliad*, apart from Odusseus' repetition of this line at 284. But the revenge that Orestes took on his mother Klutaimestre and her lover Aigisthos after they murdered Agamemnon on his return home from Troy is a common theme of the *Odyssey*. The meaning of τηλύγετος is not certain. It is especially used of an only child (or, as here, an only son), as at 482, and of Hermione, the only child of Menelaos and Helen, at III 175, so that 'beloved' or 'cherished' seems plausible.

145   **Khrusothemis ... Iphianassa:** Homer's names for Agamemnon's daughters are different from those of classical times, with no mention of Elektra or Iphigeneia, who are also not to be found in the *Odyssey*, but who are common in the Greek tragedies of the fifth century. It is to be remembered that the Greek myths did not exist in canonical versions, but that the details differed according to the circumstances in which they were told. Iphianassa here has sometimes been thought to be the equivalent of the later Iphigeneia; but if this is right, then Homer cannot have known the story which became famous later of Agamemnon sacrificing Iphigeneia at Aulis before his fleet set sail from Greece to Troy. Each of the names of Agamemnon's daughters here seems to reflect his own majesty – *Khrusothemis*, 'Golden Right': *Laodike*, 'Justice of the People': *Iphianassa*, 'Mighty Queen'.

146–147 **his own ... soothing things:** φίλος regularly has the meaning 'one's own' when it is used of parts of the body, close relatives, or possessions – thus, e.g., φίλον κῆρ, 'his own heart'; and here this meaning is extended to 'his own wife'. By ἀνάεδνον, 'without bride-price', Agamemnon must be referring to the practice whereby the bridegroom would give presents to his bride's parents, as at XI 243–5 and XVI 178. The μείλια, 'soothing things', are presumably a dowry which Agamemnon proposes to add into the bargain, as Altes did for his daughter to marry Priam, XXII 51. For the picture of marriage-settlements that emerges from the Homeric poems, see Snodgrass 1974, 114–9. Had Akhilleus become Agamemnon's son-in-law, then it is possible that by normal practice either he, or the eldest of the sons of his marriage, would in due course have been in line for the throne of Mukenai. See Finkelberg, especially 306 – 'the persistence with which the same basic situations recur suggests that kingship by marriage represents the general rule'.

150–152 **Kardamule ... Pedasos:** Homer gives variety to his list of the seven towns that Agamemnon here promises by attaching an epithet to all but the first two of them. It is not easy to explain how it could be within Agamemnon's gift to bestow these seven towns on Akhilleus. They are all on the Messenian gulf on the south coast of the Peloponnese, and so should be either within Nestor's kingdom of Pulos (though νέαται Πύλου at 153 is usually taken to mean 'just beyond the borders of Pulos'), or within Menelaos' kingdom of Sparta, or in some territory between these two – in any case, far away from Agamemnon's capital at Mukenai. It has been suggested that this passage may perhaps come from some earlier catalogue, now lost, which Homer has taken over here without sufficiently adapting it to his present context. Or perhaps he is purposely trying to enlarge the sovereignty of Agamemnon by giving him rights over territory that does not in fact belong to him. See Willcock 1978, and Hainsworth 1993, ad loc. The fourth town here, Pherai, is the same as the Phere at V 543, from where the sons of Diokles had come to Troy, 'winning honour for the sons of Atreus' – an expression which might, like this passage, suggest that Agamemnon had some rights there.

158   **Let him give in ... unyielding:** The reparations listed, Agamemnon gives his final message to Akhilleus, one that is as stern and uncompromising in expression as it is in content. His first word, δμηθήτω, rings out – all on its own at the beginning of a new line and composed of three naturally long syllables, the passive of a word which is primarily used of the taming of animals. For all its apparent magnificence, Agamemnon's offer is conditional on nothing less than Akhilleus' submission to him. There is heavy irony in ἀμείλιχος; the positive form of this word, μειλιχίοισι, was the final word of Nestor's last speech, the part of it which Agamemnon now makes clear that he has totally disregarded.

160–161 more kingly ... more distinguished in ancestry: With βασιλεύτερος Agamemnon must have in mind the same idea as Nestor expressed to Akhilleus at I 281, 'Agamemnon is φέρτερος, greater, than you are, because he rules over more people'. With γενεῇ προγενέστερος he adds a claim on the score of superior ancestry. Agamemnon traced his line back through his father Atreus to Pelops, the hero who gave his name to the Peloponnese, and so to Tantalos, a son of Zeus; but he seems to overlook, both that Akhilleus' mother Thetis was a goddess, and that through his father Peleus he too was descended from Zeus. Agamemnon makes himself, and his abiding concern for his own rank, all too clear. No wonder that no mention is made of these last four lines, either by Nestor in his reply to this speech, or by Odusseus when he conveys Agamemnon's offer to Akhilleus.

162   **Gerenian:** On this epithet of Nestor, see on VIII 80.

163–172 Most glorious ... his pity: Agamemnon has accepted Nestor's proposal, and this is enough to prompt Nestor into further speech, no less urgent and purposeful than his first one, but now concerned with the practical details of conveying Agamemnon's offer to Akhilleus. The last five lines of Agamemnon's speech Nestor wisely passes over in silence (but see the next note). They disregard entirely the ending of his own first speech, but now is not the time to say so. Nestor now expresses himself, not in proposals, but in a string of instructions rendered by imperatives and jussive subjunctives. He is not presenting matters for debate, but takes for granted the *boulē*'s approval of what he now puts forward.

164   **gifts:** the μέν after δῶρα has no corresponding δέ. There may be nothing at all in this; the unbalanced μέν, the so-called μέν *solitarium*, is common enough in Homer. But Nestor was perhaps intending to say, '*Gifts* you have offered; would that your *words* had been equally generous', and then balked at such criticism of Agamemnon at the last moment – though Taplin, 69–70, plausibly suggests that μέν could be balanced by the ἀλλ' of 165 – '*you* offer gifts; *I* will attend to the practical details'.

166   **Peleus:** The king of the Murmidons, and the mortal father of Akhilleus by the sea-nymph Thetis.

168–170 let Phoinix ... go along with them: This is the first appearance of Phoinix in the poem; and it is also surprising to find him here at the *boulē* – in view of his very close association with Akhilleus that becomes prominent later in this book, he should perhaps rather now be with Akhilleus in his tent. See Introduction, **7h**. Nestor's choice of Phoinix must be due to the close personal bond that exists between Akhilleus and him, and which Phoinix explains at length in the first part of his speech at the embassy, 434–494, a bond which enables Phoinix to exert a sort of moral pressure on Akhilleus.

Phoinix is to 'lead the way', ἡγησάσθω; and in 169, after ἔπειτ', the verb of which Aias and Odusseus are the subjects is not expressed. The ancient scholia suggested that this meant that Phoinix was to go on ahead, and that Aias and Odusseus were to follow *separately* behind. But this reads too much into the single word ἡγησάσθω. No reason is either explicitly given or comes easily to mind as to why Phoinix should go ahead on his own; and Akhilleus' reception of the ambassadors (or, by this interpretation, of Aias and Odusseus) at 193ff. does not suggest that Phoinix has already arrived. This interpretation of ἡγησάσθω arose out of the problem of the use of the dual at 182ff., on which see Introduction, **7h**.

Nestor does not give his reasons for his choice of ambassadors. Some scholars have suggested that Agamemnon should have gone to Akhilleus himself; but if Nestor had ever entertained such an idea, he would certainly have discarded it on hearing the conclusion of Agamemnon's offer-speech. Nestor's nominations widen the issue of the quarrel. Previously it had been between Agamemnon and Akhilleus alone; but now Akhilleus is to be confronted by representatives from the whole army. On Odusseus, see on VIII 97; he is the natural choice when there is diplomatic business to be done, and Antenor dilates on his oratorical powers at III 216–23. Aias is the military man; he was named as ἄριστος next after Akhilleus himself at II 768. (He was also a cousin of Akhilleus, as Aiakos was the grandfather of both; but Homer makes nothing of this connection.) So Nestor has nominated the personal friend of Akhilleus, the diplomat, and the warrior; and these will be the roles that each of the ambassadors will maintain when they address Akhilleus.

The heralds play no explicit part in the ensuing proceedings with Akhilleus, but their presence lends an air of officialdom and religious sanction to the embassy. Odios is not otherwise known as a herald. Eurubates could be the selfsame man who at I 320 went with Talthubios to fetch Briseis from Akhilleus' tent; but the word means 'traveller' (*-batēs*) 'far and wide' (*euru-*), and could be a generic name of heralds.

171–172 Bring water ... his pity: The ambassadors nominated, it only remains for Nestor to insist on the appropriate religious observances. It was essential to wash one's hands before making a formal prayer – so VI 266–8. εὐφημῆσαι is literally, 'avoid ill-omened words'; but, since *any* words might be ill-omened, it is tantamount to 'keep silent'. This practice is common enough in classical times, but does not appear elsewhere in Homer.

173 pleasing to them all: The first that we have heard of the reaction of the *boulē* as a whole to the proceedings. Up until now, it is the interaction with each other of Nestor and Agamemnon that has been all-important. Although the decisions of the *boulē* have now been taken, the Akhaian leaders still remain in Agamemnon's tent, where Odusseus and Aias find them on their return at 669.

174–177 Assistants immediately ... into each: Nestor's concluding instructions are now carried out. The young men 'crown', the mixing-bowls, i.e. fill them to the brim; the mixing-bowls are those in which, after the usual Greek fashion, the wine is mixed with water – cf. Akhilleus' instructions to Patroklos at 202–3. This mixture is then distributed to those present, after a ritual beginning, in which a few drops are put into each cup and then poured onto the ground as a libation to the gods, after which the cup is filled for normal drinking. After the libations, the prayers would have been offered, as directed by Nestor at 172. κήρυκες are most often 'heralds'; but as well as conveying messages and instructions, they also function at various public occasions, e.g. in calling an assembly, and presiding at feasts or, as here, ceremonial occasions. The ceremonies described here are all to be found elsewhere, with similar language, e.g. I 470–1, *Od.* I. 146, VII 183–4.

178   **they were setting forth:** Here we have the regular plural form, ὁρμῶντ', as the embassy gets under way; the vexed duals do not begin until 182, and there is nothing in 178–181 to suggest that the embassy does not start out together as a single group of the three ambassadors and two heralds whom Nestor nominated at 169–70.

179–180 Nestor was giving ... at Odusseus: A fine touch. The embassy has been Nestor's idea; and even at this moment of departure he cannot leave it alone, but loads it with last-minute instructions as it gets under way. μάλιστα suggests that Nestor regards Odusseus as the principal spokesman, a reasonable view to draw from the part that Odusseus has played in the poem so far, and one which Odusseus reveals himself as sharing when at 223–4 he overrules Aias' nod to Phoinix and begins the address to Akhilleus himself. There is no indication of the content of Nestor's instructions; Homer introduces a brief, imaginative, sketch, but does not overdo it.

182 – 224 The ambassadors proceed along the shore, and find Akhilleus in his hut. He welcomes them warmly, and arranges an elaborate meal for them, which they then eat together.

Homer does not in this book make clear the positions of the different Akhaian contingents; but scattered references in other books show a consistent picture of the overall lay-out. See Willcock 1978, ii, 225, with a diagrammatic representation. Facing the camp and with one's back to the sea, Akhilleus is at the extreme right; and to reach him from the tent of Agamemnon, where the council took place, the ambassadors must pass by more than half of the whole encampment. They have presumably followed Nestor's advice (171–2) to pray to Zeus before departing; but the situation is a tense one, and as they travel along the shore, they offer renewed prayers, this time to Poseidon, the god of the sea. The scene that follows in Akhilleus' tent, though brief, is very telling. We have not seen Akhilleus since his withdrawal. The ambassadors find him, as Talthubios and Eurubates had done in I when they came on Agamemnon's command to take Briseis away from him, attended by the silent Patroklos; and now he has been reduced to singing of heroic exploits, rather than carrying them out himself, and even doing so on a lyre which is the product of one such exploit. These are the first visitors Akhilleus has received since his withdrawal; and the warmth and excitement of his reception are very clear. He leaps up to greet his visitors with his lyre still in his hand; and his greeting is conspicuously effusive. The repeated ἦ, each time at the beginning of its clause, in 197, is most emphatic; and Akhilleus' tone is further enhanced by the unusual structure of this line, and φίλοι in 197 developed into φίλτατοι in 198. The openness and spontaneity of Akhilleus' reception, though characteristic of how we sometimes see him elsewhere, will change completely once the ambassadors have declared their business to him.

182–186 The two of them ... found him: On the dual forms in lines 182–198, see Introduction, **7h**.

Line 182 repeats exactly I 327, when Talthubios and Eurubates make their way to Akhilleus' tent to take Briseis from him; and Μυρμιδόνων ... δ' εὗρον at 185–6 repeats I 328–9. Lohmann, 227–231, suggests that these reminiscences of the earlier scene are purposeful; the journeys in I and IX are similar, but their purposes are completely different – the first to take Briseis away, the second an attempt to restore her, and to make good the damage that her seizure has caused.

183   **the god ... the earth:** I.e. Poseidon, the brother of Zeus and god of the sea. Poseidon 'holds the earth' because the ocean, in Homer's view, embraces and supports the earth; and he 'shakes' it, because he is the god of earthquakes, and because the waves continually beat against the shore. As they travel along the shore the ambassadors naturally pray to the god of the sea; and Poseidon is also a pro-Greek god – see the note on VIII 200.

185–225 They came ... "Hail, Akhilleus!: The ensuing events follow a very similar course to the welcome of Nestor and Odusseus at Peleus' palace at XI 768–80. In both scenes the visitors arrive; they find their host(s) doing something; they are recognised, and led inside (the second halves of IX 193 and XI 777 are identical); a meal is prepared and eaten; and only after that do the visitors announce the reason for their visit. This is the basic pattern of the 'typical scene' of welcome; there is a notable example at XVIII 369–467, when Akhilleus' mother Thetis visits the god Hephaistos at his home on Olumpos. On typical scenes as a feature of oral poetry, see Parry 1971, especially 404–7; and Introduction, **4**. Arend's analysis of the welcome-scene is on pp. 34–53. Within the basic pattern of the typical scene, Homer introduces great variety to suit the particular context – cf. Willcock 1990, 4–13. Here, what Akhilleus is doing when the ambassadors find him, and the warmth and excitement of his welcome, are both distinctive; and the description of the preparation of the meal is spun out to unusual, indeed unique, length, which is the means by which Homer conveys the particular importance of this example.

185   **Murmidons:** Akhilleus' contingent of the Murmidons appears in the Catalogue of the Akhaian Ships at II 681–94. They came from Thessaly, in northern Greece (Akhilleus is the only major warrior in the *Iliad* to come from here); and they contributed 50 ships to the expedition. This was a considerable number, equal to the contributions of the Boiotians and the Athenians.

186   **they found him delighting:** Akhilleus is whiling away the time with the same activity as the professional bards of the *Odyssey*, Phemios at Odusseus' palace in Book I, and Demodokos at the court of the Phaiakian king Alkinoos in VIII. But whereas they sing to the whole court, Akhilleus has only Patroklos for company. τέρπω (again in 189), 'delight', is frequently used of the emotions aroused by the bard's singing – e.g. I 474, *Od.* I 347, VIII 91, XVII 385; and Macleod, 1–8.
           clear-sounding: λιγύς is also used of Demodokos' lyre at *Od.* VIII 67. The word can also be used of a commanding speaker, such as Nestor at *Il.* I 248; and cf. Agamemnon's λιγύφθογγοι heralds at line 10 of this book. On the basis of his studies of Serbo-Croatian singers, Milman Parry wrote: 'Fine singing for the Greeks must have been very like fine singing for the Southern Slavs: a voice as strong as possible singing to as high a pitch as possible, a clear-cut and forceful delivery of the words, and a vigorous accompaniment upon the instrument' (Parry 1971, 457).

The lyre is a stringed instrument which one plucks with one's fingers as one sings. In painted pottery of the fifth century, the instrument commonly has seven strings; but this development did not occur until the seventh century, and the instruments of Homer's day had four or five strings. On the lyre and the bard in Homer, see West 1981, 113–25.

187 **crosspiece:** This is the piece which joins the two horns of the lyre, into which the pegs which hold the strings are fitted.

188 **Eetion:** He was the father of Hektor's wife Andromakhe. His city was Thebe, near Troy, and he lost his life when Akhilleus sacked it in one of his operations in the early years of the Trojan war – VI 414–24.

189 **famous deeds of men:** κλέα ἀνδρῶν, literally, 'fames of men'. The expression recurs at 524, where Phoinix is thinking of earlier heroes who, like Akhilleus, had been possessed by anger; and it is also used of the subjects of Demodokos' songs at *Od.* VIII 73. Akhilleus is thus singing what we should call 'heroic poetry', songs of which in aftertimes he could well be the subject himself. Redfield, 30–35, discusses how, while the bard sings of the *kleos* of the hero, he also by his singing confers *kleos* on the hero's actions. At VI 357–8 Helen laments that because of their misguided behaviour she and Paris 'will be a subject of song for the generations to come'.

190 **Patroklos:** As at the scene of the seizure of Briseis, Akhilleus is attended in silence by the faithful Patroklos. This is the first mention of Patroklos in this book, and there is powerful dramatic effect in his silent background presence throughout the exchanges between the ambassadors and Akhilleus. Akhilleus' rejection of the ambassadors will lead to Patroklos' entry into battle, and so to his death; and his death will accomplish what the present embassy fails to accomplish, Akhilleus' return to the fighting.

191 **waiting:** Patroklos is perhaps waiting to take over the singing when Akhilleus is ready for a rest from it, although elsewhere in Homer the singing is performed by one man on his own, who does, however, take breaks from time to time. Milman Parry (see note to **'clear-sounding'**, 186) pointed out the great effort that singing of this sort requires; 'a good singer after a half hour of his song is drenched in sweat. The length of time which any singer will sing at a stretch is thus largely determined by the stamina of his physique'.

196 **swift-footed:** The most common of the epithets of Akhilleus, which he is supposed to have acquired when, in an incident early in the Trojan war, he successfully pursued the Trojan prince Troilos, even though Troilos was on horseback. (This incident is not given by Homer, but was a popular one in Greek vase-painting.) That Akhilleus should be swift-footed is, of course, of no consequence to the present situation. On the formulaic epithet see Introduction, **4**.

197–198 **Welcome! ... in my anger:** Akhilleus had been astonished, ταφών, when the ambassadors first arrived; and this makes itself felt in the abruptness of his address, where the single word of welcome, χαίρετον, is followed by the clause ἦ ... ἱκάνετον which most unusually is entirely contained within the line (cf. Nestor's ἑλών ... γέρας at 111). The next four words are ambiguous. Does Akhilleus have need of the ambassadors, or they of him? Perhaps the ambiguity is intentional – 'this is a moment of crisis, for me and for you'. It is characteristic of Akhilleus that with μοι σκυζομένῳ in the next line he makes no secret at all of his feelings.

200   **chairs, coverlets:** Homer's heroes invariably sit to a meal; the reclining that is familiar from classical times did not, on the evidence of painting, come into fashion until after Homer's day. Here and Athene sat on golden κλισμοί at VIII 436. The κλισμοί are, at least in classical times, light chairs without arms; the τάπητες are coverlets which are spread over the chairs, rather than floor-coverings.

201   **Patroklos:** Akhilleus does not have a retinue of servants. Patroklos, Automedon (209), and he himself undertake the necessary preparations. Some further companions and servants briefly appear at 658.

202   **mixing-bowl:** See on 174–7. Akhilleus takes for granted that the food is to be prepared, and in his instructions to Patroklos concerns himself entirely with the arrangements for the drinking. At *Il.* IV 258–60 the mixing-bowl is linked to the feast as the aristocratic activity par excellence whenever there is no fighting to be done; see Luke 1994, with evidence from archaeology as well as literary sources, for the connection of the mixing-bowl with aristocratic honour.

204   **For these men ... dearest friends:** Akhilleus repeats the declaration of his affection that he had made at 198; Aias will pointedly remind him of this at 640. The μέλαθρον, 'roof-beam', would normally be found in a more lordly dwelling than Akhilleus' hut – for instance, Priam's palace at II 414. But there seems to be no very clear conception of the architecture of the hut.

205   **Patroklos:** Patroklos maintains his dignified and respectful silence; and after 220, though he must still be present, we do not hear of him until 620. This silence is characteristic of him when he is in the service of Akhilleus; but he proves himself a formidable fighter when he goes into action in Book XVI. Homer leaves it to us to guess at his reactions to the visitors, and to the course that their overtures subsequently take.

206–217 Then he laid ... served the meat: The preparations for the meal are given at remarkable length; cf. the much shorter account at XXIV 621–6 (where 625–6 closely resemble 216–7 here) of Akhilleus' preparations for his meal with Priam. By the proliferation of detail here, Homer conveys the importance of the occasion, not only for his listeners but also for the participants. The ambassadors had already eaten at the council (90–2), but neither Akhilleus' reception nor the ambassadors' delivery of their message would be complete without a meal. For the connection of food with honour, see Griffin 1980, 14–17.

The meal consists entirely of meat, bread, and wine. This is the regular diet of the Homeric heroes, at least on ceremonial occasions; despite 'the Hellespont teeming with fish', they do not eat fish. But the Greeks of later times were largely vegetarian; and this is one of the ways in which Homer distances his heroes from the men of his own day. No indication is given of where Akhilleus has got his abundant supplies from (but cf. 72), nor of how he stored them.

209   **Automedon:** He is the most important of the Murmidons after Akhilleus and Patroklos, and is described at XVI 145–148, when he is acting as Patroklos' charioteer. He has an *aristeia* of his own at XVII 429–539, but, like Patroklos, he is now completely and silently in his master's service.

211   **equal of the gods:** See on VIII 493, **beloved of Zeus**.

214   **fire-rests:** These are the stone- or clay-blocks at each side of the fire on which the ends of the spits rest while the meat is being roasted. The elaborate description of the preparations leads to Homer using a number of words here, of which κρατευταί is one, which he does not use elsewhere. Cf. the note on 219–220.

      holy salt: The only mention of salt at meals in the *Iliad* (in the *Odyssey* it appears at XI 123, XVII 455, and XXIII 270). We have no means of knowing why it should be 'holy'; Leaf ad loc., citing Jewish practice, suggests that it may be because of its purifying qualities – it helps to make the sacrifices fit for the gods.

216   **table:** This is a small, portable, table, which would usually be removed at the end of a meal – cf. XXIV 476.

218   **facing ... Odusseus:** Is Akhilleus' position a chance event; or does he already have his suspicions about Odusseus, fearing that he has word to bring from the detested Agamemnon? Akhilleus certainly makes no secret of his suspicions of the duplicity of the embassy the moment he has heard what Odusseus has to say, 309–313.

219–220 **to sacrifice ... the sacrificial parts:** θυηλαί is another word which occurs only here in Homer. The word is presumably derived from θύειν, 'to sacrifice', and is commonly supposed to refer to the portion of meat that is dedicated to the gods; by classical times, the word can be used on its own for 'sacrifice'. The procedure here again signifies the supreme importance of this occasion. A sacrifice may be conducted, and then be followed by a meal, as e.g. at II 402–431; but the sacrifice as one of the preliminaries to the meal which we have here can be paralleled in Homer only at *Od.* XIV 418–438, where Odusseus' swineherd Eumaios sacrifices a pig in the course of entertaining his disguised master in his own hut.

223   **Aias gave ... spotted it:** A pregnant line. The meal over, the moment has come for the visitors to state their business. The military-minded Aias is impatient that no further time should be lost, and he prompts Phoinix, the comrade of Akhilleus, to make the first move. But Odusseus will have none of this. The embassy is official business, and he the official spokesman, and so he promptly seizes the initiative himself. Was Aias' attempted prompt to Phoinix intended as a snub to Odusseus?

225–655 On the speeches of the embassy, see Introduction, **7, b** to **f.**

225 – 306 Speech of Odusseus

Odusseus' speech follows immediately on his toast to Akhilleus, and so is not introduced by a separate verb of speaking. He comes straight to the matter in hand, with no more in the way of opening pleasantries than the situation demands. First he sketches the desperate need of the Akhaians for Akhilleus in their present crisis (229–51), and then he reminds Akhilleus of what his father had once told him (252–9), before he comes to the main matter, the offer that Agamemnon has made (260–99). This he sets forth almost exactly, as far as syntax allows, as Agamemnon has expressed it; and he concludes with a brief appeal to Akhilleus' pity for the Akhaians, and a reminder of the *kudos* he will gain for himself if he will resume fighting (300–6).

      The speech is a long one (though less so than Akhilleus' reply to it); and its skilfulness has long been admired. Much has been written of Odusseus' use of such devices of rhetoric as *captatio benevolentiae* (his studious attempt to get Akhilleus onto his side) and *prosopopoeia* (his address to Akhilleus through the mouth of Peleus at 254–8); and Lohmann,

231–2, calls the speech a masterpiece of 'pre-rhetorical rhetoric'. But for all his skill Odusseus quite fails in his object of winning over Akhilleus; and this has led some scholars to find shortcomings in what Odusseus says, and/or how he says it. His speech, so it is sometimes said, lacks heart. While Odusseus is wise to omit altogether the last four lines of Agamemnon's speech at the *boulē*, he ought not to have omitted the first six of them, in which Agamemnon openly acknowledged his *atē* in his dealings with Akhilleus in Book I; and furthermore he ought to have explicitly assured Akhilleus of the sympathy he has from the other Akhaian leaders. See, e.g., Reinhardt, 221–2, and Edwards 1987, 221–2. But would this really have made a difference? It would be hard to fault the carefulness and skill of Odusseus' approach; but the sequel makes clear that this approach, which takes little or no account of Akhilleus' present feelings, has not been the right one.

226   **Agamemnon:** Might it have been wiser of Odusseus to omit this reference to Akhilleus' enemy? But both the ancient scholia and some modern critics, e.g. Edwards 1987, 221, find a shrewdness in this early, apparently passing, reference to a subject which, however provocative, cannot be avoided.

229   **child of a god:** Odusseus had not added a complimentary epithet when he began his address to Akhilleus at 225, but he introduces one now, as he begins the main theme of his speech. διογενές, vocative, is the very first word of Akhilleus' reply to Odusseus.

230-231   **whether we save ... martial spirit:** Odusseus does not air the option with which Agamemnon had begun the *agorē*, that the Akhaians should now return home. That he and his men should now return home is the first, and indeed the only, option that Akhilleus will consider in his response to Odusseus. With the personal pronoun followed by particle, σύ γε, the appeal to Akhilleus is made as emphatic as it possibly can be.

232–243 For the high-spirited ... bewildered by the smoke: The Akhaian position is presented even more bleakly than Agamemnon presented it at the *agorē*, and as he will present it again at X 43–52. Lohmann, 233, points out that Odusseus represents the dangers facing the Akhaians in three blocks of four lines each –

    232–5, The Trojans have taken up position outside the city;
    236–9, Hektor, confident of Zeus' support, has gone wild;
    240–3, He intends to set fire to the ships on the next morning.

    In what he says of the Trojans' present ambitions, Odusseus reveals a knowledge of the events of the previous book within the Trojan lines that strictly he could not have; see on VIII 180–3 and on **the immortals honoured** at IX 110.

233   **high-spirited ... far-famed:** ὑπέρθυμοι and τηλεκλειτοί are regular epithets for the Trojans and their allies, and the former fits well with what Odusseus is saying here. ὑπέρθυμοι is not used of the Akhaians generally, although it is sometimes applied to individuals on the Akhaian side, e.g. II 746. The Trojan allies are enumerated in the catalogue at II 815–877.

234   **lighting many fires:** The Trojan fires *outside* the city are again symbolic of their success in the past day's fighting, as they were for Nestor at 76–7.

236–238 favourable signs: ἐνδέξια is literally 'from left to right', and signs in this direction were taken as favourable. So II 353. Zeus' lightning, and the Akhaians' terrified response to it, have been related at VIII 75–7; see also 170–1. The three successive enjambed lines expose the compelling urgency with which Odusseus is now speaking – as perhaps also does the rhyme between the endings of 236 and 237, although Leaf denies that any special effect is intended by this.

237–239 Hektor ... come upon him: Odusseus uses even stronger language of Hektor than Teukros did at VIII 299, where see note. He comes near to contradicting himself when he says in the same breath that Hektor trusts in Zeus and that he has no respect for the gods.

241 stern-posts: Hektor will hack away the tops of the ships' κόρυμβα so that he may have them as trophies of his victory.

247–251 But up ... the Danaans: Odusseus at last gets to the main point at issue, and as he does so he chooses his words with the greatest circumspection. From what he has already said, the conclusion is plain – 'You **must** save the Greeks now'. But Odusseus does everything he can to leave it to Akhilleus to make the decision for himself – hence, 'If you are minded ... consider how you will ward off'. His method is similar to that of Nestor at the *boulē*, where he touched on the matter of Briseis, but left it to Agamemnon to make the decision to seek rapprochement with Akhilleus.

249–250 grief ... cure: The jingle ἄχος/ ἄκος is perhaps an intentional effect as Odusseus reaches the climax of the first part of his address.

252–253 Good sir ... to Agamemnon: The opening ὦ πέπον gives a friendly, personal, tone to the next section of Odusseus' speech, in which he reminds Akhilleus of the injunctions he had received from his father Peleus, a tone that is strikingly different from the more formal and studied one which he has adopted so far. Nestor uses ὦ πέπον when he reminds Patroklos of his father's words to him at XI 765. Odusseus' verbatim quotation of Peleus' parting instructions to his son and his precise time-reference at 254 give his words an air of conviction – so Edwards 1970, 252–3. Akhilleus in his reply makes no explicit reference to this section of Odusseus' speech.

253 Phthie: Akhilleus' homeland touches the Malian gulf in the south, and runs northwards to the plain of Thessaly. But his own men are the Murmidons, whereas there is a separate contingent of the Phthians, which was led by Philoktetes and Protesilaos – so XIII 686, but see Janko on XIII 685–8. On the geography, see further on 395 and 447–8. Phthie is not a particularly notable area for the chief warrior on the Akhaian side to come from; but, *pace* Page, 126, there is nothing exceptionable about this – it is his fighting that Akhilleus is known for, not his place of origin. See Hope Simpson & Lazenby, 129. There are further instructions from Peleus to Akhilleus at XI 783–4.

255 proud heart: The same expression that Nestor used of Agamemnon at 109 in connection with his seizure of Briseis. It is used again of Akhilleus by Aias at 629; and Phoinix speaks of his μέγαν θυμόν at 496. Phoinix's use of the expression makes clear that it is not necessarily pejorative, but rather 'the mighty heart of a hero'. For 'stubborn', and 'stubbornness', words like ἀγήνωρ and ἀγηνορίη are used – e.g. at 635 and 700.

256 good feelings between friends: Odusseus does not himself develop Peleus' instructions on φιλοφροσύνη; but the idea that 'No man is an island, entire of it self' will play an important part in the speeches of Phoinix and Aias.

261 **give up your anger:** Odusseus repeats verbatim the condition that Agamemnon made at 157, and he returns to it at 299; but he prudently passes over what Agamemnon said next.

262–299 Seven tripods ... your anger: The changes of person apart, Odusseus reproduces Agamemnon's offer exactly, with only the two exceptions noted below. Such verbatim repetition is normal when messages are delivered, instructions and orders given, reports made, etc.; see on VIII 412. Kakridis 1971, chap. 4, discusses parallel procedures in modern Greek folk-poetry and elsewhere. That the oral poet should be able to recall exactly 37 lines from Agamemnon's speech seems a considerable feat of memory; but in their fieldwork in Yugoslavia Milman Parry and Lord found that the oral poets did have unusually well-developed memories.

269 **so much as the prizes:** It would have been possible to reproduce line 127 here with just the change of the second word, μοι, to οἱ, 'for him'. But then 'him' would not have been clear. It should, of course, refer to Agamemnon; but it might be taken as the unnamed ἀνήρ who is the subject of this sentence.

276 **something that ... and women:** Line 134 could have been repeated exactly here; but the vocative ἄναξ here would be impossible at 134. The first four words of this line have been used by Nestor at line 33; and perhaps 134 is a variation on an already existing 276, rather than the other way round. See Willcock 1978, ad loc. Leaf says, but without further explanation, that the rhythm of 276 is an improvement on 134.

300–306 But if ... brought here: The offer delivered, Odusseus returns, by ring-composition, to his original theme. But in doing so he introduces two ideas which will be important in what follows, the idea that Akhilleus might show pity to his fellow-warriors, and the idea that he will win *kudos* for himself by returning. The idea of pity Akhilleus does not take up in his reply at all; but both Phoinix and Aias remind him that he has obligations to other men besides himself. Odusseus reasonably assumes that Akhilleus will be attracted by the prospect of *kudos*; but much of Akhilleus' reply to him is concerned with saying that he is not, and his only response to what Odusseus says at 304–6 is the reminder that while he was fighting himself Hektor never rampaged like this (352–5).

307 – 429 Akhilleus' reply to Odusseus

Akhilleus forthrightly and utterly rejects everything that Odusseus has offered and requested, not by reasoned, point-by-point, argument, but by 'an explosion of rage at the impossible position he finds himself in' – Redfield, 17. The contrast between Odusseus' painstaking diplomacy and Akhilleus' spontaneous outburst of wrath could not be greater. Many of the points that he now makes he has already made in his speech at the quarrel at I 149–71 – Agamemnon's shamelessness, his own lack of a motive for fighting at Troy, the loss of his *geras*, the unequal division of the spoils, his intention now to give up and go home. But he did not there set these points within the framework of total, blank, rejection that he does now. In his towering rage, he asks questions to which there is no answer (337–41), and makes demands that it is impossible to meet (379–87). It is in his response to Odusseus' final point, the prospect of greater *kudos* for himself if he will return to the fighting, that Akhilleus is most revealing. At XII 310–328, Sarpedon makes his celebrated statement about the hero's life, in which he says that the hero receives honour from his subjects, and must make himself worthy of such honour by deeds of valour; there is, that is, 'a perfect correspondence between individual prowess and social honour', Parry 1989, 3. In his rejection of Agamemnon's offer, Akhilleus, uniquely among the heroes of the *Iliad*, rejects that correspondence, and so makes the impasse in the present situation complete.

On the character of Akhilleus' speech, and on how it fits with his characterisation elsewhere, see Lohmann, 279, n. 118, Griffin 1986, 51–7, Parry 1989, 1–7.

308–311 Child ... the other: After the one-line address to Odusseus, Akhilleus immediately makes his mood clear, with the emphatic δή in both 309 and 310, each time accompanied by a second particle, and the derisive τρύζητε in 311. ἀπηλεγέως, 'forthrightly', is a word that only Akhilleus uses. The following ἀποειπεῖν could have the meaning 'deny', as at 510; but 'declare', with ἀπο- conveying the idea of completeness, as in, e.g., ἀπομηνίσαντος at 426, seems to fit better with what follows at 312–4; it is only after 314 that Akhilleus comes on to denying Agamemnon. At 310 Akhilleus comes close to repeating what he heard from Athene when she appeared to him at the quarrel at I 212.

312–313 For that man ... something different: We expect Akhilleus to say something like, 'I will not mince words with you'. So he does, but not until 314, after he has delivered this powerful outburst against hypocrisy which, though explicitly directed at the impersonal κεῖνος, can only have Odusseus and Agamemnon as its object. For Akhilleus the offer is nothing more than a stealthy attempt to coerce him into doing what he has no wish to do.

315 **Agamemnon the son of Atreus:** In his offer-speech Agamemnon never used Akhilleus' name, but Akhilleus often uses Agamemnon's. He always accompanies it with the patronymic Ἀτρείδης, which certainly at 332 and 339, where it is the first word in the line, and perhaps elsewhere as well, we should imagine him spitting out in bitter disgust.

318 **There is ... alike die:** Having declared his rejection of Agamemnon's offer, Akhilleus expands on his present position by rattling off three proverbial-looking expressions, each exactly one line in length. The effect is very powerful.

323–327 But as a bird ... their wives: Griffin 1986, 36, observes that Akhilleus is unique in the *Iliad* in the frequency with which he introduces similes into his speech. The point of this simile lies in the mother-bird getting no reward for herself when she brings morsels to her fledglings, although Akhilleus does not make this explicit when he returns to himself at 325–7.

327 **battling with ... their wives:** Akhilleus is referring to the practice of the victors seizing the wives of their enemies when a city is sacked, as at the sack of Lesbos at 128–30. The fall of Troy was followed by wholesale acts of violence against the Trojan women by the Akhaian victors.

328–329 I have sacked ... fertile Troy: On Akhilleus' raiding exploits in the earlier years of the war, see the notes on 128–32 and VIII 370–2.

334–336 The other prizes ... taken away (my prize): Akhilleus has just said that Agamemnon, while staying behind himself, nevertheless kept most of the booty for himself. Now he makes what is substantially a new point, that Agamemnon has given out the prizes to the other leaders, and has deprived only Akhilleus of his. But at the quarrel it was maintained, both by Akhilleus himself at I 123 and 162, and by

Agamemnon at 135, that the prizes were distributed, not by the leader, but by the whole army. Akhilleus is representing Agamemnon's conduct in the worst possible light; his emotions get the better of logic and of factual accuracy. Likewise at 367.

336–337 the bride ... enjoy himself: Akhilleus is becoming carried away by his anger; Briseis was his captive, not his wife. Agamemnon has offered, *both* to restore Briseis to Akhilleus, *and* to give him one of his daughters in marriage; and Akhilleus at 394 envisages finding a wife once he has got back home. But his point here leads on well to his next one – Menelaos has not been prepared to lose his wife (so why should I lose mine?). With **Let him lie with her** Akhilleus ignores Agamemnon's solemn oath that he has not touched Briseis.

336–341 Let him lie ... love their wives: Akhilleus' emotions come to a head as his speech reaches its first great climax. Four times in five lines his sentence, or question, runs without stopping over the line-ending and ends after a single word in the next line has come to the first syllable of the second foot, and this word is each time an especially important one. Now that he has got onto the subject of Agamemnon's depriving him of his *geras*, Akhilleus is quite beside himself; that Agamemnon has now undertaken to restore Briseis untouched is of no account to him at all.

341   good, sensible: ἐχέφρων, a compound of ἔχω and φρήν, the seat of reason, is commonly and appropriately applied to Odusseus' faithful wife Penelope in the *Odyssey*. Here the expression ἀγαθὸς καὶ ἐχέφρων looks almost paradoxical, since what is expected of the *agathos* in the *Iliad* is self-assertion, rather than self-restraint.

343   won by the spear: Briseis was captured at Lurnessos, a city at the foot of Mount Ide – II 690. It was in the course of the same raid that Agamemnon acquired Khruseis, the subsequent loss of whom, when her father Khruses, the priest of Apollo, asked for her back, led Agamemnon to demand Briseis from Akhilleus – I 366.

346–377 But, Odusseus, ... of his wits: For the moment, Akhilleus has said what he has to say about Agamemnon and his *geras*, and he now goes on to his intention to depart immediately. But he will return, by a process of ring-composition, to the *geras* at 367.

347   keep the consuming fire: Akhilleus prophetically envisages the scene that begins at XV 592, when Hektor breaks through to the Akhaian ships. But his words also call to mind what in the previous book Hektor had said to the Trojans, and also what Zeus had prophesied to Here – VIII 526–41 and 470–7.

348–350 he has certainly ... stakes in it: The particles at the beginning of 348 and 349 are said in a heavily sarcastic tone; Akhilleus mentions Agamemnon's accomplishments only to ridicule them, and to declare that they will not have the success that he has had in keeping Hektor at bay. At the end of Book XII, lines 445ff., Hektor smashes down the gates of the Akhaian wall, and the Trojans swarm over it.

351–356 murderous Hektor ... godlike Hektor: Akhilleus centres the Trojan war-effort predominantly on Hektor, whom he now mentions by name three times within 6 lines. At the end of a line Hektor in the genitive case may be either ἀνδροφόνοιο as here, or ἱπποδάμοιο, 'horse-taming'. This is one of the very rare exceptions to the general rule, which was an important part of Milman Parry's researches into the oral nature of Homer's poetry, that in each position in the line each hero has one, and only one, epithet. See especially *The Epithet and the Formula I: The Usage of the Fixed*

Epithet, in Parry 1971, 37–117; and Introduction, **4**. In the present context it is clearly more to the point that Hektor is 'man-slaughtering' than that he should be 'horse-taming'.

354   **the Skaian gate:** Homer does not use πύλη in the singular. He regularly envisages the Skaian gate as the main gate leading from Troy to the battlefield; and the association of the gate with the oak-tree is also at VI 237 and XI 170. The episode of Hektor and Akhilleus having already almost come to blows is not found elsewhere.

356–363 **But as ... Phthie on the third day:** Akhilleus had briefly thrown out the threat of returning home forthwith at the quarrel, I 169, but now he develops it at more length. This threat is the one aspect of his position that Phoinix and Aias will succeed in modifying – see 618–9 and 650–3. Lohmann, 279, n. 118, shows how impulsiveness, and a tendency to throw out ideas that he does not then abide by, are consistent features of the characterisation of Akhilleus.

359   **you will see, if you care to:** Akhilleus uses the same words that Zeus used in his prophecy to Here at VIII 471. This may not be accidental – Griffin 1980, 88; in his towering rage Akhilleus is more like a god than a man.

360   **the Hellespont:** The narrow strait that divides Europe from Asia at the point where the waters from the Black Sea run out into the Aegean. Troy is by the southernmost tip of the Hellespont.

361   **the men:** There is no question but that Akhilleus' withdrawal will mean the withdrawal of his whole contingent as well.

363   **on the third day:** The speed of the voyage home will be about 75 miles a day. At *Od.* III 180, the voyage from Tenedos, just off the coast of Troy, back to Argos in Greece takes four days.

364   **plenty of possessions ... made my way:** As Akhilleus talks of his return home, a fresh reason occurs to him for refusing Agamemnon's offer – he has so much wealth already at home, and at Troy as well, that he does not need Agamemnon's gifts. ἔρρω, 'make one's way', is often used of a journey that one has reason to regret – so 377, and VIII 239, with the note there.

365   **red bronze:** The phrase χαλκὸν ἐρυθρόν does not occur elsewhere in Homer. Possibly, but not certainly, Akhilleus means copper, a metal which is the principal constituent of bronze, and which by late Mycenaean times may have been in use as a primitive form of currency – Taylour, 133. For Mycenaean sources of copper, see Lorimer, 54–8, and Taylour, 144–54.

367   **assigned ... special prize:** Akhilleus distinguishes between the gold, etc., that he has been assigned, ἔλαχον, and his special *geras*, Briseis. The former is easily replaceable, the latter is not. It is the *principle* of the *geras* that matters – so much so that there is no need to mention Briseis by name at all.

368   **insultingly:** The idea of *hubris*, so familiar from classical Greek literature, is not common in the *Iliad* – besides here, only at I 203 and 214, XI 695, and XIII 633. All four of these occurrences are, like the present one, in speeches; and the first two of them also refer to Agamemnon's treatment of Akhilleus. The word is much more common in the *Odyssey*.

372–377 **he would not dare ... his wits:** The loss of the *geras* again renders Akhilleus almost apoplectic, as it had done at 334–43. This time his fury makes itself felt with οὐδ' and οὐδέ beginning four clauses within the course of as many lines, and then by the enjambment of 375 and 376, where three short, sharp, statements, οὐδ' ἂν ἔτ' ... ἔκηλος ἐρρέτω, each begin and end in mid-line.

377   **Zeus ... his wits:** i.e. Zeus has visited *atē* on Agamemnon. Agamemnon had, of course, acknowledged this at the beginning of the offer-speech, but this part of the speech Odusseus did not convey to Akhilleus. Akhilleus recognises the *atē* of Agamemnon, but does not share his conviction that the offered gifts can now redeem it.

378   **I hate his gifts:** So far Akhilleus has concerned himself with the request that he should return to the fighting. Only now does he turn to the subject of the gifts that Agamemnon has offered. But from what he has already said it is clear that the gifts mean nothing to him at all, and his eventual consideration of them is little more than a renewed outburst of anger and hate.

379–387 **Not even if ... grieves my heart:** Akhilleus' rejection of Agamemnon's offer takes the form of a thunderous 9-line sentence, which in its structure is a conditional sentence, with a multiple protasis of 7 lines (379–85) followed by a two-line apodosis. As at 372–5, the remorselessly hammered-out οὐδέ creates a powerful effect, the more so here when it begins both the sentence as a whole at 379 and also the apodosis at 386. Akhilleus uses similar language when, once more in a paroxysm of fury, he tells Hektor that, once he has killed him, nothing will save his corpse from the ravening dogs and birds – XXII 349–54.

381   **Orkhomenos:** On the north-west side of Lake Kopais in Boiotia. Archaeology has revealed that it must have been one of the leading Greek cities in late Mycenaean times, but it is not particularly important in the *Iliad*, and this is the only reference to its wealth. It was the centre of the Minuans, whose leaders Askalaphos and Ialmenos (II 511) have appeared as commanders of the guard at 82.

381–384 **Egyptian Thebes ... horses and chariots:** Thebes, the modern Luxor, 400 or so miles down from the mouth of the Nile, had once been the capital of Egypt, and its wealth is mentioned several times in the *Odyssey*, e.g. at III 301 and IV 127, which is almost equivalent to 382 here. But this is the only mention of it in the *Iliad*. Some scholars have rejected lines 382–4, and without them the Thebes of 381 would be the one in Greece which, like Orkhomenos, had been a leading city of Boiotia. But there is some evidence that Boiotian Thebes had already been destroyed before Troy was – see II 405 and IV 406, and Kirk 1985, 193 and 196; and Willcock 1978, on 384, suggests that 381 may indeed once have stood on its own, but that 382–4 were added later, either by Homer himself or by another poet, after it had been realised that Boiotian Thebes was not a good illustration of the point that Akhilleus is here making about massive riches. There is an interesting discussion of these lines by Lorimer, 95–9, who suggests that the memory of Egyptian Thebes goes back to before the late Mycenaean age, and that the hundred gates are a fiction ('Thebes never was a fortified city') which may have arisen from the great pylons of the Egyptian temple. Mentions of Egypt in the *Iliad* and *Odyssey* have sometimes been thought to shed light on the date of the composition of the poems, with some scholars arguing that they arise out of contacts between Greece and Egypt in the *seventh* century – i.e. later than the late eighth century date that is most commonly suggested for Homer's composition; but the results of such discussions have been inconclusive. See Burkert 1976, Kirk 1962, 110f.

388–400 I shall not marry ... Peleus has gained: The climax to the rejection comes with the rejection of one of Agamemnon's daughters in marriage. This is in fact the only item of the offer on which Akhilleus wastes much breath. At 397 he deliberately re-uses the words Agamemnon had used in offering his daughters at 146, which were repeated by Odusseus at 288. Akhilleus still has those words in mind when he talks in 397 of how he will find a wife for himself from the noblewomen of Hellas and Phthie.

389　　　**Aphrodite, Athene:** Goddesses of love and of handicrafts respectively.

392　　　**more royal:** That Akhilleus had not in fact heard Agamemnon use the word βασιλεύτερος at the conclusion of his offer-speech at 160 does not diminish the fine effect of its being repeated here. This is the only time that the comparative is used by anyone but Agamemnon (Nestor used the superlative, βασιλεύτατος, of Agamemnon at 69), whose preoccupation with rank is one of the principal issues between Akhilleus and himself.

394　　　**Peleus:** Akhilleus' reasons for introducing his father are quite different from those of Odusseus at 252, which Akhilleus ignores throughout his reply.

395　　　**Hellas and Phthie:** For Phthie, see on 253. Hellas came in classical times to mean the whole of Greece, but Homer never uses it like this, but always, as here, for what is, presumably, an area of southern Thessaly. At 447, it looks as though Hellas is distinct from Phthie – or at least that it was so at the time of which Phoinix is there speaking. See the note there.

400　　　**possessions:** Peleus commands all the riches that Akhilleus needs. Agamemnon's offer of more is unnecessary, intrusive, and insulting.

401–416 For to me ... come upon me quickly: Akhilleus comes back to his original point, that the Akhaian cause is not worth fighting and risking his life for, and whereas before it was a matter of there being no *timē* in it for him, his point now is that no amount of material recompense will make it worthwhile. Now that he has expressly rejected the gifts, his position has a terrible logic that it did not have before. To appreciate the full force of what Akhilleus is here saying, one should again refer to Sarpdeon's speech to Glaukos at XII 310–328, which Hainsworth 1993, on XII 310–21, calls 'the clearest statement in the *Iliad* of the imperatives that govern the heroic life and their justification'. Sarpedon there says that the hero must make himself worthy of the honour that his subjects pay him by his deeds of valour, accepting as the price of this the near-certainty of eventual death in battle. For Sarpedon, it is a matter of *noblesse oblige*, a system of obligations and rewards. But Akhilleus shows himself blind to the obligations and dismissive of the rewards, and so the prospect of death is one which, unlike Sarpedon, he does not accept. See Introduction, **7b**.

404–405 the Archer God ... rocky Putho: The Archer God is Apollo; ἀφήτωρ is probably drived from ἀφίημι, 'let fly'. Putho is Apollo's great centre at Delphi, on the lower slopes of Mount Parnassos in northern Greece – the epithet πετρηέσσῃ is very appropriate. The word Putho, whicl one also finds in Apollo's Delphic priestess, the Puthia, was supposed to have come from Apollo's exploit in slaying the Puthon, a mighty dragon, when he established his sanctuary there. The wealth of the place will have derived from the dedications that had been made to Apollo. Although the Delphic site is one of great antiquity, it was only around the middle of the eighth century, not long before the probable date for the *Iliad*, that it began to assume especial importance throughout the Greek world – see Burkert 1985, 115–7. Homer's only explicit reference to the oracle at Delphi is at *Od.* VIII 81.

406–409 Cattle and fine sheep ... barrier of the teeth: Another eloquent and forceful climax. 406 is contrasted with 407 – ληϊστοί, 'seized in war', κτητοί, 'acquired in peace' – one line each; and then 406–7 is contrasted with 408–9, two lines each. 406 and 407 each begin with the predicate, with the rest of the line being made up of the subject, with εἰσίν in each line omitted; and these predicates are recalled with λεϊστή and ἐλετή in 408–9.

411–416 For my mother ... upon me quickly: This is the only place where Akhilleus has alternative destinies; elsewhere he is always doomed to a short life – e.g. I 352. Critics have sometimes felt uneasy about this, especially in connection with XVI 36–51, where in replying to a question from Patroklos Akhilleus flatly denies that it is some warning from his mother that is now holding him back from fighting himself. Akhilleus' denial there could be explained by what he then goes on to say – that it is still Agamemnon's insult that holds him back, the effect of which would be diminished if he were to add that his mother's prophecy is doing so too. A more serious difficulty that the passage in XVI presents is over why Patroklos, who is present here as Akhilleus addresses the ambassadors, should put his question at all, since he should already know the answer to it. Willcock 1978, on IX 410–16, makes the suggestion that the alternative fates here may have been invented for the purposes of the present passage. This would then be one example – among several – of some apparent faultiness in the editing of IX in relation to the rest of the poem; the passage in XVI has not been brought into line with the invention that has been introduced into IX. See Introduction, **7g**.

417 And I would advise..: Having said what his two *kēres* are, Akhilleus has no need to say which one he now prefers; the *kēres* passage is the conclusion, rather than the introduction, to his argument.

419–420 Zeus has extended ... confident: Akhilleus summarises the content of the previous book. In doing so, he adds little to what Odusseus has said to him at 236–43. But the acknowledgement that disaster now faces the Akhaians, which led Odusseus to implore him to return to the fighting, has led him to the decision to return to Greece and to leave the fighting to others.

426 consumed with anger: ἀπομηνίω is formed from the noun μῆνις, which is the very first word of the *Iliad*, when the poet declares that his subject is to be the anger of Akhilleus. But Akhilleus is the only human of whom the word is used; otherwise it is reserved for the anger of the gods, and χόλος is the word for the anger of humans. Akhilleus' anger has a superhuman dimension to it; cf. on 359. In the following speech, Phoinix refers to Akhilleus' anger as μῆνις at 517, but his first word for it is χόλος, 436.

427 let Phoinix ... compel him to: Akhilleus ends his speech by turning to Phoinix, and in so doing for the first time in his tremendous speech displays quiet and warmth in what he says. Phoinix is the commander of a squadron of Akhilleus' men, the Murmidons – XVI 196; and so it is less surprising that he should now stay with Akhilleus than it was suddenly to find him at the council in Agamemnon's tent when Nestor bade him lead the embassy at 168. Akhilleus' courteous and welcoming invitation to Phoinix prepares the way for both the tone and the content of Phoinix's following speech.

430 – 605 Speech of Phoinix

Akhilleus' speech is met by stunned silence. Finally Phoinix renews the ambassadors' appeal. He first reminds Akhilleus of his own tutelage of him, and then, in the parable of the Litai, of how the Apologies are the daughters of Zeus, who must be respected and accepted when apologies are offered by one man to another. Finally, Phoinix recalls the story of Meleagros, and from it draws the lesson that Akhilleus should accept the gifts while they are still on offer.

In both its approach and its tone and content Phoinix's appeal could scarcely be more different from Odusseus'; the official spokesman has given way to the personal friend and well-wisher. Akhilleus has shown himself inaccessible to the appeal of the commander-in-chief; by his more personal approach, in which he says very little about the matters of *timē* and *kudos* which have dominated much of the debate so far, Phoinix gently but significantly shifts the ground of the issue.

On Phoinix's speech, and some of the serious difficulties of interpretation that it presents, see Introduction, **7, c, d,** and **i.**

430–432 So he spoke ... addressed him: Here again the different elements of Homer's description are all ones that appear elsewhere. See on VIII 28–30 and IX 49–50. For ἀπέειπεν, see on 308–311.

432 **driver of horses:** This epithet recurs at 438, of Peleus, and at 581, of Oineus; and elsewhere it, or ἱππότα, are used of Nestor (52), Phuleus, and Tudeus, the father of Diomedes. Both epithets are positioned so that they end at the end of the fifth foot in the line, and so need to be followed by a two-syllable personal name for the sixth foot, of which the first syllable is long. It is often observed that the men to whom the epithets are applied are all now old, and did their fighting in earlier campaigns than the Trojan war, which has been taken to suggest that chariot-fighting belongs to an earlier period than the war. Certainly in the *Iliad*, chariots are used much more as a means of transport than for the fighting, and it has been thought that Homer scarcely understood their use in battle. See the Nestor-episode at VIII 80ff., and Willcock 1976, to IV. 297ff., and 1978, Appendix B, 279–80.

434–605 If, indeed ... the war: Phoinix builds his speech almost entirely from three great *paradigms* – excursuses that either lead into some exhortation, or else reinforce one that has already been made. (Odusseus had briefly introduced a paradigm when he dwelt on Peleus' instructions to Akhilleus at 252–9.) His speech may therefore be subdivided thus: –

A. 434–445: If you leave, I would not want to be left behind.
    446–495: For, Paradigm 1, I have devoted myself to bringing you up.
B. 496–501: Tame your great heart. Even the gods give way to prayers.

502–512:   As is made clear, Paradigm 2, by the functions of the *Litai*
            and *Atē*.

C.   513–523:   Therefore, accept Agamemnon's offer.

524–599:   As is the lesson from, Paradigm 3, the story of Meleagros.

D.   600–605:   So, accept the offer, and return.

Phoinix sometimes speaks with the garrulity of an old man, at one moment
digressing from his main theme, at another expressing it in an elliptical and allusive
manner which seems to rely on the outlines of his story being known to the audience
already. But underlying his three very different paradigms is his consistent regard
for Akhilleus as an individual, and his conviction that Akhilleus is now acting
wrongly in continuing to isolate himself from his fellow-Akhaians.

435–436 ward off consuming fire: The prospect of the Akhaian fleet being burnt is here, as
commonly elsewhere, taken as the equivalent of the total defeat of the Akhaian
expedition. E.g. Hektor at VIII 180–3, Odusseus at IX 240–6. In the event, the
Trojans will begin to fire the Akhaian fleet, but will then be repelled.

437   dear child: In his first line, Phoinix had addressed Akhilleus with a formulaic
epithet, φαίδιμ' 'Αχιλλεῦ. But he loses no time in introducing the form of address
that foreshadows the thrust of the whole of the first part of the speech, his close
personal relationship with Akhilleus. He is striking a quite different tone from that
of Odusseus; and φίλον here hints at the new approach to the present issue which
will reach its climax with Aias' words to Akhilleus about the φιλότης ἑταίρων at
630. So Rosner, 315.

438   alone: οἶος gains emphasis by its position at the beginning of the line, after
enjambment. Likewise νήπιον, 'a little child', 440. Phoinix returns, by ring-
composition, to his present point, that he does not wish to be separated from
Akhilleus, at 444–5, having in the intervening section adumbrated the theme of the
first part of his speech, his care for Akhilleus in his youth.

440   the same for both sides: The meaning of ὁμοίιος is not known. It is used by
Homer elsewhere of old age and of death, and is commonly assumed, though with no
precise authority, to be equivalent to ὅμοιος, 'alike', and so used of things which are
the same for all.

442   to teach: The idea of Phoinix as Akhilleus' tutor has perhaps been specially
invented for the present passage. We do not find it elsewhere, and Akhilleus' tutor is
usually the centaur Kheiron. Homer does not give a prominent role to fairy-tale
figures such as centaurs, and it would be quite unlike him to ascribe Akhilleus'
tutelage to one – Griffin 1977, 39–53. Why Akhilleus was not tutored by his mother
Thetis is not clear; indeed at XVIII 57 Thetis claims that she did rear her son.

443   speaker of ... of deeds: The two qualities for which Nestor commends Diomedes at
the beginning of his address to him at the *agorē*, 53–4. Phoinix's tuition will repair
the shortcomings of the youthful Akhilleus at 440–1; but while the speech that he has
just delivered has made Akhilleus' powers as an orator very clear, Peleus' hopes that
he would excel at the *agorē* are unfulfilled throughout the *Iliad*.

447–495 when I first left ... shameful ruin: Phoinix's first, autobiographical, excursus, may
          be subdivided:

A.   447–78:   His flight from his own home;

B.   479–95:   His reception with Peleus, and his bringing-up of
                  Akhilleus.

But no more than a comma separates these two sections at the end of 478; Peleus' reception was the immediate consequence of Phoinix's flight. Each of the sections may also be subdivided –

A.   447–73:   Phoinix's quarrel with his father Amuntor;
     474–78:   His flight.
B.   479–84:   Peleus' reception of Phoinix;
     495–95:   Phoinix's tutelage of Akhilleus.

On some of the difficulties of this section, see Introduction, **7, i, I**.

447–448 Hellas, Amuntor: The geography seems confused. From what is said here and at 478–9, it looks as though Hellas is the kingdom of Amuntor, and is *separate* from Peleus' kingdom, to which Phoinix fled on leaving his father; but at II 683 Hellas is described as being part of the kingdom of Akhilleus (the son of Peleus). A further difficulty over this passage concerns Amuntor, who at X 266 is said to have come from Eleon, which is not in Thessaly, but Boiotia. It is perhaps better to accept that there is confusion here, rather than trying to explain it away. For Phoinix's narrative, it is sufficient to suppose, either that Hellas embraces the separate kingdoms of Amuntor and Peleus, or that within Thessaly there is a kingdom of Amuntor, Hellas, and a separate kingdom of Peleus, Phthie. See also on 395. In assessing Homer's apparent vagueness over some aspects of Greek geography, one should remember that he virtually certainly did not come from mainland Greece himself.

448   the reproaches of my father: Both Phoinix's own story, and his subsequent one of Meleagros, begin from strife within the family.

451   (clasping me) by the knees: Phoinix's mother adopts the conventional position of a suppliant before her son. One supplicated a person by sitting before him, putting one hand on his knees and the other on his chin.

454   Erinues: Phoinix has met his mother's wishes, but in doing so he has shown disrespect towards his father, and so Amuntor calls on the Furies of the Underworld to punish him – successfully, as appears from 493–4. Similarly, Meleagros' mother at 566–72 calls upon the Erinues to respond to the parent's curses upon the child.

457   Zeus beneath the earth: Presumably Hades, or Plouton, though Homer does not name him like this elsewhere. Persephone was the wife of Hades.

458–461 [I planned ... the Akhaians]: These lines are not in our mss., but they are quoted by Plutarch (c. 100 AD.) at *de aud. poetis* 8 (*Moralia* 26), who says that Aristarkhos athetised them 'in fear of what they said'. They have been restored by modern editors, and they certainly make Phoinix's resolve to leave his family home more plausible. Although the lines record that Phoinix was thwarted in his intention to kill his father, they may perhaps arise from the quite common situation of a murderer leaving home, and coming as a suppliant to the ruler of another country. Both Epeigeus and Patroklo' were received by Peleus in these circumstances – XVI 570–4, XXIII 84–8; and see also Theok'umenos at *Od.* XV 224.

465   **entreated me:** The kinsmen are presumably closing ranks; but it seems strange that Phoinix does not make the object of his kinsmen's intervention more clear.

466–469 **They were slaughtering ... drunk from jars:** The ceremonies follow the same lines as a sacrifice, and just like the sacrifice, they are aimed at restoring a sense of fellowship among the participants.

468   **singed:** The singing is necessary to burn away the bristles.

472–473 **one of them ... the bedroom-doors:** Amuntor's palace, *megaron*, has a colonnade in the courtyard separating it from the outside world (αἴθουσα αὐλῆς), and another one at the entrance leading into it. The latter seems to have been a vestibule, off which there were rooms, in one of which Phoinix slept. These rooms and the αἴθουσα would have formed the πρόδομος. See Lorimer, 406–22, especially 415–22; and the diagram of Odusseus' palace at Jones, 11.

479   **I reached:** The root of ἐξ-ικ-όμην is the same as that of ἱκέτης, 'a suppliant', who is 'one who comes to seek aid or protection' (LSJ.). See on 458–61.

481–483 **loved me ... many possessions:** One can only speculate as to why Peleus cherished Phoinix at least as much as his own son.

483   **He made me ... many people:** Peleus gave Phoinix what Agamemnon has just unsuccessfully offered to Akhilleus.

484   **Dolopes:** The only mention of the Dolopes in Homer. But they are recorded in later times as having come from the country inland from Phthie.

488–491 **before I, ... childish helplessness:** The length at which Phoinix dwells on the details of Akhilleus' childish helplessness is a measure of the importance he attaches to the theme; his help to Akhilleus when Akhilleus was himself helpless now entitle him to appeal to Akhilleus. The diet of meat and wine is exactly what we have already met at the *boulē*, at the reception in Akhilleus' hut, and at the feasting at which his kinsmen tried to prevail upon Phoinix to stay with his parents.

493–494 **the gods ... child of mine:** The consequence of Amuntor's curse on Phoinix at 453–7.

494–495 **But you ... shameful ruin:** Phoinix at last reaches the point of his narrative, but expresses it in less than two lines. His direct appeal in the next line-and-a-half is equally unassuming and unobtrusive. He is largely content to allow his paradigms to speak for themselves, and to leave Akhilleus to draw the required conclusions from them.

496   **tame:** Phoinix's use of this word is quite unlike that of Agamemnon at 158, even though it is again in the imperative, and again directed at Akhilleus. Agamemnon used it in the passive – Akhilleus was to subdue himself to him; by the active here Phoinix means no more than 'curb'.

498   **greater though ... strength are:** The greater *aretē*, *timē* and *biē* of the gods are what, apart from their immortality, differentiate them from men.

499–500 **sacrifices ... burnt offerings:** The necessary concomitants of human address to the gods. The burnt-offering is equivalent to the sacrifice. The libations have already appeared in this book at 177, where they were presumably accompanied by the prayers which Nestor had prescribed at 172.

501   **entreating:** λίσσομαι points the way ahead to the parable of the *Litai*. Phoinix's point is that, as the gods are amenable when men ask for forgiveness, Akhilleus should be also. But by this use of λίσσομαι and *Litai* he is somewhat misrepresenting what has happened in the interests of his argument. Agamemnon has offered gifts, and Phoinix gives full weight to that at 515–9; but neither Agamemnon nor anyone on his behalf has gone so far as to ask for forgiveness. Nevertheless λίσσεσθαι continues from now on to be used – in the paradigm of Meleagros at 574, 585 and 591 (also λιτάνευε at 581), and in relation to the embassy at 520 and 698.

502–514 **For there are ... the great ones:** For some of the difficulties of Phoinix's parable, and its application to the present situation, see Introduction, **7, i, II.**

503 **lame ... squint-eyed:** These epithets have been transferred to the *Litai*, when strictly they apply to the miscreant, who is 'lame' because of his reluctance to apologise, 'wrinkled' because of the mental turmoil that he is undergoing, and 'squint-eyed' because he dare not look his victim in the face. By being applied to the *Litai*, however, they make a fine contrast with the sure-footed *Atē* at 505. The unusual rhythm of this line enhances the idea of the slow-footed Litai: | - - | - - | - ᵛ ᵛ | - - | - - | - - | – five spondees, with -αι τε at the end of the first and the beginning of the third feet – with the caesura *after* it, τε being a postpositive (see Introduction: Scansion: The Homeric Hexameter 2), and χωλαί filling up the first foot, but the endings of the next four feet not coinciding with the end of a word.

513–514 **But do you, ... daughters of Zeus:** *Atē* has struck Agamemnon, and in its wake have come the *Litai* which, by Phoinix's present version, he is now offering to Akhilleus. So it is now up to Akhilleus to respect them, rather than to reject them and so bring *Atē* upon himself. Phoinix builds up his appeal to Akhilleus step-by-step: at 496, no more than, 'Tame your great heart'; now, 'Respect the *Litai*'.

515–523 **For if ... your anger:** Phoinix's appeal to Akhilleus is adapted to what he has just said. Agamemnon has been raging intolerably (516) – the original *Atē*; but now he is offering gifts – the *Litai*. Phoinix does not say what will happen if Akhilleus continues in his rejection of them, simply that Akhilleus' anger was hitherto justifiable (523), but that Agamemnon's offer has completely changed the moral aspects of the situation. What Phoinix is here saying is repeated, more directly, but with no more success, by Aias at 636–42.

524–526 **Even so ... persuaded by words:** On the κλέα ἀνδρῶν, see on 189. ἥρως is a difficult word to understand in Homer, but in the *Iliad*, though not in the *Odyssey*, it is applied predominantly to fighting men. By Homer's day it was coming to be applied to men who were worshipped after their death, whether they had been warriors or not. See Burkert 1985, 203–8. In talking generally of men quarrelling with each other Phoinix uses the unusual word ἐπιζάφελος, which, in its adverbial form, he used of Agamemnon at 516. His words here suggest that the theme of a quarrel between fighting men was a common one. Besides Agamemnon and Akhilleus, and the following tale of Meleagros and his family and countrymen, we hear at *Od.* VIII 75–82 of a quarrel between Odusseus and Akhilleus at the beginning of the war. A fine late sixth century black-figure vase in the British Museum, commonly titled 'Heroes quarrelling', and attributed to a painter of the Leagros Group (*BM. Cat. Vases* B 327), also suggests that this theme was a generic one.

The clear statement at 526, **they were open to gifts and could be persuaded by words,** is in the event developed in an unexpected way. Meleagros was, eventually, open to gifts and persuaded by words; but in his conclusion at 597ff. the point Phoinix makes is that this change of heart came too late, when the gifts were no longer on offer, and that Akhilleus should not repeat this mistake.

527   **action of old:** By setting it firmly in the past, Phoinix gives an air of antiquity and dignity to the forthcoming tale. If the chronology is pressed, Meleagros in fact lived no more than one generation before the Trojan war, being the half-brother of Diomedes' father Tudeus. See the stemmata given by Hainsworth 1993, in his note to 555–8.

529–599 The Kouretes ... evil for nothing: For discussion of some of the difficulties of Phoinix's paradigm of Meleagros, see Introduction, **7, i, III**.
The paradigm may be divided thus: –

A. 529–49: The war between the Kouretes and the Aitolians;
B. 550–72: Meleagros' withdrawal;
C. 573–99: The pleas to Meleagros, and his eventual return to
                    the fighting.

Within the first of these divisions, the story of the Kaludonian boar, which provides the cause of the war, occupies lines 533–46; and in the second of them the digression on Meleagros' wife Kleopatre occupies 557–64.

529–549 The Kouretes ... stout-hearted Aitolians: Phoinix begins with the fact of the war, continues at 533 with the Kaludonian boar story, and only at 547 makes it clear that this is the explanation for the war.

529–530 Kouretes, Aitolians, Kaludon: Aitolia is on the northern side of the gulf of Corinth, at its western end, on the plain (577) of the river Euenos. In this account the word is used for the realm of Meleagros' father Oineus only, and Kaludon is the capital of this realm. Oineus' opponents, the Kouretes, come from Pleuron, which is about ten miles west of Kaludon.

533   **Artemis:** The goddess of hunting, who therefore naturally sends a boar, the common object of the hunt, to cause the required distress among mortals. So at the beginning of the *Iliad* Apollo, who is the god of healing, sends a plague to punish the Akhaians.

534   **first fruits ... his garden:** The θαλύσια are the offerings made at the harvest-festival. As the following line shows, the offering includes meat as well as produce.

535   **were feasting on hecatombs:** For the hecatomb see on VIII 548–52. That the gods should be feasting on the offering is most unusual. More commonly, they do no more than partake of its savour, while the sacrificial meat is consumed by the human participants in the ceremony. But things were perhaps different in the times prior to the Trojan war; so Griffin 1980, 187, n. 22, and Kirk 1990, 10.

537   **Either he forgot ... dreadful mistake:** Oineus' error had been unintentional; Agamemnon, who used ἀασάμην, the verb from *atē*, at 116, no doubt thought the same of his. But it was not the intention, but what happened – or failed to happen – which mattered. The first half of this line provides the explanation for the second half; 'either Oineus forgot or he did not think; in either case he made a dreadful mistake'.

547–549 But Artemis aroused ... stout-hearted Aitolians: I.e. Artemis remained as angry as ever, and caused war to break out over the division of the spoils, which we know well enough from elsewhere, but with little help from Phoinix here.

552   outside the wall: Meleagros' Aitolians have been on the defensive within their own city (531), so this should mean that Meleagros now drives the Kouretes back from outside the wall of *Kaludon*, into, presumably, their own city of Pleuron. But on Meleagros' subsequent withdrawal the Aitolians are back on the attack and at the walls of Kaludon again (573–4). 'A strangely mobile war in Aitolia' – Willcock 1978, note to IX 550–2. In the account of the fifth century lyric poet Bakkhulides (V 90–154) Meleagros does indeed drive the Kouretes back into their own city; and it seems possible that Homer has innovated on this version and introduced the attack by the Kouretes on Meleagros' city of Kaludon in order to get as close a parallel as he can with the situation of the Akhaians and Akhilleus at Troy. 'While Meleagros/Akhilleus was fighting, things went badly for the Kouretes/Trojans, and they were not able to stay outside the wall (i.e. their own wall)'. But in the main action of the *Iliad* the Trojans have now driven back the Akhaians towards their ships; and so to maintain his parallel Homer has brought in the story of the Kouretes attacking the Aitolians (standing for the Akhaians in the main narrative) within their own city. Willcock 1964 suggests that Homer may in his paradigmatic stories regularly adapt the traditional version of the story so as to secure the best possible fit with his paradigm.

553–554 anger came ... excellent sense: With the mention of χόλος, the similarity of Meleagros' situation to Akhilleus' becomes clear; χόλος was the word Phoinix used of Akhilleus' anger at 436. With 'even men of excellent sense', he seeks to prevent the similarity from giving offence, very much as he had done in the *Litai* parable at 514. As with the account of the war between the Aitolians and the Kouretes, Phoinix states the fact of the anger, but postpones the explanation of it – here until 565–6.

555–566 then he, angry ... of his mother: On the considerable difficulties of the story of the discord in Meleagros' family, and within that the digression on Kleopatre, see Introduction, 7 i, III (i) and (ii).

555   his own: The basic meaning of φίλος is 'dear', but here, as elsewhere in Homer, the meaning is rather the possessive 'one's own'. As was observed by an ancient commentator, Althaie is anything but dear to Meleagros at this point, when she has just pronounced her curses on him.

Althaie: She was the daughter of the king of the Kouretes, so that her feelings in the present war would have been divided. But that is not a factor in her present anger with her son, which is explained, very briefly, in 567, and repeats the discord-within-the-family theme of Phoinix's own story.

559–560 he even ... beautiful ankles: The story was that, after Idas had carried Marpesse away from her father Euenos, Apollo wished to carry her away from Idas. Idas resisted him, and Zeus intervened, asking Marpesse to make her own choice between the two, at which Marpesse chose Idas.

563   sharing the fate ... kingfisher: literally, 'having the fate', meaning that Marpesse mourned as the kingfisher was believed to mourn for its lost mate.

565   Meleagros lay ... his heart: With παρκατέλεκτο, 'lay beside', Phoinix recalls the idea of κεῖτο, 'lay', in 556, immediately before the digression on Kleopatre which is now concluded.

The last three words of this line, with πέσσει indicative instead of the participle πέσσων here, have already been used, by the god Apollo, of Akhilleus' anger at IV 513. Such a similarity is unsurprising when a comparison is being developed between the angers of Meleagros and Akhilleus. The metaphorical use of πέσσω as 'brood on' is striking; the basic meaning of the word is 'digest'.

566–572 She was making ... from Erebos: Althaie's curses on her son are given at impressive length, and they closely follow the course of Amuntor's on Phoinix, 454–7 – except that hers are heard by the Erinus, whereas Amuntor's were heard by Hades and Persephone. Phoinix advisedly pursues this part of the story no further, and omits to say how the Erinus responded. The upshot was in fact the death of Meleagros, not something Phoinix wants to bring in to his parallel between Meleagros and Akhilleus.

567   death of her brother: Althaie's brother (in other versions Meleagros killed more than one of his uncles) would have been on the side of the Kouretes, and so Meleagros would have killed him in the struggle over the spoils of the Kaludonian boar. Phoinix makes no attempt to make his story intelligible at this point to those who do not know it already. Our most accessible account of the story of Meleagros is that of the Roman poet Ovid (43 B.C. to c. A.D. 17) at *Metamorphoses* VIII 273–525.

573–599 Soon the ... for nothing: The family histories behind him, Phoinix proceeds to the final part of the story, which he tells in a straight-forward manner which is quite unlike what has gone immediately before. The parallels with the situation in the Akhaian camp become closer and closer. Meleagros is approached, first by the imploring citizens, then by his kinsmen (Althaie has apparently had a complete change of heart, 584) and finally by his comrades; and Phoinix repeats at 574 and 585 the verb λίσσεσθαι which he had used at 501 of the embassy (note also λιτάνευε at 581). Meleagros, like Akhilleus, is offered generous gifts, and, while he remains adamant, his city is set on fire (589), as the Akhaian ships will be before Akhilleus relents (cf. 602). But finally Meleagros relents; and we expect Phoinix to say to Akhilleus, 'Do you also relent'. But instead of that Phoinix introduces a last twist, and tells how by the time Meleagros relented the gifts were no longer on offer, so that his message is, 'Do not leave relenting too late, as Meleagros did'. Ultimately, Akhilleus is told not to follow Meleagros' example!

574–585 The elders ... companions: That his companions should supplicate Meleagros *after* his own family is perhaps strange; the appeal of Meleagros' kinsmen might have been expected to be the climax. Lohmann, 258–63, suggests that the order of the approaches to Meleagros is modelled on the order in which the ambassadors address Akhilleus – the official representatives of Kaludon refecting the official spokesman Odusseus, the kinsmen reflecting Phoinix, and the comrades reflecting Aias. The appearance of Meleagros' mother Althaie at 584 is also unexpected; we have not heard of her since she cursed her son at 568–71. But Kakridis 1949, 14, 37, and Appendixes i and iii, points out that a list of suppliants such as this is a common motif of folk-tale, within which the appearance of the mother of the person supplicated is entirely to be expected.

577–580 great gift ... open ploughland: Phoinix leaves it to his hearers to draw the parallel with the present situation. The offer to Meleagros, though less extensive than Agamemnon's, is still a handsome one. We do not know the exact extent of the γύης, but at *Od.* XVIII 374 four γύαι are represented as what the best oxen can plough in one day's work, and now Meleagros is being offered fifty. On the τέμενος, see on VIII 48.

585   **refused:** Phoinix aptly repeats the word ἀναίνετο that he has used of the man who rejects the Litai at 510.

589   **city:** The exact nature of the ἄστυ is not certain. Lorimer, 428–9, suggests that an ἄστυ may have been included *within* the palace, to accommodate the king's civil and military staff; she bases herself on what is said of Troy at VI 390–3, and recognises that this will not apply here. But lines 591–2 rather suggest that at least here the ἄστυ and the πόλις are identical.

590   **fair-girdled:** The girdle (cf. βαθυζώνους at 594) is regularly found with women's dress (but not men's) from Homer's day onwards, with a fold from the upper part of the garment hanging over it, but this appears to be a change from Mycenaean times – Lorimer, 363–70, and 377–83.

591–594 told him ... deep-girdled women: As Kleopatre enumerates in general terms the consequences for the defeated of the fall of a city, she brings the eventual fate of Troy vividly to mind. At VI 414–28 Andromakhe recalls to her husband Hektor what happened when Akhilleus overcame her native city of Eetion.

598   **giving way to his feelings:** I.e. to the change of feeling that has overtaken him on hearing Kleopatre's catalogues of the misfortunes of the fallen city.

        After his long account of the story, Patroklos gives its climax, and the point of it, with a telling directness and brevity. He was very sparing in his direct instruction to Akhilleus at the end of his own story – just the three lines 496–8; but he became more expansive after the parable of the *Litai*, with 513–23 addressed directly to Akhilleus.

598–604 But they ... ward off the war: In making his point, Phoinix begins with the gifts, but moves from there to the matter of Akhilleus' *timē* at 603. Akhilleus had begun by saying that there was no *timē* for him in fighting, and then gone on to reject the gifts; but now Phoinix says, in his usual unobtrusive manner, that the gifts and the *timē* are connected with each other in a way that Akhilleus gave no trace of suspecting. The conclusion to his appeal is thus very much what Odusseus' was at 303–6, with verbal reminiscences of 302–3 at 603; and it reverses the position that he had taken at the beginning of his speech. There he had taken seriously Akhilleus' threat to return home; but now he has come to a position where Akhilleus must stay and fight and defend the Akhaian ships.

601   **my friend:** Phoinix ends his address with the same personal tone in which he had begun it (437, 445). Neither Odusseus nor Aias addresses Akhilleus as φίλος.

606 – 713 In his brief reply to Phoinix, Akhilleus repeats his implacable anger towards Agamemnon, and again invites Phoinix to remain. Aias and Akhilleus exchange short speeches, and the embassy breaks up. Odusseus reports the failure of the embassy to the

Akhaian leaders, and Diomedes proposes that for the moment there is nothing more to be done, but that in the morning Agamemnon should reassemble his forces for battle. The Akhaian council disperses.

Phoinix had ended by connecting Agamemnon's offer with Akhilleus' *timē* (604–5); but Akhilleus does not see this connection. Four lines (607–10) are all that he needs to repeat that he has *timē* enough already, before proceeding to repeat that his anger with Agamemnon remains unabated. There is therefore little further to be said. Aias' speech, presenting the soldier's point of view, brings in the matters of φιλότης and αἰδώς, but these too are lost on Akhilleus in the face of his continuing anger. When the ambassadors, Phoinix apart, return to Agamemnon's tent there is likewise little that can be said. The embassy has failed in its object of placating Akhilleus; that it has had some success in modifying Akhilleus' first intention of returning home the following day into, first, being prepared to consider this the next morning (618–9, his reply to Phoinix), and then into an undertaking that he will return to battle, but only when Hektor and the Trojans are setting fire to the Akhaian ships (650–5, the reply to Aias), is of no account beside his refusal to take up arms again immediately. The book is rounded off neatly, with Diomedes again advancing a practical proposal, as he had done at the beginning, but this time one which finds favour, and the Akhaians then making libations and retiring to their tents, in contrast to their restless despondency at the start. They too will now await the dawn, just as the horses were doing in the final line of VIII.

607–608 Phoinix, aged ... this honour: Akhilleus begins respectfully – contrast the beginning of his reply to Odusseus at 308–13! ἄττα is hardly translatable, but it gives a tone of deference and affection to what is being said. It is commonly used by the youthful Telemakhos in the *Odyssey* when he addresses the faithful old servants of his father. The words γεραιέ and διοτρεφές appear together elsewhere only at XI 648 and 653, when Patroklos addresses the venerable Nestor.

609 **by the beaked ships:** Akhilleus unconsciously gives a hint that he may no longer be inflexibly bent on returning to Greece. This is confirmed by his final words to Phoinix at 619–20.

611–613 But I ... son of Atreus: Akhilleus has no more to say on the points that Phoinix has just addressed to him at such length. He either totally rejects, or else totally fails to understand, the point that Phoinix had made after his parable (515–23), that the situation is quite changed now that Agamemnon has made his offer.

613 **hero:** On ἥρως, see on 524–6. Akhilleus may be using the word sarcastically here; he is certainly not using it to impute heroic stature to Agamemnon.

615 **a good thing:** A most unusual use of καλός in Homer for moral values. Elsewhere it is most commonly used of a fine physical appearance, often in conjunction with μέγας; and it is rare to find it as a moral term before the sixth century. See Adkins 1960, 43–4, and 1972, 35.

617–619 These men ... stay here: Akhilleus dismisses the other ambassadors without even addressing them. His offer to consider in the morning the question of whether or not to return to Greece is a matter for him and Phoinix alone.

620–622 He spoke ... from the tent: For Akhilleus there is now no more to be said, and so he seeks to bring the proceedings to a close immediately, without even hearing from

Aias. A bed is to be made up for Phoinix as a sign that the moment has come for the rest of the embassy is to depart.

624–642 Child of ... all the Akhaians: On Aias' short but significant speech, see Introduction, **7e**.

624–625 Child of ... let us go: Aias begins with the same one-line address to Odusseus that Akhilleus had begun with at 308. He is a man of straightforward thinking, and few words; and his advice for the moment is conveyed by just the single word, ἴομεν, brought in as soon as it can be.

629 **mighty heart:** Peleus had previously urged Akhilleus to curb his mighty heart (255), and Phoinix's 'Tame your great heart' at 496 amounts to the same thing. At 109 it was Agamemnon's mighty heart which Nestor said was the cause of the quarrel with Akhilleus. Aias here says that Akhilleus has himself 'made savage his mighty heart', but at 637 that it is the gods who have put a savage heart in his breast. This ascription of emotions both to the person concerned and to the gods is common in Homer; cf. 703, where Diomedes says that Akhilleus will rejoin the fighting 'whenever his heart bids him and the god arouses him'. See the note to VIII 218.

630 **hard man:** Aias is not the man to make a secret of his feelings. Agamemnon had used σχέτλιος of Zeus at 19; Akhilleus is like a god in his unrelenting and uncompromising anger. See the note to 426.

Both σχέτλιος here, and νηλής, meaning much the same thing, in 632, gain emphasis by being placed in the 'run-over' position – i.e. at the beginning of a new line, as an addition to the line that has gone before. Akhilleus has employed the same effect at 335–41. See Hainsworth 1993, to IX 625–42 – 'in emotionally uncharged situations sentence and verse tend to coincide. By overriding this tendency the skewed sentence expresses the passion of the speakers'.

631 **we honoured:** Aias accepts what Akhilleus has just said about the honour that he enjoys already, but diverges from him over what that now makes it proper for him to do. As Aias thinks of the Akhaian forces generally, he appreciates that the *timē* that they have paid to Akhilleus now deserves some reward; but he is largely blind to the *dis*honour that Agamemnon has done Akhilleus in taking Briseis.

633 **recompense:** The family of the murdered man may accept blood-money, and then give up their hostility towards the murderer. The same idea appears again on the Shield of Akhilleus at XVIII 497–508; but side-by-side with this we also hear, e.g. at II 664–6, of a practice whereby the family was obliged to kill the murderer unless he fled the country.

For Phoinix the right course for Akhilleus arose out of the parable of the personified *Litai* and *Atē*. Aias sees things more plainly than that, and the practice in the case of a murderer gives him all he needs by way of an example to Akhilleus.

635 **high anger:** Aias uses the same expression, θυμὸς ἀγήνωρ, of the murdered man's relative that Akhilleus has used of himself at 398. See the note to 698–700.

638 **(just) for a single ... seven:** For the straightforward Aias the Briseis-issue is simply a matter of arithmetic! He cannot see it as Akhilleus sees it. Briseis and the seven other women are the ones who are already available, and whom Agamemnon promised at 128–32 (= 270–4). The further ones that will be available in due course, including a daughter of Agamemnon (139–47/281–9), Aias ignores.

640–642 respect your ... all the Akhaians: The ambassadors have been received under Akhilleus' roof, and so a bond exists between Akhilleus and them, and Akhilleus is failing in his duty to them, and to the whole army, of which they are the official representatives, by rejecting them. Akhilleus had indeed accepted the ambassadors with honour when they first came to his tent; but as his words of welcome at 197–8 and 202–4 make clear, he was accepting them as friends, with no thought for the official capacity in which they had come. Aias' use of μέλαθρον for Akhilleus' tent here is perhaps intended as a reminder of Akhilleus' similar use of it at 204.

644–655 Aias, child ... for battle: Akhilleus divides his reply to Aias equally between dismissing him and the embassy, and stating the conditions on which he will eventually resume fighting (644–9/650–5). His tone is respectful – he concedes that Aias has spoken 'in accordance with my feelings', and when he returns once more to his anger with Agamemnon he does not use the imperative tense that he had used to Phoinix at 612; but for the moment he is as unbending as ever. But then he adds his remarkable concession. He will return to battle, but only when *his* men, *his* positions, and *his* ships are under attack. His return will be on his own terms, not on Agamemnon's. By snubbing the embassy Akhilleus has come at least a little way towards granting what it had requested.

649   But you, go: No more than one line is necessary for Akhilleus to send the embassy on its way. He has said even less in answer to Aias' points than he did to Phoinix's.

650–655 For I shall ... for battle: The first four words of 650 are very nearly identical to the beginning of Zeus' prophecy to the gods at VIII 473. Zeus and Akhilleus foresee what is to happen in much the same way, with the crucial difference that Zeus also foresees the death of Patroklos. In the event, Hektor forces his way through to the Akhaian ships at the end of Book XV, which leads in XVI to Patroklos taking up the fight, and so to his death, the event that will at last bring Akhilleus back to the fighting. What Akhilleus says here does become true – but not at all in the way that he here foresees.

652–654 the tents ... black ship: Akhilleus does at least think of his own contingent, the Murmidons, though not of the Akhaian force generally, as Aias had wanted him to do. His thinking remains self-centred (cf. τῇ ἐμῇ at 654); but is he at least thinking of Meleagros, who returned to battle only when his own city was on fire (587–9)?

657   making a libation: Wine is poured onto the ground as an offering to the gods, as it had been at 177, before the embassy set out, and will be again at 712, as the *boulē* in the Akhaian camp disperses. On each occasion the ceremony marks the end of the present proceedings.

661   fleeces ... nap of linen: The bed for Phoinix is an elaborate affair; the nap of linen is not included when Kirke's attendants make up a bed for her and Odusseus at *Od.* X 352–3. This would function as a sheet, with the fleeces and rug on top as blankets.

664–668 Lesbos ... Enueus: Akhilleus' Lesbos campaign was mentioned by Agamemnon at 129; but his operations at Skuros are not otherwise known. Skuros is the island just off the eastern coast of Euboea, and so the episode may have taken place during the course of the Akhaians' original voyage to Troy. The naming of Diomede's father may suggest that her family had been of some consequence in Lesbos, although neither she, nor Enueus, appears elsewhere. The maidservants of 658 were no doubt spoils of war as well.

669   **tents:** At 90, the gathering of the *boulē*, and at 178, the departure of the ambassadors, the singular was used of Agamemnon's tent. The plural conveys some sense of grandeur to the commander-in-chief's quarters.

670   **sons of the Akhaians:** I.e. the elders who had gathered for the *boulē* at which the embassy had been decided on, and who are now found to have stayed with Agamemnon throughout the course of the ambassadors' exchanges with Akhilleus.

671   **standing up:** The leaders are so anxious for news that they now rise as they pay the necessary courtesies to the returning ambassadors.

673–709 **Come, tell ... among the foremost:** The book ends, as it had begun, with three speeches from the Akhaian leaders – yet more ring-composition

673–675 **Come, tell ... mighty heart:** Agamemnon has just one thing to ask of the embassy, and so he asks it, in no more than three lines. He makes no mention at all of his offer, which is subsidiary to the question of whether Akhilleus will return or not. His question is largely composed from language that has appeared already – 674 in Akhilleus' first speech at 347, ἀπέειπε in the narrative at 431 (Akhilleus' response to Odusseus), χόλος in Phoinix's and Akhilleus' speeches at 436 and 646, and μεγαλήτορα θυμόν at Odusseus' recall of Peleus' words to his son at 255 and in Aias' speech at 629.

673   **much-celebrated:** πολύαιν' could also be translated actively, 'teller of many stories'. But the passive fits better with the following 'great glory of the Akhaians'. 'Teller of many stories' would better suit Odusseus' role in the *Odyssey* than in the *Iliad.*

680–687 **He orders ... are confident:** Odusseus reports, with considerable verbal repetition (cf. 684–7 and 691–2 with 417–20 and 428–9 respectively) what Akhilleus has said to *him*, and gives no hint of the modifications of his position that Akhilleus has expressed to Phoinix and Aias. But he has no reason to do otherwise – Akhilleus' concessions in no way alter the prospect of imminent catastrophe that now faces the Akhaians, and that it was the object of the embassy to remedy. With ἄμ' ἠοῖ φαινομένηφι at 682 Odusseus does recall the expression that Akhilleus used to Phoinix at 618; but this is simply a metrically convenient replacement of Akhilleus' ἦρι μάλ' to Odusseus at 360.

688–692 **these men ... compel him to:** The message is such a solemn one that Odusseus wants to have it confirmed by the other members of the embassy – including the heralds, of whom we have not heard since Nestor nominated them at 170. This naturally leads to an explanation of why Phoinix is not now present, where Odusseus again sticks closely to the original words of Akhilleus (427–9).

693–696 **Thus he ... spoke:** See Introduction, **4** on how these lines are made up of elements that appear elsewhere.

697–709 Most glorious ... the foremost: Diomedes' speech is well balanced. The six central lines in which he addresses the gathering at large and again makes a proposal for meeting the present situation are preceded by four, and followed by three, lines addressed only to Agamemnon. As in his first speech, he is still smarting under Agamemnon's reproach to his ἀλκή – it is perhaps no accident that this is the last word of that part of his speech that is addressed to the leaders (706), before he rounds once more on Agamemnon. But he is not this time responding to a proposal by Agamemnon which he regards as wholly unacceptable; and his own proposal now is a thoroughly sensible and practical one, and one which concerns the army *en masse*.

698–699 you should not have ... countless gifts: Diomedes comes straight to the point. With λίσσεσθαι he repeats Phoinix's version that the offer to Akhilleus was in the nature of an apology to him (see on 501), although he has of course not heard that. From what he then goes on to say, Diomedes presumably means that no approach should have been made to Akhilleus at all – an *ex post facto* judgement; he had not objected when the approach was proposed at the *boulē*.

699–700 proud man ... his pride: On ἀγήνωρ and ἀγηνορίη, see notes to 398 and 635. At 398 Akhilleus would not have been using ἀγήνωρ in criticism of himself, but some criticism is surely intended by Aias at 635 and Diomedes here. A scholiast's note here renders ἀγήνωρ as 'excessively arrogant', ἄγαν ὑβριστικός. Griffin 1986 shows how Homer's characters in their speeches much more often make criticisms of each other than Homer himself does.

702–703 he will fight ... arouses him: Diomedes correctly infers that Akhilleus' refusal to Odusseus was not the end of the matter, and that Akhilleus will one day return – on his own terms. For Akhilleus being prompted both by his own heart and by the god, see on 629 and VIII 218.

707   beautiful rosy-fingered Dawn: Cf. the different formulaic description of Dawn at VIII 1.

709   you yourself ... among the foremost: With αὐτός Diomedes adds weight to his implied criticism of Agamemnon's leadership – 'you *will* this time take your rightful place (though you did not do so before)'. The criticism is a fair one. Agamemnon played a less prominent part than Diomedes, both in the fighting which began at IV 446 and when it was resumed at VIII 60. Diomedes' words also hint at the *aristeia* of Agamemnon with which the fighting on the following day begins at XI 15 ff.

712–713 And then ... gift of sleep: The quiet in the Akhaian camp with which the book ends contrasts sharply with the ubiquitous turbulence with which it began. The question of what to do next has at least been satisfactorily resolved, even though the outlook remains as bleak as ever. The quiet finality of the lines is enhanced by their metrical similarity; in all but the fourth foot they scan identically, and they also have in common a weak caesura in the third foot.

Index

accusative of respect, 33

Agamemnon, and Akhilleus, 10–12; ancestry, 221; and *atē*, 25, 218, 234; character and leadership, 18–19, 210, 250; speeches – in VIII, 191–2, 194–5: at Akhaian *agorē*, 210: at *boulē*, 218

agorē, 205: and *boulē*, 177, 203, 210

Aias, son of Telamon, 222; ambassador in IX, 11, 222; body–shield, 134; speech in IX, 19–20, 247–8

aigis, 195

Aineias, 185, 187, 196

Akhaians, compared with Trojans, 14; the Akhaian trench and wall, 188, 190, 197, 214; their positions, 191, 223

Akhilleus, character, 233; epithets, 7–8, 198, 225; and Patroklos, 26–7; raids around Troy, 2, 189, 219, 249; reception of embassy, 223–4; re-entry into battle, 12; replies to the embassy, 18–21, 230–1, 248; *timē*, 21; two fates, 22, 236–7; See also under 'Agamemnon'

Althaie, 28–9, 244

Amuntor, 25, 239

Andromakhe, 188–9, 219

Argos, 210, 220

Aristarkhos, 16, 17, 23, 25, 179, 182, 189, 205, 210, 211–2, 240

atē, 26–7, 192; See also under 'Agamemnon' and 'Zeus'

Athene, in III, 10; pleads with Zeus, 13, 179–80; as Tritogeneia, 179–80; See also under 'Here'

Atreides, 209

basileus, 213; and *anax*, 194

blood money, 247–8

caesura, 43–4

chariots, 183, 188–9, 237

conditional sentences, 39–40

correption, 46

dactyls, 43; effects with, 46–7

Danaans, 178

Dardanians, Dardanos, 187

Dark age, 1–2, 5

deipnon, 181, 188, 214, 226–7

Delphi, 5, 236

Demodokos, 6, 13, 224

digamma, 46

Diomedes, character, 18, 211; formulaic epithets, 8; insulted by Agamemnon, 211; and *kudos,* 187; and Odusseus, 184–5; speeches – at Akhaian *agorē,* 211; at end of IX, 250; See also under 'Nestor'

dual, forms, 31, 32, 34, 36; in VIII, 182; at IX 182–98, 23–5

end–stopping, 47; in IX, 211

enjambment, 47; in VIII, 181, 190, 204; in IX, 229, 232, 234, 238, 247

epic cycle, 2–4

Erebos, 198

Erinus, Erinues, 25, 239, 244

foreshadowing, 11–12, 202, 248

formulas, 7–10; in VIII, 177, 178–9, 180–1, 182; in IX, 211, 215–6

Gargaros, Gargaron, 180
genitive, causal, and of separation, 33
gephuras ptolemoio, 199
gods, discord among, 14, 177; hostility to Troy, 206; and humans, 14–15, 191, 247
Gorguthion, 14, 195–6

hekatombē, 206
Hektor, character, 184, 187, 195, 197, 204; death, 12; epithets, 233; speeches in VIII, 187–9, 203–5
Hellas, 208: see also 'Phthie'
Hellespont, 237
Herakles, 2–3, 198
Here, 189, 191; and Athene, 11, 15, 178, 197–203; opposition to Zeus, 10, 13
hērōs, 241
Homer, 4–7; address to Muse, 194; attitude to Greeks and Trojans, 14; battle-scenes, 15; and epic tradition, 3–4; the Homeric question, 7; workshop of, 24–5
Homeridai, 5

Ide, 180
Iliad, date of composition, 5; 'original version', 22; papyrus fragments, 6; when committed to writing, 6
Iliad, Books VIII and IX; action of, 10–11 and future action, 10–12
Iliad, Book VIII, action, 15; inconsistencies, 16, 202; papyri, 16–17, plus-verses, 16–17; and the rest of the *Iliad*, 12–13, 177; text of, 16–17
Iliad, Book IX; contrast with VIII, 17; duals at 182–98, 23–5; inconsistent with passages elsewhere, 21–22
Ilion,Ilios, 212
indefinite clauses, 40

Iris, 200–1

kērukes, 223
klea andrōn, 225
Kleopatre, 28
krētēr, 191, 226

Lemnos, 191, 214
libation, 222–3, 248–9
lissomai, 241
Litai, 19–21, 26–7
Lukia, Lukians, 188

marriage settlement, 220
Meleagros, Phoinix's story of, 3, 27–9, 242; tradition of, 29
metaphor, 185
Mycenaean age, 1–2

Nestor, character, 212–3; Gerenian, 183; proposals in IX, 11; rescued by Diomedes, 4, 186, 189; speeches – at Akhaian *agorē*, 212–3: at *boulē*, 216, 221

Odusseus, 222; ancestry, 184; character, 184–5; formulaic epithets, 7–8; speech in IX, 19–20, 227–8; See also under 'Diomedes'
Olumpos, 177,189
optative, uses of, 39–40
oral poetry, 5–10

paradigm, 25–9, 238, 243
parataxis, 214–5, 218
Paris (also Alexandros), in III, 10, 14; shoots Nestor's horse, 4, 183
Patroklos, companion of Akhilleus, 10, 18, 225; entry into battle and death, 12; See also under 'Akhilleus'
Peleus, 221, 235, 239
personification, 208

Phemios, 6, 224

philos, 220, 243–4

Phoinix, 221–2; and Akhilleus,11; flight from home, 25–6; speech in IX, 19–20, 25–9, 237–8; tutelage of Akhilleus, 238

phratry, 213

Phthie, 229; and Hellas, 235, 239

Poseidon, 201; epithets, 224; rebuffs Here, 190

possessive dative, 33, 34

postpositives and prepositives, 44

prosody, 45–6

repetitions, in VIII, 178–9, 199, 201–2; in IX, 9, 210, 212, 215–6, 224, 233, 237, 249, 250

ring-composition, in VIII, 196, 207; in IX, 17, 209, 230, 238, 249

sacrifice, 206

Sarpedon, speech at XII 310–28, 19–20, 235–6

Schliemann, 1–2

similes, in VIII, 194, 196, 197, 206–7; in IX, 208–9

Skaian gate, 181, 233

Skamandros, 203

spondees, 43; effects with, 46–7

Sthenelos, 185, 212

subjunctive, uses of, 39–40

synizesis, 46

talent, 219

Tartaros, 178

temenos, 180

Teukros, archery, 11, 13, 194–6; half-brother of Telamonian Aias, 194

Thebes, Egyptian, 234

themes, 9–10, 224

Thetis, and Akhilleus' fate, 22, 236; appeal to Zeus, 198; See also under 'Zeus'

trace-horse, 183

tripod, 195, 219

Trojan war, 1–2

Trojans, character, 186, 187; epithets, 228

Troy, 1–2, 237

vulgate, the, 6

Zeus, and *atē*, 25; balances the scales, 182; design for the war, 191; forbids gods' intervention, 11–13, 177; portents, 14–15, 186, 188, 189, 192–3, 229; promise to Thetis, 10; and the Titans, 202; towards Here and Athene, 200–2